M. H. WOODSCOURT

# THE WINTER KING

BOOK TWO

WINTERVALE

Cover art by GetCovers

Published by True North Press

www.mhwoodscourt.com

ISBN: (Hardback) 978-1-959619-08-6

ISBN: (Paperback) 978-1-959619-09-3

*DEDICATION*

*To the brave men and women who fight for freedom on every battlefield.*

*In particular, to Captain Nathan Hale of the American Revolution, whose sacrifice and patriotism have been my inspiration throughout the writing of this book.*

*Rest in Peace*
*September 22, 1776*

# Content Warning

The following pages contain war violence and death, along with topics of slavery, cannibalism, and regicide.

While such matters are handled with delicacy, they may not be easy for tender hearts to handle.

Proceed at your own discretion.

—M. H. W.

Ilid
Swan Castle
Fraelin
Keep Canad
Keep Arch
Keep Montré
Dorshen Heights
The Channel
Serrelle
Crane Castle
Hear ye, hear ye. No magic shall be used within the mighty realm of Simaerin, by order of the Crow King.
Mount Vinwen
Vinwen Province
Delesar River
Siarn Woods
Keep Lirial
Suffon
Misoril Province
Simaerin
Kender
Hesh-Kasal
Keep Talbethé
Yast Port
Kellion
Glashon Province
Londolin
Crowwell
Vaymeer Sea

# PART I

# THE BATTLE FOR BAYTON

# Chapter One

The mouth of the cave gaped larger than Nox's worst nightmares could ever paint. It smelled worse too. Gnawed bones littered the pathway around patches of snow.

Nox shuddered. From his vantage point, huddled in a thicket of frost-bitten spice berries, he couldn't deny he'd reached his destination.

That was *good*. It was also really, really bad.

Turning toward the familiar, oft-encouraging face of his friend, Nox recoiled upon finding Nathael's complexion green, his lips pulled down in a grim frown, his eyes leaden. Nathael pulled those dead eyes from the cavern and tried the limpest smile never recorded in history.

"I think we found it," he said in a wooden voice.

Nox grimaced and nodded. "I'm afraid you're right."

"Now what?" asked Nathael.

Nox swallowed hard. His friend was the brave one, always stalwart, always unshrinking, while Nox followed where he could, too timid to lead. But this had been *his* idea, and while Nathael supported him, Nox couldn't bring himself to shirk responsibility now, when it well and truly mattered.

He turned back to the path strewn with the bones of countless animals, especially deer. "I must go in."

He pushed through the thicket, shriveled berries dropping at his feet, until he broke free of the wasted undergrowth to stand unprotected. He halted, trembling.

*Now or never.*

Squaring his shoulders, he wended around the bones, growing increasingly conscious of his considerable girth. He'd never been a small child, and his sweet tooth was inferior only to his discerning palate. Nox *liked* food. A lot. Perhaps that came of being a baker's son. Only now did he perceive an unforeseen danger in weighing twice what Nathael did.

He might be eaten.

The faint crunch of footfalls sounded behind Nox. He glanced back to find Nathael tailing him. The encouraging smile was back, though it still lacked its usual luster.

"Y-you don't have to come," Nox whispered.

Nathael shrugged and said nothing. As Nox moved forward, Nathael followed.

The two were as close as brothers, though they weren't related. Nathael had been a waif, orphaned young, and half-wild when Nox's father took him in and offered him an apprenticeship in the bakery. Hollow-legged and quick-witted, Nathael learned fast, developing a special eye for detail so vital in crafting delicate breads and confections.

Nox's mouth watered just thinking about Nathael's skills.

The crunch of a bone underfoot shattered his appetite. His knees knocked together.

The cave loomed near: high, dark, and terrible. Nox halted at its border, just where the winter sun lost its claim on earth. Shadows played at the entrance, whispering dread secrets on the wind.

Heart raging like a blacksmith's hammer, Nox crossed into the darkness, fingers itching for a blade he didn't own. Only faith brought him here: faith in something most people scorned. Except Nathael. Nathael never scoffed when Nox became serious about something.

The cavern sloped into the earth, and the air grew colder and, strangely, less pungent.

Nox licked his lips with his parched tongue.

"Tell me when I need to stop," Nathael whispered behind him. Nox glanced back but couldn't tell his friend from the pitch black enfolding him.

"Stay here. It's close now."

"Be careful, Nox. May Afallon be your guide."

Nox nodded before he remembered Nathael couldn't see him. "Thank you. I'll be back soon." He trudged down the tunnel.

As he walked, contemplating his mission and his dire need for success, his heart hammered less. His arms swung. He'd come here because he must. More than that, he'd come because King Gwynter *believed* him.

Since Nox was a little boy, he'd harbored a secret dream. A wish of sorts. As he grew, he'd developed a theory around it. Except for Nathael, the few people Nox confided in had scorned the idea.

But King Gwynter hadn't mocked him when Nox stood before the war council and asked to try something insane. It was their only hope of taking Bayton. And driving the Crow King's army from that town was crucial.

There was so little time. Though Nox and Nathael had traveled as fast as they could, the going had been slow. If Nox failed, he would make it back to Dorshen Heights well after events played out. But if he succeeded — if Nox's dream proved true — victory might become a certainty.

The problem was, though Nox had dreamed and theorized and prayed, he hadn't a shred of evidence proving he could achieve his goal.

After all, who had ever heard of anyone taming a dragon?

## Chapter Two

The cry of a crow brought Gwyn's head up from prayer.

He fell still under the elm tree where he knelt, muscles tense and ears straining, but the crow never called again from the neighboring trees in the naked copse. Letting out a sigh, Gwyn watched his breath appear as a cloud under the gloom of a winter morning. He climbed to his feet and wrapped his tattered cloak tighter across his chest.

A dusting of snow had fallen in the night, bringing a chill that ached in Gwyn's bones. Dead foliage bore the brittle touch of frost. Through the stillness of the cold, the clatter of camp stirring upstream drifted toward him.

Gwyn picked his way along the bank of the frozen stream, searching the solid depths for any sign of a fish. His stomach rumbled, but Gwyn saw no hope of breakfast.

He breached the camp's border, hand aloft to alert the sentry seated on a tree limb. The soldier saluted him as he passed, and Gwyn trudged on to the tent he called home. Aluem stood before the flap. The magnificent unicorn tossed his head in greeting, silver and gold twined horn bright under the dismal sky, pearlescent eyes warm.

Gwyn rested a hand on Aluem's muzzle and rubbed. "Good morning."

A voice like rushing wind filled Gwyn's head. *'Good morrow to you, fair king and brother. How were your prayers?'*

"Peaceful until the last moment. I heard a crow."

Aluem nodded, eyes reflecting Gwyn's concern. The unicorn stepped aside to let Gwyn slip into his tent. A table adorned the center of the inner space, cluttered with maps and half-used candlesticks, sealing wax, and a hastily scrawled, half-finished missive.

Gwyn passed the table by and slipped through a second flap into the back chamber he shared with Lawen. Gwyn hovered over Lawen's makeshift bed, watching his elder brother snore softly. He must be cold. He had only one blanket and used his tabard for a little added warmth.

"Lawen," Gwyn whispered, and bent down to shake the man's arm. "Wake up. Lawen."

The soft snores faded, and Lawen opened one eye. It glinted in the faint light. "Mmm?"

"I heard a crow just outside of camp. It was very close."

"Mmm." Lawen turned onto his side in his bedroll. Gwyn reached out to shake him again, but Lawen shot up, as though someone had stuck hot pincers under his back.

"A crow?" Lawen looked around, wild-eyed, black hair disheveled.

"Outside of camp," Gwyn replied, smiling faintly. "Good morning, brother."

Lawen moaned and rubbed his face. "Was that necessary, Gwynter?"

Gwyn straightened. "It wasn't a joke. There was a crow. I came back to tell you."

Lawen slid his hands from his face to shoot Gwyn a glare. "You went off alone again, didn't you?"

"I was praying." Gwyn shrugged. "I needed privacy."

Lawen growled. "Gwynter, you can't do that anymore. You're a wanted man! The Crow King has demanded your head! You're worth ten thousand denn. *Ten thousand!*"

Gwyn nodded soberly. "Yes, I saw the posters."

"You promised to keep Kive with you. At least that. Where is he?"

"Kive hasn't come back from — from hunting, and I needed to speak to Afallon. Urgently."

"Couldn't you do it here?"

Gwyn grinned. "Through *your* snoring? Afallon wouldn't have heard a single word."

Lawen scowled, wadded up his tabard, and threw it at Gwyn, who caught it and threw it back. Lawen took the hit full in the face and allowed himself to fall onto his bedroll. He sighed wearily beneath the wad of cloth before dragging it from his face.

"In all seriousness, Gwyn, you mustn't be alone. Please."

Gwyn bobbed a nod, his cheeks warming. A night plagued by bad dreams had driven him half-conscious from the tent, out into the predawn world, where he'd sought solitude. Comfort. Afallon alone seemed able to provide that these days.

"Do you think the crow saw you?" asked Lawen, rising from his bedroll to pull the blue threadbare tabard on over his head.

"Very likely, though I never saw him."

Sighing again, Lawen pulled his boots over his britches. "It was only a matter of time, I suppose. We'd best pull back into the main camp. You'll be safer there."

Gwyn nodded and knelt before his own bedroll to pack it up. He preferred that anyway. Generals Haratin and Leelin had insisted he leave the main body of camp to hide with a smaller contingent in the nearby woods. Magical protections held better across a small perimeter, and Gwyn's safety was their foremost concern.

But Gwyn hated to hide, ignorant of his army's movements, more of a prisoner than a commander. He must lead the armies under his command. The people expected it, and — just as important — Gwyn wanted to do something, not just stand around like a banner flapping in the breeze.

General Haratin always contended Gwyn was more a symbol than a mortal man. Better that he stayed safe and alive rather than risk himself on the battlefield. Gwyn suspected the general's motivations were self-serving. Haratin wanted charge of the army and the glory of leading it to victory.

How long might it be before Haratin's thirst for fame allowed the Crow King to buy his loyalty back? The rebellion's ragtag forces weren't exactly winning the war.

Gwyn sighed and rolled his bedding. He tied it and tossed it next to Lawen's bedroll.

"You did it on purpose, didn't you?"

Gwyn looked up at his brother looming above him, arms crossed. "Did what?"

"Risked yourself, so we would return to Haratin's camp."

Gwyn scowled. "Haratin's camp, is it?" He inhaled and silently counted until his temper boiled down to a simmer burning in his stomach. "Do you know, Lawen, what destroys the seeds of change, the very seeds of hope for liberty and renewal?"

He glanced toward the flap, listening to the wind picking up beyond the canvas. "At first our forces stood a chance — a genuine, powerful chance, even against such odds as the Crow King and his order. But now we're in shambles. Half our numbers have vanished. Not from bloody battles, oh no. But because of greed. Peasants, soldiers, even knights swelled our ranks just last autumn. A mere year later, we're sinking as a ship caught in the tirades of winter storms. We have no food. We have no proper shelter. Why? Because we haven't any money."

He stood up and turned to face his brother, meeting the green of Lawen's even gaze. "A just cause is destroyed because those who were at first content to fight for a dream now require distinction, class, power, and most of all, money — while I would dissolve *all* those things if it only brought peace." He closed his eyes and exhaled. "What can I do, Lawen? We have no money. No hope of finding it. No whisper of a chance without it, for it's true the people are starving. We've left the fields unworked." He shrugged.

"But could I turn such earnest men from the cause? Should I have? Especially the former slaves?"

"You're worrying too much." Lawen placed a hand on Gwyn's shoulder. "When this detestable winter mellows, our numbers will swell again."

Gwyn frowned. "Not by half. And who can blame them? We've no proper victories to our credit. All that compels such men as Haratin to remain is the knowledge that the Crow King would sooner draw and quarter him than make him a general under the Crow Banner now. The *best* he could hope for on the enemy's side is a pardon and a modest parcel of land once we're crushed."

"You're gloomy indeed today, Gwynny." Lawen squeezed his shoulder. "Have patience and faith. To whom have you been praying?"

A soft smile touched Gwyn's face, soothing his writhing insides a little. "I do have faith, but I also have fear, and both are in constant turmoil. I can't say which will win in the end." He pulled his cloak closer as the wind howled and the tent walls shook. "We're in desperate need of a miracle, Lawen, and I cannot help but doubt Haratin will be the instrument of it. We require a strategy. We need a sure victory. Just one. If we can manage that, perhaps those who have deserted our cause will return. Perhaps they'll remember that the Crow King is a tyrant still, and our aim remains to topple him.

"That's my greatest frustration, Lawen. The people of Simaerin have so quickly forgotten that we're fighting, not to put me on the throne, but to remove a madman from it."

Lawen shook his head. "It's both, Gwyn. An empty throne is worse than one filled with a despot. Chaos is a crueler master by far than even tyranny."

The tent flap flew aside and the wind roared louder. Gwyn and Lawen spun toward it, hands flying for their swords.

In the doorway, mouth stained red with blood, stood Kive. The fallen fae smiled, his pale, blue-tinged skin stark against the tangles of long black hair that tumbled down his shoulders and framed his tattered robes. "Hello, Shiny. Hello, Hawk."

Gwyn's smile returned. "There you are. Come here, Kive."

The Ilidreth skipped into the tent and to Gwyn's side. "Yes, Shiny?"

"Did you eat well, Kive?"

"Oh, yes, Shiny. I found such nice juicy rats. So plump, with loooong tails."

Gwyn patted Kive's head. "I'm happy for you. While you were hunting, Kive, did you see any crows or big rats skulking about?"

"Only one, Shiny, up on the cliffs. But the juicy rat won't be skulking any longer, Shiny. Such a nice rat." His red eyes twinkled.

Gwyn exchanged a glance with Lawen. "Where on the cliffs, Kive? How close?"

"Not close, Shiny. The rat was searching. Searching. Sniffing. But now he's not."

Gwyn pushed down a smile. Despite the horror of Kive's eating habits, his demeanor remained so innocent that sometimes Gwyn forgot to feel the disgust he ought. There was also a kind of relief knowing Kive could dispatch enemy scouts without raising a ruckus.

With a sigh, Gwyn patted Kive's head again and moved to the tent flap. He drew it aside and fixed his gaze on the cliff heights looming in the southern sky, ominous and mocking.

Beyond those cliffs lay Bayton, the once-thriving port city long under the Crow King's tyrannical grip. Last year a band of mage sympathizers had tried to rescue as many condemned mage children as possible, smuggling them from Bayton in the night. But the Order of Corvus — the Crow King's elite mages — had discovered the operation and slaughtered anyone involved, as well as their families, including infants.

That had been the gale that moved most of Gwyn's followers to stand against the Crow King. Dubbing magery evil was one thing. Burning babes was something else.

Since the massacre, dissidents had flocked to Gwyn upon

hearing that he openly opposed the Crow King. At the time, Gwyn had made no such move, but those who knew his lineage had published it across Simaerin. Gwyn accepted his role as a rebel, but he still wanted nothing to do with being king.

It didn't matter. Gwyn had a war to win. Later he could sort out the right way to govern Simaerin.

The key was Bayton. Daily, the Crow King squeezed the port city as tight as he could, drawing the blood of mages, or possible mages, or mage sympathizers. He wouldn't allow food into the city. The ports remained closed. Trade had virtually halted. The people trapped within Bayton's walls were dying — rebels and loyalists alike.

Gwyn *must* find a way inside. To do that, he had to breach the walls. Yet the Order of Corvus and the Crow Army stood in his way, defenses in place against any frontal assault.

The only hope Gwyn's army had lay on Bayton's north side, guarded solely by the cliffs above. Dorshen Heights. Knowing only nature stood guard there, Gwyn had marched his army in a wide circle around the city and camped on the cliff's back side. If he could conquer this route, he might attack the one viable weakness in Bayton's walls.

But getting up there unnoticed had proved challenging. His army would be exposed on the heights. It was madness to try.

*Madness might be all I can use against such odds.*

"The conundrum is magic," he murmured.

"What do you mean?" asked Lawen, standing beside him to consider Dorshen Heights.

"The Order of Corvus is braced against magic. They know how to block it. How to deflect it. Even to outlast it. But just as Dorshen Heights stand by Afallon's will, our best chance is to forgo magic and try using man's natural ingenuity as our defense. It will bring us closer. Maybe even close enough. It's our only recourse, should Nox fail."

"But, Gwyn, we're exposed up there."

Gwyn nodded. "We don't need forts or keeps, merely a wall of earth to be our shields. We'll bring weapons for defense, but as I said, if we can reach the top it ought to be close enough. From there, Adesta and I should be able to negate the city's defenses. After that, magic won't be effective for *either* side. We'll level the playing field. It might even shake the enemy enough that we won't need to outlast them."

"There are only two of you against a dozen of Corvus."

"I still think it will work. Either way, we can't afford to wait any longer. Nox might not return, and our supplies grow thinner, as do our soldiers."

"You sound mad, you know. It's a terrible risk."

"Not if we climb to the top of the heights under the cover of night."

"The moon's full, Gwyn. Any crow would spot a force climbing the cliffs, no matter the hour. And lest you forget, magic isn't an option. We're blocked from seizing the elements. No cloud cover, no wind noise."

Gwyn smiled grimly. "There is one force the Order of Corvus cannot block against. We shall pray for Afallon to aid us."

# Chapter Three

General Haratin had nothing kind to say about Gwyn's strategy, but though Lawen had his doubts, he backed Gwyn up with vehemence at the war council. Protests notwithstanding, Gwyn had the final say.

To distract the Crow King's forces stationed outside the walls of Bayton, Gwyn ordered General Haratin to take a force of five hundred men and position them within the forest boundaries near the highway leading to the port city. The general was ordered to barrage the enemy with arrows each day at eventide for three days, changing up their location now and then to keep the enemy guessing and exasperated.

Now, on the third night, a force of three hundred men waited for true night to begin their assent up Dorshen Heights, bearing picks, shovels, and bows and arrows. Gwyn stood at their head, watching the few wisps of cloud clustered around the full moon, useless and faint. Should any crows or other spies of the king be watchful tonight, Gwyn's plan would fail.

The situation within the walls of the city grew more desperate every day. Gwyn must aid them now or it would be too late. Tonight at the latest Nox was due to return. If he never came, this was the only option left. Gwyn must make his move, or crawl back home, defeated and condemned to the Crow King's justice.

*Afallon above, please lend us Thy victorious sword. Shroud us from the enemy.*

He uttered the prayer again and again.

But the moon remained bright, the clouds sparse, the wind a mere whisper. Gwyn heard every shift and murmur of conversation like a shout in his ear.

Lawen stood to his right, Aluem to his left. Both companions stayed silent and grim. What the unicorn thought of Gwyn's plan, he didn't divulge.

The contingent waited as long as Gwyn dared to let it. But conditions never altered, and he sighed. "Move out."

Lawen issued the birdcall signal and three hundred soldiers climbed the slope leading to the heights along a narrow pathway.

Gwyn rode Aluem along the path, scrutinizing the way.

He blinked.

The scouts he'd sent ahead had vanished in a growing haze. A fog crept in, thick and frigid. The moon blazed far above, but Gwyn couldn't see around him more than a foot or two. A smile broke across his lips and he urged Aluem on a little faster.

Two hours trickled away before Gwyn crested Dorshen Heights. Thick fog hung in the air as he peered down into the shadowed city of Bayton. Not a single candle lit the streets. A pall seemed to hover over it, despite the full moon.

"Behold Bayton," Gwyn whispered, "the city whose soul has been decimated by an ancient tyrant."

The first twenty men of the contingent heaped up earth along the heights under the cover of the fog, while a second group set up a series of small catapults Gwyn had commissioned from a sympathetic blacksmith. Crafted for fast disassembly to make transportation from location to location easier, Gwyn had been itching to try them out for weeks.

He'd only risked bringing three catapults up the cliffs tonight, but three would be more than enough to insight nervousness in the enemy. Volleys of loose rock were impossible to block from such a vantage point if Gwyn could suppress the magery of the Order of Corvus.

*If Nox fails, it's all we can hope for.*

The fog persisted while the soldiers took shifts to build their dirt battlements. At dawn, the listless sun rose and burned the fog away at a slithering pace. Noon arrived before the last of the shroud vanished under the sun's rays, revealing the new formation atop Dorshen Heights.

Gwyn ordered his banner raised. Under the bright sun, whipping and streaming in a breeze, a gold-threaded unicorn galloped and glistened across a white field.

A cry swelled up from the Crow King's army positioned around the walls of Bayton. The city guard dashed along the battlements below.

Gwyn glanced at the blue sky. No sign of Nox. He padded to Lawen's side at the nearest catapult. "Give them a warning. Make it clear."

"As Your Majesty commands."

With a crack, a single craggy stone pitched over the ledge. It soared through the air, pebbles breaking from the mass. Throbbing magic rippled across the air as Corvus mages snared the wind to halt the projectile's progress. Gwyn seized his chance. Adesta's magic pulsed on the far side of the dirt fortification, following his lead.

Every mage borrowed from the Weave, the core of life, to manipulate nature. The Crow King's mage order had claimed the Weave within a certain radius of Bayton and blocked it from anyone beyond those who had harnessed it.

Only those granted access could wield the Weave inside that border — but there was a single way around that rule. Gwyn and Adesta could travel the same path, the one granted by the Order, tracing it to its source as they might follow a single hole in a funnel traveling backward. There, they could block the Weave at the one access point that the Order must keep open to use their own magic.

A weak mage, one who housed no magic within himself, who only manipulated beyond his frame, would have no chance. But Gwyn had been tapping magic within himself, rather than beyond, since he'd first learned to wield magery. While that was just two and a half years ago, a dam of magic had been building inside him since his infancy. Within Gwyn dwelt an access point no mage could bar. All the Order of Corvus could do against him was block nature itself.

In open warfare, Gwyn's inner magic made little difference, for his body weakened quickly in combat. He must rely on the surrounding elements to sustain his defenses against multiple oncomers. But *this* coordinated defense was different. Against Lawen and Adesta, Gwyn had practiced igniting his defensive magic in a unique offensive strike, stoppering his opponents at their magic's access point, like a shield used to cut off a man's limbs.

Adesta — strong in magery as well — became adept at following Gwyn's trail and using his own core magic to fortify Gwyn's, turning that shield into a battering ram.

They traveled now across that inner funnel, threads of magic weaving into an attack strong enough to shatter Corvus's defenses. The battering ram struck and the mage barrier surrounding Bayton tumbled like water bursting from a dam.

The wind howled and rippled out in all directions, shuddering through the forest near the Crow King's armies.

Silence thundered through the sky following the shockwave.

*Let us win the day, Afallon. Let us rescue Bayton.*

A savage roar cut across the heavens and fire blossomed above.

Shrieks sounded from the army below, from Bayton itself, even from Gwyn's forces. Gwyn turned his eyes upward with a wide grin, heart soaring.

Glistening like emeralds and sapphires, wheeling across the wide blue expanse, sailed a dragon. Small, nearly imperceptible upon its back, rode two common, unassuming figures.

Lawen let out a hearty laugh. "By Afallon, he's done it! He's really done it!"

# Chapter Four

Not a drop of blood spilled. From Dorshen Heights, Gwyn watched the armies of the Crow King retreat en masse from within and around Bayton. The dragon circled overhead, streaming smoke from its great maw as though to encourage the enemy to move along a little quicker.

After the initial shock, Gwyn's band of men had whooped and cheered. Someone shouted, "It's our dragon. Ours!"

Even with the winged beast in view, Gwyn had refused to loosen his grip on the enemy's magic. A handful of powerful mages might risk standing against the dragon. Gwyn mustn't let that happen.

Evening fell before the retreating forces vanished from view in the south. General Haratin must have been watching, for his troops flooded the city at once, tore the Crow King's banner from the watchtower, and raised Gwyn's galloping unicorn.

'*Shall we go down?*' asked Aluem, pawing the ground with one hoof. '*I am eager to greet yon dragon.*'

Gwyn nodded, stomach knotting. Bayton would need food and other supplies he couldn't provide straight away. He would also need to fortify the city's defenses while he made ready to use the dragon to push toward Crowwell, where the Crow King sheltered in his castle for the winter.

Gwyn must press his newfound advantage, but he lacked the tools to do so.

He swung up onto Aluem's back and released his control on the Weave. A weight fell away as his body trembled and his vision wobbled. Motion caught his attention. He glanced left and found Adesta Gilhan approaching. The young man always looked pale, with long fair hair and large blue eyes, but in this moment, he appeared like a wisp of cloud that might fade away to nothing.

"Difficult to believe we succeeded," said Adesta in his heavy Fraeli accent. He bowed his head as he reached Gwyn's side. "The little dreaming fool came through with his dragon. It appears I've lost a few wagers."

Gwyn smiled. "And I have won a few."

Adesta chuckled. "I shall pay you soon. The result is well worth the loss of a little gold." He wavered on his feet. "Are you heading down?"

Gwyn nodded. "Do you want a ride?"

The Fraeli nobleman shook his head. "No, no. I shall find my own way. Unicorns are not for petty soldiers to ride. Go on, Your Majesty. I will be along."

"You aren't a petty soldier, Master Mage. I honor you for your work today."

Adesta laughed. "You, sire, would honor a cow for its milk, or a chicken for its eggs, or a bee for its honey."

Gwyn frowned. "That I would, Lord Gilhan. Perhaps if we honored such achievements more highly than we do lesser things like gold or sport, we would finally find that ever elusive state called peace."

Adesta's smile faded. "I was in jest only, sire."

Gwyn sighed and scrubbed a hand over his face. "And I well know it. Forgive me, Adesta. I'm exhausted and out of humor."

The Fraeli mage nodded, a smile twitching at his lips again. "I think you can be forgiven a slight defect of character now and then, my royal friend. It is a pleasant reminder that you are merely human like the rest of us."

Gwyn managed a grim smile. "Perhaps royalty is the most human of any line. Except for those descended from crows. And if being inhuman requires such a state as his, I welcome my defects — countless though they be."

Adesta snorted. "Your greatest shortcoming, my lord, is your self-depreciation. You're a good man. Someday the entire world will know it and shall laud your name for centuries to come."

Heat climbed Gwyn's cheeks. He swallowed down the urge to bolt and shook his head. "Enough of your flattery, you serpent." He patted Aluem's neck. "Let's go before this creature ruins me with his lies."

The unicorn trotted off, but Adesta's laughter rang in Gwyn's ears, welcome in its sound, but heavy against his shoulders. While the flattery of his friends warmed his heart, his gut wrenched. The Crow King had been of the Ilidreth once; a fae being, fair as sunshine and gentle as moonlight. Something had changed him.

Gwyn could recite the names of countless kings and queens throughout history whose benevolent reigns had become tinged with the blood of warfare and the greed of the power-hungry. Tales of once-noble kings turned tyrant sang out a warning to any who might hearken.

What stained a man's character so? Where had he taken his first misstep? What had been his first whispered temptation or the last before he fell?

How could Gwyn avoid such a fate, where so many other great souls had not?

# Chapter Five

Straw and rubbish littered the streets of Bayton. Buildings of commerce stood scorched from fire, slumped open, plundered, and desecrated.

A pall of despair hovered over the citizens of the once-thriving port city. Hungry eyes peered between curtains in the townhouses Gwyn passed as he rode under evening's gaze to Bayton's square. A handful of mounted men followed at his back. General Haratin remained at the main gates, awaiting his return. Before Gwyn discussed their next strategy, he wanted to take in Bayton's condition for himself.

A smell wafted from ahead, growing stronger. The twin odors of death: Iron and urine, mingling with smoke. As he neared the square, Gwyn braced himself.

Aluem's hooves faltered. The unicorn's ears flicked back, and his nostrils flared. '*Dark magic, Gwynter.*'

Gwyn sensed it too. The tint of corrupt magic dusted the square, invisible to the common eye, but writhing like myriad ants to a mage's view.

The dissident dead had been drawn and quartered. Four bloody heads jutted on spikes above the charred remains of dismembered limbs upon a pyre.

Someone had nailed a slab of wood to a separate spike, its message painted in blood:

*Beware all ye who look upon this sight, for this is the fate of all who defy Divine Afallon and His Crow King's will.*

Insides churning, Gwyn tasted bile on his tongue. He turned away. Tears burned his eyes, but he blinked them back. Lawen trotted to his side upon his dappled mount and rested a hand on Gwyn's arm.

"Find out who they were," whispered Gwyn, when he found his voice. "I would honor their sacrifice."

"Yes, sire."

Gwyn turned from the square, searching the surrounding buildings. "What now, Lawen? What hope can I give them? I don't even have the food they require."

"We'll get it," Lawen murmured. "Your council is striving every day to obtain the promised goods from your backers."

Gwyn grunted. His *council*. His *backers*. Towwen Brym, Brioc Ffyr, and even Gwyn's childhood friend, Towwen Stone — or as Lawen called them: "The Towwens' Brymstone and their friendly Ffyr" — had formed a council, inviting into their circle all who supported Gwyn's claim to the throne. A claim he had yet to make.

The council was twenty strong now and growing by Brioc's reports. They had settled in Charquae, the single high-profile city in open defiance against the Crow King. There, the council put out the word: *The line of Wintervale hasn't failed.*

Daily, the council labored to gather backers to support Gwyn's army. Merchants and tradesmen and even plantation owners had come forth to pledge their goods and service in Gwyn's name — but most had yet to make good on that pledge. Meanwhile, Gwyn's army starved. It lacked weapons and decent armor. Horses were scarce.

*Perhaps the dragon might encourage them to come through a little faster.*

A gust of wind snared Gwyn's gaze. The dragon circled low, long, and lithe, bright even in the dusk.

Aluem raised his head and bayed a sound. A rumble like thunder descended in answer, and the dragon circled lower. Nox waved from his place where the dragon's neck joined the rest of his graceful body. Behind him rode Nox's quiet friend Nathael.

"Tell them to land outside Bayton's gates," Gwyn said. "We'll meet them there."

Aluem bayed again, relaying the message. The dragon changed course, and wind rushed by Gwyn again, thumping his light brown ponytail against his back.

"Come, my friend," Gwyn said, stroking Aluem's neck. "Time to meet the dragon. There's little else to see here."

Perhaps with the dawn, Bayton would stir. Fear had been too faithful a companion for the past year to withdraw in a single day.

Aluem carried Gwyn from the square and its gruesome display. As they reached its edge and entered the main thoroughfare leading to the gates, a breeze stirred on Gwyn's left. An arrow whistled as a bowstring hummed. He turned his head toward the sound, magic stirring in his veins. The arrow missed him by half an inch, whispering past his ear.

Gwyn's gaze settled on the man peeking from the broken doorway of a sagging townhouse, a bow clutched in his hands. Wrath and panic burned in the man's eyes. His cheeks were sunken. His skin appeared gray as ash in the pallid dusk.

"Down with the Winter Traitor!" the man shouted, voice cracking.

"Gwyn?" asked Lawen, arrow nocked and aimed at the man.

"Feed him," Gwyn said. "Then take him prisoner. Don't let him harm my men, nor let them harm him. He's done me no injury."

Lawen nodded. "As you wish." At a signal, two of Gwyn's entourage dismounted from their horses and seized the man, dragged him from the house, and tied his wrists behind his back.

The man made no sound, but as his eyes collided with Gwyn's, he spat on the ground.

"Bloody traitor. You'll burn for treason and heresy!"

Gwyn turned away. "Feed him well. He's thin as a reed."

"As you wish, sire," replied a soldier.

The prisoner scoffed. "I'll not take food from rebel scum! Better to kill me now. I want none of your so-called benevolence."

Gwyn glanced at the prisoner. "You might not take from rebel scum, but what of the fields of Afallon? He grows the crops. Take from Him and give thanks for the sustenance."

He urged Aluem on. The contingent followed. Gwyn's hands trembled as he adjusted his grip on Aluem's mane.

*'Are you well, Gwynter? Did the man frighten you?'*

Gwyn shook his head. How could he describe the feelings roiling in his core? Not fear, not anger. Determination, yes. His very soul yearned to overthrow the tyrant who had inflicted so much harm on Simaerin and its people. But could Gwyn succeed? Had he the skill and the fortitude to see this war through?

Long gone were the days of his youth when he'd dreamt of leading armies to distinguish himself in combat. Now, there was little choice and little chance, yet the cause mattered far more than past squabbles with the Fraeli or the Ilidreth.

*I must find a way.*

Only by Afallon's will could he win. Afallon, and those sent by His will to guide Gwyn true.

The gates loomed closer. Gwyn allowed himself a grim smile. Beyond that barrier stood a mighty fire-breathing chance, thanks to Nox and his friend. It was far more than Gwyn had before. Even the Crow King must acknowledge that much.

But what might the tyrant send in reply?

The gates parted as Gwyn approached. He glanced overhead to find his banner flapping in the night breeze, then he crossed under the portcullis and stepped out onto the plains sprawling before Bayton. There, in terrible majesty, stretched Nox's dread dragon, glistening with green and blue scales as vibrant as the Vaymeer Ocean.

The heavy-set youth stood before the dragon, waving a hand over his head. "Your Majesty, you see? We came in time! Just as I promised, I tamed a dragon!"

As Aluem cantered toward the youth, Gwyn found himself laughing. "So you did, Nox. Very well done!"

Nox beamed so bright that his eyes looked like the stars appearing above. He gestured to his friend as Gwyn flung himself from Aluem's back. "You recall Nathael, my friend and accomplice on my mad quest?"

"But of course." Gwyn nodded to Nathael as he took Nox's hand and shook it heartily. "My thanks and congratulations to you both, Nox. You've won the day for us, just when we needed such a victory most." He grinned. "Your feat will go down in history no matter how this war ends, and you shall likely be hailed as the maddest adventurer who ever lived to tame a dragon."

Nox laughed, face flushed. "I'm only glad I could help, sire. Truly, it's a wondrous day for our cause." He turned toward the dragon. "His name is Parsha of the Azure Isle of Wayfaring Dreams. In short, sire, he's quite a poetic soul. Not at all fearsome — unless provoked."

"Noted." Gwyn took a step toward the dragon called Parsha and bowed low. "Greetings, Friend Dragon. I thank you warmly for your aid this day."

The dragon fixed his white-blue eyes on him, slitted pupils shrinking to narrowest slivers. Parsha inclined his head, and the mane of hair that draped down his long neck shimmered like it held tiny gems, while smoke streamed from his nostrils. His voice poured into Gwyn's mind like a torrent of rain in a thunderstorm. '*Greetings, tiny king of the mundane world. You rather resemble your late great-great-great-great-grandfather. A bit taller, though, for something so tiny.*'

Gwyn caught the glint in the dragon's eye. "My thanks for such *lofty* praise, mighty one."

The dragon bared his fangs in a grin. '*It is good to know you are not without humor, Wintervale.*' His eyes slid to Aluem. '*Mighty prince of unicorns, what brings you out in these turbulent times? Does the mundane lad carry promise enough that you would brave such woes as war brings?*'

Aluem tossed his head. '*Do not worry so for me, Parsha the Poet. This lad is a mage and not mundane at all.*'

Parsha's eyes returned to Gwyn. '*Aye, so it seems.*'

'*Besides,*' Aluem continued, '*You are here. What compelled you to slither from your dank cave?*'

Parsha's grin stretched. '*The boy who brought me here. He came to my cave, not to slay me, but to* tame *me. Of all the strange notions of this world, I've never heard its equal. When he declared it, I could not help but laugh. And laughter is so contagious, the robust child laughed with me. Soon we were friends, for laughter secured that bond at once. Thus, when he next implored me as a friend to become tame and let him ride me into battle, I assented. It feels good to stretch my wings.*'

Aluem shook his head. '*Beware, Parsha, for this war is not like other mortal affairs. The Crow King is Ilidreth, and far fallen.*'

'*Aye, that I knew. I am not so removed from the mundane world as unicorns oft-times attempt to be. But you, Aluem of the Crystal Vale, are either very brave or very foolish. Perhaps the former secures the latter. Never mind. Shall we remain friends in this engagement?*'

Aluem nodded. '*Our companions are allies, so I recommend that course.*'

The dragon gave his own, great nod. '*Excellent. So it shall be.*' The dragon turned his head toward Nox, and seemed to communicate with him, but Gwyn heard none of his words, cut off from the dragon's mind.

"I gather he's here to stay?" whispered Gwyn.

Aluem nodded. '*Aye, my kin and king. He will stay. But do not rejoice overmuch, for two reasons: First, the Crow King will seek his own ally of the winged beasts, and some can be bought if not chained. Second, and this is of immense importance: Parsha is a dragon poet, but that does not make him any good. Do not ask him to recite a single verse. Not even once. Am I clear, young Gwynter?*'

Gwyn nodded vehemently.

'*Good. One wrong phrase from his fanged snout, and our armies may well lose this war at once.*'

Gwyn's eyes widened, and he wondered if the dragon could be so bad as that, or if Aluem — honest, worthy friend — was perhaps exaggerating. Gwyn decided it might be best if he never found out which.

# Chapter Six

A fitful night on the plains compelled Gwyn from his bedroll early. Lawen sat awake on his own bedroll, perhaps fearing Gwyn would wander off on his own and get himself killed.

But Gwyn wasn't foolish enough to seek solitude so close to Bayton. Yesterday's incident with the hungry bowman had been a striking reminder of the hostility festering there. Though the Crow King had locked more people than mage sympathizers in Bayton for the past fifteen months, Gwyn's forces made a steady target for those loyal to the Crow Crown to blame.

Bayton was a dangerous place no matter whose side you stood on, and Gwyn well knew it.

He strode from his tent, Lawen at his side. A mist hovered on the plains, forming shades and shadows to taunt one's vision. Kive appeared ahead, so slender and pale, he looked like a phantom of the mists.

"Hello, Shiny. Hello, Hawk."

"How was your night, Kive?" asked Gwyn.

"I said hello to Fairy Wren. She was with Rabbit."

Gwyn frowned. "How is Rabbit?"

"Still dying," Kive replied rather cheerily.

It wasn't true, but Kive didn't understand fevers, just as he didn't understand people. He viewed Adesta as a rabbit and claimed the mage lay dying, though it was common for mages to grow sick after they drained their magic reservoirs. "Fairy Wren" was tending to him until the fever broke.

Gwyn thought of the girl with a smile. Nathaera ren Lotelon, the disowned daughter of Lord Traycen ren Lotelon, a now-deceased mage once in the Crow King's service. Nathaera was a stubborn young woman, insistent on marching with the armies rather than staying at home and sewing quilts. When Gwyn had encouraged her to live with his mother and sisters in a safehouse outside Charquae, she'd refused.

Over a year ago, she'd declared feelings of love for Gwyn. He'd never broached the subject since, at first afraid he would hurt her, and after a while, afraid he'd waited too long.

Surely, she didn't entertain the same feelings anymore. By now she'd formed a close connection with Adesta, who had helped her escape to Fraelin two years ago to save Kive's life. She and Adesta were nearly always together now. Adesta adored her; anyone could see that. His countenance lit up whenever she approached him. That must be why Nathaera stayed with the army. Adesta was here, helping in the war — the man who'd always been there for her, as Gwyn only tried to be.

What Gwyn's feelings for her might be now, he didn't ask himself. Why explore them when it was obvious he'd missed his chance? Besides, the war was too important to spare time for his private life. He had no private life now. Everything he was, everything he did or said or thought, was published by those around him. He'd become a symbol. A king.

Lawen's soft voice speared Gwyn's reverie. "Your thoughts are heavier than the mist. Where are you, Gwynny?"

"Sorry. I'm worried about Adesta. His fever should have broken by now."

"What about you? Any symptoms?"

"I didn't tax myself too much. I'm afraid Adesta took the brunt as we withdrew from the blockade." The world wobbled beneath Gwyn's feet, but that was normal when he used magery. It would pass. "Should we check in on him?"

Lawen searched his face. "Certainly. Nathaera would enjoy seeing us. I'm confident she has much to say." He clapped Kive on the shoulder. "What say you, my good man? Shall you lead us through this unsavory mist to yon maiden?"

Kive stared at Lawen.

Gwyn smiled. "Take us to Fairy Wren, Kive. Please."

"Oh!" Kive danced toward the northerly tents. "Oh, yes. Fairy Wren. This way, Shiny. This way, Hawk. Fairy Wren is cooking Rabbit."

The brothers chuckled. Kive's world looked vastly different from theirs, and they welcomed the distraction it carried.

Mist pulled at Gwyn's feet as he moved forward, hair damp, cloak sodden. Soon he reached the tent where Adesta lodged. It was ornate compared to the surrounding tents, commissioned from Fraelin, where fashions were extravagant. The exterior was made of lavish patterns and threaded in silver, while the interior stood plush and warm, full of rugs and pillows, lamps, and incense.

Kive pranced inside ahead of the brothers.

Adesta lay across an imported chaise lounge, pale and perspiring. Nathaera knelt before him, a cloth dripping in one hand, frozen in mid-motion. Her green-blue eyes pinned on Gwyn. "Sire!" She tossed the dripping cloth aside, sprang to her feet, and curtsied low. Her golden hair bobbed along with her, then settled against her homespun dress of dull gray. Despite the plainness of her garb, the lady was no less fair than she'd been as a noblewoman. Indeed, against the gray, her eyes glowed brighter, cheeks pinker, and her slight, lithe frame appeared more graceful.

Gwyn flushed. "There's no need for such formalities among friends, Nathaera. I only came to see how Adesta is faring."

"Ah. Right. Of course." She bit her lip and turned her back on Gwyn to face the lounge. "He's still fevered, but I think it will break soon. He strained himself a little too much. I suspect he was trying to take the brunt of the assault against Corvus. That sounds like him."

Gwyn came closer. "It certainly does." He towered more than a foot above her, and she glanced up at him with her wide, friendly smile.

"How are you, Gwyn?" she whispered.

Gwyn caught her infectious smile. "A little tired, but otherwise I'm well. And you?"

"Oh, well enough, I suppose. Except I do long for a decent bath now and then. Creek-bathing in the winter is utter rubbish and hauling water in to boil just takes so long. We need proper bath tents as the Crow King's got."

"Shall we borrow some of his?" asked Lawen, approaching.

"His rats?" asked Kive as he leaned over the back of the chaise lounge to finger Adesta's nose. "Rabbit. Twitch. Twitch, Rabbit."

Adesta's nose obediently twitched.

Gwyn chuckled. "Leave him alone, Kive. Rabbit is sleeping."

"Sleeeep, Rabbit," Kive whispered in his drawling tones.

"That's probably good for him," Nathaera said. "His slumber is fitful. Perhaps Kive's command will give him a deeper sleep to fight that fever. Well done, Kive."

"Thank you, Fairy Wren," replied the fallen fae, still fingering Adesta's nose. "Rabbit is sleeping."

"I'd like very much to borrow a lot of the Crow King's goods," said Nathaera. "But we can't get that close. Even the dragon won't easily break his magical barriers. Neither you nor Adesta has the strength to keep pulling the stunt you did yesterday."

The bleakness of his situation closed in again around Gwyn like giant hands wrapping around his soul, squeezing. His shoulders slumped and he sighed. "Yet we can only press on. Nox has done us a great service, and I'll not waste the hope it provides, even should that hope be a sliver."

"I wouldn't call a dragon a sliver," said Lawen.

Nathaera nodded, hands on her hips. "Nor I, even should he look like one — which this one doesn't. Dragons are temperamental by all reports."

"Parsha seems nice," Gwyn said.

"Is the giant lizard staying?" asked Kive, looking up from his slumbering prey.

"For now, yes."

"Will I eat him?"

Gwyn snorted. "I'd not try, Kive."

"Of course not, Shiny. *Shinies* don't *eat* lizards. Kives do. And I'm Kive. Will I eat him?"

"Don't," answered Nathaera. "You'll likely get a bellyache like that time you ate that entire bucket of toads. Dreadful."

"I did not get a bellyache," Kive shot back. "The toads just didn't like being eaten."

"Exactly. Imagine how much worse it would be to have a giant lizard living in your belly, not enjoying having been eaten."

Kive's eyes widened, and he draped himself over the lounge and leaned close to Adesta's face. "Rabbit. Don't eat giant lizards. It makes them grumpy. Also, don't eat Fairy Wrens, for it makes them likewise. Shhh. Sleep."

Gwyn, Lawen, and Nathaera laughed until their mirth rang hollow.

"What's your next plan?" asked Nathaera.

Gwyn's chest tightened. "We march for Crowwell."

Nathaera blinked. "But we don't have the resources. And it's the dead of winter."

"I realize that. But if we delay, our dragon won't be the only firestorm upon the field. We'll lose the single advantage we possess."

"We have two advantages," Lawen said with a reassuring smile. "Our cause is righteous, and thus we have Afallon's blessing. That's something the Crow King forsook in his madness if he ever believed."

“Three advantages,” said Nathaera, stooping to pick up the cloth she’d abandoned. She straightened and met Gwyn’s eyes. “The Crow King can’t kill you. His magic won’t let him — by the grace of Lady Shalesta of Swan Castle.”

There were crueler fates than death, but Gwyn pushed a smile to his lips and nodded.

# Chapter Seven

Crowwell, the royal capital of Simaerin, stood five hundred miles southward, across countless winter wastes, fallow fields, icy rivers, and legions of the Crow King's armies. Gwyn ordered Nox to fly ahead on Parsha's back to scout out the way, while he and the war council dealt with Bayton's dilemma. The rotund boy eagerly obeyed.

Nox's friend, Nathael, stayed behind and asked to meet privately with Gwyn on the first gray morning after the army settled outside the port city. Snow fell, dusting the camp in white powder.

Gwyn sat behind his desk within the command tent, aides and generals dismissed, though they'd dragged their feet about it. In the tent's gloom, a single candle bobbed in a stray breeze, and shadows played around it, painting the maps and walls in shades.

Nathael stood before Gwyn: A slight, youthful, comely figure, flaxen hair tied back, clothes plain and patched, but clean. A frown on his lips etched deep lines against his forehead, like he wanted to say something, but didn't know quite how. His hands tugged at the hem of his shirt.

"What did you wish to discuss?" asked Gwyn, smiling to ease

the young man's nerves. It never grew less strange that a man several years his senior felt uncomfortable in his presence.

"Forgive me, sire," said Nathael, gasping out the words.

"For what?" asked Gwyn, tilting his head to one side.

"I know your generals feel this audience is far above my station. They're right. Only, I have something to say — to ask — and I can't be silent any longer."

Gwyn nodded. "Apparently not. Though I must refute the idea that your station is beneath mine. I'm human, just like you. I'm Simaeri, just like you. Does that not make us equal under Afallon's heaven? Say on."

The lines on Nathael's face smoothed. His cheeks reddened and his blue eyes shone. "Thank you, sire. It's this: I have always feared the Crow King. I've seen his tyranny from my early youth. While he coddled and bribed nobility, we of the peasant caste were mere cattle to be used as he saw fit. My father died in combat in a war overseas. What the cause was, I hardly know. Something that barely affected affairs in Simaerin. He had no choice. He was a serf. Not a slave, for his skin was fair, but serfs are little better treated — only easier to conceal when they're dragged from their homes and sent by boats to fight.

"My mother and I never saw him again. She was with child but starved to death before she gave birth to my little brother or sister. I fled from those who would sell me and lived on the streets of Charquae until Nox's good father helped me shed that life.

"By rights, sire, I'm a runaway slave. By rights, I should be drafted into the Crow King's army by now, fighting against you. Only divine Afallon's intervention spared me that dread fate. But though I've lived well learning the trade of a baker, and though I'm skilled in that trade, yet my heart has been troubled by the goings-on within Simaerin. I asked myself how I could live under the banner of an evil man whose reign is dyed in red and rot. And then I heard about you.

"At first, your name was merely one more among the Crow King's lackeys. You were more skilled than most, and more just than most, but still a man of the king, so sworn. Then came the glad news of your lineage. Of your banner. Nox and I both resolved at once to find you and join your cause. Nox is a kind soul, and his heart is pure. He serves you because he believes you're the rightful king. I don't."

Gwyn held Nathael's eyes steadily. "Why do you serve me?"

"Because, rightful king or otherwise, your cause is just. You promise liberty for the nobleman *and* the slave. You promise mercy, for the freeman and the bondsman. You promise Simaerin renewed, cut loose from the chains that have long held her fast to a legacy of murder and deceit. I believe you mean to keep your promises. You could be the illegitimate son of a farmer's daughter, for all I know — but I would follow you, for you bring hope where I've long held fear and hate."

Nathael shuffled his feet. "We well know your character in the streets of Charquae, sire. Even in the Crow King's service, you enforced discipline and reverence in the troops you commanded. You killed no more than was needful. You heeded the cry of the oppressed. Now you stand to oppose the Crow King, and though your forces are few and your supplies scant, you still stand. Such integrity hasn't been known in an age, at least."

Gwyn bowed his head, shoulders tight. Drawing a long breath, he stared at his hands folded against the top of his desk. "You do me too much credit, friend, but I thank you for your faith." He looked up. "Why do you make this grand speech?"

"I do have a purpose in presenting myself, sire," Nathael said. "Only let me make my intentions clear: I swear my fealty to you, King Gwynter ren Wintervale. My life is yours."

Gwyn squeezed his palms together. "I accept your fealty, and gladly."

Nathael smiled, eyes shining brighter. "I'm your man, sire, and thus I make one request."

"What is it?"

"Let me serve as your spy, sire. Nox rides the clouds, but I can play my part upon the ground just as well. My time on the streets has taught me how to blend with the crowds of any city. My ears are sharp, my wit sharper still. Let me play the spy, and I will gather whatever information I can glean in Crowwell to aid us."

Gwyn's shoulders relaxed. "Let me ask but one question before I grant your request. You've seen me ride, I presume."

"Aye, sire. Often."

"What do you make of my steed?"

Nathael's eyes lit up. 'Tis the fairest creature I've ever beheld. I'd never thought to see a unicorn in my life, sire."

Gwyn's smile deepened. "Your request, Nathael, is granted. And I thank you for your willingness. You may go with my trust and"—he rose and grabbed a leather purse lying upon the edge of the desk—"take this. It isn't much, but it will help you along your journey. Also, take one of the officer's horses. The fastest." He tossed the purse. Nathael caught it deftly.

"Thank you, sire." The young man bowed low.

"Find a priest called Rindermarr Lorric. He can give you shelter while you stay in Crowwell. May Afallon ride with you, Captain."

Nathael blinked, then grinned. "And with you, Your Majesty." He bowed and strode from the tent, the proudest promoted serf's son Gwyn had ever beheld.

Lawen appeared at the entrance in the next heartbeat. "Are you well?"

Gwyn nodded and bowed his head to hide the tears in his eyes. "Were all men as noble-hearted as he, this world would become Afallon's heaven."

# Chapter Eight

A solitary armored figure rode into Gwyn's camp as night settled dark and grim over the plains. Bened Arnnor, a once-decorated knight in the Crow King's army, presented himself to Gwyn and fell to one knee.

"I swear unwavering fealty to the King of Wintervale, rightful heir of Simaerin," Bened declared before Gwyn's officers and aides within the council tent. "My sword, my cunning, and my heart belong to you, sire."

Gwyn considered the kneeling man for a long moment from his chair atop a makeshift dais. Bened Arnnor was a man in his prime, with dark hair and dark eyes, an aristocratic nose, and a well-muscled, tall frame. "What of your oath of service to the Crow King, Sir Bened?"

"My oath is to the rightful king, and he is not that man. Thus, my honor is not spoiled, but is elevated by my actions here."

"Well said," murmured General Leelin.

General Haratin sported a sour frown as he strode from his place near Gwyn's chair. "I know of the Knight of Arnnor. You've lost several campaigns against the northern Fraeli Keeps. For what were you decorated? Feats of outstanding stupidity?" He barked a laugh and several seasoned generals joined him.

Bened colored and lifted his head to meet Haratin's derision with a sneer. "My campaigns in the north were well plotted and executed. Had we more men and resources than the Crow King afforded us, we'd have taken Keep Montré. As to Keep Canad, it was an ill-advised effort. I told the Crow King as much. He was a fool not to heed me. Regarding my decorations, I was honored with them for different campaigns, no more or less worthy than my northern battles. A loss does not undo the glory of other days."

"But losing lives in battle is the responsibility of he who commands," Haratin growled.

"Indeed, General Haratin." Bened's eyes gleamed in the candlelight. "Such as at Suffon and Kender."

Haratin turned a brilliant red and Gwyn feared he would explode in his rage. "How dare you broach a subject you know nothing—?"

"On the contrary," said Bened in a low, calm tone. "I know a great deal. I've studied your shoddy war tactics since my infancy and found glorious sport in improving each one." A smirk crawled across his lips.

Haratin lurched forward, drawing his blade. Bened fleetly rose, pulling his sword to meet his challenger.

Gwyn pushed from his chair and raised a hand. A barrier sprang up between them, shimmering with a faint pearlescent sheen, harder than rock. Haratin's sword met the barrier with a deafening clang, and he stumbled back, sword slipping from his fingers.

Lawen took a single step forward where he stood on Gwyn's right side. "There will be no duel before the king, my lords. Contain yourselves and behave as sensible Simaeri soldiers under the Unicorn banner."

Bened sheathed his broadsword and dropped to one knee, clapping a hand to his breastplate. "Forgive me, sire. I provoked General Haratin needlessly."

"It isn't my forgiveness you must seek," Gwyn replied quietly, "but that of the man whose pride you've injured."

A vein pulsed near Bened's eye, but still kneeling, he angled himself toward Haratin and bowed his head low before the barrier. "My humblest apologies, General, for thoughtless words in a moment of heat. I failed to give you the proper respect afforded to an officer so long dedicated to the service of his country, no matter the ineptitude of its execution."

Haratin's eyes widened as splotches of red dotted his face. He spluttered and whirled toward Gwyn, stabbing a finger at his offender. "You see, Your Majesty? This uncouth pup has insulted me yet again! I demand satisfaction."

Gwyn stepped from the dais. The hum of the barrier murmured in his ear as he stood before Bened. "You will have it, General Haratin, though it will not be by the drawing of blood. Sir Bened Arnnor, do you deny that your words to General Haratin have been intentionally injurious?"

"No, sire. I meant every one to cut."

"Why?"

Bened shifted to bow toward Gwyn and raised his eyes. "Because he's a fool, and every student of warfare knows it well."

"Yet you said yourself that years of service to his country affords the general a certain level of respect, did you not?"

"I did, sire."

"Are you a man of your word, sir?"

"Yes, sire."

"And you have sworn your fealty to me," Gwyn said quietly.

"Yes, sire. Wholeheartedly."

"Then you will submit to my judgment?"

"Whatever it be," said Bened, "I will view it as justice."

"Then you will act under General Haratin's command as his aide for three months."

Bened's jaw fell open. "B-but, sire—"

Gwyn spoke over his protests. "*If* during that time you prove yourself as loyal as you say, and *if* I am satisfied by your efforts to place respect where it belongs regardless of your personal opinions, I will give you a contingent of your own and you will stand equally with Generals Haratin and Leelin at my war council. I have heard of your cunning and bravery. Let me see them and you will be rewarded."

Bened closed his mouth and bowed his head for several heartbeats. "Sire, your judgment *is* fair, but I fear for my wellbeing. General Haratin nearly cleaved me in two for my insolence. Will he not make my duties hard beyond enduring to be avenged?"

"Possibly he will," Gwyn said, nodding. "And if that should happen, I will reverse your roles over the next three months so that the general knows better the demands of justice." He turned toward Haratin. "Do I make myself plain, General?"

Haratin scowled but inclined his head. "I'd not stoop to such a level, Your Majesty. I too value the knight's cunning and I will make full use of it."

"Very good." Gwyn looked again at Bened. "I would have a private word with you on another matter. This council of war will resume on the morrow."

The armored men filed from the tent, leaving Gwyn and Lawen alone with the decorated knight.

Gwyn sighed. "Please rise."

Bened climbed to his feet.

"I'm sorry you had to provoke General Haratin that way," Gwyn said. "I'd much rather have given you your own force of arms immediately." His eyes narrowed. "But I won't allow pride and arrogance to run amok among my council. You should have held your tongue before a seasoned officer, Sir Knight."

"I realize that now, sire. I fully understand your actions. They were just."

"I'm glad you see sense. Enough on that. I placed you with General Haratin for two reasons." Gwyn strode to his chair and sat. "First, to teach you some much-needed humility. But also because General Haratin is *not* a competent strategist. His plans are simple to predict. He spreads his forces across a field in perfect rows to be picked off easily. You, Sir Bened, have a more unique approach to combat which may give us the edge we need in this war."

Bened nodded, eyes bright. "Stealth, sire."

"Exactly. Our tactics must carry an unpredictable element."

"Such as with your dragon." Bened grinned. "It was a brilliant stroke, sire. I was already on my way when I learned of your victory at Bayton. I came with greater haste after that, eager to serve a king whose cleverness is such as yours."

"That was not my cleverness, but the heroic genius of one of my men. You see, Sir Knight, a war isn't won by one man's prowess, but by the careful blending of many minds. That is how we'll win if win we can."

"Sire, we will win," Bened said, "for I cannot long abide failure."

## Chapter Nine

Two days later Gwyn received word that supplies would arrive at Bayton within the week. Relieved, he entered the port city again and rode to the square, now cleared of the remains of the dead. A tinge of dark magic still permeated the air. Aluem shifted as Gwyn studied the three men standing before him.

The city's magistrates, Lord Breye, Lord Tull, and Lord Succunder, stood somber and silent in robes of scarlet bearing the crest of the Crow King.

Gwyn inclined his head. "Thank you for meeting with me."

Lord Breye, eldest and senior of the three heads of Bayton, sneered. "We do so as prisoners. We do not acknowledge your claim to Simaerin, nor that you are anything more than a malcontent youth thirsting for power and blood. What right have you to bombard our city with your rebel forces and drive away the Crow King's protection?"

"Protection?" Said Gwyn. "You astound me. He locked you within Bayton to starve, yet you declare his act a noble one?"

Lord Succunder scoffed. "He taught a valuable lesson to the rabble who would openly defy him. Those vile souls who wield magic brought the king's wrath down upon Bayton. We approved of his actions against such blasphemers."

Gwyn's hands curled into fists. "You *approved* of the death sentence the tyrant king sealed upon your city? Blind, foolish, heartless souls! Do you care one whit what happens to your fellows? Women and children have *died* these past fifteen months. Your trade has halted. Your food stores are used up. Even your fresh water is nearly depleted. Bayton dwells by the east sea, but you're virtually cut off from its riches — and you *approved* it? Did you desire so much to die in the name of loyalty?"

Lord Breye raised his chin. "We die by Afallon's will. Had you not invoked the Crow King's wrath, this would not have gone on so long. It's at *your* feet that the blood of the fallen rests, Gwynter ren Terare! Your rebellion will quake Simaerin for decades to come, and what befalls your rabble army is no one's fault but your own. Can you in good conscience plunge this country into civil war? Is the throne so important to you? Pah! You'll never sit upon it, little boy. We loyalists shall never bow the knee to a usurper."

Lawen urged his horse forward several paces. "Oh? How odd then to see so many doing just that. You're the fools. You've bowed to a usurper these many years. The Crow King is no Simaeri king. He's not human at all. The Crow King is Ilidreth."

Gwyn reached a hand toward his brother. "Enough. We've no evidence to present to them. Your words sound ludicrous."

The magistrates stared at Lawen.

"Ahh," said Lord Tull, speaking for the first time. He was a short, balding man, with sharp eyes and a viperous smile. "I see. A clever move, Lord ren Terare. Gather the madmen and lunatics to your banner. Use them to win your throne. Well played, but it will avail you nothing. The Crow King shall long stand watch over Simaerin, and none shall be his end."

A chill raced through Gwyn, crawling like ants along his insides. "You're a mage of Corvus. I know your kind well."

The magistrate's smile widened. "I'm but a servant of the Crow King."

"Just as Lord Traycen ren Lotelon was," said Gwyn. "The Crow King's mindless puppet, a mere extension of his hand. This is how he's slithered his way into the great cities of Simaerin. You already know the truth, Lord Tull. You know the Crow King's blood, and you care not a whit."

He turned from the mage and caught Lord Breye's gaze. "Food and clothes will arrive here soon from Charquae. You would be foolish to refuse them. Let your people eat at my expense and know that I freed Bayton not for my sake or yours, but for the oppressed people of Simaerin."

He wheeled Aluem around and trotted from the square, Lawen, Haratin, Bened, and several other officers at his back. Along the street, Gwyn caught sight of a little girl leaning from a second-story window of a scarred townhouse. She waved at him, a shy smile on her lips, dark hair long and loose against her shoulders. Next second, someone pulled her inside and drew the curtain tight.

He smiled to himself, relieved children still survived here. The Crow King hadn't murdered them all.

# PART II
# CROSSING THE DELESAR

# Chapter Ten

Camped on the banks of the Delesar, Gwyn stared at the missives clutched in his fingers. He sat on a rotted-out log, listening to the rush of the ornery old river as it carried chunks of ice toward the eastern channel.

The two letters contained the second and third strands of unwelcome news in recent hours. The first had come last night, bearing a report that Charquae, seat of Gwyn's greatest support, had fallen under attack. The Crow King had sent a dragon — a red-scaled, fire-breathing behemoth. Gwyn could only pray that Nox and Parsha, whom he'd sent out as soon as they'd returned from their daily scouting, would reach Charquae soon enough to stop the dread beast's barrage.

Even then, with two such warriors in the sky, what damage might descend upon the unprotected city? Were his mother and sisters safe?

The Crow King's reply to Gwyn's victory at Bayton had come at last. Even with a recent influx of new recruits to double the Winter Army, this boded ill for Gwyn's infant forces. The Crow King's trained and capable force of arms had far outstripped Gwyn's present numbers already. Now, with a dragon on the Crow's side, only a miracle would grant Gwyn the might to defeat such odds.

He prayed daily for such a miracle.

Once, he would have ridden to Charquae's defense with Kive, for the fallen fae could order the dragon to retreat, but Gwyn suspected the Crow King wanted him to make such a move. Gwyn wouldn't risk Kive's life. Not when the Crow King wanted so badly to destroy him.

Today's news matched Charquae's situation. His latest supply wagons had been ambushed and pilfered en route. That meant no food, no weapons, no clothes, and no money to pay Gwyn's officers. Again. This was the third time Charquae's supply wagons had been waylaid, and under the present aerial threat, nothing more would come from that city for the time being. Perhaps ever.

The last missive, sent by Captain Nathael en route to Crowwell, sank Gwyn's spirits into the depths. The Crow King had allied himself with the Heshi. A mercenary army hired to destroy Gwyn's rebellion. The Heshi hailed from Hesh-Kasal, a prosperous country eastward across the channel. The mercenary force fought upon the order of their prince, Freyder, who kept for himself what they earned in their service.

Nathael's report revealed the location of several Heshi camps. The nearest lay across the Delesar in a hamlet called Trayton. A force of some fifteen-hundred men waited for Gwyn to cross the river.

The Winter Army couldn't hide. Crow Loyalists reported regularly to the enemy. Gwyn had no advantage, only a desperate need to cross the river and march on to Crowwell. He must find a way to ambush the Heshi, but the mercenary force remained on high alert, ready for anything.

Gwyn could only sit, and wait, and pray.

"Am I intruding?"

He started up and turned to find Nathaera approaching, bundled in a ragged blanket, her nose red with the cold.

"Not at all. Please." Gwyn motioned to the log. "I welcome the company."

She sat. Together they stared at the raging river.

"Rumors are circulating in camp about the contents of your letters," Nathaera softly said. "General Haratin is particularly agitated."

Gwyn gripped the letters tighter. "I'm not ready to tell them yet."

She nodded. The river rushed on.

Gwyn sighed. His breath misted before him. "Where's Kive?"

Nathaera wrinkled her nose. "Off eating something diseased, no doubt. I told him to stop doing that around Adesta. It makes the poor man ill."

Gwyn smiled. "How is Lord Gilhan?"

"Fully mended, except when it comes to the eating of rats. And who could blame him?" She turned her head toward Gwyn. "I don't want to talk about Adesta. How are you, Gwyn? You look pale and thin. Why do you always look pale and thin? You're not eating enough."

"Who is?"

"You're not sleeping either."

"It's this blasted cold."

She laid her hand over his. "Gwynter."

He met her eyes, deep, gentle. "Yes, Lady Nathaera?"

"How might I help you? What pebble in your mountain of troubles might I hold to extend some measure of relief?"

He stared. This was no longer a girl, but a woman, slight yet strong, beautiful, and brave. Warmth swelled in Gwyn's chest. His lungs constricted against its pressure, and he leaned close to Nathaera's face, eyes lingering on her lips.

She leaned close. Their lips met, shy, tentative. Gwyn pulled back, struck by the impropriety of his actions.

He turned to the river, flushed cheeks aching in the cold. "Forgive me, my lady. That was—"

"What I've longed for ever so long," whispered Nathaera.

Gwyn blinked and stared at her. Tears brightened her eyes. Her nose shone redder than before. "Nathaera—"

"I know you don't love me," she said, wringing her hands. "I've wished you did. I've even prayed you would — but why would such a man care for a little wisp like me? I've said that before, haven't I?" She rose from the log and stood before him. "I told you once that I loved you, and I meant it. I still do. I ache for your kiss, Gwynter. Never have I met anyone I could love more dearly. But I expect nothing in return. I desire it, but I don't expect it. Don't think I do. This moment, whatever it was, I will always cherish."

She started to walk away, but Gwyn pushed to his feet and caught her wrist.

His mind reeled, heart hammering, limbs quaking. He pulled her close and embraced her. Her head rested against his chest.

"Nathaera," he whispered. "I'm a fool. A blind, insensible, conceited fool."

She laughed. "Oh, Gwyn, aren't all men?"

"I, more than most." He loosened his grip until she could tilt her head up to look at him. "Forgive me, Nathaera."

"I can't forgive you for something you've not done. I know you can't love me. You needn't apologize—"

"That isn't what I mean." He brushed his finger against her cheek. "I thought you were in love with Adesta."

Her jaw dropped. "With *him*? Oh, Gwyn, I—"

"Sire!"

Gwyn released Nathaera just as a foot soldier appeared from the shadows, panting, breath clouding around him.

"What is it?"

"Forgive me, but you've received another, er, message." The soldier proffered a thick package sealed and hastily addressed: *To King Gwynter ren Wintervale of the Winter Army somewhere in the Wilderness.*

Gwyn's heart faltered. He recognized the handwriting as Towwen Brym's. The printer dwelt in Charquae. Gwyn accepted the package and untied the string, broke the seal, and unwrapped the contents. Inside lay a slip of parchment and a tapestry carefully folded. Gwyn's hands trembled as he unfolded the tapestry to find his own lineage through his mother, dating further back than he'd ever seen. It traced directly to the first Wintervale king of Simaerin, and even to that king's father, King Cygmund of Fraelin.

The slip of parchment shouted at him:

*Try to argue against truth if you dare.*

*–T. Brym.*

"Thank you, soldier," said Gwyn, refolding the tapestry. "Where's the rider who delivered this?"

"In your tent, sire. He insisted."

"Has he any word on Charquae?"

"None, sire. He didn't ride from there. He comes directly from Fraelin."

Gwyn hurried past the soldier. Nathaera followed.

General Haratin and Bened Arnnor stood before the tent.

"What's all the news?" demanded Haratin.

"Not now," said Gwyn, pushing past them. He entered his tent and faltered. He'd expected to find a soldier in armor, but he found a youth, thirteen years of age or less, dressed in the ornate garb of a Fraeli nobleman.

The youth smiled. "Greetings, King Gwynter of the noble line of Wintervale. I am Fayett sae Marqwen, Crown Prince of Fraelin. I am most honored to meet you at last."

His accent wasn't as thick as Adesta's. He held himself with such dignity that Gwyn felt like an awkward, gangling stablehand before him.

"Your Highness," said Gwyn, inclining his head. "I had no word of your coming..."

"I sent no word," said Fayett, smiling brightly. "Not to you, nor to my father. Only Towwen Brym knew of my journey, and only as a messenger from Fraelin, not by name. He sent his package via

Fraelin to avoid unwanted attention, and I took it upon myself to deliver it to you. But I do bring a promise from Fraelin which may bolster your heart in so turbulent a time.

"My father, Crane King of fair Fraelin, has agreed to send our fleets to your aid. They will be needed for the siege against Crowwell if you are to succeed. Such will not be possible until the spring thaw, but Fraelin is your ally, King Gwynter."

# Chapter Eleven

The Crow King's troops held the nearest bridge with a force of four thousand men, and there Gwyn lost one of his generals. He received word of General Leelin's capture near dawn, two days following Prince Fayett's arrival from Fraelin.

Several days before reaching the Delesar, Gwyn had sent General Leelin ahead with eight hundred men to scout the only means of crossing within a hundred miles unless they could secure boats. If possible, the general was ordered to seize control of the bridge, and then hold it until Gwyn's arrival. The general never reported back, so Gwyn sent his aide, Aleteer Hemonn, to find out what had happened.

Upon returning to camp, Aleteer bowed on one knee before Gwyn, a frown carving lines around his eyes. "He left his men camped one mile east of the bridge and stayed in a tavern along the highway, sire. The enemy captured him while he ate breakfast, according to the lass I questioned. He put up no resistance."

Gwyn closed his eyes, his stomach twisting. "The general's resolve has long been wavering. No doubt he finds the Crow King's prison more hospitable than our present famine."

Aleteer didn't hide a scowl. "Mayhap he'll change his mind when his head is severed from his body, sire."

"Likely," answered Gwyn, "but there's no cause for wishing that upon any man."

"The general is a coward, sire. He abandoned his post to sleep in a tavern and dined on pheasant and cheese while his men starved and shivered in the cold."

Gwyn sighed. "Aye, but he reaped his reward. See to your own flaws, Aleteer, and let Afallon judge your fellows for theirs."

Aleteer colored. "Yes, sire. Forgive me."

"No need. You've done me no injury. Now, stand. Call for my remaining generals. They'd best know the fate of our missing ally."

The aide rose, bowed at the waist, and hurried from the tent. Gwyn took the chance to throw off his cloak to dress, then bundled himself in the ragged cloak again.

Soon the generals assembled: Lawen, Haratin, Mershen, Grene, along with Colonel Cluv and Sir Bened Arnnor.

"Forgive the early hour, but word has reached me of Leelin's fate," Gwyn said. He explained what he'd learned and then fell silent. His eyes lit on the candle flickering upon his desk. "I've been contemplating our options, and there are few. To the east, we're cut off by a force of Crowsmen and by the Delesar, which is impossible to cross without boats. To the west, our means of crossing by bridge are made treacherous at best and fatal in the most likely case. It's too well guarded. We're virtually cut off from the south, which is where we must head or we'll starve.

"Prince Fayett's promise of aid from Fraelin has offered us a chance to win this war, but only if we survive until spring. To do so, we must cross this river, but more than that, we must procure the supplies we so desperately need. General Mershen?"

"Yes, sire."

"As a physician, what is your opinion on the condition of our men?"

"Most are ill, sire. Few are properly shod, and our rations are little better than a thin soup once a day. We'll run out before two weeks are up, and then starve unless those supply wagons reach us."

Gwyn sighed. "Those wagons won't come and Charquae can ill afford to send anything more."

"You make our situation sound very bleak, sire," said Grene.

"Rather fatal," Haratin said shortly. "Are you proposing we surrender, Your Majesty?"

"Nothing of the kind." Gwyn moved to his desk and tapped a map. "We're here, my friends. Here is the bridge along the highway, thirty miles west. And here," he slid his finger across the river and southeastward to a tiny dot, "is Trayton, nine miles away. It's in this tiny hamlet that the nearest troop of Heshi make their camp, no doubt to discourage our crossing of the Delesar by any means other than the bridge."

"Rightly so," said Haratin. "We'd be mad to face the Heshi as we stand now. They're the most disciplined and skillful warriors in the world. The Crow King was wise to hire them."

"Sire, what *are* you suggesting?" asked Grene.

Gwyn sensed eyes probing him. He looked up to meet his brother's gaze.

"You mean to cross the river by boat," said Lawen.

Gwyn nodded. "We must. There's a harbor three miles eastward on this side of the river where a brewery stands. There, large boats are docked between shipments sent downstream to Phinion, where the bridge stretches across the Delesar. I mean to commandeer these boats and take our army across at nightfall on the eve of the Feast of Afallon. The Heshi will have celebrated all night and will probably be in a drunken sleep if we attack at dawn."

"Forgive me, sire," said Haratin, "but this scheme is madness. We can't possibly secure enough boats to cross in one night and arrive in Trayton by dawn to surprise the Heshi. Apart from that, surely not all of them will be asleep!"

Gwyn smiled grimly. "We can but try. There's no other course."

"The Feast of Afallon is still a week away," said Mershen. "We'll barely have enough supplies to subsist on, and no strength. When we reach Trayton our men will be too exhausted to fight. And if they learn that they're fighting the Heshi, they'll desert before we can cross the river."

"If we can take Trayton," Gwyn said, "then we'll have the supplies we need. The Heshi are well provisioned, and we'll take what food, weapons, and blankets we require. I know this is madness, but we have no choice. We cross and fight or we sit and starve. Or we surrender. But should we do so, gentlemen, our lives are forfeit, and the liberty of Simaerin is lost before it's won. What say you? Will you cross with me? Shall we take a leap of faith, believing in Afallon's mercy?"

# Chapter Twelve

Voices clambered for Kovien's attention.

He stood before the window of the highest turret in Crow Castle, staring down on the city below where thousands of mindless Simaeri milled about this mild winter day. Leaning out, Kovien tried to ignore the voices and dwell instead on Gwynter.

He camped out there, somewhere along an ice-filled river, trapped between Simaeri and Heshi forces, starving.

*Starving.*

One of Kovien's favorite tactics. He used it often to cow those who opposed him.

"But it's such an ugly death," said a faint voice.

"Hush," said another. "He'll starve you next."

"Too late," Kovien whispered. "I already did." He glanced behind him, but today the tower room stood empty, his ghosts invisible — merely voices. "You're much too loud today. Leave me."

"We'll never leave you," replied a deep, musical voice, horribly familiar. "You'll never let us go."

"Leave," whispered Kovien, closing his eyes. "You, at least."

"I cannot, my son."

Kovien clenched his jaw and shook his head. "I am not your son, but the Crow King of Simaerin. You are dead. Long dead. I watched you die."

"But I remain."

"Be silent, please. I cannot hear over all your shouting."

"I'm not shouting, Kovien. I've never shouted."

Kovien softly laughed. "No, not even once. Not even when I killed you." He turned again toward the empty room, disappointed when he couldn't witness the wounded expression on King Roth's face. He turned back to the window. "Never mind. You whisper loudly. Leave me."

A chill ran across Kovien's cheek, like icy fingers brushing against his skin. The Crow King yelped and stumbled sideways, rubbing his face where his skin burned. "Enough! Enough. Leave me to my solitary torment. You've haunted me long enough, demon king."

"I am not the demon," whispered the dread voice.

Kovien chuckled, bowing his head. "You're right. You're right. The demon is out there. Beyond the castle. He marches to steal my throne. My throne. Why? Have I not paid the price for peace? Are my sacrifices not sufficient? Foolish child! He knows not what he unleashes upon the world. All that I've done to protect it from its own miserable failings. But he will learn. He must learn. I must teach him."

"Why, Kovien?" whispered the dead king. "Aren't you sick yet of death and war?"

Kovien returned to the window and glowered at the city far below. "Sick of them? Why would I be sick of my cleansing? Soon, King Roth, soon I shall finish my work."

"Do you even know what your work is anymore, my son?"

Kovien hunched away from the voice behind him. "I am the Crow King. Not your son. Your son is out there." He jabbed a finger to the north, the faraway north, where Gwynter kept the fallen Ilidreth close at his side. "Soon, very soon. They think to spare him, but he is mine. Yours. Not theirs. And he will finish falling. After that, I will cleanse the world."

"Too late, Kovien," said the king's gentle voice. "Kive is waking to himself. It is evident in the broken seal. Magic is flooding Simaerin again. You've already lost."

"Never," hissed Kovien, whirling to face what he couldn't see. "Never. Kive is mine. I am his master. I broke his mind, and what is broken will not be mended."

"The Winter King defies you," said the ghost, and a howling mass of voices echoed him, drumming into Kovien's ears.

*He defies you. Defies you!*

He doubled over and covered his head. "Hush. Enough. ENOUGH!"

The voices ceased. The wind outside died. All the world fell silent.

"I am the Crow King of Crow Castle," he said, straightening to defy the voices, though they were still. "I alone rule Simaerin. I alone command the Ilidreth. I shall burn Fraelin to the ground and swallow Hesh-Kasal in the sea. These oaths I will keep, and no *boy king* shall stand long to oppose me. Kive will fall. Fall from the last of his grace, into the deepest wells of despair, where hope can never blossom. Magic will fail and fade. And then, at last, at last! I shall find peace."

"No, Kovien," whispered the familiar deep voice. "There is no peace for the damned."

A sob escaped Kovien's lips before he could steel himself. He whipped around to the window and slammed a fist against the stone frame. "Burn! Burn, Simaerin! I shall show you my displeasure. I shall show you the wrath of the damned!"

He spun and stalked across the dusty room, snatched up his feather-lined cloak from the floor by the door, and flung it across his shoulders. He strode from the tower and descended the winding stairs. At the bottom of the steps, waiting in perfect solemnity, stood Traycen ren Lotelon, head of the Order of Corvus.

"With me," Kovien whispered, and the man followed, perhaps a little stiff in his movements. Resurrecting the dead was difficult and disturbing, but Kovien had done it for Traycen — for the man was loyal as few others. Besides, the pact Kovien had made with the Order of Corvus granted long life. The others would lose faith if their leader remained dead.

Traycen didn't behave quite the same as he had in life. Though he responded to commands, and spoke and ate as he had before, he was not strictly the same nobleman. The soul remained, but the body... that had been tricky. Gwynter and his little band of heroes had buried Traycen somewhere in the True Wood, and Kovien didn't wish to dig up a rotting corpse. Instead, he'd borrowed another body, one freshly killed, and stowed Traycen's captured soul there, then wove magic around the man's features to make him appear as the nobleman had.

Securing the soul had been the simple part of his work. The Order of Corvus belonged to *him*. Their souls were *his*, by magical contract. The soul had returned to Kovien here in Crow Castle shortly after his death as the contract had specified.

Sticking the soul to a different body became tedious, even frustrating, but Kovien knew how to be patient. It was solid work. Only two or three mages in the world would be skilled enough to see through the deception.

"Londolin," Kovien said aloud.

"The old capital, sire?" said Traycen, lifting an eyebrow.

"Yes. Burn it. We've no need of ancient relics. The line of Wintervale *is* dead, no matter what dubious sources might claim. Best we put to rest any ideas of reestablishing the old world. Gwynter will never find a throne." He smiled. "Except perhaps in his Afallon's heaven."

GENERAL CADOGAN REN Silverard mused over the northern map on his desk, finger tracing the Delesar to his best estimation of where the Winter Army camped. The army lay virtually pinned, but when last the Crow Army had assumed as much, the blasted rebels had produced a bloody fire-breathing dragon.

Cadogan would never again underestimate the resourcefulness of his enemy. It shouldn't surprise him. He'd been Lawen ren Terare's commanding officer for four years, and he'd seen the lad's skill for himself. He'd also noted Gwynter's war tactics and his ability to inspire the men under his command. Cadogan recognized a lethal force when he saw one. The brothers together made such a force, drat them both.

A knock tore Cadogan's gaze from the black ink strokes beneath his finger. He sighed. "Come in."

Traycen ren Lotelon entered, expressionless and grim. "Might you spare a moment, General?"

"Like it or otherwise, yes." Cadogan gestured to the chair before his desk, then leaned back in his seat and folded his arms over his flat stomach. "What does our king instruct?"

"He has commanded that Londolin be destroyed," said Traycen, taking the proffered seat.

Cadogan hesitated for a heartbeat. The order made sense as he considered it. "Destroy a symbol the rebels might try to use to incite the people." He nodded. "It's a good move."

"Naturally. The Crow King is wise."

"He is farseeing." Cadogan leaned forward to pull a map from the bottom of his stack. He laid it out to study the ruins by the Vaymeer Sea, west of Crowwell.

Londolin, last relic of the reign of Wintervale, last of the ancient realm of kings. It was almost a pity to burn the city. According to theologists, Afallon Himself had walked the length of that hallowed place, when it had been only a seaside village. The Blessed God was born there, and so the line of Wintervale claimed it as a holy site and raised up a city to worship Afallon long after the God had ascended to His divine throne.

"I assume he desires this to be done as soon as possible."

"It's your priority," said Traycen.

Cadogan nodded. "I'll assemble my men this very day. We'll march at first light for the holy city."

Traycen rose to his feet. "See that no stone is left standing. Destroy it, Cadogan."

"I understand. His Majesty's word is law."

Traycen excused himself, leaving Cadogan to consider his march against the abandoned city. He would lament his part in its end, but he understood well the need of such extremes. Should Gwynter ren Terare march there rather than to the well-fortified present capital, he might inspire legions of Simaeri to follow his cause. There was something about Londolin that drew out faith, or perhaps superstition. Cadogan didn't know which had greater power.

One thing was certain. The church wouldn't be happy, Crow King's orders or not. It was at the church's behest that Londolin remained standing in the first place, and the first Crow King had allowed it.

First Crow King. Who was Cadogan fooling? He knew the truth. Had known it long. This Crow King was the first, his life prolonged by the blessing of Afallon...

Yes, that was why. Cadogan rose from his chair and began rolling up his maps. Londolin stood several hundred leagues from here, much closer than Gwynter's distance from the holy ruins. Even should the boy consider changing his destination, he'd not make it ahead of Cadogan. At least, not with his army. Only alone, upon his unicorn's back.

And then, he could do nothing to stop Londolin's fall.

# Chapter Thirteen

"Shiny?"

Gwyn looked up from the rushing river. "Yes, Kive?"

"South."

Gwyn blinked. Did Kive now know directions? How had Nathaera managed that? "South, Kive?"

Lawen shifted in his ragged blanket where he sat on the rotted log under the waning moon. He rose to join Gwyn and his fallen fae, breath misting before his face. "Do you think something's happening in Crowwell?"

Gwyn shook his head. "I'm not sure. Kive, what is south?"

Kive lifted a trembling finger to the southwest, expression grave. "South. There. Going."

"What's going south, Kive?" Gwyn shivered as a premonition crawled up his spine.

"The Crow's hand."

Neither man corrected Kive's bird anatomy. They listened and waited.

"South, south." He paused. "West from the tower, south toward the sea. There they'll destroy it and then destroy me." Kive smiled to himself. "Heigh ho, Shiny. Kive made a rhyme."

"Yes," said Gwyn, frowning as he stared into the darkness of the far shore. "Kive did."

"Do you understand what he means?" asked Lawen.

"I think so," whispered Gwyn. "I'm afraid so. He means Londolin. West from the tower, south toward the sea. From Crowwell, that's exactly right. Only a few hundred leagues."

Lawen shook his head. "Why destroy a ruin?" He sucked in a breath. "They think we would take it?"

"There's a chance. I'd already considered it once, but we're too slow moving. It would have drawn the Crow King's attention. Apparently, that doesn't matter now."

"What can we do?"

"We? Little." Gwyn rubbed a hand across his arm. "I could race there upon Aluem, but holding the city by myself? With Aluem, perhaps. But then I would abandon my forces to save an empty fortress. Though it's a beautiful symbol, it isn't worth that cost."

"Then we let Londolin fall?"

"I'm afraid we must." Gwyn sighed and rubbed his hand across his face. "I'm so tired, Lawen. How can we accomplish this?"

His brother wrapped his arm around Gwyn's shoulders. "By the will of Afallon, or we die trying. There's no other recourse now."

"True." Gwyn stared into the black river. "We must win our freedom."

"Aye." Lawen squeezed Gwyn's shoulder and released him. "Our choice is made, Gwynny."

"It's a choice made anew each morrow that comes," whispered Gwyn. He bent down and picked up a stone from the frozen ground. Rubbing his thumb against the smooth, icy surface, he contemplated the path ahead. "I choose not only my own life, but I also march mere lads and wizened men alike to an untimely end. May Afallon forgive me."

He turned from the river. "When Londolin falls, there will be some who become disheartened. We must have a victory in Trayton. The dragon's appearance at Bayton isn't enough."

"I agree, though it's a mad venture, Gwyn. Even with every boat, it will take hours to cross the Delesar."

"I'm aware." Gwyn turned to Kive. "You said the Crow will come for you after Londolin falls?"

Kive canted his head. "Shiny?"

"In the south, Kive. Will the Crow come for you when the south falls?"

"Oh. The Crow is waiting. Breathing. Sleeping."

"Will he come, Kive?"

"Oh, yes, Shiny. Master will come for Kive, always."

"We must be ready. I don't know why the Crow King has waited so long to destroy Kive. Perhaps a wisp of familial affection remains, or perhaps there's some other factor, but Kovien *will* try to end Kive's life before this war is done."

Kive faintly hissed, though whether at Gwyn's words or something downstream, it was impossible to say.

The Feast of Afallon would fall in three days. He must remain patient. No news had come from Charquae, and the entire camp waited each day for word, nerves taut. The Crow Army remained at the bridge, content to let Gwyn's forces starve on the riverbank.

Sighing, he turned from the wrathful river and moved toward camp. Lawen trailed after him.

"Where are you going?"

"To visit my men." He held his hand out and silently beckoned to Aluem. The unicorn trotted from the darkness and allowed Gwyn to mount him.

"Should I come with you?" asked Lawen.

"No, I'll be fine. Rest, Lawen." Unicorn and rider cantered onward, Kive keeping pace on foot.

Visiting the patched-up tents was Gwyn's painful routine, made worse at night. As they navigated the wide paths between rows of sagging shelters, Aluem's hooves sloshing through mud and reeking waste, Gwyn listened to the ragged coughs of over half his army. He'd marched five thousand men from Bayton, and already four hundred had vanished: either dead or run away.

A thousand lay gravely ill. Three quarters of the whole suffered with fever, some plagued by dysentery. All huddled in their shelters, starving and cold. What wounds the troops carried had come from marching, or gangrene, or in-fighting.

The Winter Army must be the most ragtag, pathetic force Gwyn had ever beheld. Witnessing the state of his men pierced his heart. His eyes burned with tears and weariness. What could he do? The destitution was so great, would anyone have the strength to fight the Heshi at Trayton, let alone beat them?

*Yet there's no alternative. To surrender would ensure torture and death for all of us.*

"Your Majesty?"

Aluem halted, allowing Gwyn to glance back toward a sagging tent among so many just like it. Standing before the weather-beaten canvas, a man in his forties leaned against a crutch, his leg bandaged, bare feet exposed and blackened from frostbite. Stubble and scratches adorned his firm jaw and his eyes glowed with hunger above his sunken cheeks.

Aluem wheeled about to face the man.

"What is your name, soldier?" asked Gwyn.

"Brisht, sire. You are him, aren't you? King Wintervale?"

Gwyn hesitated. "General Wintervale, Brisht, if you please. I'm your commanding officer in war, not yet crowned."

Kive circled around Aluem to eye the man. "Is he a rat, Shiny?"

"No, Kive. Hush."

Brisht shrank from the Ilidreth.

"Don't be afraid," said Gwyn, lifting his hand. "He won't harm you. His preference is for crows' feathers."

A grin lit on Brisht's face. "Oh, aye, sire. There's been rumors of such. So, it's true he's a tame Ilidreth."

"Not tame," Gwyn said. "Friendly. I've allied myself with the Ilidreth in the past, and I'll tell you straight: They're not wild and savage as the Crow King claimed. Rather, they're solitary as they grieve the loss of their great kingdom. Some are fallen, and therefore mad like Kive, but many are sane and fair. I would sooner tame a — well, a dragon, than dare to tame an Ilidreth. They're people, Brisht, same as you and I, and I'd thank you to pass that word along to your fellows and see they don't slander the name of the woodland people any longer."

Brisht's eyes grew wider as Gwyn spoke, and he bobbed his head. "Aye, sire. General. Sir. Only, does this mean we've Ilidreth allies on the way?"

Gwyn frowned. "I hardly know. A friend among the Ilidreth told me over one year ago that he would try to gather his people to arms, though he made no promise. But time flows differently for the Ilidreth, and perhaps to them the length of one year is how we perceive a fortnight. Mayhap they'll still come." He glanced toward the northwest, fancying he could make out the far-off ancient wood against the dark night.

"Sire? Eh, General, I mean."

Gwyn tore his eyes from the shadows. "Yes?"

"I want you to know, I support you." It was dark, yet Gwyn felt certain Brisht's face burned red. "Your cause, that is," the soldier went on. "I was but a humble farmer before, a serf serving his lord in the far west province of Misoril, and I thought nothing could change. But news spread of your revolt. Of your lineage and claim. For the first time, my lord, I looked up and considered the Crow King. Considered that something might be wrong in his way of ruling. I threw down my pitchfork straight away and ran from my duties that very night. Marched across rivers and woods to reach you. Brought several runaway slaves with me. Now here we be, for what that may be worth." He gestured toward his makeshift tent. "That there is Rafer and his son, young Dura."

Warmth spread through Gwyn's body like a summer's breeze as he spotted Rafer's dark face peeking out from the tent. The runaway slave's feet stretched before him, wrapped in bloodied rags. Tears pricked Gwyn's eyes.

He swung from Aluem's back and clasped a hand to each of

Brisht's shoulders. "It means more than kingdoms, my friend. I thank you, all of you, from my soul."

Brisht's face beamed even in the gloom. "You humble me, sire."

"No," Gwyn said, quietly, firmly. "You, sir, humble *me*." He met Rafer's eyes. "Each of you."

## Chapter Fourteen

The red dragon shimmered against the cloud banks above, a dread specter, lithe and long.

Nox sat beside Parsha in the wide-open fields before Charquae, hidden in plain sight. Dragons were remarkable creatures, as Parsha himself declared. His favorite talent was what he called *camouflage*; a word he'd borrowed from the Fraeli, no doubt. Apparently, it meant blending in with his environment.

Nox wasn't certain lying in an open field in the midafternoon was quite the same as blending in, no matter how well concealed Parsha somehow made himself. It was nothing short of magic. Wonderful, dazzling magic.

*If only Nathael could see this.*

"Parsha?" asked Nox, settling back against his dragon's gleaming hide. "What exactly are we waiting for? Should we not strike down the enemy dragon before he destroys Charquae?"

Parsha remained still as a statue as he answered. "That dragon is a *she*, my little fat friend, not a *he*. There is a very great difference between the two in terms of temperament and fighting style. She circles wide, not to intimidate a city she already perceives as destroyed, but to lure *us*. The Crow King, it would appear, has won himself a very patient dragon. Though *how* he won her, I could only guess. Female dragons are difficult to bribe or threaten unless you steal their eggs. I suspect that is not the case here."

"How do you know?" Nox asked, straining to see the distant red form better, and failing.

"Had he done so, Charquae and half of Simaerin would already be in flames. She is too patient, too strategic. Almost..." He stopped, then rumbled a faint growl. "She is obedient to someone else's will."

"Did the Crow King cast a spell to enslave her?"

"Doubtful," said Parsha. "It is extremely difficult to enslave a dragon's will. I said she is obedient, and certainly not to the king himself."

"To whom then?"

"Who can say? A woman. That is all I know."

"I don't understand."

"That does not surprise me, round one. You are not a dragon, and though I am very fond of you, I do not feel inclined to explain a dragon's nature at the present time. Suffice it to say, this dragon is *compelled* to serve the Crow King through rather foul tactics."

Nox shook his head. "Very well. I don't understand, and that's all right. The question is how do we proceed?"

"We cannot defend Charquae for long." Parsha sighed. "In open combat, I might not win against her, and that would mean the ending of many souls. Too many. That leaves two options. Either we evacuate the city — which isn't wise, I grant you — or we attempt to reason with the she-dragon."

The blood flowed from Nox's face. "Reason with her?"

"Aye, little friend. Should she be willing or able to tell us her trouble, we could both solve the mystery of her alliance with your enemy and perhaps dissuade her from continuing in her present course. Which, I might remind you, is our demise."

"But...how can we initiate conversation with her? If we so much as twitch, she'll torch us."

"That is simple. Well, it will be once you have supplied for us a diamond."

Nox's jaw dropped. "A what?"

Parsha's eyes narrowed. "Surely, you've at least *heard* of diamonds, Nox. Have humans become so ignorant of the earth's riches?" His tone was a blend of horror and pity.

"O-of course I've *heard* of diamonds. I've even seen one set into a noblewoman's necklace. B-but, how do you expect me to find one, now, here?"

"Oh, is that all that troubles you?" Parsha chuckled. "Nothing to worry about. I am confident that once you enter Charquae quite stealthily and find the leaders of your rebellion's council, they'll be very happy to accommodate your request when you explain that it will save their beloved city."

The blood might well have drained from Nox's body. He sat, numb of mind, cold of limb, staring at the frostbitten grass before him. "Just like that? You genuinely believe yourself, don't you?" He turned his head up to offer his own pitying look. "Perhaps I'm ignorant in the ways of dragons, but you're equally so in the ways of humankind. King Gwynter's council has never even *met* me before. They would have my word, and nothing to recommend me otherwise. It would be like a young dragon — a *very* young dragon — coming up to you and demanding a portion of your hoard to keep a knight from skewering you."

Parsha blinked his eyes. "In such an event, I would gladly lend what was required."

"Truly?"

"Well..." Parsha considered. "How young a dragon?"

"Very, very."

Parsha nodded. "I see. You're yet untested."

"A complete unknown to these great men, in fact," said Nox. "They would sooner trust a crow."

"Hm. Well then." Parsha blinked slowly. "Very well. We have but one course, though I despise it." Before Nox could ask what the dragon intended, there was a peculiar popping and clicking noise, and Nox felt himself sinking. No, not sinking. Falling back because the dragon was *shrinking* in size.

Nox jumped to his feet as the dragon came to stand at a horse's height, and then his frame shifted; legs lengthening, heightening; tail dwindling; muzzle diminishing into a human face.

Nox stared, horrified. Bewildered. Fascinated. Within mere moments, the dragon had changed into a tall, comely, regal-looking man in his prime. Parsha the Human had the same white-blue eyes, though now long golden hair trailed down his back. He stood garbed in exquisite robes of blue and green glistening with tiny gems. Bare toes stuck out from under his apparel.

"I dislike taking on this form," said Parsha, flexing his fingers. "It feels so confining, so minuscule."

Nox kept staring. "You're human."

Parsha grimaced. "Nonsense. I merely took on the shape of a human. We dragons can do so when required. How else do you think we have survived the endless quests your knights embark upon to claim our hides?"

It made sense, Nox supposed, but the idea of such mighty beasts wandering around the cities and hamlets of Simaerin wasn't precisely comforting.

"Do not fret," said Parsha. "We prefer not to take this form most of the time. Too inhibiting, as I said. Now, shall we?"

"Y-you're coming with me to Charquae?"

Parsha had begun to walk but paused now to glance at him with such a look of patient pity, Nox's cheeks caught fire.

"I mean, is that really a good idea?"

"Of course. You said your council won't listen to you. Well, they will listen to me." His tone rolled like quiet thunder, firm and confident, and Nox had a hard time believing the council *wouldn't* listen to him. Nox certainly intended to heed the dragon's every word, as he much preferred being the dragon's friend to being his breakfast.

Together, dragon and boy marched toward Charquae, while red death wheeled above them in the sleet-colored sky.

NOX HAD IMAGINED terrified crowds parting before the impressive specimen that was Parsha the Human — but he needn't have worried. The streets of Charquae were like that of a ravaged field of corn. Littered with random articles of clothes, bits of spoiled food, a doll, a shoe. Devoid of people. Doors sagging open. The only sound beyond Nox's feet was the whisper of a breeze.

Charquae no longer resembled the city of his youth.

"Where have all your people gone?" asked Parsha.

"They ran from the dragon," Nox murmured.

"I could guess as much, my friend, but where did they run *to*?"

Nox considered that. Where would the people run in such a time of crisis? His eyes shot upward, and he pointed to a steeple towering above the other buildings of the once-industrious city. "There, the churches."

The man-dragon eyed the nearest steeple for a heartbeat or two. "Ah. Faith." He started down the thoroughfare, Nox at his side.

"Are you skeptical?" asked Nox, wondering for the first time what dragons believed in.

"No," Parsha said, smiling. "The faith of humans is commendable and exceedingly powerful when harnessed appropriately. Churches are infused with that faith. I was merely pondering the fickle nature of humans."

"Fickle?"

"Indeed. Were all Charquae's citizens so devout yesterday? I think not. The problem lies in your nature to doubt, which is weakened only in times of crises. This is not a criticism, Nox, but an observation of a very young, impulsive, stubborn race. You do learn, either to douse yourself in faith or doubt before the end."

"What do you believe in?" asked Nox. "Afallon or some other god? Do dragons have a religion of their own?"

Parsha's smile deepened. "I believe in the Weave, which is life.

You believe in Afallon, who is life. Perhaps they are the same, known by different names."

Nox folded his hands behind his back and considered. "You don't sound certain, yet you call my nature young and fickle."

The man-dragon laughed. "True. True. Perhaps we are not so different, man and dragon. We journey along life's many pathways, questing, ever questing, for knowledge divine."

"That's pretty," said Nox, running the words through his mind. "Is it one of your poems?"

"Nay," said Parsha, laughing. "That was mere thought. Poetry is more than words or visuals, but an expression of the soul. A movement, like water flowing, or music singing."

Nox nodded, unable to think of any other response.

They reached Charquae's largest church, its spire stretching toward the heavens. Nox took the steps up the stone edifice and pulled on the door, but it flung aside to admit him. He snatched his hand back before it got crushed.

A cloaked and cowled figure stood in the entrance, a sword pointed at Nox's prominent belly. "State your business, ruffian. This church isn't a sanctuary for the common masses. It belongs to the council of King Wintervale. If you seek shelter, find another holy house."

Nox blinked, then grinned. "Good! That saves us a lot of searching." He gestured to Parsha. "We've come at His Majesty's behest with news from the Winter Camp."

The figure's sword lowered marginally. "What news?"

Nox hesitated. "Have you heard of the Winter King's dragon?"

"Aye. And now we've another flying overhead if you've not noticed. How have you entered the city? The gates are secured."

"A pointless action," Parsha said, pointing up, "considering the dragon's general location."

"Well," said the cloaked man, flames in his tone, "we couldn't well let travelers enter to risk their own lives, and an evacuation would have encouraged the dragon to attack sooner."

"So, you sit like a goose in the hearth." Parsha shook his head.

"There is a very simple solution to your circling problem, only we need a diamond."

Nox winced. "Uhm, Parsha."

Silence fell between the three men.

The man's sword raised again. "A diamond?"

"Yes, a very large diamond of the first water."

Nox tried a laugh and caught Parsha's arm to keep him still. "We need to meet with Brioc Ffyr or Towwen Brym, please."

"About a diamond?" asked the man in wooden tones.

"About a dragon," Nox replied. "*Two* dragons, in fact. Please. It is urgent."

The man sighed. "Name?"

"Nox, son of Hemm."

The man stiffened beneath his cloak. "Hemm? The baker?"

Nox perked up. "Yes."

"I thought you looked familiar. You and your twiggish brother sometimes work the shop, do you not? A better knot of bread I've never tasted than Hemm's."

Nox flushed and smiled. "Indeed, sir. Though the twiggish boy you mentioned is only like a brother to me. We're not related."

The man stepped aside. "Enter in peace, Nox, son of Hemm, and perhaps we can convince you to stay long enough to magic up a proper meal. I'm Remien, son of the sea for all I know. I bid you welcome. Come in and be comfortable."

Grinning, Nox led Parsha inside the stone church, down a short passageway, and into the chapel itself. The wooden pews had been pushed aside to make way for tables laden with candles, parchment, scrolls, ink wells, tomes, and trays of half-eaten gruel and dry bread, as well as a few tankards and empty bottles smelling of ale.

Standing or sitting in various attitudes of thought, at least two dozen men crowded the chapel, most of them young, a few bearing the seasoning of declining years. At the center table sat four men with their heads together, poring over what must be a map, one man tracing his finger along some road or other, while the others stared hard as though the map would answer their unasked questions.

"Gentlemen, my lords, and fellow rebels," called Remien, voice ringing through the vaulted chamber. "May I present the honorable Nox, son of Hemm the baker, and his rather well-dressed companion, whose name I failed to obtain 'aforehand?"

Several men dipped their heads in greeting, but those at the center table didn't look up, too engrossed in their discussion.

Remien tried again. "Nox here, fine fellow that he is, has braved the world beyond our dragon-plagued city to reach us, bringing with him word from our Winter King."

Someone dropped a quill to the flagstones. Every eye turned toward Nox, whose face burned. He bowed at the waist. "G-greetings from His Majesty Gwynter ren Terare ren Wintervale. I've come at his behest to bring Charquae from the brink of destruction."

Chairs shrieked against stone as those at the center table rose to their feet. The youngest of their number, perhaps younger than Nox himself, spoke in clear, carrying tones. "What hope do you bring, Sir Nox? We would hear what our king requires of us."

"A diamond," Parsha piped up. "All we require is a diamond of the first water. I won't say it again."

## Chapter Fifteen

Diamonds could be obtained, certainly. But a diamond of the first water — one that met with Parsha's approval — *that* was a different matter altogether.

Nox waited with the dragon inside the church at one of the pilfered tables. Remien hovered nearby, while the other rebel leaders had abandoned their shelter in search of Parsha's especial request. The dragon remained relaxed for the first hour but when Towwen Stone — one of the council members and Gwyn's childhood friend by his own report — brought in a sack filled with gems and dumped them across the wooden planks of the table, Parsha grimaced.

"A city filled with second-rate riches is hardly worth saving," he murmured as he poked through the gems with disdain. "Have humans no *eye* at all?" He caught a single ruby between his finger and thumb and squinted at it for several seconds, then scoffed and tossed the precious stone over his shoulder.

Nox gawked as the ruby clattered to the floor near the high-rising lectern. "Is it fake?"

"No, far worse. Whatever fool cut that gem had no talent nor any heart to speak of. He ruined it. It's little different from a pebble."

"It's not worth anything?" asked Nox, perplexed.

"Oh, it might purchase a few acres of land, but frankly, no one should ever be subjected to the study of such poor workmanship."

Nox let out a whimper and scooted from his chair to collect the hapless ruby that was still worth so much. Dragons were the oddest creatures.

Towwen Stone watched Parsha until Nox returned to the table, ruby in hand. The scholarly councilman smiled at Nox and sat to await Parsha's verdict of his remaining gathered riches. "Tell me, Master Nox, how fares the Winter Army?"

Nox frowned and ran a finger over the knots of the polished tabletop. "It desperately needs supplies, i' truth. Few wagons sent from Charquae have ever arrived. Men are without shoes, let alone armor, weapons, or even food."

Towwen frowned and nodded. "Alas, we're in no position to send more aid, especially if the wagons are only waylaid time and again. We're only strengthening the enemy in our efforts, such as those efforts be, under siege as we are." He glanced at Parsha. "Tell me, Sir Dragon, how will this diamond save our fair city?"

Parsha eyed Towwen Stone for a long moment, perhaps weighing his character as Nox might weigh the quality of a freshly baked loaf of bread. When Parsha had first declared his need of a diamond, the room had exploded with indignation and laughter, Towwen being of the latter temperament. But Nox had silenced all by kicking a chair hard, sending it clattering.

"You laugh at no man, but a fierce beast!"

Laughter had roared across the room, swallowing up the indignant few. Nox had tried to shout over the crowd of men, but then Parsha had lifted a hand and summoned fire to wreathe above him, flames bright and hot.

"Heed me, humans, or there shall be *two* dragons tearing stone from mortar!" His voice had rung across the still room, sharp and commanding.

"He's a dragon," Nox had said into the silence. "He's taken on this form in order to enter Charquae. We really do need a diamond."

It took a little more persuasion, but not much. When Brioc Ffyr, oldest resident mage, had confirmed that the Weave surrounding Parsha looked unlike any man's magery, the other men began to sweat.

Now Parsha tilted his head and offered a toothy grin, showing very inhuman fangs to Towwen Stone. "The diamond is not unlike the Fraeli's parley, though perhaps it is more of a bribe than mere negotiation. Should the she-dragon treat with me, your city might be spared. If not, you will need to flee by nightfall, for I must at that point duel her over this territory."

Towwen paled to the shade of a summer cloud. "How likely is it she'll accept your invitation to treat?"

Parsha's smile widened. "There is no dragon alive who would not at least come down to examine a diamond of the first water. But let me assure you, if I proffer up a diamond or other precious stone of *lesser* quality, I and this entire city — indeed this entire province — will be reduced to cinders in the merest flicker of a moment."

Nox shifted at the prospect of becoming cinders. He carefully rested his inferior ruby away from the pile of gems under Parsha's scrutiny, afraid to offend *this* dragon and set him off. These beasts, Nox suspected, were never *fully* tame.

The door to the chapel opened.

Towwen turned as Nox and Parsha eyed the door. In streamed the rebel leaders, grim as they spread across the room to make passage for a newcomer.

Nox straightened, recognizing Lady Delyth ren Cryven, the recently widowed wife of Charquae's leading lord and former governor of Vinwen Province. Nox knew as well as anyone else that House Cryven didn't support King Gwynter's cause. In the months preceding his death, Lord ren Cryven had sentenced several affluent citizens to death without a trial after accusing them of treason and magery. Many rebels considered it Afallon's judgment when the elderly tyrant had died in his sleep shortly afterward.

Lady Delyth was an elegant old woman, willowy and frail as embers. Her face, said to be fair in years gone by, held lines like a spider's web — yet there was something beautiful about her eyes. She was gowned and bedecked in velvet and emeralds, and she leaned on the arm of a young man Nox thought might be her grandson and heir to House Cryven. He looked comely and well dressed, also adorned in precious gems and rich cloth.

Towwen Stone stepped forward and bowed low. "My lady does us honor by her visit."

Lady Delyth lifted a hand as though to swat the youthful man aside, though she never touched him. Her eyes fixed upon Parsha, dark and glittering. "Brioc Ffyr calls you a dragon. Is this truth?"

"It is, faded one," said Parsha, rising to tower before the slight figure.

She nodded once, curtly. "He also tells me you have the means of saving Charquae from the Crow King's death sentence."

"I only lack a diamond," Parsha replied.

"I do not believe in the Winter King's cause," Lady Delyth said. "House Cryven has long served the line of Crow Kings, and even aided in overthrowing the line of Wintervale in days of yore. I am proud of my husband's heritage, just as he was before his death. But I also love Charquae. This is my home and the home of my children. My grandson has lived here always." She nodded to the boy supporting her. "I do not wish Charquae to fall before the wrath of a dragon, even if that dragon belongs to the Crow King. What I do now is treason. My beloved husband would likely behead me for my actions here, yet I do them, for the sake of life. May Afallon have mercy upon me."

She lifted a velvet pouch in trembling, wizened fingers. "Take this, mighty dragon, and save Charquae — for the children of now and still unborn."

Parsha nodded. "Nox, bring me the pouch."

Nox rounded the table and reverently accepted the lady's offering, bowing his head as he backed away. He whipped around the table and placed the pouch in Parsha's hand.

Lady Delyth turned and drifted toward the exit. Brioc Ffyr strode across the chamber to peck her cheek at the door.

Nox glanced at Towwen Stone. "Do they know each other so well?"

"She's his aunt," Towwen Stone replied, then waved at Towwen Brym as the printer crossed the room.

"Well?" said Towwen Brym. "Open the pouch, dragon, and let us see a diamond of the first water."

Parsha eyed the man flatly, then untied the pouch's string and upended it. The diamond fell into his palm, and Nox breathlessly considered the stone. He cocked his head. It looked no different from the other diamonds Parsha had examined as far as Nox could tell.

The dragon lifted the diamond between his finger and thumb, squinting. "Ah," he sighed, "now *this* is a diamond." He tilted it from side to side. "Observe the fine cuts, precise and nearly perfect. And colorless! Not an ounce, not a tint! Few diamonds have I seen so well crafted by man. It still carries the Weave. This is exactly what we need."

He dropped the diamond into his palm and looked up to face the men gathered at the table. Nox glanced around to find every face in the chapel pinned on Parsha, intense, eager.

"Then," said Towwen Stone softly, "she'll accept your parley?"

"It is not a parley, as I said. But yes, tiny human, she will converse with me, at the least. No dragon, none at all, could do otherwise with such a gem as this."

# Chapter Sixteen

General Cadogan would normally call a halt on the eve of Afallon's feast and allow his army to celebrate before continuing their march. Such had been the tradition for centuries. But the Crow King's command had been urgent, and Cadogan felt that urgency deep in his bones: Destroy Londolin, *now*.

He pressed on, praying Afallon would understand the need, and perhaps bless his cause. Doubtful, though, considering which city Cadogan marched upon.

He was a devout man, for he'd seen the divine hand of Afallon directing his course through years of victorious military campaigns, but Cadogan was foremost a man of the sword, and he would do whatever it took to obtain that hard-won victory — even destroy the holy city.

Surely Afallon hadn't led him to this point only to fall before a ragtag band of rebels under the command of an adolescent leader with claims to a long-dead line of kings. Worse still, those kings had fallen to the Crow King because they were weak; prone to fits of mercy when the law demanded justice.

Yes, Cadogan believed in Afallon, but not as other men did.

Afallon was not some frail child filled with love for all men and countries, as women and babes believed. Instead, He was a forceful, glorious being, intent upon Simaerin leading the world into an age of order and purpose.

The Crow King had been divinely selected to guide the country toward that future.

Cadogan never shared these thoughts with others, especially priests. The church already clashed with the Crow King's philosophies. Any more tension between the two factions might lead to the church's isolation. Should that occur, the people — torn between fealty and faith — might make a foolish choice.

The Crow Army marched through the holy night. With the dawn Cadogan called a halt long enough for his men to chant prayers in honor of Afallon's Feast before he called them back to order.

They marched most of the day, and in the late afternoon, Cadogan eyed the distant spires of Londolin, Silver City of Afallon, a scape of cathedrals erected for Divinity. To the west stood the southernmost border of Simaerin's ancient wood. No Ilidreth dwelt this far south these days, but still the trees crouched across the land, ominous, as though poised to strike.

*Utter rubbish*, Cadogan thought, and avoided looking toward the forest again.

The army reached the holy city at eventide. Part of Cadogan preferred the idea of destroying the looming walls of the fortress capital in the dark, but that was cowardice speaking. He required precision to puncture the walls and bring them down swiftly, which meant waiting for sunrise. Calling a heavy watch for the night, Cadogan retired to his tent early and tried to rest.

In his dreams, strange banners streamed in a curling mist at the forest border.

THE DAWN CAME LATE. A hush hovered on the air.

Cadogan washed his face, then donned his armor. His fingers were clumsy as he latched his breastplate, buckled his sword, adjusted his cloak. He tucked his helm under his arm and motioned for his aide to follow him out into the camp.

The army lay exposed. The ancient road leading to Londolin stretched wide, wending between flats and hills dotted with ancient trees, forcing the encampment to pitch tents around the towering trunks, hiding some from view.

Cadogan didn't like it, despite no outlying threats. The only living souls within leagues of Londolin, apart from Cadogan's forces, were the two dozen priests dwelling inside the holy city, dedicated to preserving its architecture. Those same priests must be relocated.

Cadogan strode through the camp with his aide, his page, and several officers until he reached the high gates to the city. "Ho the watch!"

A black-robed priest poked his head through the tower window beside the gates. "What brings the Crow to the Silver City?"

"The Crow King has issued a command. I must speak with the head of your order."

"Does it take an army to bring His Majesty's missives? This is a city of peace. No man of war may pass through the gates."

Cadogan scowled. Most of the priests sent to Londolin were ordered here by the Arch Priest because they were deemed overzealous or disgraced. None would be easy to handle. "I carry the Crow King's seal. Let me enter and speak with your High Priest, or by Afallon, I swear I shall use force to break down the gates."

The priest studied Cadogan's encampment. "You've brought catapults."

"Of which I will happily demonstrate the destructive capabilities, unless you open the confounded gates, man!"

The priest considered him, huffed, then vanished within the tower. An age passed before a second priest popped his head out the window to peer long at the army spread before the city.

"State your business," called the priest.

Cadogan rolled his eyes. "My business is this city, or I would not be here. I would speak with High Priest Douva *immediately.*"

"You would," the priest agreed, "but you can't. He's... indisposed."

"Short of death, there's no excuse he can provide which will satisfy. Open these blasted gates, let me inside your blasted city, and take me to your blasted High Priest."

The priest shrugged one shoulder. "But as you said yourself, sir, death is a reasonable excuse. Yes?"

A tremor ripped down Cadogan's spine. The hairs on his neck bristled. "High Priest Douva is dead?"

"Yes, very lately."

"How?"

"An arrow, sir. Shot in the head." The man pointed his finger toward the southern trees. "It came from there and was made in the fashion of Ilidreth weaponry. We buried High Priest Douva on the Eve of Afallon's Feast."

Cadogan whirled toward the trees. In the same moment a cloud passed over the rising sun, darkening the world. There, just at the border, Cadogan imagined he saw a line of men beneath streaming banners. The morning mist hadn't yet been chased from the shaded treeline, and it coiled there, ominous in its silent revelation.

In Cadogan's dream, he hadn't been able to discern the crest upon the enemy banners, but he knew them now.

For three hundred years, the Ilidreth had been fractured, disordered, mad.

Now they stood before the Crow Army, still and calm beneath the Swan banner billowing in the morning breeze.

"Open the gates!" Cadogan screamed.

"Londolin is a holy city. We cannot allow soldiers to—"

Cadogan drew his sword and pointed it up at the man in the window. "Open the gates, priest, or I will have my archers pierce your skull, and then I shall stand aside to let the Ilidreth defile your *holy* city. Let us enter!"

The priest disappeared inside. Within moments, the gates creaked aside to admit Cadogan's scrambling force of arms. As the soldiers filed into the city proper, Cadogan weighed the implications of an Ilidreth army so near the sea, so near Londolin. Had they come to destroy the Silver City themselves? If so, why? If not, why had they come here? The Ilidreth weren't organized anymore. They didn't have the strength to defy Simaerin outright, not after all the Crow King had done to them.

Then why?

Was entering Londolin the best move? Did the Ilidreth intend to trap them here? The city was impregnable. Fortified by the Crow Army, the Ilidreth stood little chance of taking it.

Yes, entering Londolin was Cadogan's best chance. Caught in the open, the Crow Army would suffer too many losses. The Ilidreth were ghostlike, swift, and silent, using the trees to conceal themselves. In such terrain, Cadogan's disadvantages were too many. Best to let the Ilidreth try laying siege if they attacked at all. This might be only a bluff.

Inside Londolin, Cadogan ascended a steep staircase leading to the gate tower. He entered the room where the two priests had wasted so much of his time. Empty now. Cadogan rushed to the window and stared out at the forest. The Ilidreth remained there, unmoving, perhaps content to watch the Crow Army stream inside the city.

*Why are they doing this?*

Only a few Ilidreth continued to defy the Crow King, and only ever in conjunction with Fraelin. Yet that was no Crane banner shimmering in the glowing sunlight. It was a Swan banner. An emblem which hadn't been raised for centuries.

The Ilidreth didn't care about Londolin. It meant nothing to them. They didn't believe in Afallon. Didn't swear fealty to the Wintervale Kings of old. Didn't claim the sea for themselves.

"So then, why?" growled Cadogan, pounding the stone windowsill.

The general whirled and left the tower to bark instructions at his men in the street below. "Set a watch. Get the stragglers inside. Be sure the gates are barred immediately afterward. Find the dratted priests. Don't just stand there. Now!"

Soon his orders were fulfilled, including the rounding up of the two dozen priests who inhabited Londolin. The robed clergy stood in calm repose on the main city thoroughfare, unruffled by the threat beyond the walls. Cadogan eyed them with an equal measure of curiosity and annoyance.

"Well? Which of you is in charge now that High Priest Douva is dead?"

"No one, General," answered a slim, balding man. "We await the word of the Arch Priest on this matter."

"Then you have no leader?"

"We're led by Afallon," answered a young man, barely grown.

Cadogan rolled his eyes. He really should have expected that answer. He paced before the priests. "All right. Can any of you tell me when the Ilidreth were first spotted on the forest border?"

"Three nights ago," answered the balding priest. "High Priest Douva saw them during his nightly walk along the battlements. He mentioned it during morning mass, but he said it might be a mere trick of the moon. Those trees don't seem natural ofttimes in the watches of the night."

"You sound rather superstitious for a priest."

The balding priest held Cadogan's eye. "I follow the Light of Afallon, but there remains the Dark of Thiavos even so. For each rising sun, there is a rising moon also."

"Never mind that," said Cadogan, cross and tired and not in the mood for religious zealots. "High Priest Douva was killed two evenings ago, was he not?"

"He was."

"Yet my army comes straight from Crowwell, and we've seen no trace of your messenger riding to report Douva's end or your need of instruction from your Arch Priest. Curious indeed."

"We sent a messenger pigeon, General," replied the youthful priest.

"Ah. Very well. It hardly matters anyway. The Crow King has sent us to Londolin to destroy the city. Your time here in exile has ended. We will escort you back to Crowwell as soon as we've dealt with the Ilidreth."

The priests shifted to exchange looks, but none appeared surprised.

Cadogan raised an eyebrow. "Is there a problem?"

"No, General Cadogan. We expected such an order would arrive soon. High Priest Douva prepared us for the possibility."

"Will you object?"

The priests again exchanged a look.

The young priest spoke. "Would our objections hold any weight? You're following the Crow King's will."

"Excellent. Then you will stand aside while my men burn Londolin. Once the Ilidreth see the fires across the Silver City, whatever stirred them up will settle, and they should soon return to their forest dwellings."

Again, the priests eyed one another. Calm. Irritating.

"If you have something to say, say on," Cadogan growled. "Otherwise begone. I've important matters to attend to."

"We have nothing more to say," replied a tall, plain priest with a prominent nose. "Good day, General. May Afallon attend thee to the end."

The priests turned and ambled toward the cathedral where they'd been found. It was a grand old structure, adorned by statues of holy men ordained of Afallon in ages past. Cadogan turned from the sight, fighting a wave of nausea. He hated to burn Londolin.

*But I must.*

"Light the torches. Burn every building."

A cry sounded on the wall. Cadogan spun to watch as one of his guards tumbled toward the ground at the wall's foot. The man hit with a sickening thud, an arrow jutting from his chest.

"They're attacking!" shouted Cadogan, then he froze, eyes fixed on the top of the wall.

The Ilidreth didn't attack from without. The Ilidreth stood

*inside* Londolin, along the battlements — *hundreds* of them — all with arrows nocked and pointed down at Cadogan and his men. But *how*?

His eyes searched for some sign of weakness in the wall, then he turned toward the city spread before him. His eyes fell on the two dozen priests hovering before the Holy Cathedral of Afallon. They stood watching, calm, composed, unsurprised.

"How?" whispered Cadogan.

They were priests of Simaerin. The Ilidreth were the enemy.

"Why?"

## Chapter Seventeen

The eve of Afallon's Feast fell, painting a dense fog across the Delesar River. Gwyn stood on the bank, watching his ragged men board the commandeered boats and start the painstaking crossing of the icy river.

Only so many men could fit into each boat, and the river took longer to cross and return for more soldiers than Gwyn had hoped. Still, he had little choice but to advance his forces toward Crowwell.

"Now, now, sire. Don't look so grim."

Gwyn turned to find Nathaera approaching, a cloak wrapped around her slim frame, eyes dancing with a light nothing could extinguish, not even the winter fog. Beside her strode Kive, immune to the cold in his tunic and trousers, barefoot despite Nathaera's constant insistence that he wear the boots Adesta had gifted to him. The two came to stand at Gwyn's side, and he smiled down at Nathaera.

She pulled her hood over her head to fend off the chill as she studied the river. "Ice chunks?"

Gwyn nodded. "Quite a few. But the boats are sturdy, and the rowers are careful. Hopefully, we'll cross without incident."

She nodded. "There will be incident enough on the other side. How far is Trayton from the river?"

"Roughly nine miles."

"Shall Kive and I cross with the next group?" She glanced up at Gwyn, smiling.

"Nathaera, it's dangerous. Cross with the last party and by then we will have taken Trayton."

"Nonsense. Kive is useful on the battlefield, and he won't let anything happen to me. I won't stay behind with the supplies."

Gwyn turned fully to face her, and she turned toward him.

"Yes, Gwynter?"

"I want nothing to happen to you."

She smiled. "With Kive I'm perfectly safe."

"Kive is easily distracted."

"No," chimed in Kive, shaking his head. "Not distracted. Only Kive. Kive is Kive."

"That's what he meant," Nathaera said, patting Kive's arm. "Don't argue with Shiny, Kive."

Kive turned to eye the river and hummed tunelessly.

Nathaera met Gwyn's gaze again. "I don't seek danger for the thrill of it, but because I want to be near you. I can't abide the thought of waiting out of sight for word of your safety. I had to at Dorshen Heights, and the pain was unbearable. Don't make me wait afar off again. I expect nothing more than that, sire. Only let me stay nearby and I shall be content."

He opened his mouth to answer but found no words for a reply. She stood before him, a fair and graceful maiden of high breeding and intellect, eyes sharp, tongue sharper still, and all she asked was to stand at his side through whatever dangers lay ahead. Why? What did she see within him that persuaded her to risk her life on his behalf?

"My dear lady," he whispered, "I could sooner command the river to cease its flow or the stars to disappear in the heavens than deny your request, so heartfelt as it is. But please don't make me regret this granting by losing you."

Her smile brightened like a sunbeam. "I wouldn't dream of it, my lord." She caught up her skirt and curtsied low, eyes twinkling. Straightening, she placed her finger to her brow. "As I said before, don't look so grim, sire. You'll wrinkle here, and you're much too young for wrinkling."

Gwyn laughed and ran a hand across his forehead. "I fear this war will turn me gray very young indeed."

Over the next hour, Nathaera hovered near Gwyn while Kive skulked along the riverbank, examining who-knew-what in the icy water.

Lawen appeared in the fog and nodded to Gwyn. "It's time."

Gwyn pulled his cloak a little tighter, then smiled at Nathaera. "Come with me. It's time to cross."

She patted her skirt. "Come, Kive. We're going."

Kive bounded to his feet. "Yes, Fairy Wren. Coming, Shiny." He followed Gwyn and Nathaera to the boats, slinking like a shadow against the night gloom.

Sleet fell from the sky, bitter against Gwyn's face as he helped Nathaera into the bobbing vessel. He staggered into the seat beside her, uncertain on the water. Kive leapt in next, and the boat violently rocked hither and thither until the oarsmen coerced it back into its natural motion.

Gwyn clutched the side. The boat pushed out into the current, filled to its capacity with his officers, save for Bened Arnnor who had volunteered to oversee loading the last of the soldiers. Chunks of ice battered the side of the boat, and the oarsmen rowed hard against the river's incessant pull. Wind howled, flinging fog and sleet into any face that dared glance up from the protection of their cloak.

Kive alone seemed oblivious to the cold, black hair whipping free in the storm, arms extended as he howled with the wind. Gwyn didn't bother to silence him. No one could tell the difference between his cry and that of nature, and somehow Kive's fearlessness heartened Gwyn.

It took an age to bring the ship into a natural harbor on the south side of the Delesar. When he stumbled from the boat, pulled ashore by Lawen's sturdy hand, a thrill of gratitude for solid ground flooded Gwyn's body, warming him a little. He suspected he'd have found the life of a sailor disagreeable.

Nathaera tripped onto the shore beside Gwyn, laughing a little. "Well, that was terrifying. Good thing Kive loved it, or we'd all have sunk in his panic." She frowned. "What of Aluem, Gwyn? He can't cross in the boats, can he? We must leave all the horses behind, too."

Gwyn shook his head. "Aluem said he could get the horses across the river, but not in a conventional manner. I left him to it."

"You don't know what he's going to do?"

"No."

"Going under way," Kive chimed in. "Going under way, Shiny."

"Under way? Where is that, Kive?"

Kive pointed down. "Under way of the water. Thundering, thundering. Allll the horses are under way."

Nathaera and Gwyn exchanged a look, and the girl shrugged. "There you have it. Aluem's taking them under way."

Gwyn nodded. "Beneath the river. Somehow."

"If he can do that for the horses, why not us?" asked Nathaera. She gathered her skirts and ascended the slope away from the river, toward a makeshift station assembled for meager shelter.

"Horses are protected by unicorns," said Gwyn, swiping water from his face as he followed Nathaera under a canvas lean-to. "Magic that might aid them won't necessarily work for us. Perhaps for me, as I'm connected to Aluem, but not for any other riders, and not for the foot soldiers. That's my guess, at least."

Gwyn and Nathaera waited two more hours while the army crossed the Delesar, each soldier carrying his own weapons and his few possessions. It took longer than Gwyn had hoped it might, but night yet remained, and the march ahead was brief enough, they should arrive in Trayton in the wee morning hours. If luck allowed and by Afallon's grace, the Heshi would still be slumbering in a drunken stupor.

When Bened Arnnor arrived with the last of the men, Gwynter divided his army in half and ordered General Haratin to take the direct northern route to the hamlet. Meanwhile Gwyn and his force would circle around from the south to surround and contain the Heshi army. A report from one of Gwyn's aides, an earnest man named Rohkye — who had scouted out Trayton in the guise of a traveling cobbler — informed the War Council that a single guard-house stood just south. Likely those on duty would be awake if not alert.

Gwyn sent his other aide, Aleteer Hemonn, ahead of his force to dispatch the Heshi guards. Aleteer was a skilled swordsman, lean and agile, and Gwyn prayed he would be stealthy enough to silence the watch before an alarm sounded. Gwyn had contemplated sending Kive ahead for a midnight meal, but the fallen fae was too easily distracted, and Gwyn didn't savor giving him verbal permission to eat people under any circumstances.

As Gwyn's force took up the nine mile march to Trayton, Kive walked beside him, staring wistfully ahead into the darkness where Aleteer had been swallowed by the night.

Gwyn had walked about ten minutes when he halted, spotting a white figure amidst the hammering sleet ahead. He smiled as he recognized Aluem drifting near, ghostlike against the storm.

'*Greetings, young King Gwynter,*' said the unicorn in his head. '*Your horses await you in a glade just up the path. Follow me.*'

He quickened his pace and soon found the horses standing near one another for warmth under the harsh elements. Exclamations filled the ranks. Gwyn grinned as he mounted Aluem and ordered his riders to mount their own steeds. The foot soldiers looked on, shivering, barefooted, but grinning broadly, as though this had been Divine Afallon's intervention.

Spirits lifted after that. But as Gwyn rode down the ranks, offering encouragement where he might, his heart throbbed as he found the snowy tracks of his soldiers stained by their own bloody feet.

Prince Fayett sae Marqwen rode toward the rear of the march

upon a stallion of pure black. The prince inclined his youthful head toward Gwyn, smiling. "Your Majesty."

"Your Highness," answered Gwyn, returning his nod. Aluem matched the stallion's pace. "Are you certain you wish to engage in this battle?"

"I have no doubts, but might you, Your Majesty?" asked Fayett. "And are those doubts due to my age or the matter of my Fraeli blood?"

Gwyn hesitated. "Your age, Your Highness. And your station. This war has already claimed too many lives of immeasurable value."

Fayett nodded. "I well understand your concerns, Majesty, and they are valid. Nevertheless, I am resolved. I pledged my heart to your cause, King Gwynter, and I shall not betray it. If my lot is to die in Simaerin under the Unicorn banner, it is a worthy end. Far better than to die abed while the Crow banner still flies in the world."

"But what of your father and mother? They don't know where you are, nor what you're about," said Gwyn quietly.

"Quite true. Nor shall I write them now or in the future, until at last this war is decided."

Gwyn's brow wrinkled. "But they'll worry themselves ill."

"Unlikely. They think I'm away for my education. I have my letters routed from there."

Gwyn stared. "But surely the academy has alerted them."

Fayett laughed. "No, no. The professors there are quite under my thumb. I assure you, they'll not spill my secret."

"Not even to the king?"

"Especially not to him, else they might lose their heads. So they fear, at least."

Gwyn shook his head, caught between laughter and wonder. "But if you're killed here, surely the professors will lose their heads at that point."

"I've made provisions for that as well," said Fayett, but he didn't expound. His eyes turned toward the marching soldiers ahead.

"While I'm honored by your concern, Your Majesty, now is the time to focus on your next battle. The Heshi are not a force to take for granted, as I'm sure you know. Ride proud for your men, inspire them upon your exquisite white mount, and lead them to victory."

Gwyn stroked Aluem's neck and nodded. "You're right. I must be present. Come, Aluem."

He charged ahead.

## Chapter Eighteen

Thin fingers of sunlight stretched between dark clouds as dawn ascended.

The Winter Army stood on the border of the tiny hamlet, the scent of wood smoke strong on the air. Not a soul in Trayton stirred. Rohkye sat on his gelding beside King Gwynter's fair horse, assessing the ordered state of Trayton. That came as no surprise, for the hamlet had been erected in recent years and named after one of the Crow King's closest advisers: Traycen ren Lotelon. The man was well known for his organizational skills, tactfulness, and precision. Each house in Trayton looked roughly the same size and style, leaving no room for personality.

Upon visiting the hamlet a few days ago, Rohkye had determined he would despise living in such a place. How could he tell the difference between his home and someone else's, for Afallon's sake?

Aluem shifted, drawing Rohkye's focus from the buildings back to his king. Gwynter sat upon Aluem, gray eyes scanning the area with such severity, such alertness, Rohkye tensed in response. Gwynter must be the most disciplined youth Rohkye had ever seen — and he'd seen plenty of youths in former days spent tutoring the nobles of Crowwell.

Among his caste, Gwynter was exceptional. Not for his looks, though he was comely — or for his charm, though he was polite and kind — but for his intellect and air of command. Gwynter stood taller than most, and he used his height instinctively to cow dissenters.

Rohkye had first beheld Gwynter when the youthful commander had entered Crowwell following a successful campaign in the north, shortly before he'd declared war against the Crow King.

At the time, over a year ago, Gwynter had ridden on the back of his white horse into the capital city, half of his men in accompaniment — the other half dead or missing — and Rohkye had been struck by the authority in Gwynter's bearing. His sharp eyes and severe expression.

Rohkye had shuddered to consider what this boy would grow into under the guiding hand of the Crow King. What nations might topple beneath Gwynter ren Terare's scrutiny? Would he become Traycen ren Lotelon's successor, only to transform into a more terrifying specter?

Shortly thereafter, following a birthday celebration in Crow Castle, Gwynter had left Crowwell in company with his brother, and only a month had passed before word reached Crowwell of Gwynter's dissension.

What had changed? At first, Rohkye couldn't guess, but he recalled the severity of the boy's presence, and he feared for Simaerin. Though Rohkye held no love for his sovereign king or the ruling class, he feared far more the reign of the Crow King's student. Rohkye went that very day to a chapel and prayed for deliverance from tyranny. There he encountered a priest named Rindermarr Lorric, who had listened to Rohkye's fears and laughed them away.

"That boy was never the king's man," said the priest, clapping Rohkye upon the back. "He served under threat alone, and *that* accounted for what frightened you. One does not long suppress a ren Terare's spirit!"

The priest had urged Rohkye to leave Crowwell, ride to Mount Vinwen, and join himself to the dissenter's cause. In what Rohkye then believed to be a bout of madness, he obeyed the priest and rode as quickly as he might into the rebel camp to declare himself before a much different young man than he'd remembered. Gwynter ren Terare had smiled in a soft, kindly way, and welcomed Rohkye into his service warmly.

Since becoming Gwynter's aide, Rohkye had seen the boy in his moments of strength and weakness, and had been privy to his private suffering as few others. Now Rohkye could declare this young commander stood as a man among men, better equipped in his humility to lead Simaerin than any king within the world.

While Gwynter was inexperienced, he was also steadfast and quick to learn. The day Gwynter took the throne of Simaerin, the world would change.

*And now I witness his path to achieve that height.*

"There."

Rohkye followed Gwynter's finger and spotted a banner bobbing on the far side of the hamlet. The signal that General Haratin's men were in position.

Gwynter took a deep, steadying breath. "Afallon be with us."

He drew his sword and raised it high. A heartbeat passed, then he dropped his sword forward, ordering the attack to commence. He said no word, gave no shout, for that would alert the Heshi. The Winter Army surged forward, hooves thundering, feet beating the earth, snow flying behind the charging force.

Someone in the hamlet shouted. Two men darted from one house to race toward the central building.

Rohkye galloped behind Gwynter. Aleteer rode on the king's other side, having finished his gruesome task in the guardhouse twenty minutes before.

Rohkye nocked an arrow and let it loose, satisfied when his target fell screaming before the door of the central building.

The second Heshi fell to Aleteer's feathered projectile in the next second.

General Haratin's forces appeared even as half-dressed Heshi officers stumbled from the houses, swords in hand.

The Heshi commander burst through the door of his quarters, sword drawn, only to find half of his men running pell-mell before his eyes, while others had dropped their weapons in surrender.

Enraged, the Heshi commander shouted savagely in a foreign tongue and charged Gwynter upon his white horse, but Aluem lowered his head and charged the man back. The Heshi commander fell with a cry, chest drenched in blood, though Gwynter's sword remained clean.

Rohkye stared at the sight, then looked around at the Heshi soldiers.

"Who here will sound the surrender for your commander?" demanded Gwynter, trotting forward. "I will allow no more bloodshed this day. Speak!"

A man wearing only his trousers came forward and spoke in guttural tones.

"He is second in command," said a youthful voice.

Rohkye glanced behind him as Gwynter turned toward the source.

Prince Fayett rode forward, grimly smiling. "He speaks for the Heshi in his commander's death, and he begs a peaceful surrender."

Gwynter nodded curtly. "He shall have it, once all his weapons are confiscated."

Prince Fayett repeated the order in the same guttural tones.

The man nodded and barked orders at his men. Soon a mountain of swords, sheathes, knives, bows, and arrows piled before Gwynter.

"Lawen," said Gwynter, and his brother rode forward. "See to the supplies. Find out what we can feed our soldiers. Sir Bened." The knight came next. "Count our soldiers and tell me how many we've lost. Mershen, see to the prisoners. Get an exact count. Haratin, secure the perimeter and watch the roads for any sign of the Crow's army. Rohkye, Aleteer, see to any person residing in Trayton who is not a Heshi soldier. Don't let them come to harm."

Rohkye started at once for the nearest door. Soon it became clear that any common folk who once inhabited Trayton had gone elsewhere. He hurried to find the king.

Upon reporting the news to Gwynter, who had taken up temporary residence in the central building, Rohkye stood at his king's side and listened to Lord Lawen's report on supplies.

"It won't last very long, but our men will have a decent meal tonight and in the week to follow, even if we feed the Heshi prisoners. I've already given orders for none of the men to raid the supply house or wagons, and I've taken the liberty of flogging anyone who attempted to rob the Heshi as well."

Gwynter nodded. "Good. We can't become thieves under any circumstances."

Bened Arnnor entered, expression grim.

Gwynter straightened in his chair. "Well, Sir Knight? How many?"

"Of the Heshi, twenty-two men were killed in the skirmish. Of our own number, two froze during last night's march. In the skirmish, sire...none fell."

Gwynter blinked. Rohkye looked between the two men.

"None?"

Arnnor nodded. "We lost not a single man in combat, sire."

Gwyn sighed and leaned back in his chair. "Thanks be to Afallon."

# Chapter Nineteen

During the battle, if so it could be called, Nathaera stood beside Kive on the outskirts of the hamlet, her eyes fastened on Gwyn.

She watched his quick movements as he barked out commands during the engagement, and she nearly screamed when the Heshi commander charged him — though she felt silly when Aluem skewered the man with his horn.

Gwyn was always safe upon the unicorn's back, not to mention the protective nature of his defensive magic. Aluem had claimed him as his kin and held a ceremony before the Winter Army had left the hills of Vinwen to begin their long and arduous war against the Crow King.

Nathaera envied Aluem his place in Gwyn's heart. She only wished she could be as dear to him, even if Gwyn only saw her as a sister. Anything was better than being kept apart.

Her mind slithered back to the kiss upon the banks of the Delesar, and she chewed her lip.

*Don't think about that. You don't know that it meant anything! He might've been delirious with fever.*

Yes, that was it. Nothing had come of his actions since, after all.

"My lady?"

She turned and smiled at Adesta as he approached, a grin on his lips, eyes gleaming.

"You look proud of yourself, my lord."

He laughed, but his smile faded. "You've been standing here for quite a while, though we've taken the..." he gestured to the few buildings "...village, is it?"

"Hamlet, which is smaller than a village, though I hope that doesn't weaken your victory." She laughed.

He shook his head. "We've outwitted the Heshi, so-called strongest army in the world. I shall accept no ridicule, not even from you, my lady."

"And I shall provide no further ridicule. Gwyn was brilliant to attack as he did."

His grin slipped a little. "It was a bold and ingenious move."

"Is something wrong?" asked Nathaera, tilting her head.

"Rabbit is sad," murmured Kive, and stroked Adesta's fair hair with his slender fingers.

The Fraeli nobleman stiffened. "Please Kive, don't pet me. Especially with those fingers. How many times must I ask you?" He sighed. "Nothing is wrong — save perhaps Kive's hygiene — but I would inquire if my lady has decided yet?"

Nathaera winced and turned away. "Oh, Adesta. I told you already, I can't yet. Not amid everything. I — I just need to think a little longer."

"I understand, and I'll wait as long as I must, but I fear for a less than favorable answer, and...I long to hear otherwise."

Nathaera twisted her skirt around her finger. "I'm not ready yet, my lord. Give me more time."

"Of course, my lady. I'm sorry to pressure you. I won't inquire again."

She turned to watch Adesta walk away, then let out a gasp. "Why do men *do* that, Kive?"

"Men?" asked Kive. His eyes followed Adesta's retreating figure.

"Do you mean Rabbit, Fairy Wren? What did Rabbit do, Fairy Wren? Shall I eat him?"

"No, no, Kive. Remember, you don't eat rabbits anymore."

"Oh yes. I forgot." He turned from Adesta, interest lost. "Fairy Wren?"

"Yes, Kive?"

"Are you upset, Fairy Wren?"

She sighed and squatted down to hug her knees. "Yes, Kive. I am. Adesta — Rabbit wants Fairy Wren to marry him, but Fairy Wren can't, you see. She's in love with someone else. Someone who doesn't feel the same way. And while Fairy Wren could never marry Rabbit under those conditions, and though Fairy Wren is very used to speaking her mind — even when it's a terrible idea — for some reason Fairy Wren *can't* tell Rabbit no! It's so difficult, when I know I'll only break his heart, and he has such a good heart. I don't think I could sleep once I saw his face twisted in agony.

"Oh, why do men have to look so earnest in their declaration, and then so devastated when they're rejected? What makes them so confident that they can just ask a woman such an important thing without first *knowing* the heart of the other?"

She paused as she recalled her own declaration of love to Gwyn. Unheralded, unrequited, unwanted.

"I suppose," she murmured to herself, "Fairy Wrens do that too. How silly of us all. Why do people fall in love?"

"It's rather inconvenient, is it not, my lady?"

Not Kive's voice. She yelped and jumped to her feet to whirl around. Bened Arnnor stood before her, a faint smile on his lips.

She rested a hand over her galloping heart. "You startled me, Sir Knight."

"My heartfelt apologies, my lady. That wasn't my intent."

"Well," she said, smiling, "if you meant to announce yourself, there are better ways."

"Again, forgive me."

Her heartbeat slowed a little. "It seems you inflicted no permanent damage, so I'll forgive you wholly, sir. But pray, what brings you out here? Aren't the officers attending the king?"

Bened Arnnor hesitated. "So they are, but I am recently demoted, and felt a little out of place and rather useless, so I escaped the close confines of the interior."

She glanced at the central building. "Your demotion, sir — does it make you bitter?"

"No, my lady. The king's judgment was just." He inclined his head. "Allow me to take this opportunity to formally introduce myself, though it's hardly proper. I'm Sir Bened Arnnor of Glashon."

She grinned. "Oh, in the wilds of Simaerin, perhaps this is the proper way, else no one would know anybody. I'm—"

"Lady Nathaera ren Lotelon, Lord Traycen's only daughter, am I right?"

She blinked. "Yes. You are. Have we—"

"I've seen you at court, though we've never spoken," Bened said, lowering his eyes. "My father has had dealings with Lord ren Lotelon frequently. You were lately betrothed to Sir Windsur ren Cloven of Yastport."

"That was nearly two years ago. I've heard he's since become betrothed to another maiden. One of unequaled beauty."

Bened nodded, dark eyes gleaming. "Ah, yes. The lady Arianwen ren Targeth."

Nathaera nodded, recalling the willowy, raven-haired young woman of House Targeth. Arianwen seemed an otherworldly creature, so quiet, sweet, and composed, every other lady at court envied her appearance and decorum, for both were impossible to mimic or mock. Nathaera envied the lady's height, though not the pallor of her skin or the sorrow etched in her face.

"She's such a solemn girl," Nathaera said. "Windsur will ruin her."

Bened smiled faintly. "He seems an amiable man."

"True, so he does seem. But seeming is not the same as being, and while Windsur is quite good at being many things, what he seems isn't one of them."

"Would you call him a scoundrel, then?" asked Bened, his eyes wide while a teasing smile twitched at his mouth.

"Once, I wouldn't dare. But, bless Afallon, I'm free of the creature and so I must confess I suspected him of such. You may tease, sir, but truth will out, now or someday."

Bened's smile fell away. "Do you believe the lady Arianwen to be in any danger?"

"Nay," said Nathaera, shaking her head. "Not straight away, for appearances matter to Windsur above all else. He would never harm her before the marriage. After that, I shudder to consider...and to think, not long ago I was bound to him. The treacherous snake!"

"Come, come," said Bened. "Surely you exaggerate, my lady."

She sighed. "I know nothing for certain, but the rumors were thick around Crowwell. He's never ventured to steal the virtue of a noblewoman, but he's rather fond of scullery maids, and knowing what I do of his impatience and his temper, I believe those rumors now that I'm not overshadowed by any promise. But listen to me! Gossiping as other ladies at court. I confess, it feels relieving to say it aloud. I've always feared marrying Windsur, but it was a matter of fact, unalterable. So I thought."

Bened arched an eyebrow. "So, then. You don't regret being disowned by your father and your House to live the grueling life of — well, a soldier, my lady?"

She laughed softly. "Indeed not, sir. Do you?"

He smiled. "I suppose you're right. The cause is just, and the sacrifices: worthy cost."

"You seem very concerned for Lady Arianwen," said Nathaera, torn between teasing him and genuine concern. "Is she special to you, sir?"

"That lady? Nay. I hardly know her. But I fear for anyone clutched in the claws of a scoundrel, no matter how sullen her disposition."

The sound of feet approaching brought Nathaera around. One of Gwyn's aides stopped just short of the two.

"Sir Bened?" asked Rohkye, bowing. "His Majesty would like a word with you."

"I'll be right there." Bened bowed to Nathaera. "I take my leave for now, my lady."

"Good day to you, sir." Nathaera curtsied.

The knight strode away, black cloak billowing in the chill wind.

"Fairy Wren?"

She blinked and turned. "Kive, were you still here?"

"No, Fairy Wren. I was there." The fallen fae pointed to a pile of chopped wood beside the nearest hut. "Hiding from the rat."

"Hiding, Kive? You didn't want to eat him?"

"No, Fairy Wren. Not that rat. Nooo." He shuddered.

Frowning, Nathaera cocked her head. "Because that rat is on our side?"

"Side, Fairy Wren?"

"Er, because the rat fights with Shiny. For him. Um. Because he protects Shiny, that's why you don't want to eat him, right?"

"Rat doesn't protect Shiny," Kive said, and hissed.

"Yes, he does. He came here to help, Kive."

Kive vigorously shook his head. "No. Nooo. No, Fairy Wren. Rat is with Crow."

Nathaera laughed. "Oh, of course. Yes, Kive, he used to work for the Crow King. So did Shiny, and a lot of other people. But now they oppose him."

Kive shook his head again. "Not that rat, Fairy Wren."

Nathaera's smile faded. "Kive, are you...are you certain? That rat works for the Crow King? Bened does?" She pointed toward the far-off knight as he slipped inside the central building.

The fallen Ilidreth turned toward the woodpile. "Caught in the web of a juicy spider. Maybe not a rat at all. Maybe a fly. Small, juicy fly. Flying, flying, flying. Caught!" Kive snatched at the air, though it was too cold for any flies to be buzzing about.

Nathaera's skin crawled, and she eyed the central building.

Should she say something to Gwyn? Kive's instincts were often right, but he was also paranoid and mad, prone to mistrust anyone new in his sphere. It had taken him months before he'd accepted Adesta into his menagerie of pet animals, thus dubbing him a rabbit rather than the commonplace, succulent rat.

Since then, Kive had added many animals to that same special realm of his mind, but most people were still rats, with a few flies and spiders on the side.

"Kive, what do you mean about the fly in the spider's web?" She glanced toward the Ilidreth, but he'd vanished, likely chasing a winging bird.

Sighing, she shook her head and started toward the central building. Kive's instinct might be right or it might be very wrong. Blind accusations would only hurt Gwyn's cause, so Nathaera must be vigilant and determine for herself if Bened Arnnor was trustworthy or a traitor.

It was all she could do.

# Chapter Twenty

Rats were Cadogan's only company his first night in the dungeons of Londolin.

While the priests of this place had spent most of their lives maintaining the ancient city, preserving its architecture and history, none had apparently thought to clean the cavernous cells of the castle's dungeon.

Alas, Cadogan's initial hope that neglect would make escape possible had crumbled upon examining the door of his present abode. Blacksmiths of yesteryear had been more skillful. That, or the iron had been enchanted not to rust. Either way, Cadogan was doomed to remain here until someone released him, or he died of disease.

Pungent odors lingered on the air, rendered by rat waste, stagnant water, and a pale fungus growing upon the walls. A bed of sorts cowered in the chamber, carved from the rock. Once, perhaps, a pallet of straw had rested against the hard surface, but it had long ago decayed, leaving a smudge of filth behind.

He coughed out every breath.

Worst of all, Cadogan's mind kept poring over the humiliating events of the previous day. His utter failure.

His men had been so spooked by the Ilidreth's sudden appearance on the walls, many had thrown their weapons aside and surrendered on the spot. The rest had scattered, no matter how Cadogan shouted at them to regroup. He couldn't blame them, too shaken himself to react as a soldier should. The priests' betrayal galled and frightened him most. He could only pray these priests had acted independently, a dark bruise against the church's unflagging loyalty, nothing more. But Cadogan had to wonder how deep the wound ran.

Did the church really support the Crow King? How many Wintervale sympathizers cankered the ranks of the clergy?

A door shrieked open somewhere beyond Cadogan's private dungeon chamber. Where his officers were kept, he didn't know, though the obvious strategy was to keep him apart. It would diminish morale in his men and decrease his chance for retaliation.

Cadogan rose from the stone bed and crossed to peer through the iron bars of the window in his impenetrable door. Torchlight grew in the corridor beyond. Footsteps scraped and echoed off stone. Shadows fled before the light. Soon Cadogan spotted three figures approaching, two robed like priests, the last in a long cloak of motley hues.

The three figures stopped before his door, faces contorted by light and shadow in the guttering flame.

"General Cadogan ren Silverard, step away from the door."

Cadogan backed up.

The tallest figure entered the gloomy chamber and threw back his cowl to reveal long black hair, piercing blue eyes, high cheekbones, and pointed ears.

Cadogan held his head high and gazed steadily at the Ilidreth warrior. "Are you to be my executioner?"

"I am High Lord Celin'Laen clo Vae'nan, guardian of the *Chesevwé,* champion of *Shaeswéath*, ally of the Winter King, and protector of High Prince Kive ave'ar Edelin of Ilid. Thus, I come to Londolin to declare war upon the usurper whom you serve. I denounce the Crow King as ruler of Simaerin and pledge my life to the cause of his enemy."

Cadogan frowned. "But what of your allegiance to the rightful ruler of Ilid?"

"What claims High Prince Kovien ave'al Edelin once held in Ilid are forfeit, for that high prince is no more. In his stead stands a creature consumed by madness and cruelty. His one rightful claim is his death as a tyrant and a traitor."

"I don't believe as you do, Ilidreth. My king is the greatest ruler Simaerin has ever known. From his own lips, he has declared the Ilidreth a savage race intent on our demise. How can I do anything other than wipe you from the face of this world?"

The Ilidreth leaned near, eyes burning in the torchlight. "Does savagery warrant feeding the flesh of my brethren to your Ilidreth prisoners? Is that not savagery as well? And what of the Crow King's edict to slaughter children because they wield magic? Tell me, General, if your own child came into his magery, would you follow that edict? Does loyalty to king justify wanton murder?"

For a heartbeat Cadogan hesitated. "Yes," he mumbled, "for without loyalty to my king, without perfect obedience, Simaerin will plunge into chaos. If all harbored the same unwavering devotion, there would be no war, no famine, no crimes. If he asked me to kill my own son, I would accept that sacrifice."

The Ilidreth's eyebrows drew together. "I see. Indeed, if everyone followed blindly as you do, that could well be so. But, General, that is not the case, and despite your soulful devotion, Simaerin yet plunges into chaos even now. No amount of sacrifice, not the shedding of innocent blood or the selling of one's soul, will change that. The truth, young human, is this: There will always be tyrants, and there will always be heroes who rise to oppose them."

Cadogan shook his head. "I will not believe that."

"Truth. You *will* not, and a man's will defines him. You contradict your own philosophy, human, but you are blind to that. It is just as well. I cannot persuade you."

"What will you do with me?" asked Cadogan.

"I? Nothing. The priests may require your services. Until then, you shall remain in this dungeon and maintain your delusions."

"Why did you come here if not to kill me?"

The Ilidreth faintly smiled. "I wished to see the face of a man in service to the Crow King. I desired to glimpse his vision. I see now precisely what I feared. Once, High Prince Kovien was a being of light and gentle wisdom, revered and nearly worshiped. But alas, darkness and doubt crept into his heart. Madness settled there, leeching hope, and Kovien fell to give rise to the Crow King. He slew his father, High King Roth, and trapped his mother in eternal slumber. Worst of all, he imprisoned his younger brother, the fair and lively Kive, within the dungeons of *Shaeswéath*, where he tortured him and fed him rats and likely worse things, until at last the young prince's mind and soul shattered."

Cadogan scoffed. "A sad tale, indeed, if it is true. Where were you through all of this? Where were the Ilidreth to aid their royal family?"

"One year ago, I could not tell you, but in the changing tides, my memories are returned to me," said the Ilidreth, tones forlorn. "I was locked outside the castle grounds. Kovien cast a spell. After he murdered the king and brought taint into the realm of Ilid, most of the Ilidreth fell.

"Light lost, hope robbed, those of us who did not fall tried to break through the magical shield surrounding *Shaeswéath*, but we had no success. When at last Kovien removed the shield, we were much too late. He had vanished, and Kive had been broken beyond aid. When no sign of Kovien could be discovered, I and my brethren thought he had gone off to die, and we slipped into the last Vales of Ilid to bide our time until the taint would touch our magic and we too would fall into madness and ruin. And so, we forgot much. Perhaps we chose to forget.

"Meanwhile, the Crow King rose in Simaerin, slaying the line of Wintervale in Londolin. Within this ancient city, I can still hear the ghostly cries of the dead softly on the wind. When he had removed all threats among humankind, Kovien turned his sights on the

Ilidreth. We knew not that he was once our prince. It is only recently that I remembered that truth. But now all is clear. The Crow King will not rest until every remnant of his sin is removed from the world. Even unto the destruction of his own people. Even should it require the tainting of the Weave itself.

Celin'Laen canted his head. "But he shall not succeed, General. The Crow King will fall a great deal farther than as Kovien he ever could, and it will be at the hand of the Winter King, who shall usher in a spring of renewal. By the Winter King's hand, Prince Kive is mending, though I and my brethren had given him up as lost forever. Gwynter ren Terare ren Wintervale shall undo all the Crow King has done, and he shall be remembered far longer than your tyrant lord."

"My king is no tyrant," Cadogan said. "He's making the sacrifices necessary to usher in the very spring of which you speak."

The Ilidreth's eyes searched Cadogan's carefully. "Tell me plainly, General, do you truly — to the very depths of your soul — believe that is so? Can anyone — human or Ilidreth — cease destruction after he has begun it? The Crow King has not merely executed criminals and heretics. He is guilty of genocide. Countless deaths are on his bloodied hands." Celin'Laen shook his head. "General, do you not ask *why*?"

Brow furrowed, Cadogan lowered his eyes to the floor. "He has been called, appointed by Afallon, for this loathsome task."

"Nay, Cadogan red Silverard. Even you do not believe so. High Prince Kovien ave'al Edelin succumbed to fear and prejudice. The Ilidreth are not immune to such, though many once believed so. We, just as humans are prone, grew proud and haughty. Many of our kind thought ourselves superior. Not the king and his lady, mind you. She was human, after all. But Kovien could not abide his mixed blood, for he feared that it weakened him. He saw his father's kingdom, the wealth and wisdom, and feared how it might fare over time in our alliance with Simaerin and Fraelin.

"Disturbed and doubtful, Kovien left the woods of Ilid, with a handful of protectors, in search of answers. They sailed far from this land across the sea. What they found in the end, I do not know. What Kovien suffered in spirit, I cannot guess. But he came back changed and alone. Clad in wrath and steeped in blood, Kovien purged the Ilidreth. So he called it. A *purging*.

"What did it accomplish, General? What did he gain? Was it worth the price he paid?" Celin'Laen bowed his head. "I cannot believe so. 'Twas a waste and a tragedy. The ache within my breast shall never mend. The tears I have shed cannot be counted. The mar upon Ilid shall ever be a scar, unfading, throbbing with memory and regret. *This* is your Crow King. *This* monster is the man to whom you bend the knee and pledge your life and honor. But what honor is found in senseless death? What answer can you give me from your heart?"

Cadogan's hands curled into fists. What answer could he give? He knew already that the Crow King was of the Ilidreth, a prince by blood with a vision for a future unlike the past. But was that future the right one? Did Cadogan serve a madman?

He knew the answer already. Yes. *Yes*, he served a madman, and not even a Simaeri royal. A usurper.

But Cadogan was bound to him by oaths both temporal and magical. He could hardly break those. And he had long believed the Crow King's course was *right*, though brutal.

*Am I deluding myself? Have I been wrong all along, too blind, too stubborn to see?*

Lifting his head, Cadogan met those striking eyes again. "If what you say is truth — if the Crow King *should* be dethroned — how can a mere boy accomplish this? The Crow King's magic is unmatched. His reach is long, his wrath terrible, his mind cunning."

Celin'Laen smiled gently. "Alone, no man can accomplish such a feat. But the Winter King is not alone. He stands with truth, and with allies, human and Ilidreth alike. It is in unity, not in tyranny, that strength is found. Young Gwynter is not alone."

# Chapter Twenty-One

Parsha bade Nox to remain within the walls of Charquae, but that seemed a pointless exercise as the dragon himself had stated that should he fail to obtain a truce from the she-dragon, all would be lost.

When Nox told Parsha as much, the man-dragon shrugged his shoulders and started off for the city wall. Nox took that as a sign that he could follow, so he did. He doubted he would be any use, but he couldn't stand back and twiddle his thumbs while his beloved city stood between two opposing dragons.

Parsha the Human strode through the brittle grass, not taking the road. He returned to where before, as a magnificent beast, he'd lain in plain sight, hiding.

Glancing at Nox, Parsha offered a fanged smile, then pulled the velvet pouch from his robe pocket, and upended it to drop the diamond into his palm.

It might be a coincidence that the dragon wheeling above suddenly changed directions. Sweat beaded across Nox's brow.

Parsha fingered the diamond, sighed, then pinched it between forefinger and thumb to hold it aloft. Sunlight sparkled in the diamond cuts.

Nox had no knowledge of gems and their quality, but here, now, he thought this diamond the most exquisite in the world — for it may well save Charquae and all its inhabitants.

The dragon flew toward them. That was certain now. Nox clasped his hands together and muttered a prayer.

The dragon approached with such speed, Nox feared she'd lower her jaw only to scoop up Parsha in his human form, along with Nox, and devour them whole. She was large enough. Maybe she didn't like diamonds. Or maybe she found them tasty.

Those wings pounded across the air, forward, back, forward, back. Grace and power and death. But as Nox shrank into himself at her approach, the she-dragon slowed and shifted just as Parsha had. In the last seconds of flight, her form became human, long black tresses flowing down her back, dark eyes lit with fire, clad in flowing robes of bloodred. Human feet, bare and slim, lightly touched the earth.

"Parsha of the Dreaming Eye," she said in silken tones much too quiet, much too gentle for the fearsome beast she'd been moments before. "*You* are the Winter King's ally?"

Parsha nodded. "Greetings, Demréal of the Golden Stream. I had not guessed you would serve the Crow."

"I do not serve the Crow," she said, teeth bared to remind Nox of her true form. "I serve another, more fair, though just as troubled."

"Is this other human master or friend?"

Demréal hesitated. "Do you know much of the Crow's court?"

"Nay," said Parsha.

"Then you would not know her."

"Your bonded?" asked Parsha.

Demréal shook her head, tresses bobbing. "Nay, but perhaps a friend. She spared my life and now I am indebted to her. I do the Crow's bidding to spare her life in return. Thus, you see it is a debt from which I cannot be dissuaded."

Parsha frowned. Nox looked between them, wondering who the lady at court might be.

"In what way is the lady threatened?" asked Parsha.

The she-dragon hissed, sending a shudder down Nox's spine. "She is trapped within Crow Castle, bespelled to take her own life, should I or one other make a single foolish move."

"You and one other?" asked Parsha.

Demréal nodded. "I know not the poor fool's name or purpose, only that someone else suffers as I. Either Charquae must fall or she will. Perhaps the other creature's task lies elsewhere. I know not."

"The Crow will not set her free even after you accomplish your task," said Parsha quietly. "Surely you see that you are now his lifelong slave."

The fair woman-dragon bowed her head and sighed. "This I know, but I am bound to my honor."

Nox shook his head. "It seems to me that if honor binds you to do something dishonorable, it makes moot what you attempted to begin with. In that case, there's no honor in following honor." He froze, then flushed as he realized he'd spoken aloud. "I—I'm sorry."

Parsha offered him a faint smile. "The round one speaks a kind of wisdom, I believe. After all, what would the fair maid say did she have her wits about her? Surely she would not thank you for staining her hands with the blood of Charquae."

Demréal turned her dark eyes on Nox and stared long. "You may be right. Perhaps. Hm." She turned back to Parsha. "Let me see the diamond."

He proffered it. The she-dragon plucked it up and stared into the gem's depths. "There is no taint upon its soul," she murmured. "It may even be enough..." She looked up. "I shall accept this in trade for Charquae. But where I fail, the Crow will send another to triumph."

Parsha grinned toothily. "He must find the fair city first. Indeed, that was my original proposal. Let me *hide* Charquae. Tell the Crow it is fallen. It will be weeks at least before he can confirm so for himself. Any other eye will be deceived, save a dragon's. It buys you time, and me as well."

"Do as you will, Parsha," said Demréal. "I must return to Crow Castle to try to free my human friend." She glanced at Nox. "Farewell, rotund sage. I shall ponder your philosophy."

She moved a long way off, then shifted and altered until she was the long, lithe, serpentine beast once again. The ground trembled beneath her mass. Nox thought her much prettier and less fierce than he had at first.

As the dragon soared into the sky on powerful, beating wings, Parsha glanced at Nox. "I told you I could save Charquae. I did not foresee that you would contribute. Well done, my spherical companion. Let us return to the church of your god and share the good news. I understand humans enjoy every chance to make merry."

# Chapter Twenty-Two

"Prince Marqwen, how do you fare?"

Fayett looked up from the scroll in his hands and smiled at Gwynter standing at the flap of his tent.

"Ah, welcome," Fayett said. "Come in, please. I'm quite well, thank you for your inquiry." He gestured to the chaise lounge across from his plush chair. "Please sit, Your Majesty."

Gwynter entered in his tattered blue cloak and sat rigidly in the proffered seat. Fayett resisted a smile as it twitched at his lips.

Surrounded all his life by royalty and noblemen, Fayett had never seen one like Gwynter ren Wintervale: Quiet, humble, even a tad awkward — not in his mannerisms, but in his dealings with Fayett. Understandably so. After Gwynter's encounters with the Crow King, he must not trust royal blood overmuch. Fayett had resolved to do all he could to rectify that, but he was only one prince, inexperienced himself.

Studying the Wintervale heir, Fayett liked what he saw. Gwynter was tall, lean, naturally graceful, and often grave. His eyes took in everything, swift and sharp. Fayett suspected Gwynter could read his character at first glance. He moved with purpose and authority, though he seemed unaware that he possessed that commanding air in every situation. When Fayett entered a tent filled with men, his eyes invariably caught on Gwynter, no matter what the young king was about, sitting or standing.

"I heard reports of your skill with a blade at Trayton," Gwynter said.

Fayett's smile deepened. "I am quite handy with a sword, true. It is the pride of Crane Castle that we of the royal line are skillful warriors. No king should ask more of his people than he can first provide himself. That includes protection and knowledge of warfare and stratagems. So decreed King Cygmund of Crane Castle, and so we have adhered as his heirs."

"'Tis a noble philosophy," said Gwynter.

Fayett smiled. "Would you care for tea or wine?" He motioned to his manservant stationed in the shadows of his tent.

Gwynter lifted a hand. "No, thank you. I won't take from your stores, Your Highness."

"Nonsense. Tonight, I'm celebrating the last of those same stores, as I've distributed the rest to your soldiers alongside the Heshi supplies you procured. I also gifted what remains of my coins to your paymaster to compensate for your losses to a small degree."

Gwynter stiffened. "Your Highness is too generous. I cannot possibly accept—"

"I foresaw your protests and so I acted on the sly. 'Tis too late, my good king, and you must accept *that*."

The young king bowed his head. "I humbly thank you."

"Which is more than enough in return, Your Majesty. Do not think the suffering of Fraelin at the hands of the Crow King does not warrant some retaliation on my part. If my supplies can sustain the enemy of that unjust tyrant, I am happy to play some part in his demise. I shall write tonight for more to be brought from Fraelin and add that to my contributions."

"I'm overwhelmed," replied Gwynter, hands clutching his knees, eyes still lowered.

"This is just a sliver of what I wish to do to aid you, King Gwynter. I would have Fraelin and Simaerin become allied as once they were in ages past. We are kin, you and I. Our forefathers were brothers, each the son of King Cygmund. So, let the oaths of old be renewed. Let us fight together for a land free of torment and greed, insofar as any man can make it so. What say you, Your Majesty?"

Gwynter sat still. He slowly lifted his head, eyes bright in the burning braziers circling the plush interior of the tent. "Nothing would please me more, and I accept your proposition wholeheartedly, Prince of Fraelin."

Fayett grinned. "'Twill gladden my father's heart greatly once I dare to tell him." He laughed. "Should he give me the chance to explain anything when he learns of my whereabouts, that is."

Gwynter chuckled. "Indeed, Your Highness. Let us pray he is not so impulsive as his wayward heir."

"It is good to hear you laugh, Your Majesty. I had begun to wonder if you knew how."

The young man dropped his eyes and his smile faded. "I think I'd forgotten how. This war is not like others. It isn't a distant thing against some foreign force." He glanced up and shrugged. "Even against Fraelin, it seemed less personal somehow, I regret to say."

"That makes sense." Fayett waved away Gwynter's apology with a hand. "It is something else entirely upon your own soil. I do not wish to fathom how painful it must be to fight against your own countrymen and even to defy the standing king, tyrant or no. By Sweet Afallon, 'tis a cruel fate."

Gwynter nodded, studying his hands. "Aye, and far from finished. But we must survive until spring if we're to stand a chance. We march farther south to escape winter's bitter chill, where shelter and food might be found. But I can think of only one course to protect us until the thaw, else we'll be overrun and slaughtered by the Crow Army. We must take Keep Talbethé."

Fayett recoiled. The Fraeli well knew that keep, where once the dread Lord Chiaven had made his home one thousand years ago, before Simaerin and Fraelin were two separate countries. It was Lord Chiaven who had finished the Blessed Afallon's work when he'd executed the mild-mannered god within the keep itself, immortalizing Afallon's teachings forever.

From that time until now, most Fraeli and Simaeri called Keep Talbethé cursed — though the Church of Afallon declared it a hallowed place.

Whispers proclaimed only wicked men could long abide living within the keep. Historically, those who lived there became inhumanly strong, but cruel and barbaric on the battlefield. Until the fabricated line of Crow Kings, the church had maintained the keep, but since the Crow banner rose over Simaerin, its halls and courtyards teemed with people again. Not any people — but the Order of Corvus, the Crow King's personal army of mages. A more wicked lot, Fayett couldn't name. Dark magic ran rampant there, according to his father's spies. Fayett could well believe it.

"Your Majesty," said Fayett, tentative. "Surely there is another shelter we can use...?" His mind ran over the maps he'd seen of the land between Trayton and Crowwell, searching for any route other than the Winter King's choice.

Gwynter shook his head, eyes stormy. "I'm afraid not, Prince."

"But the keep is out of our way. Can we not take the east road through Dilian and—"

"There is no hope of shelter along the eastern coast. A garrison of the enemy stands between Dilian and Keep Hathoss. They would slaughter us."

"Talbethé will slaughter us faster," said Fayett, heart quickening.

"Not necessarily. Consider, Your Highness: You feel certain that we would be crushed if we attempted to take Keep Talbethé."

"Aye, because we *would*."

"You are convinced of this?"

"Most assuredly."

Gwynter's smile appeared again, stretching slyly across his lips. "*That* is why we shall stand a chance. The Order of Corvus knows this is how we feel. They wouldn't dream any more than you do that the Winter Army would march on Keep Talbethé, stronghold of Corvus. The element of surprise is on our side."

"Surprise, *sui*, but nothing more," said Fayett. "No level of planning will give us an edge sharp enough to overwhelm Keep Talbethé. Forgive me, Majesty, but this is folly. The fortress is impregnable. And — and even should you take the keep against all odds, that would shatter the very defenses you seek to gain for your army."

"True. *If* I marched my army to its front gates and announced my presence. A siege would fail."

"You intend to *sneak* inside the keep?" The implications, all the problems Gwynter wasn't stating, the improbability of success, flashed across Fayett's mind. "You must have some other scheme, not mere infiltration."

Gwynter nodded. "I realize that a frontal assault will not penetrate the keep. I also recognize that taking a handful of men inside the keep by night and attempting to assassinate or overpower the Order is next to useless. I intend to sneak inside, but my plan isn't murder at that point."

A spark had ignited in Gwynter's eye, and Fayett found himself drawn to the flame of quiet enthusiasm burning there. A yearning to believe that this man's scheme could work swelled up, though it was madness. "What do you intend?"

Gwynter's smile deepened further. "Trickery, Your Highness. I intend to fool them into believing we've already won. However, there is one other matter I must see to first."

## Chapter Twenty-Three

"No," snarled General Haratin. "I will not be party to such reckless, disgraceful, foolhardy plots! I say again, sire, *no*. You go too far."

Gwynter ren Wintervale looked up from the table splayed with maps, eyes flickering in the candlelight. Rohkye stared between his liege lord and the officers assembled, each hooding their feelings as best they might — except for General Haratin, red-faced, nostrils flared.

"You will not obey my orders?" asked the Winter King, tone soft and laced with warning.

"Nay, young king," said Haratin. "I cannot. Any effort to take Talbethé will fail, no matter how clever you think yourself. We haven't the strength of arms, we haven't the provisions, we frankly haven't anything. Charquae is fallen by now. Your source of support is ended. We're a mere phantom army, haunting the barren winter fields until at last the men disband or worse — turn on their leaders! Well, I've had enough of starving and freezing in the name of a mere pup, ambitious and overeager to prove himself. I'm finished pretending."

"What will you do, General Haratin?" asked Gwynter.

Tension crackled in the air, every face fastened between king and general, breathless. Rohkye didn't dare to move, though he'd been pouring out diluted ale for the officers. Now didn't seem an appropriate time to serve drinks. Or to twitch.

"I shall retire to my estate, Your Majesty," said Haratin. "Unless you intend to stop me. But by Afallon, if you try, I shall fight my way free or die in the effort."

The Winter King considered Haratin for several heartbeats, eyes dark as a stormy sea. "Would you swear an oath, Haratin, not to betray our plans to the enemy? On pain of death and by your very soul, would you swear to keep silent?"

"This is madness, sire," piped up Mershen, hands raised in a placating gesture. "Haratin can't well go back home unmolested. The Crow King knows of his acts of treason. Surely *you* recognize the danger, Haratin. If you return, your life's forfeit. We're all committed to this fight, whether or not the circumstances are ideal."

Haratin sneered. "Ever the faithful lapdog, Mershen. Laying siege to Talbethé is tantamount to suicide. I'll have no part in it. I won't lead my men to death for this — this — this *whelp* who calls himself a monarch!"

Lawen slammed his fist against the table. Rohkye nearly leapt out of his skin, and sloshed ale down his ragged front.

"Firstly," said Lawen, green eyes as dangerous as Nox's dragon, "Gwynter has *never* declared himself king, yet other men have called him so, for that title was inherited at birth. You've seen the proof. We all have. Whatever claims you make, let them be truth at the least, Lord Haratin. Secondly, do not use protecting your men as an excuse for your cowardice. Say aloud what you think: You're afraid, General. Talbethé scares you spitless."

"I admit it!" The red splotches deepened across Haratin's face. "Keep Talbethé is impenetrable. None can breach its walls. Only madmen would consider taking it, and none would succeed." He turned back to Gwynter. "I won't march on Talbethé. I won't march on Crowwell. I denounce you. You're a weak and inexperienced fool. What glory is there in this mad crusade? I say none!"

"And you shall say no more," said Gwynter firmly. "Go, Haratin. Leave this camp, leave my men, leave your honor, and begone from my sight before dawn, or I shall burn you as a traitor."

General Haratin raised his chin to look down his nose at the king, but Gwynter stood taller than him. Rohkye turned back to pouring ale. The other men resumed studying the maps across the table. For a moment longer, Haratin stood in defiance, but when King Gwynter rested a hand on the sword strapped to his hip, the general stepped back. He hesitated, then sniffed, and spun to storm from the tent.

Silence ruled long after hooves thundered away outside. Gwynter turned to Rohkye. "You may serve the drinks now. The men are thirsty."

Rohkye shook himself and handed out the tankards, two at a time, as Gwynter motioned to the maps.

"Gentlemen, now that we've rooted out the rat, which would no doubt delight Kive..."

Nervous laughter trickled through the officers.

Gwynter tapped the dread spot against the canvas map. "We must take Keep Talbethé. We all know it, whether or not you can admit it to yourselves. Should we march for Crowwell, assuming we first survived this winter in the cold, the Order of Corvus would undoubtedly send forth the forces of Talbethé to hinder us. Likely, that would result in complete annihilation. Can anyone dispute me?"

No one spoke. Several officers sipped their ale.

"I thought not." Gwynter sighed. "I admit that Talbethé is a terrifying specter. We took Bayton because only a handful of the Order of Corvus oversaw its barricades. They underestimated us. Again, just now in Trayton, we overpowered the Heshi — alleged strongest army in the world — not because we were stronger, but because they underestimated us. But if we march on Crowwell, the Crow King will not underestimate us, especially after these victories. He will send a wave great enough to crush us where we stand. That wave is gaining momentum even now. The defeat of the Heshi has guaranteed that.

"This leaves us just one option. We must take Talbethé before the Crow King can conjure his reply. We must strike a third chink in the enemy's armor, or we lose all. And besides, Talbethé is the only fortress large enough to imprison our Heshi guests, which we must do before they gain enough courage to stab us in the back.

"I spoke of besieging the keep with our full force of arms. That, gentlemen, was a lie. Haratin has long doubted my plans and his motivations have been self-serving. No matter what scheme I presented to this council, I knew he would protest loudly and likely withdraw his support. That won't surprise anyone here, very likely. Thus, I knew I must present a false plan, one that would tip the scale at last and show Haratin his own true colors. In this I've succeeded, and I ask you to forgive my subterfuge.

"We will *not* be laying siege to Talbethé. We will instead infiltrate it to topple its defenses from the interior. General Haratin was correct in one regard: We *are* as a phantom force, but *that* will lend us strength. Let us become like specters, stealthy, unseen, *powerful*. This is our single advantage. We shall conquer Talbethé, we shall dethrone the Crow King, and we shall give rise to a new nation built for the people and not for the tyrants of ages past. This we can do, by Afallon's grace.

"Gentlemen, I ask you to ride with me even through madness. What say you?"

Silence answered.

Lawen clapped a fist to his chest. "My liege, I will ride with you into the very pits of Hell, should you ask it. And i' truth, I believe this time you do."

Laughter, nervous but strong, rippled through the officers. One by one they clapped their fists to their armored chests and bowed their heads.

"Into the fray we ride, sire," said Mershen.

"Come what may," added Bened Arnnor.

General Cluv lifted his tankard. "Let us take Talbethé, that the Crow King may understand what fear truly is!"

"Hear, hear!" cried the officers in unison, lifting their ale to drink a toast.

King Gwynter looked on, grim and silent, his ale untouched. Rohkye wondered what thoughts swirled in the young king's mind: Guilt, fear, pride? Did he think his army stood a chance? Would Talbethé hold or would it topple?

Either way, what would the Crow King do in retaliation?

# Chapter Twenty-Four

Storm clouds settled over Crowwell, reflecting Kovien's mood.

He had conjured them to do so, for though he was born an Ilidreth, and the fae couldn't control weather patterns, he was also born human, and thus he was a mage. The combination endowed him with magic fiercer, more awesome, than had been seen in any age since Afallon.

Once, long, long ago, he'd hated his power. Hated his blood and birthright. In truth, he still did. But now he was much more than High Prince Kovien had ever been. He ruled Simaerin; he had vanquished Ilid; soon he would raze Fraelin to the ground.

Such had been his plan. And from there, every isle, every peninsula, every tiny nook in the wide world would become his.

But now, seated on his throne, eyeing the bowing messengers at his feet, cramped, and confined to this tiny chamber, in this tiny kingdom, with tiny, incompetent human creatures—

Kovien stamped down hard on a swelling urge to shatter the castle walls around him. He must maintain control. He must remain calm. The Crow King never grew angry. Never became upset. He was the pinnacle of right, justice, truth. His cause would never fail.

There was no reason to panic...

"You have heard nothing of General Cadogan since his capture?" asked Kovien, keeping his voice low and level. Good, he sounded calm. Not a trace of panic, not an ounce of anger... "The Ilidreth invaders have not displayed his remains upon Londolin's walls?"

"No, sire. They hold him and his entire army within the Silver City, but beyond that we know nothing."

Kovien's heart constricted. The Ilidreth had come, *here*, to Simaerin—*and they flew the Swan banner*.

Unthinkable, unbearable.

But the Crow King must be calm, unruffled, long-suffering...

Kovien nodded. His face remained a mask. "And the so-called Winter King. What progress has he made? Still trapped on the banks of the Delesar, yes?"

"No, Majesty," answered another man bowing before him, wearing the tabard of a royal courier. "Your spy sent a missive, but it reached Keep Hathoss too late. The Winter Army has crossed the river and taken Trayton. They attacked at dawn on the Feast of Afallon. The Heshi were abed and only one escaped to send a letter by pigeon, else we would know nothing of their defeat."

Kovien closed his eyes. Rage surged through his veins like fire, hot, harrowing. "Very well." His voice drifted out as a whisper, tinged with icy anger. At least it was cold, though his bones were melting. "Any sign of which road the Winter Army is taking?"

"None yet, sire. We hope to learn their plans soon."

Kovien opened his eyes. "My spy would not fail me deliberately." His gaze slid to the third prostrating figure. "What of Charquae?"

"The dragon continues her torment, sire. The people there must be cowed by now."

"What of the enemy's dragon? Any sign?"

"None, sire."

Kovien frowned. Odd that Gwynter ren Terare had found a dragon, used it once at Bayton, and then never again. But then, dragons were difficult to capture and harder still to keep. Likely, whatever bargain he'd struck had run its course. But there was still the chance Gwynter was playing a game. That the dragon lay in wait for some greater purpose.

"Very well," Kovien said. "Send word to Arianwen. Tell her Charquae must fall *now*."

"Yes, sire." The man lowered his head more, then rose from his knee, and scurried from the room.

Kovien turned to the second messenger. "Londolin is lost to us — but dispatch an army of three thousand foot soldiers to keep the Ilidreth contained there. We do not need them joining the Winter Army in their efforts to reach Crowwell."

"Yes, sire." The messenger also bowed, then left the throne room.

"You."

The last messenger lifted his head. "Majesty?"

"Bring me Windsur ren Cloven. Tell him to hurry."

As the messenger left, Traycen ren Lotelon moved from the side of the throne to bend his knee at Kovien's side.

"What is your will, my master?"

"My spy is only human, and his word reaches me slowly. Find out what young Gwynter plans next."

Traycen nodded. "Yes, my king." He vanished on the spot.

The courtiers and servants who remained in the throne room kept silent. Kovien could hear the whistling wind beyond the walls, high and eerie. Not long ago, he had feigned that magic belonged only to heretics, but since Gwynter's betrayal, all that had changed. Now, of necessity, Kovien had revealed the truth. The Order of Corvus was his personal army of mages, and Simaerin must accept that fact.

Many nobles were uncomfortable with that revelation, but Kovien hardly cared. He must use every tool in his arsenal or he could lose this war. Indeed, he could lose everything.

In proper Traycen fashion, the mage returned within moments, and not alone. Clutched by the hair, sniffling and trembling, knelt a man in armor.

"General Haratin, formerly of the Winter Army, sire," said Traycen, and he yanked the man's head back until he elicited a whimper.

Kovien propped his elbow against the arm of his throne and rested his cheek against his palm. "Greetings, General Haratin, senile fool in the flesh. But what is this of a former rank? Have you been thrown out of the enemy camp? Release him, Lord ren Lotelon. Let him speak."

Haratin fell forward when the mage unhanded him. Gathering himself up, the general held his chin high as he met Kovien's gaze. "I was on my way to see you, Your Majesty. I've not been thrown out of Gwynter's camp. I left of my own volition."

Kovien's lip lifted in a snarl. "How commendable. So, you only had a brief bout of madness, and now you think better of betraying your liege. I'm touched, Haratin. Quite touched."

The man paled. "Forgive me, my king. I was weak and—"

Kovien lifted a hand. "None of that if you please. Lord ren Lotelon brought here you because you have news of Gwynter's next move. Supply it to me and I may spare your life, though treason is punishable by death."

Light caught in Haratin's eyes and he leaned forward. "Yes, my king. Just before I rode from the Winter Camp, Gwynter shared his next plan of attack. His goal is Keep Talbethé. He intends to lay siege to it."

Kovien stared at Haratin. He threw his head back and laughed. "Talbethé? Truly? Does the fool think he could conquer that fortress, now or in a hundred years? He lacks the men, the arms, even the magic to accomplish such a feat. He cannot flatten it as he did that old relic on the plains. Was this not some jest at your expense, Haratin?"

"Nay, sire. He was deadly serious and set upon his goal. I argued long with him about the folly of his scheme, but he remained resolute."

"And thus, you left, at last seeing his recklessness for what it is." Kovien canted his head. "But where do you stand now, General?

Not with Gwynter seemingly, yet you have betrayed me as well. Where does that leave a man, I wonder? Forsaken, I think. I said I would spare you, Haratin, and I keep my word. Your life remains yours, but I cannot tolerate traitors. You must leave Simaerin.

"I doubt Fraelin will offer sanctuary, for they are allied with Gwynter. You also helped with the taking of Trayton, and so I suspect the Heshi will not extend an invitation. Across the sea may be your only recourse. But that I leave to you. Goodbye, Haratin." He turned his head away.

"S-sire, please. Have I not redeemed myself in some degree? I would serve you faithfully. I would swear an oath—"

"As you did once to me, and once to Gwynter?" The Crow King smiled. "Yet you expect me to believe you a third time? I am no fool, Haratin. Oaths and honor mean nothing to you. You disgust me. Begone. Should I see you again, I will not stay my hand twice."

Kovien looked up and pinned his gaze on the figure striding from the back of the long chamber, head held high, arrogance rolling from his frame like smoke from a dying fire. Kovien smiled. The proud ones were so easy to bend and mold.

"Ah, Sir Windsur ren Cloven, I am glad you could come so swiftly. I have need of you."

# PART III
# KEEP TALBETHÉ

# Chapter Twenty-Five

Rain and sleet pursued the Winter Army.

Burdened with Heshi prisoners, Gwyn wondered how the army survived at all. Why had the Heshi not risen to overpower them? How far could they stretch the meager food rations? How long before the overworked, undernourished horses gave out? When would the men abandon him?

These thoughts he kept to himself, though nightmares plagued his sleep as constantly as ragged coughs broke from his chest. Most of his army was sick. Those who weren't would be soon.

Even Nathaera, bundled in furs taken from Trayton, looked pale and much too thin. Gwyn feared she was sicker than she let on.

He rarely saw her. Every day the army marched until dusk, with Gwyn at the head and Nathaera among the supply train creeping along in the rear. When the Winter Army had camped in the northern regions, Gwyn had sent the supply train ahead to arrange camp before the army arrived each day, but now, in enemy territory he dared not risk losing what few supplies he still had.

When the army halted nightly now, each man helped raise his own shelter, be it a tent, a lean-to, or his own tattered blanket tied to a brittle tree branch.

At first Gwyn had hoped traveling southward would entice calmer days, if not warmer, but no such mercies descended from on high.

On the fourth day of their march from Trayton, Gwyn rose before dawn and slipped from his tent, careful not to wake Lawen huddled in his meager bedding.

Kive stood like a sentinel outside, incognizant of the nipping cold. He turned to smile at Gwyn. “Hello, Shiny.”

Gwyn’s worn boots crunched through crusty snow as he moved with the fallen fae toward the outskirts of camp.

The guards on duty nodded and said nothing, familiar with their king’s habit.

Gwyn moved down an embankment of snow toward a grove of evergreens peculiar against the frozen plains around it. Here, undercover of the trees, Gwyn knelt in prayer as the fragrance of pine needles teased his senses. Kive hovered, silent.

Thirty minutes later, Gwyn rose, stiff and sore. A cough tore from his lips, and he tightened his cloak against his chest.

“Is Shiny dying?” asked Kive, by now familiar with the signs of death throughout the camp.

“No, Kive,” gasped Gwyn as he caught his breath. “I won’t be vanquished by a cold.”

“Good. Kive doesn’t want Shiny to die.”

“Thank you, Kive.”

The Ilidreth nodded faintly, eyes drifting toward the southern skies. “The Crow is moving.”

Gwyn tensed, but there was no use trying to glean coherent details from his fallen friend. Kive’s instinct appeared good, but Gwyn could only brace against the looming threat he already knew was coming.

“Kive, listen to me.”

The fae turned, red eyes deep as blood in the predawn gloom.

“You’ve done a lot for me, and I’m grateful. You’ve risked yourself again and again. I don’t want to risk you even more — but I need your help.”

"Yes, Shiny?"

"Will you come with me?"

"Kive is already coming with Shiny," said the fae, brow drawn.

"Yes, that's true. But I must go somewhere extremely dangerous, and success will only be possible if you come too."

Kive tilted his head, then bobbed it vigorously. "Where Shiny goes, Kive goes."

Relief warmed Gwyn a little. "Thank you, Kive. You're a true and brave friend."

"No," said Kive, shaking his head. "Just Kive."

ONE DAY GWYN would learn not to argue against Nathaera's decisions. The stubborn girl simply did as she pleased.

So it was, as Gwyn rode upon Aluem ahead of the Winter Army toward Talbethé, that with him traveled Lawen, Kive, Bened Arnnor, *and* the dratted girl. Bened had been another addition Gwyn didn't intend, but the man was familiar with the keep's interior, and that would save Gwyn time he could ill afford to waste.

There were other insistent voices, two being his aides, Aleteer and Rohkye, but Gwyn must draw the line lest his entire council ride ahead of the army, leaving it leaderless.

The morning Gwyn had planned to ride out for the keep, he'd received a visit from a local farmer of some wealth. The man and his sons knew of the Winter Army and their plight. Rather than report their whereabouts to the nearby Crow Garrison, the farmer had invited Gwyn's army to pitch tents in his fallow fields to rest, and opened one of his granaries for their use.

Gwyn had humbly accepted. Rather than ride out that day, he'd ordered his army to march to the fields and set up camp. Once they were fed, he'd allowed himself to sleep through the day and night.

Next morning, he and his assembled team mounted their steeds and started toward Talbethé. Gwyn prayed Afallon would be as merciful in this pursuit as He'd been in softening the farmer's heart.

Talbethé stood on the other end of a five day ride along the king's highway, but Gwyn and his company agreed to travel off the beaten path and cut the time down to three days, should weather permit. Miraculously the sky held its peace, though clouds dragged across the wide expanse, low and threatening.

On the second morning, Nathaera huddled in her furs, blowing into her cupped hands in a futile effort to warm herself. "What I wouldn't do for some mulled cider!" She coughed and patted the ground beside her. "Come, Kive."

The Ilidreth drew toward her from the border of the copse where the company camped. "Yes, Fairy Wren?"

"Do you see anything moving out there?"

"Only crunchy birds in the sky," said Kive, sorrowful. He plopped down. "No juicy rats at all."

"Pity." She patted his head. "Just let us know if you do see someone *before* you go bounding after him, hm?"

"Yes, Fairy Wren."

Nathaera turned to Gwyn, smiling. "Did you sleep all right?"

He managed a nod, though his thoughts raced with what lay ahead. Even far away in Vinwen, growing up he'd heard stories of Keep Talbethé. Despite not knowing of the Order of Corvus's magery, he'd felt a sense of dread whenever adults whispered the order's name, like it was something unholy. Strange that he'd not felt the same dread toward the Crow King who created the order.

Even now, knowing what he did of Kovien, having seen his madness, he felt none of the fear or malice he knew he ought. Why was that? Did he instead pity the man?

"Gwynter?" asked Nathaera, resting her hand against his arm. The cold of her fingers seeped through his cloak.

"Sorry," he whispered, laying his hand over hers. "I was merely thinking of the task ahead."

She nodded. "That's reasonable, considering."

Lawen stoked the fire for breakfast, which consisted of unseasoned oat gruel, but Gwyn was too famished to care. As Lawen coaxed the flames, he lifted his eyes toward Bened, who stood on the edge of the copse.

"When did you visit Keep Talbethé before, Sir Knight?" asked Lawen.

Gwyn looked at the knight, interested, and Nathaera shifted beside him to regard the man with narrowed eyes.

The knight stirred and glanced toward the company. "Only last year. The Crow King asked me to accompany Lord ren Lotelon to inspect it. I suspect the king was testing my fortitude. It was there I learned the depths of my courage."

Gwyn lowered his eyes and he shivered. The little company journeyed now toward what even clergymen called a manifestation of Hell.

He glanced at the knight. "Is it true the land around the keep is spoiled?"

Bened inclined his head. "Aye, Your Majesty. Nothing grows there but sharp thorns and poisonous weeds."

"No doubt fed by the taint of Corvus," murmured Lawen.

"So dark and sad," whispered Kive, staring at the slate sky. "Wanton. Needless." He sighed and lowered his eyes to meet Gwyn's gaze. "Shiny, when does it all end? When does all the last sunshine vanish?"

"It doesn't, Kive," answered Gwyn with as much conviction as he could muster. "We fight forever. When we fall, others will take up the banner of light and carry on. It doesn't end, Kive."

Kive canted his head. A smile drifted across his lips. "Yes, Shiny. If you say so, yes." As the fallen fae spoke, Kive's eyes flashed from red to a beautiful silvery hue, then back to red again. His inane madness burned there once more. Kive hummed a hymn commonly sung at burial rites. Gwyn hunched deeper in his cloak.

"Hush, Kive. None of that," said Nathaera, resting a hand on the Ilidreth's shoulder. "I've taught you better tunes. Sing me a sea ditty!"

Kive's voice rose in a tuneless chant. "Crash, sang the sea, the sea, the sea. Drive me to the reef, to the reef, to the reef."

"Halt! Enough." Nathaera laughed. "That isn't how it goes. I forgot you always change it into something morbid. Try singing about flowers, Kive. Remember the flower song I taught you?"

Kive bobbed his head. "Clinging roses climbed the vines of twining misery—"

"Columns three, Kive. Columns three. Not misery." The girl tried to hide a grin. "He has the funniest mind."

Kive went on. "And lo! Ill maiden drew to pick the fairest of the blooming weeds."

Nathaera groaned. "It's '*sweet* maiden drew to pick the fairest of the blooming *reeds*.' Here, listen." She sang the gentle ode:

'Clinging roses climbed the vines of twining columns three,
And lo! Sweet maiden drew to pick the fairest of the blooming reeds,
To weave a basket fit to bear to castle yon at dawning morn,
And set before the mighty king whose heart was lately cracked and worn.
In woven basket lay the cure to mighty lordling's deep despair:
A drop of sunlight gathered there by rain and moon and maiden fair.'

Kive chimed in. "And snow and soot and dirt and blood and aneeemals all there!"

Nathaera laughed, and Gwyn chuckled, despite the fae's imagery.

"Your voice is lovely, my lady," he said.

She pulled a face. "Thank ye for the compliment, Gwyn, but it's a plain voice for a maiden of my stature." She paused. "And I don't mean my height. Not a word on that, sir!"

He raised his hands as he vehemently shook his head. "On my honor, lady, I would never broach the subject."

Lawen cleared his throat. "I don't wish to interrupt what promises to be a thrilling verbal spar, but alas, our meager meal is ready." He held aloft the sticky mess of gruel in the smoke-stained pot.

"Ooh, that looks more appetizing than yestermorn's meal," said Nathaera. She leaned forward to accept Lawen's proffered dollop in a tin cup.

Gwyn grimaced as he accepted his helping. Of all the trials this winter had brought, he liked the fare least of all. He didn't dare study the contents of his breakfast too closely. Lawen had removed what dead weevils he could find before he boiled the oats, but there were always more. Gwyn ate the pasty gruel with rhythmic haste, chewing as little as he could.

Swallowing, he choked on a cough and doubled over as his chest constricted. Fire seared his lungs. His head throbbed. When the fit passed, he looked up to find his companions watching with concern.

He offered a wan smile. "I'm all right."

"That cough doesn't sound good," said Lawen.

Gwyn lifted an eyebrow. "Neither does yours, brother. Nor does Nathaera's cough, come to that. Indeed, I would venture to say none of us is very well, excepting the unicorn and fallen fae."

"On the contrary," said Bened, "I'm fit as a minstrel's strings."

"A pauper minstrel, perhaps," Gwyn said. "Your color, sir, is not much darker than this unsavory paste." He glanced at the sky with a shiver. "We've delayed too long. Hurry with your meal. We need to keep going."

Soon the companions broke camp and rode on. The clouds drew closer. Snow fell like feathers and stung like knives, breaking the stillness of the day. Kive rode with Nathaera, and she huddled close for what warmth he might provide. Gwyn glanced her way now and then, worried she might fall ill. Ragged coughs cut through the group, but they never halted.

Night descended as the snow thickened. An abandoned shed, sagging and forlorn, offered shelter.

Gwyn slumped against the moss-covered planks within, sighing. His chest burned in the frosty night air, and he coughed until his throat burned.

Lawen passed around a wineskin containing a few precious drops of liquid, which served to revive Gwyn a little.

He sat straight and glanced at the faces of his faithful friends. "Tomorrow we'll reach Talbethé as evening falls. We must wait until true night before we enter the keep. I know we're all afraid—" He broke off as a cough rattled his frame. After a moment, he looked up, panting. "Forgive me. We're all afraid, even doubtful of the success of our objective. But we must try, nevertheless. Thank you for coming with me. Whatever may happen, no one can doubt your courage." He looked at Nathaera. "Kive is the key to our victory. Please try to keep him focused."

She nodded. "That's what I'm here for."

"Like a beastie's handler," Lawen said, smiling. "Don't worry so, Gwynny. We've got Afallon on our side."

"And Kive," piped up the fallen fae. "Kive is also on Shiny's side. Kive is."

Gwyn grinned. "So you are, Kive. And I thank you for it."

# Chapter Twenty-Six

Growing up on the streets of Charquae, Nathael thought he knew hustle and bustle. But that city appeared tranquil and pastoral compared to the noise and mayhem of Crowwell's markets.

Bodies pushed and jostled each other as voices rose in a deafening din, competing uselessly, for surely no one could make out a single word any merchant said.

Worst of all hovered the stench: sweat, raw fish, refuse, perfume, sweet breads, hay, horses, all assaulting the senses until Nathael grew dizzy and nauseated.

He spent his first two days acclimatizing to the thoroughfares, before he could navigate to the troughs and taverns to glean any tidbits on the war. Idle gossip harbored little by way of reliable army movements. Instead, whispers centered on much nearer threads of news.

Among them, a single name caught Nathael's attention: Sir Bened Arnnor.

Another name always accompanied it.

Lady Arianwen ren Targeth wasn't a familiar courtier, but Nathael knew little of the noble Houses. His meager knowledge came from Nox, who'd daydreamed often of becoming a knight to win some fair lady's hand — but that didn't mean Nathael had paid special attention. Still, as he skulked about the tavern doorways, adopting the persona of a wandering waif, virtually invisible, he heard names he'd forgotten but now recalled. Other names, every soul in Simaerin knew by heart.

Lord Traycen ren Lotelon, for instance.

At the *Winged Sword*, a well-kept establishment off the King's Road, Nathael shrugged off his flea-bitten cloak in the nearby alley, squared his shoulders, and entered the tavern as a respectable tradesman, young but well enough off to buy a pint or two.

The tavern keeper, a middle-aged man not unlike Nox's baker father, nodded a greeting as Nathael aimed for a solitary table far from a lively bunch of soldiers. He settled near an elderly man and his plump, rather chipper companion — probably a granddaughter, whose taste for wine showed in her complexion. They weren't wealthy, nor were they paupers. Likely of the merchant class. Nathael had an inkling they would serve his purpose well.

"What can I get you, young sir?" asked the tavern keeper as he approached, routinely wiping a tankard with a white cloth.

"Mead," said Nathael, smiling amiably.

"Very good, sir." The keeper strolled away and Nathael leaned back to partake of the chattering girl's every word.

It took time — two mugs of mead for him, three goblets of wine for her — before the plump young woman landed on the topic Nathael had caught snatches of at previous establishments.

"But can you imagine?" gasped the girl between gulps. "The knight of Montré's Folly — the fool who thinks himself so aloof and superior — stooping at last to the Crow King's command? And why? For a stuck-up noblewoman! I'll grant, Lady Arianwen is the loveliest creature this side of Swan Castle. But I doubt she knows he even exists."

The elderly man seated across from the girl offered a patient smile. "One mustn't believe all one hears, my dear."

"Perhaps not, but *everyone* is talking about it. It's a secret, and *those* make the best telling. Imagine! Bened Arnnor kowtowing to the king. Not so high and mighty now, is he?"

"It's no child's game the knight plays," said the man, and took a sip of wine. "After all, he's ridden straight into the enemy camp."

"All because Lady Arianwen is in danger." The plump girl sighed and rested her chin on her fat hands. "How I *long* to be in danger. Would that some knight found me worthy to risk life and limb for!"

The man smiled his patient smile again. "Better to marry a good honest tradesman or farmer. Security is worth far more than romance and heroics, my dear."

Nathael stayed to finish his mead, though his mind reeled with the implications. Bened Arnnor was acting on the Crow King's behalf? He'd gone to the Winter Camp only to spy and betray King Gwynter? Was the Lady of Targeth truly in danger? Was that the true motive for Bened's betrayal, or was he loyal to the Crow banner?

Pressing two coins to the table, Nathael rose and started past the girl and her grandfather. The girl looked up and flashed a smile.

He nodded back and moved on, dismissing her from his mind. He must send word to King Gwynter.

Bened Arnnor knew too much already. If he sent word to the Crow King about any of Gwynter's recent plans, it may unravel everything the Winter Army struggled for.

He would send a pigeon and then seek Rindermarr Lorric. Along with shelter and sustenance, the priest could perhaps aid him in learning more of the capital's goings-on. Especially how the Crow King intended to retaliate against Gwynter for the taking of Bayton and the hamlet of Trayton.

# Chapter Twenty-Seven

"Without supplies, the Winter Army is lost," said Towwen Brym, slapping a hand against the tabletop.

"That's no reason to raise your voice," Brioc Ffyr said, frowning at his friend.

Nox looked between them, sandwiched along the table of King Gwynter's council. There'd been a heated debate in the church over the past hour, but little accomplished. The problems were many, but the answers were few.

For the moment Charquae was safe. Even now, Parsha stalked the fields outside the walled city, keeping it hidden in plain sight. He had assured Nox all was well now, and the she-dragon wouldn't return, but Nox alone fully trusted the poet dragon's words.

The present concern loomed like a storm cloud over those assembled. How could the council assist the ailing army hundreds of miles away? Nox had the chance to paint a full picture for them an hour before, and when he sat, the silence of the vaulted chamber had been palpable. Doubtless, the army's condition had worsened since Bayton. Doubtless, many had already died from exposure or worse. Did the army still exist?

No news had reached Charquae because of the she-dragon, and

certainly nothing would come now. The city had vanished from the human eye. To send supplies from here would unveil the truth: Charquae still stood.

Besides, the wagons were always waylaid en route.

There had to be another way.

Nox thought of Parsha, but the dragon was protecting the city. If he left to aid the Winter Army, he couldn't maintain the deception. Did that matter? If the army faded, Charquae would follow sooner or later. The Crow King would eventually see the truth.

"We must steal what the army needs," piped up Towwen Stone, the scholarly friend of the king. He glanced at Towwen Brym, then Brioc, shrugging. "Charquae's supplies are needed here, for we've no idea how long we must remain hidden. That leaves us only one alternative. The enemy has plenty of storehouses along the King's Highway. Granaries dot the map from here to Crowwell and even near Londolin. I propose a small band of us leaves Charquae, infiltrates one or more of these granaries under the guise of priests or soldiers of the Crow, and delivers them personally to the Winter Army.

"If we fly the Crow banner, bandits and loyalists won't dare to plunder our wagons. It's dangerous. Undoubtedly, we face death or worse if we're caught. Nevertheless, we must do this, else we must surrender now and fail the true king of Simaerin. What say you, gentlemen?"

"One issue," said Towwen Brym, raising a finger. "We don't know *where* to deliver the stolen goods once we've got them. Assuming we live that long."

"We know they're heading south by one route or another. That's enough to start."

Brioc spoke up. "Where will we obtain armor or robes to disguise ourselves for the heist?"

"Here," said Towwen Stone. "The Crow King's soldiers must have left accoutrements behind when they abandoned the city. The Crow banner is easy enough to find. We have but to choose which granary to take from and begin our journey."

Nox watched as the men around the table murmured assent. There were a few half-hearted protests, but everyone seemed to understand the stakes. This was the best option open to them.

The council pored over maps, debating squiggles and dots drawn in ink.

Eventually, Brioc tapped a fortress drawn on the largest of the parchments. "Here. The Winter King will go here."

Another man scoffed. "You're losing your wits, man. That's Keep Talbethé. *No one* would go there."

"But he must," said Brioc. "If he doesn't take that keep, he won't reach Crowwell. The Order of Corvus has regained too much strength this past year. Should he pass the keep by and march to Crowwell, his army will be wiped from Simaerin before the spring thaw. Knowing this, he'll make for the keep."

"It's suicide," said Remien, shaking his head.

"Doesn't matter. He must take it or fail."

For a moment no one spoke. A voice broke the silence. "Are we doomed then? Was this all a dream?"

"Aye," said Towwen Brym with some heat, "naught but a dream, but one worth striving for. Surely, it's better to pursue such a dream than to live a nightmare. And if we fail? Why then, we fail with glory!"

"Not much glory in starving to death," muttered a sullen-faced man down the table.

Towwen Brym turned on him, but before he could retort another man rose. "For my part," the man said, voice clear and strong, "give me liberty or let me burn!"

"Well said, Henris!" cried Towwen Brym, slapping the table again.

As other voices thundered their approval, Nox's spirits lifted.

Though nothing in their situation had changed, surrounded by such brave, eloquent, determined men, Nox thought he might succeed at anything he tried — and the fight was worth whatever cost.

If only Nathael could be here now to witness this historic

moment. These men, few in number but vast in courage, were changing the very world.

Brioc Ffyr and the Towwens Brym and Stone took charge as the energy in the chamber lessened a margin or two. Choosing a course was one thing. Plotting it was something else. Any mention of Keep Talbethé had ceased, as though it had never come up. Even when referencing the army's likely destination, only the land around the keep was alluded to.

Nox considered the map as voices rose and fell around him. He turned to Remien, who sat in silence beside him.

"What about the Crow King?" asked Nox, frowning.

"What about him precisely, Nox, son of Hemm?"

"Well, if Master Ffyr can predict the Winter King's plan to take Talbethé, surely the Crow King can too. Won't he act?"

Remien shook his head. "No. While the Crow King finds King Gwynter a reckless youth, he would still never think him so foolhardy as that. Which must be part of the Winter King's scheme: No one would see it coming."

"But Master Ffyr sees it," said Nox.

"Aye, but Brioc is as foolhardy as his liege — perhaps more so. Philosophers usually are."

"Master Ffyr is a philosopher?" Nox glanced at the middle-aged mage with renewed admiration. "I thought he was only a printer."

"Philosophers are often attached to a trade, lad," said Remien, grinning. "Philosophizing of itself pays very little. They must find a way to fill their bellies, same as other men."

Nox considered that. "What does he philosophize about?"

"Who knows? I can't keep his thoughts straight." Remien turned back to the maps, eyes darkening as they fell on the region of Talbethé. "Never mind cryptic thoughts and antics for now. Pray to Afallon, lad. Pray hard. Anything short of a miracle will be the end of our army, and if that happens, we'll all burn just like Master Henris said."

# Chapter Twenty-Eight

Lady Arianwen ren Targeth caught a snowflake in her palm and watched it melt, envious of its escape.

Flicking the water away, she drew the curtains of the window shut and turned to the darkened bedchamber. The bed crouched like a giant beast waiting to snare her, but she moved there anyway and sat upon the feather mattress as she wiped her palm dry against her gown. She didn't bother to wipe her eyes.

With a sigh, Arianwen fell back against the coverlets to stare into the shadows above the four-poster frame. Tears slid from her eyes to roll into her black hair.

"Let them fall," she whispered, so softly she hardly heard herself.

"Who, my dear lady?"

She shot upright, eyes wide as her heart thundered in her chest. There, near the window. Shrouded in shadow.

"Your Majesty," she murmured, bowing her head.

"Let who fall?" asked the Crow King in silken tones, so gentle, so kind.

She let every emotion slip from her face. Let them melt like that tiny snowflake. He must see nothing of her heart. "No one, sire. I was speaking of the snow outside."

"Ah." He reached a hand out and drew aside the curtains to let in a sliver of gray light. "Charquae is fallen, my lady?"

Arianwen hesitated a heartbeat. "Yes, my lord. So the dragon said."

"You've done well. I told your intended so before he left."

Arianwen resisted a frown. "You sent Sir Windsur away?"

"Just so. He will join Sir Bened in his quest to thwart the Winter King at Keep Talbethé."

"I see." She folded her hands into her lap and stayed as still as possible.

"Aren't you pleased? Both suitors are quite in earnest to win you."

"Hasn't one suitor already won my hand?" asked Arianwen in icy tones.

"So he believes, but war is an ugly affair, my lady. So many noble souls fall upon the field." A smile laced the Crow King's voice. "So Sir Bened hopes. Perhaps they will duel one another before the end. Which shall be the victor, I wonder? Which would you bestow your favor upon?"

She turned her head away. "Does my favor matter, Your Majesty?"

"Not really. I was merely curious."

Muted footsteps approached the bed. She stiffened but remained where she sat. Where could she run?

Long fingers brushed her cheek. "Thou art fair, Arianwen," whispered the king, "and cold as the northern climes of Fraelin. I shall break your spirit yet." The hand retreated and the king drew back.

Arianwen turned her eyes to the looming figure. "What are you waiting for? Why have you not harmed me?"

Faint laughter came as a song. "You think I desire your body? Nay, lady fair. I am not some brute in search of pleasure. My needs, my goals, are not so petty as man's. I keep you here for other reasons. My own reasons. I need not elucidate. All you need know is that you shall never leave. Is that not enough?"

She stared at the shadows of his face. For one year, one dreadful year, she'd waited here, fearing the time he would come to her bed and rob her of her virtue — but if not that, what could he want? What could she possibly provide?

She opened her mouth, perhaps to beg, perhaps to scream in defiance, but then she shut it. What was the point in asking? He wouldn't say. They both knew as much. He intended to make her suffer, that much she guessed already. Bowing her head, she listened to his footsteps fade away. If he left by the door, she heard nothing of its opening or shutting.

At last she looked up and had the room once more to herself. For a moment more she didn't move. Then she leaned forward and pressed her hands to her face.

She choked on a sob. "Blessed Afallon! *Why?*"

# Chapter Twenty-Nine

"Gwynter, may I ask you something?"

Gwyn rolled over in his bedding, ignoring the aches in his bones, and caught the light of his brother's eyes in the predawn glow. The dilapidated floorboards of the shed moaned beneath Gwyn as he shifted. Light snaked in through termite holes in the eastward wall, illuminating the slumbering lumps huddled beneath thin bedding.

No one else stirred apart from Lawen who lay beside him. Kive roamed somewhere outside, probably hunting.

"What is it?" Gwyn whispered.

"We both know General Haratin is a snake. Even Kive would agree, despite his preference for rat flesh. Your council knows it too. So why did you tell him about Talbethé at all, especially if you intended to let him leave? I'd bet one thousand *denn* he's going to tell the Crow King. Anything to elevate himself."

Gwyn smiled grimly. "Aye, that he will, though he's a fool if he thinks the Crow King will reward him after all he's done." He pulled his blanket closer. "He *is* a snake, but I counted on that."

Lawen's brow wrinkled. "You played him. How? The Crow King will send his forces here."

"Some, possibly. But I doubt he'll supply many. He'll react, for he's underestimated our strength twice already, and won't do so again. But he won't weaken Crowwell's defenses until he's certain we're doing as Haratin reports. Little doubts will rest in the king's head: Was Haratin fooled? Does the Winter Army intend to march straight for Crowwell and take the city while the Crow protects the Order of Corvus?"

"All right. So, he'll not send his entire army to wipe us out. But why do you want the Crow King to know?"

"Because in his doubt, he'll send his best man to thwart us if we strike. And if we remove the Crow's right hand, we'll stand a better chance overall. The Crow King will expect us to besiege the keep, and his right hand will aim to destroy us openly. Thus, his guard will be raised against an outside assault. Neither will expect our infiltration, for the keep is impenetrable. Ask anyone."

"It's a dangerous ploy, Gwyn."

"Yes, 'tis." Gwyn rolled onto his back and studied the cobweb-cloaked ceiling. "But necessary. You say you killed Lord Traycen in the True Wood."

"Aye."

"But he appears yet to live. Why? Does some imposter wear his face? Or does the Crow King protect his own especially?"

The floorboards creaked. Lawen sat up to stare down at Gwyn. "You want to lure the Crow King."

Gwyn met his brother's eyes and said nothing.

"That's madness," Lawen hissed. "If the king comes—"

"Sir Bened came to me with the idea, and I agreed with him. I want to end this at Talbethé if I can, Lawen. I don't want to storm the capital. Our army may not last until spring as it is." His chest constricted and Gwyn rolled to one side. Coughs ripped through his throat. The fit lasted until his eyes streamed with tears. Lawen's hand rested against his shoulder, soothing.

"What's done is done, I suppose. Just rest, Gwynny. If you can..."

Choking on swelling emotions, Gwyn caught Lawen's cool hand to rest it against his face.

Lawen's arm stiffened. "You're burning up." The fingers of his free hand pressed against Gwyn's forehead, cold and welcome.

"It doesn't matter," Gwyn whispered. "We must enter Talbethé on the morrow, well or otherwise. I shan't let a fever stop me."

"But, Gwynter—"

"No, Lawen. We ride on. We take the keep. After that, I'll rest for a little while."

"If you ride like this, we won't reach the keep."

"Aluem won't let me fall." Gwyn closed his eyes. Weariness washed through him, stifling, heavy...

"You're using too much magic. You're trying to sustain yourself with it, aren't you? Gwynter, that kind of abuse kills mages. It can drive them mad."

Gwyn smiled. "Worrywart." He sighed faintly and let sleep take him, down, down, to a place of blissful darkness.

❦

AN HOUR'S sleep granted Gwyn some strength, and he used it to rise and mount Aluem even as Lawen protested.

"You're fevered?" asked Nathaera, stepping from the shed, cheeks red in the cold.

"Just a little," said Gwyn. "I'll be fine. We must keep moving."

She took another step, lips parting as though to argue, but then she nodded and mounted her steed. "Kive."

The fallen fae trotted from around the back of the shed. "Yes, Fairy Wren?"

"Ride with Shiny if you please. Keep him upright."

Kive bobbed a nod and clambered onto Aluem's back behind Gwyn, who didn't protest. Indeed, he welcomed the support as he relaxed his throbbing muscles against the bony frame of the fallen fae. The pounding in his head eased a tad. Sunlight stung his eyes as he turned his attention toward the path ahead.

The company moved out. Every hoofbeat against the earth pulsed through Gwyn's body.

'*Can you keep this up, young Gwynter?*' asked Aluem.

Gwyn set his jaw and nodded. The unicorn didn't push further. Gwyn called a halt once to partake of a meager meal of salted pork. After that, they pushed with all they had to reach the keep by dusk.

As the sun drew its last threads of light from the sky, Gwyn spotted the looming walls of Keep Talbethé highlighted by countless torches. The keep was made of black stone, rough and sharp, with jutting metal spikes glistening in the guttering flames. The walls rose, solid and heavily manned with armored guards stalking the battlements above. Around the keep spread a vast wasteland of ice. Snow fell heavily.

Gwyn shivered. The atmosphere of this place was dark — darker than the growing night. The frigid air tasted like sorrow and cruelty in conflict.

The company stayed hidden within the last stand of trees before the keep, waiting until true night swallowed the world.

Gwyn turned to the fallen fae. "All right, Kive. It's time to do as we discussed."

"Eat the rats?" asked Kive.

"No, Kive," said Gwyn, smiling. "Remember the gate?"

"Oh, yes, yes. I must tell the rats to let you enter because you are an ally."

"Yes, Kive. Exactly."

"Won't they remember after a moment?" asked Nathaera.

"Not before it's too late to stop us," said Gwyn steadily. "Kive and I have been experimenting with his manipulation. I'm confident that wording isn't what's important. Kive could tell me to stand perfectly still and I would do so. He could also tell me to find the nearest cliff and jump to my death, and I would start off to find that cliff — but the accomplishment of his order depends, not on the nature of the command, but upon the conviction with which he states it.

"Should he tell me very casually to jump off that cliff, I would likely fight it off long before I had to jump. Should he, however, *insist* earnestly that I do so, I might not be able to resist before it was too late, if I resisted at all. I've timed Kive's most earnest command. Without fail, it lasted nearly an entire day and night. I've also tested to see if the number of people under the command's sway would alter the length of its influence. It didn't."

"Just how did you test all this?" asked Lawen, eyes narrowed.

Gwyn smiled faintly. "I assure you, Kive did no worse to my council than to belay its fears a few times. I've worked more closely with Kive independently. I also tested the group potency, but that I did using ignorant Heshi prisoners before we started toward Talbethé—to keep them from killing us in our sleep. Still, I'm confident in my conclusion." He rested a hand on Kive's shoulder. "Before you head for the gate, Kive, tell me very strongly to have a clear mind and not feel the effects of my fever."

Kive moved to stand before Gwyn, looking up into his eyes. "*Shiny, have a clear mind and do not feel the effects of your fever.*" His tones rang deep, silken. Insistent.

Gwyn's thoughts broke through the murky fog and he sighed. "That should last at least through the night."

"But, Gwyn," said Lawen, "you're still sick."

"Yes, but now I can fight." He turned to Nathaera. "One flaw in Kive's ability is the matter of perception. His wording *does* impact the effects, not just his tone or intent. Should he tell a guard to turn around, for instance, the guard may make a full circle rather than turn his back on us. Simple, precise commands are best."

She nodded. "I understand well enough. I'll keep him straight."

"Good. Then it's time to go. Sir Bened, the banner?"

The black knight proffered the Crow banner he'd kept tucked in his saddlebag. It was now tied to the tor of a long, straight stick. "Ready, Your Majesty."

A shadow passed over Gwyn's heart as he considered the black crow against the red field. He curled his hands into fists and bowed his head. "May Afallon be our shield this night. We ride."

# Chapter Thirty

Thundering toward the gates of Talbethé, banner streaming against the chill wind, the Winter King's company stayed behind Kive, who sprang up as he reached the gateway. He darted up the wall among the spikes until he crested the battlements and disappeared from view.

"Ho the keep!" cried Lawen, as the horses slowed before the towering entrance.

"Who goes there?" boomed a voice from the left gate tower.

Lawen said nothing. A moment later the portcullis lifted with a rumbling of apparatus. Two guards appeared in the entrance, spears in hand but not pointed at Gwyn's company.

"Enter, allies," said one guard in a gruff, distant voice.

Gwyn nudged Aluem forward, nerves taut, straining for any discordant noises to indicate a trap. The clatter of hooves behind him rang loud in his ears.

The entire keep might easily stir. Was this a mistake? What if Kive's command wasn't enough to control so many Corvus mages? What if the fallen fae lost his focus midplan? What if the Crow King came to Talbethé rather than a subordinate?

*Am I prepared to meet him in combat?*

Wind rushed through Gwyn's mind. *'Steady, Gwynter. Be bold.'*

Kive scampered into view to Gwyn's right, waving vigorously. "Shiny, I told them. I told them we're allies. They're listening, Shiny."

Gwyn smiled despite himself. "Well done, Kive. Very well done."

Kive glowed with pleasure, then turned to the armored man standing beside him. "Let them through. *Let them through. They're allies.*"

The two guards remained stationary. Gwyn glanced at the banner flapping above the keep. "Lawen?"

His brother dismounted, grabbed a folded Unicorn banner, and sprinted toward the steps leading up to the battlements.

"Nathaera?"

The girl was already racing to Kive's side. "Come, Kive," she said breathlessly, "we must alert the officers that the keep has fallen to the Winter King!"

"Oh, yes. The keep has fallen," declared Kive.

"Don't tell me!" laughed Nathaera as she dragged Kive by his wrist toward the inner tower where the officers and mage leaders would soon assemble to direct their forces.

Gwyn waited a moment, then turned to Bened. "Sound the alert, Sir Knight."

Bened moved to the nearby battle horn and blew into the mouthpiece. A deep, resonating sound shook the earth, waking the compound. Scurrying feet flooded the corridors and slapped against the flagstones. Metal clanged and rattled. Troops of armored men and cloaked figures formed rows. The long-bowmen strung and nocked their weapons, prepared to let fly their arrows upon whatever force lay beyond the walls.

Gwyn waited at the open gate, not daring to breathe, willing his heart to stop drumming against his chest. Had Kive and Nathaera made it to the tower unscathed? Would the Ilidreth's command do what it must?

A shrill cry broke from the wide tower window. Gwyn's heart convulsed.

*Dear Afallon, let that be one of Kive's victims and not Nathaera.*

A voice rang out across the bailey, strong and familiar. "Look at all the rats, Fairy Wren!"

The army shifted. Several cloaked mages lifted their heads higher to listen. Gwyn resisted the urge to flinch, though no one could see him in the shadows of the gate. He dismounted Aluem.

"Listen, rats," cried Kive's voice unseen in the tower. "The Winter King has besieged the keep! The gate has fallen! *You are overrun by your enemy!*"

Murmurs rose and cries filled the night sky. Above the din, Kive's voice rang on, repeating the words Nathaera fed him, his tones thick with power, heavy, adamant. Urgent.

"*Attack, rats! Attack your neighbor! Attack your friend! He is the enemy! He is a traitor of your king!*"

Gwyn stood apart from the soldiers and mages of Talbethé, unaffected by Kive's words, already being a traitor of the Crow King and not a rat. Turning, Gwyn smiled toward Bened, but the man had vanished in an ocean of soldiers as they drew their swords on one another.

The clash of weapons and screams of the dying stained the wind.

Guilt surged through Gwyn's soul as the cracks between flagstones seeped with blood and snow, but he drew his sword and started forward into the melee.

Lawen joined him, panting slightly. "That was brilliant, Gwyn. Very effective, from what I saw on the wall."

Gwyn nodded. "Unfortunate, though. Not all these men are evil."

"Few are, I suspect."

Conversation died as a pulsing wave of magic berated Gwyn's soul. He staggered but righted himself and searched the scrabbling crowd for the mage challenger.

There, on the stone steps that spiraled up the command tower, a cloaked figure stood in repose, the calm in a storm. Gwyn started for him, stretching forth fingers of his magic to knock aside any soldier who approached. Lawen fended off any stubborn combatants, using his sword like a master, keeping near of Gwyn.

"Go," Lawen said, as they reached the bottommost step. "I'll be right behind you."

Gwyn stared up at the cloaked figure. Traycen ren Lotelon had come, and Nathaera hid within the same tower. Had she encountered him? What was the source of that scream? Was she well, or—

A sound like crashing thunder broke through Gwyn's thoughts. He wheeled around.

Boulders rained down from the battlements above. Laughter filled the sky — booming, manic.

Lawen flung himself aside, narrowly escaping the barrage.

A jeering voice followed the mad laughter. "Hold fast, Winter King! It is I who will destroy you."

Gwyn spotted a man leaning over the walkway on the wall above. As the dust from the boulders swept aside in a rising wind, Gwyn frowned. Windsur ren Cloven? Why had he come here? He was no mage, no soldier, not even a formidable noble. Only his wealth allowed him to aspire to any ambitions.

But then, he had a grudge against Gwyn. That much he'd proved when he'd turned Gwyn over to the Crow King's justice for using magic to save Lawen's life. No doubt, the source of his grudge had been the turning of Nathaera's affections.

Gwyn sighed and raised his sword toward Windsur. "A duel would be best undertaken upon even footing."

Windsur barked a laugh and lunged from the wall with a shout. Gwyn exclaimed and shot out a hand as though he could break Windsur's fall—

But Windsur didn't fall. He glided toward the earth, expression torn between glee and shock.

There. Tied by a cord to Windsur's neck, a black stone pulsed with magic. The man landed on his feet between Lawen and Gwyn. Both brothers pointed their blades at him.

Windsur grinned. "I've yearned for this moment, Gwynter ren Terare. I've dreamed of nothing else."

"That isn't healthy," said Lawen, eyes glinting, tone mocking. "Have you spoken with a physician?"

Windsur scowled. "Silence, demon. You shouldn't be alive! Only Gwynter's heresy preserves you."

"His heresy?" Lawen scoffed. "If by that you mean magic, what was it that aided you just now when you stupidly jumped from a forty-foot wall?" He stabbed a finger toward the battlements.

Windsur grinned. "The grace of Blessed Afallon."

Gwyn bristled and Lawen took a step forward, jaw clenched.

"I've no interest in *you*, m'lord farmer," said Windsur. He raised his hand, the stone at his chest pulsed, and Lawen flew backward. He crashed into an armored soldier long-since hacked to death.

Lawen untangled himself and charged toward Windsur, magic weaving at his fingertips. A rope of watery light shot from each hand, and the tendrils wrapped themselves swiftly around Windsur, binding him even. The noble sputtered. Few knew that Lawen, too, was a mage.

"Go, Gwynter," Lawen growled. "I'll see to the half-pint knight. You have a keep to take."

Gwyn nodded and turned back to the tower steps. The cloaked figure still stood there, observing, perhaps coldly, perhaps with amusement. Traycen had never been easy to read.

Gwyn started up the steps. "Lord ren Lotelon," he said evenly. "I'd heard you were dead."

"Once," said the familiar voice, strangely remote. "But my lord and master has revived me to serve him a while longer."

"Show me your face," said Gwyn, disturbed by the shadows hiding the mage's features under a heavy cowl.

The figure lifted an arm to pull back his hood. Gwyn shivered. The mage's movements were too fluid, too silken. The cowl fell back, and Traycen ren Lotelon stood before Gwyn, exposed, the same as he'd been before — but somehow changed. The life was gone from his face. His skin glowed a pale hue, stretched too tight.

The features were right, yet terribly wrong. But the man's eyes were his own; cold, fathomless, save for the flicker of fervor burning there: A zealot in service to his idol.

"Have you harmed Nathaera?" Gwyn asked.

"No," answered the master mage. "She is nothing. I've come for another purpose."

"Do you intend to kill me?"

Traycen smiled, chilling Gwyn to his core. "Not *you*, Winter King." His eyes flicked behind Gwyn. "The Crow King sends his condolences."

Gwyn whirled. Windsur had been knocked to the ground. Before the man stood Lawen, gasping for breath, sword hovering above the noble's chest where the pendant no longer hung.

The din of fighting raged on.

Snow fell quietly from the pitch-colored sky.

The caustic breath of iron pervaded the air.

Gwyn could sense Traycen behind him, unmoving. What was he missing? He looked again, desperation clawing at his stomach.

Something *was* wrong. He could sense that much.

There.

Gwyn's heart tripped.

"Do you yield?" asked Lawen, voice strangely loud, echoing in Gwyn's mind.

Windsur glowered up at him, hands fisted at his side, sword out of reach. But the pendant wasn't gone. It was in his hand, glowing, pulsing. Bloodlust poisoned the air around the knight.

"Never!" screamed Windsur, ignorant of the danger, assuming himself invincible. He didn't understand. He didn't perceive the Crow King's cruelty.

"Lawen, no! Windsur, it's a trick!"

Too late. Gwyn was too late.

Windsur held the pendant aloft. The magic within, charged with murder, erupted. The pulse scattered across the ground like a ripple, too low to touch Gwyn or Traycen on the steps.

The wave of power swallowed every soldier, every mage, every living being who stood upon level ground within the keep. Snuffing out life like breath against a flaming candle.

Swords clattered to the flagstones. Bodies dropped, soulless, to the ground.

Gwyn screamed. His eyes sought Lawen. Found him, fallen, motionless. He screamed again and bolted down the steps, but strong arms wrapped around him, holding him fast.

"Fool," breathed Traycen into his ear. "The magic still thrives. Enter its path and your life will be forfeit."

Gwyn wrenched against the mage with every ounce of strength. "Release me! Let me go!"

Traycen lost his grip and Gwyn stumbled down the steps, tears searing his eyes. The magic was fading fast, and as he stepped into its remains, he felt only a tingling stroke against his soul.

There, lying so still, so very still...

Gwyn fell to his knees before Lawen, vision swimming, hands shaking. He reached down and touched Lawen's face, sought breath against his lips. Found none. Already Lawen's flesh felt cold as ice, pale as snow, and his eyes stared heavenward.

Tears fell harder. Gwyn whimpered. "No, please. Please don't, Lawen. You can't. Not now, not like this. I need — need you. I can't fight without you. Lawen." He gripped his shoulder and shook gently, as though he might wake him from slumber. "Lawen, please. Come back. Come back. *Come back*!"

He crumpled forward and pressed against his brother's chest. Sobs racked his frame.

Lawen was gone. The Crow King had taken him, had sacrificed the mages of Corvus to do so, had fooled Windsur into using his own life to see it done. And Traycen ren Lotelon had known.

Gwyn lifted his head and turned.

Traycen stood nearby, his face the same impassive, hardened exterior it always was. Just a puppet, a mere doll. Wrath filled Gwyn with a surge of heat so terrible, he thought he might wither. He rose, caught up his sword, and faced the Crow King's faithful servant.

"You've stolen my brother. Return him to me."

Traycen smiled. The gesture was empty. "As I said, the Crow King sends his condolences."

Gwyn choked against a scream. Tightening his grip, he charged, swinging his blade. Traycen drew his sword in time to deflect the strike. Gwyn stumbled back, threw his leg forward and lunged again. Hitting, striking, hacking.

He threw himself into every assault, letting instinct guide his sword, too blinded by tears and burning fury to see well.

Traycen fell back, and Gwyn kept at him, hitting, swinging, thrusting.

His muscles ached. His vision cleared. The mage struggled to fend him off, brows pinched. The mage's grip weakened against Gwyn's relentless onslaught.

He would kill this man. Traycen should be dead already. Lawen had killed *him*, not the other way around.

Anger gnawed at Gwyn's insides. He screamed again, a long, pain-filled cry. His next blow knocked Traycen's sword from his hand. The mage stumbled backward, losing his footing.

Gwyn lifted his sword and swung it harder, sheering through the man's neck, severing his head.

Hot blood spattered against Gwyn's face.

The head toppled and rolled.

Gwyn slumped against his broadsword, panting, sweating.

Weeping.

He stood within the courtyard of Keep Talbethé, surrounded by the dead. Utterly alone. He could hear the snow landing like soft kisses against the faces of the dead.

The wind had ceased.

All held still beneath the storming sky, save for his grieving heart. Save for his wrath.

"Gwynter."

He gasped and staggered around to find Nathaera standing close by, Kive at her side. The woman's eyes were wide, lips trembling.

"Nathaera," he whispered, and sank to his knees, head bowed. "He killed Lawen. He..."

Footsteps echoed across the vast courtyard, drawing close. Nathaera knelt before Gwyn, caught his face in her hands, and lifted his head until he met her gaze.

"I saw everything, Gwynter. I saw. I understand." Tears slipped from her eyes. "I'm so sorry. I'm so sorry, Gwyn."

"I saved him," Gwyn whispered, barely hearing his own voice. "I saved him, Nathaera. He wasn't supposed to die."

"He lived, Gwyn. You saved him from dying in a horrible, horrible way. He lived and fought with you a while longer. It's what he wanted most. He loved you, Gwyn. He still does. Now weep, my love."

She drew a handkerchief from a hidden pocket of her ragged dress and dabbed his cheek where Traycen's blood had landed. "Weep for your brother. Weep for the anger and the pain and the loss. Let it out and hold nothing back. I'm here, I'll stay with you, it's just us. Shut out the rest of the world and cry, Gwyn. I'll hold you tonight."

He slumped forward, let his sword crash to the flagstones, and fell into Nathaera's arms.

She held him, kissed his head, and said no more. All that night, Gwyn wept beneath the winter sky among the fallen, longing for years far gone, when all had been soft, and sweet, and safe.

Summer would never come again.

# Chapter Thirty-One

Kovien staggered sideways and caught himself against the wall. His heart throbbed. Magic flooded his body, potent, cold, full of fear and malice. He gasped and pressed against the wall to keep from tumbling down the tower steps.

"Breathe, my son," whispered the voice of King Roth.

Kovien hissed through clenched teeth, unable to reply, unable to command the ghost to depart. The pain would pass. He would not be overcome.

Finally, the flood of magic faded into a dull ache, familiar, even welcome.

He smiled softly. "Traycen must have been successful. Lord ren Cloven is dead, as are the other mages. And Lawen, too. Excellent." He started up the stairs again, headed for his private tower. He'd known the Weave would attack him soon, but it had come more quickly than he'd expected.

Ah, well. His plan had borne fruit.

"Gwynter will come here next," murmured Kovien, easing himself up the last steps. "He will try to kill me in his rage. I long to see the hatred burning in his eyes. Humans succumb so easily to such emotions. Come soon, Gwynter. Hurry, so that we may end this mad war. So we may end it once and forever."

"You cannot slay the Winter King," whispered Roth.

Kovien pushed open the door to his tower and slipped inside. He shut the door, locked it, and leaned against the barrier. Tears slid from his eyes.

"It is just as well, for he cannot slay me either. How then shall it end? What madness will win the day?" He laughed. "There is but one way to settle our dispute, for neither can kill the other. But Gwynter may be convinced to kill himself."

"I won't let you."

Kovien opened his eyes and smiled at the new haunt standing before him, pale, translucent, and shimmering.

"Greetings, Lawen ren Terare. I thought you might come."

# Chapter Thirty-Two

At dawn Kive carried Gwyn into an officer's sleeping quarters, where the young king tossed in a fevered sleep.

Nathaera ordered the fallen fae to remain with him while she sought a means of treating the illness. She entered the courtyard and flinched under the bright sun of a cloudless day. As her eyes adjusted, she blinked at the sight of Aluem trotting toward her across the yard where a blanket of snow covering the many dead.

'*How fares Gwynter?*' asked the unicorn.

"Not well. How did you escape Windsur's magic?"

Aluem tossed his head. '*Unicorns cannot be so easily destroyed, though it rendered me unconscious for a time. I regret not being able to rescue brave Lawen. Too many mages stood between me and him. Gwynter's heart is shattered. I feel his grief as though it were my own.*'

"Lawen was a man of highest honor." Nathaera blinked back tears. "I counted him as a dear friend."

'*What do you require for Gwynter's care?*'

"Herbs." Nathaera wiped her eyes. "I fear his grief has brought him very low. His will to fight his illness might be crushed, but I can't let him die like this if I might aid him at all."

Aluem nodded, turned, and trotted toward the inner complexes. Nathaera followed but faltered as a figure appeared in the doorway of the nearby barracks.

"Sir Bened?"

The knight inclined his head. "My lady, I'm glad that you were spared. Where is His Majesty?"

Nathaera hesitated. "Help me find herbs, and then I'll bring you to him."

"What herbs do you seek?" asked Bened, following her into the building Aluem had already entered.

"How did you survive, Sir Knight? Anyone upon ground level was instantly killed in the magic's thrall."

"I wasn't on the ground, but fighting upon the battlements," Bened said. "Has the king's fever overtaken him, my lady?"

She turned to the knight. "Yes, Sir Bened. Gwyn is terribly ill, made worse by the death of his brother."

Bened blinked. "Lord ren Terare fell?"

Nathaera nodded and turned away to hide her tears. "After that, Gwyn slew Lord ren Lotelon. If you were on the battlements, how did you not see what I've described?"

Bened pushed aside his mop of unruly hair to reveal a large goose egg of an ugly purple hue across his forehead. "I was knocked unconscious, my lady. I've only surmised what occurred afterward by the unwholesome tinge of the Weave still upon the air, and the corpses sprawled across the courtyard and within every building. What became of the army leaders and mage commanders within the tower where you and Kive were?"

Nathaera grimaced and glanced at the knight. "Kive was hungry."

Disgust etched lines into Bened's face, and he said no more.

Aluem waited for them toward the back of the barracks, having found an apothecary storeroom filled with all Nathaera might need to tend to Gwyn. She filled Bened's arms and then her own with poultices and phials, and together they returned to the chamber where Gwyn lay. Aluem remained outside.

Kive sat beside Gwyn, dabbing at the sheen of sweat against the young man's face, just as Nathaera had instructed. The Ilidreth looked up. His eyes lingered on Bened for a long moment. "Hello, Fly."

Bened strode forward and set his supplies on the edge of the cot. "He looks very poorly."

Nathaera dropped her armful beside his. "Of course he does. He's pressed himself harder than anyone else in this war, and now he's lost his elder brother — whom he loved more than anything of this world. 'Tis a wonder he's fighting his illness at all."

"It does seem a shame," Bened said, almost to himself. "After all Gwynter did for his brother, willing to sacrifice his very life, only to lose him now..." He reached down and caught up a dried herb to twirl it between his fingers.

"He did what he must, then and now," said Nathaera with some heat.

"That's quite true." Bened turned to her. "Sir Windsur is dead, yes?"

She bit her lip and nodded, dropping her eyes. "Yes. Foolish dunderhead. He used the Crow's magic, no doubt thinking he'd be protected, but he was only a pawn."

"Disposable," whispered Bened with an upward quirk of his lips.

"You find that funny somehow, Sir Knight?"

"Perhaps appropriate. The lady Arianwen is spared his crass habits. Is that not well?"

"Aye, but so many died."

"Your enemies," said Bened.

"Yes. But 'tis still a tragedy."

He raised his brows. "Tragedies occur daily in war, my lady. The cost of freedom is high. Perhaps you and your king should have considered that before you raised a banner against the Crow King."

Nathaera bristled. "Just a moment, *sir*. You raised the same banner. You've been fighting the same war."

His smile widened and his hand fell to his sword. "Not quite." He drew it, blade flashing with light from a nearby brazier. "The farce is no longer necessary. I've done my service to the king. Windsur ren Cloven is dead. His Majesty cannot deny me any longer. You'll have to quarter here in Talbethé for the winter, and come spring you'll have nowhere to go, for we will be waiting without the walls. Bring in your miserable, starving troops, fair lady, and let them fatten up. A last feast, you might say."

Nathaera tossed hair over her shoulder. "You think this revelation is a blow to me, don't you? Well, Sir Knight, I have a surprise in reply: Kive saw through your deception. He called you a fly caught in the spider's web. I assume that means your love of Arianwen has trapped you, though whether she's the spider or someone else is I don't know or care. You think to leave this keep and claim fair maiden's heart? Think again."

Bened's lip curled into a sneer. "You think me a soft simpleton. My goal was never Arianwen alone. Don't think for a moment I did all this just to woo a maid. The Crow King has promised that I will stand as his right hand in Traycen's place — and now both he and my rival in love are dead. As for your *ploy*, I thought you suspected me, but what good has it done you? Gwynter listened to me when I suggested we take Talbethé, and again when I proposed we lead Haratin to the Crow King to lure him here. Your feelings and suppositions have changed nothing. Now you stand in my way: A little girl without an army at her back."

Nathaera folded her arms and glowered at the black knight. "I don't need an army, sir. I have a Kive."

The fallen fae slipped from the shadows of the small room, and stepped up behind Bened, canting his head. "May I eat the fly, Fairy Wren? Is it time now?"

Bened's eyes widened. "But he's full. He ate the mage leaders. And he only eats rats."

Nathaera allowed herself to smile, though it was a frigid gesture, cold and distant like her insides. "Wrong. Kive only eats rats because I tell him to only eat rats. He also likes crunchy birds and juicy flies. Besides, he ate those men last night. It's morning now and time for breakfast."

"You won't let him," said Bened, perspiration forming on his brow. "You don't approve."

"There are many things about war of which I don't approve, Bened Arnnor, yet they must be done. Give me a better reason. Tell me why I shouldn't have Kive eat you here and now."

Bened trembled as Kive leaned close to his neck and gave a long sniff.

"Juicy fly," whispered the Ilidreth.

Bened crashed to his knees. "Please, my lady. No one should die like this. I've only done my duty to Simaerin. I've served my king as a dutiful knight. I deserve mercy. For Afallon's sake, don't let him eat me!"

Nathaera shook her head. "What then can I do, Sir Knight? Let you depart and return to your king as a cowering mongrel? Would *he* show you mercy under these conditions, I wonder? I can't well let you stay here to harm Gwynter or myself. Give me an alternative and I'll consider it."

"Tie me up," said Bened. "Treat me as a prisoner of war."

"Kive will still eat you when I'm not looking."

Bened's eyes darted across the room with a desperate glint, as though he might perceive some answer to his dilemma. With a sudden cry, he threw himself backward, knocking his head into Kive's stomach. The fae tumbled backward and Bened leapt to his feet, spun, and rammed his sword through Kive's chest.

Nathaera screamed.

Bened turned to her, panting. "So much for your pet. I'm leaving now. Don't give me cause to kill *you*."

Tears spilled down Nathaera's face. Her hands curled into fists, shaking. "I'll *destroy* you, Bened. I'll find you and kill you myself."

The knight smiled dryly. "You're quite welcome to try, my lady." He bowed his head, then trotted toward the door. "Your king won't last long, you know. He's fading even now. Perhaps a blade can't end his life, but illness can take him all the same. It's just you now, Nathaera — all alone in the ancient fortress of Talbethé, with the ghosts of ages past. I do hope they don't drive you mad."

Nathaera held her head high. “Never fear, Crow Knight. Afallon is on my side.”

The knight scoffed. “In the place where he fell, how much good shall that do, I wonder?” He turned and slipped through the doorway, footsteps swift and heavy down the corridor.

Nathaera rushed to Kive’s side, a sob escaping her lips. “No, my dear friend. Please don’t leave me.”

Kive lay still, so still, and pale, not breathing.

She ran a hand along his cold cheek.

Kive coughed and opened his eyes. “The fly killed me, Fairy Wren. That was very rude.”

Nathaera shrieked. “You — Kive, you’re alive!”

“Yes, Fairy Wren,” said Kive, patting the ear she’d screamed into. “Kive can’t stay dead like aneemals. Kive is Kive.”

# Chapter Thirty-Three

Towwen Stone studied the wagons that rolled and bounced along the weather-beaten road below the dense treeline.

He and his band of marauders — for what else could the bedraggled men call themselves? — crouched upon the snowy hillock and shivered in their cloaks, waiting, waiting.

Was this it, at last? Had they found the stores of food they'd long sought?

The original plan to infiltrate a granary and take its stores had ended in humiliation. The Crow King must have guessed their move, for the granaries along the route to Talbethé had all been emptied before Towwen and his force ever arrived. Frustrated but committed, Towwen had determined to pilfer the supply trains going from garrison to garrison — but here, too, the Crow King had foreseen foul play. Every line of wagons the marauders attempted to commandeer were full of soldiers rather than food.

Empty-handed, the band pulled back barely alive. Towwen's force of fifteen men had been cut down to twelve. He could scarcely afford any more casualties, but he must steal supplies before the Winter Army starved.

King Gwynter's army might somehow take Keep Talbethé, but

that was unlikely without the proper accoutrements, warmth, food, and medicine. Towwen must hurry. He felt that urgency; it boiled in his blood, but how could he succeed?

Each day looked more hopeless than the last.

Until now.

This wagon train was like all the others, except for one key factor: It wasn't en route to a garrison. Where then was the shipment being taken?

At first glance, the backwoods road led nowhere of consequence, but when Towwen had consulted his maps, he found that the path meandered along the hills a day or two before it split, and one of those roads led to Talbethé.

That begged a question: Why would the fortress need supplies unless it faced the chance of a siege?

The Crow King must have ordered the wagons to take an inconspicuous route, and Towwen's band had only happened upon it by chance.

The only question left was whether this was a trap, or the wagons carried legitimate supplies?

Either way, Towwen wasn't certain he and his fellows would survive this encounter. The wagons were guarded more heavily than most, while his band huddled in the cold, battling exhaustion, low on provisions. If the band failed here, there would be no more opportunities. This was Towwen's last chance.

He glanced at Remien. The other man nodded, his mouth a grim line. He understood. They all did.

Inhaling, Towwen rose, fingers trembling as he drew his bow and aimed at the crow emblem emblazoned upon the ranking officer at the front of the train. He tried to calm his racing heart, tried to focus on his target.

The pounding of hooves shattered his concentration. He lowered his weapon and watched a horseman advancing hard on the wagon train from the rear.

A courier, or—

Towwen's heart faltered, and his jaw fell. The galloping figure was no messenger of the Crow King, nor a soldier, nor even a human. Clad in motley shades of gold and red, with long hair of glossy black, Towwen couldn't mistake the Ilidreth for anything.

He expected the soldiers in the train to draw blades or point lances to slay the intruder — but the wagons rolled on, only a few of the Simaeri contingent glancing his way.

The Ilidreth rider came level with the Crow officer, and they exchanged words. Nothing more.

"What devilry is this?" whispered Remien. "Does the Crow now enlist the aid of his foe, and do they now heed his call?"

Towwen shook his head. "It could be a rogue Ilidreth. Just one. Perhaps he's fallen?"

The ground cracked with rumbling thunder. Towwen and Remien turned to watch as a cavalry of some three hundred Ilidreth stormed over the southern hills, Swan banner streaming in the wind.

The Simaeri commander never called his men to arms. The wagons kept rolling.

One of the Ilidreth riders broke away from the whole and galloped toward the hillock where Towwen and his band hid.

With a hammering heart, Towwen drew back his bowstring again. "Come no closer!"

The rider slowed his pace. "Greetings, friends of the Winter King. We've heard of your struggles against the Crow as you've sought to steal food for your army. In answer, we bring those same supplies from the central granary in the southern fields of Lemlin, which we recently burned to the ground as tribute to the tyrant king. Come, come! We are bringing your food to your king at Talbethé. Join us and be welcome."

Towwen and his men exchanged bewildered glances.

"How can we trust you?" demanded Remien, ever cautious.

The Ilidreth smiled. "You can hardly afford not to, Simaeri, though the choice remains yours."

"What of the Crowsmen who ride with you?" asked Towwen. "Your prisoners?"

The Ilidreth smiled. His horse pawed the ground. "Our allies. We are pleased to call General Cadogan ren Silverard such. He and his men have sworn their allegiance to a new king."

Towwen raised his eyebrow. "The Crow's General swears to serve King Gwynter?"

"Nay," said the Ilidreth. "His oaths are sworn to High Prince Kive of *Shaeswéath*. Such an alliance offers certain magical protections against previous oaths. But it is not my place to say more. Our leader, Celin'Laen, would better explain."

"Well?" asked Remien, gaze fixed on Towwen.

There really wasn't anything to deliberate. Either the Ilidreth told the truth or he didn't. Towwen was in no position to win free should this be a trick.

He shrugged. "I say we accept a free ride to Talbethé."

❦

HIGH LORD CELIN'LAEN couldn't meet with Towwen Stone until evening fell, when a halt sounded above the forested hills. The wagons made a circle upon the road around the camp of General Cadogan's men, while the Ilidreth army slept apart without fire or tent to warm them. Perhaps they had no need of such material things.

The Ilidreth horseman who had called to Towwen's band earlier now guided him and Remien to the tent of General Cadogan, where the man himself and Celin'Laen waited within.

The rest of the band stayed in a large tent provided by the Crowsmen, with nothing more than Towwen's reassurances that all would be well. Towwen prayed his instinct was right on that point.

The scholar and his warrior friend entered the General's tent together, and warmth enveloped them. The tent was large, covered in colorful tapestries, lit with six braziers circling the interior. Plush cushions lay about the chamber, along with trays of fruits and a decanter of wine.

Against several cushions lounged a well-dressed man in his

middle years, with sun-kissed skin even in midwinter, gray-flecked brunet hair, and dark brown eyes that held secrets: General Cadogan ren Silverard, dragon-slayer, seasoned knight, and the Crow King's finest blade.

Across from the human sat the Ilidreth who must be Celin'Laen. He wore the motley garb of his people, with pointed ears peeking from under sleek black hair running the length of his spine. He didn't lounge as Cadogan, but sat upright and rigid, blue eyes searching Towwen and Remien in turn.

"You are acquainted with the Winter King," Celin'Laen said. "I scent him upon you, young scholar."

Towwen started. How did the Ilidreth know he was a scholar? What had given him away?

Celin'Laen offered a faint smile. "Your hands are dyed with ink, and knowledge fills your eyes. Both are qualities of a bright and inquiring mind." He glanced again at Remien. "A warrior, illegitimate but proud. You do not let a dark past shadow a noble future. What are your names?"

"I am Towwen Stone, and this is my friend and compatriot, Remien Seafarer."

Celin'Laen lifted his hand and uncurled his fingers toward Cadogan. "This, as you've surmised, is Lord General Cadogan ren Silverard, now sworn to serve the High Prince of Ilid. You needn't suspect him. In the dungeons of Londolin he considered most carefully his options and found his service to the Crow King wanting in honor."

Towwen raised his eyebrows. "The dungeons of Londolin?"

"Yes," said Celin'Laen. "He was until lately my prisoner there. But just as his heart was turning, we heard the first whispers of Talbethé's fall and the Crow King's trickery."

Starting, Towwen clenched his hands. "I've heard nothing of Talbethé, save Brioc Ffyr's prediction that the Winter King would try to take it. You know more?"

"We do," said the Ilidreth, inclining his head. "The whispers first came from the birds winging southward. After that, Aluem raced into the Silver City, past the Crow's watch, and informed me of what had transpired. We know all."

"Please tell me."

Celin'Laen nodded and motioned to the nearest cushions. "Sit, Simaeri. Be comfortable."

Towwen dropped onto the cushion, eager for news, whether good or ill. His childhood friend and king had truly brought Talbethé to its knees? And what of the Crow King's trickery? In the end of it all, who had been the victor?

Remien settled beside Towwen, stiff, brows drawn.

Celin'Laen began in a low voice. "The Winter King took Talbethé over one week ago. His plan was clever and simple, but the Crow King foresaw trouble and set a trap. It seems he tricked a man named Windsur ren Cloven into activating a spell that stole the lives of most who were within the keep. Gwynter was spared, for he stood upon steps above the Weave's destructive path — though it is likely he would have lived either way, for his protections are strong. Aluem assured me that Lady Nathaera and High Prince Kive are also alive.

"Alas, Lawen ren Terare fell upon the field of combat beside Windsur ren Cloven, after which Gwynter succumbed to fever. Also, in the aftermath, Sir Bened Arnnor revealed himself as an agent of the Crow King and fled. Aluem gave chase, but from the sky a winged beast swept down and caught up the knight to carry him away. Aluem said the beast seemed something like a crow, though considerably larger, and made of a dark substance: A tainted creature. It made Aluem ill to be near it." Celin'Laen shook his head. "This is what we know."

Towwen bowed his head. He had known Lawen all his life. The man was noble-hearted, brave, and kind. Gwyn idolized his brother. A heavy blow indeed. Would Gwyn recover from such a loss?

Celin'Laen spoke on. "Before Aluem brought us word of the keep, he went first to the camp of your Winter Army, carrying a missive from Lady Nathaera that the army could march to Talbethé and quarter there for the winter. Once there, they will be warm and well fed, but the supplies within the keep will not hold against the long months ahead. We are bringing more to sustain them, and we also bring men to increase their number. My contingent is three hundred strong. Cadogan has enlisted the aid of fifty-four soldiers who loyally serve House Silverard rather than the Crow King.

"The remainder of his army lingers in Londolin under the careful watch of a few of my own forces, while one thousand of the Crow King's men camp unwittingly outside the city's gates and think all is well. They do not know of the secret paths beneath Londolin.

"From the Vales of Ilid I have been promised another one thousand warriors in the spring. With their coming, should the Winter Army not lose more of its precious souls, we might stand well against the Crow and his forces. I've dispatched messengers to Fraelin as well to enlist their aid. Some alliances remain from bygone days.

"Of a certainty, I know we may count on Keep Montré in the high north. The Fraeli commander there is a friend, and whether the Crane King agrees to fight against the Crow King or not, certainly Duke Dontri shall. That will increase our number by another five hundred bowmen and three hundred cavalry."

Despite the tragedy of Lawen's death, Towwen found himself heartened. He didn't know the present count of the Winter Army, but he could guess it had been greatly reduced since Nox's report now over a fortnight before. Should the numbers have been reduced to under a thousand men, that number would soon triple between the Ilidreth and Fraeli allies, with the chance of even more support.

"Thanks be to Afallon," breathed Remien. "We might actually survive this."

"You think so?" asked Cadogan, speaking for the first time.

Towwen's heart skipped a beat. The knight's voice pealed smooth and commanding, like thunder in a rainstorm.

"Certainly," said Remien. "The Order of Corvus is wiped out. The Crow King himself saw to that. That gives us quite an edge."

Cadogan smiled wryly. "You know little of the Crow King if you believe that. You think he sacrificed his mages in some desperate effort to thwart Gwynter's bold strike? The Order of Corvus has never been more than a front and a tactic. Its presence has long kept the church where it is, for it feared annihilation. But its purpose was always to be as fuel for a fire. What that fire is, I couldn't say for certain, but the Crow King has sacrificed large groups of mages since he took the throne of Simaerin. I've always suspected it feeds his own power — the power to dominate and control an entire kingdom — but that's merely a guess. Lord ren Lotelon knew more."

Towwen leaned forward. "Knew, sir?"

"Aye," said Cadogan. "The unicorn said King Gwynter killed Traycen ren Lotelon after Lawen fell. Just as well. The master mage was no longer human. I regret far more the loss of Lawen ren Terare. He was a good soldier. A good man. These days, there aren't too many of his caliber in both regards."

Towwen's eyes narrowed. "You saw the unicorn? You didn't see a horse instead?"

Cadogan's wry smile returned. "Does that baffle you, Master Stone?"

"I' true, yes. As far as I knew, only the pure were able."

"The pure and the powerful," said Celin'Laen. "But General Cadogan is not a mage. His only source of magic is the sword he wields — a gift from the Crow King, I suspect. He is not powerful, and so, despite your mistrust, Cadogan must therefore stand among the pure. Do you understand now, young scholar? In any force, there will stand together men of good or wicked intent. Can you judge which be which?"

Towwen considered that, his eyes fastened on the general. "Why the change of heart? What makes you turn from the Crow King?"

"I'm not a particularly devout man—at least by the church's standards," said Cadogan, shrugging. "Blind faith has done nothing to rid the world of wars. The Crow King promised a solution. I still believe he means to keep his promise. But his methods..."

The general sighed. "I've grown hard in my years of campaigning. As I spoke with High Lord Celin'Laen, it brought to mind all I'd forgotten of honor and mercy. I've spilled ample blood for my country, but the blood I've spilled has been that of my countrymen. As I pondered this, the unicorn arrived in Londolin, and Celin'Laen brought me from the dungeons to hear the creature's words."

Cadogan scowled at the rug under his feet. "As I said before, Lawen is — was a man I admired. Even as young as he was, he stood firm upon his principles. He balked against the deeds I performed for the Crow King's sake. He confronted me and refused to follow my orders until I threatened his younger brother, knowing he cared for none better. And then, as Lawen performed the tasks set before him, he grew ill. His distress awakened his latent magery. His guilt caused it to destroy him. I think some part of him wanted to die. In a way, I sentenced him to death. Perhaps that was where it started. I believe Lawen ren Terare exhumed my buried humanity. In his death, he restored it to life. I fight now against the tyrant king in his name."

The general's words hung in the air. Finally, Towwen nodded. "Stated as a man of honor. I welcome you to the cause, General Cadogan, as I'm certain the Winter King shall. You knew of Lawen's magery, but you never reported him. Did you know he was the leader of our own order of mages?"

Cadogan smiled. "He led the Order of Cygnus? That doesn't surprise me. Are you of the same order?"

"I am," said Towwen. "My aspect is words."

"Ah, like the printer. Brioc Ffyr, isn't it?"

Towwen nodded.

Cadogan rubbed his chin. "There may come a time for your skill to flood the streets of Crowwell. Words have great strength to influence. Is your preference spoken word or written scrawl?"

"Scrawling is my mastery," said Towwen. "I'm no skilled orator."

"And can your mage pen be read by all?"

"All," said Towwen. "Even a babe in arms."

"Very good." Cadogan turned to Celin'Laen. "We'll need his skill in Crowwell."

"That's not possible," Towwen said. "We've lost contact with Rindermarr Lorric. There's no way into the royal city anymore. Brioc meant to take me there, but our access is cut off."

"Nonsense. You think I don't have connections of my own?" asked Cadogan.

"Loyal subjects to the king?" asked Towwen flatly.

Cadogan smiled. "I'm well acquainted with those out of favor with the Crow King. More than a few of Crowwell's citizens are not quite law-abiding. There are many routes into the city used by smugglers."

Towwen folded his hands on his lap. "I'll consider your words, but we must reach Talbethé first and make ourselves useful to the Winter King. His goals will decide my course."

# Chapter Thirty-Four

Sunlight bled beneath Gwyn's eyes, coaxing him awake. He resisted. Something within whispered to lie still and think as little as possible. Muddled images floated in his mind's eye, heavy and gray. His breath caught and his heart flinched.

He must avoid thinking. Mustn't think. Must only breathe and remain asleep.

"Gwynter?"

Nathaera's voice. Near, worried. Must he answer? Must he stir?

Could he not remain in oblivion, where sorrow lapped against the shore of his mind, then pulled back, ebbing, distant?

"He's waking," the girl said, shattering his last effort to climb back into a dreamless pit.

His eyes fluttered open. Light stung, harsh, vivid. Alive.

Why did that wound him?

"Afallon be praised! You're awake." Nathaera's voice caught on a sob.

Gwyn sought her against the brightness. There. She stood above the bed where he lay. Her hair framed her face, soft and fair, eyes filled with tears as a smile grew on her lips.

Those same eyes widened, and she threw out her hands. "Don't move just yet."

He hadn't considered it.

"You're still very weak," she went on. "Your fever nearly claimed you, Gwyn, but last night you triumphed. After a week of dreadful fighting, you're on the mend. Thank Afallon." She sank to her knees beside the bed and caught his hand in her warm fingers.

Weariness etched dark circles under Nathaera's eyes and leeched color from her skin. Worry surged through Gwyn like a winter wind, and he opened his mouth to chasten her, but as frigid air filled his lungs, a fit of coughs took him. Harsh, ragged. Searing.

Nathaera gripped his hand until his fit calmed. "You're still mending. Don't strain yourself. Don't try speaking if it causes you effort."

*Lawen.*

Memories swelled up and broke across Gwyn's mind. Talbethé. Lawen. Dear, strong, noble brother. Gwyn squeezed his eyes shut as tears built, choking. They rolled down his cheeks, scorching his eyes, his throat, his chest.

"Oh, Gwyn. Gwyn," whispered Nathaera. "I'm sorry. I wish..." But she didn't finish her wish, for they both knew it was beyond mortal power to fulfill.

Gwyn stayed still and let his tears fall. Anger had consumed him long enough to kill Traycen. It would no doubt surface again, driving him to face the Crow King. But now, in this sacred, harrowing moment, he mourned for his dearest friend. Lawen was gone now.

Until Afallon saw fit to claim Gwyn, there would be no more summer days with Lawen in the fields of Vinwen. No more hunting trips, or wrestling matches. No more campaigns together. So much would change, and the pain would be ever present, but he must carry on, or Lawen's death would be for naught. Gwyn had brought him here to Talbethé, and here he fell.

To turn back now, to lower his banner and concede defeat, would declare Lawen's sacrifice meaningless.

He would never allow that.

“Nathaera,” he whispered, voice ragged.

“Yes, Gwyn?”

“We must win. We will win. The Crow King shall fall.”

“Yes,” she said, tones soothing but firm. “And his fall shall sound with a mighty, thundering crash that will shake the foundations of the world.”

# Chapter Thirty-Five

Two days more brought Gwyn to his unsteady feet.

Nathaera supported him as he climbed the stairs to the battlements where he could watch his haggard army trudge into Talbethé. At first, she'd protested, but studying his face, she knew arguing was a waste of breath.

"We've lost so many," whispered Nathaera atop the wall, sorrow clutching her heart.

"We will lose more still," answered Gwyn. "For those who can't fight, we spill the blood of the brave."

She glanced at her king and found his gray eyes steadfast, light-filled. She knew all too well the grief hidden beneath his stoicism, but relief washed through her to see more than the color of his flesh returning. The fire of his soul had reignited. Though the Crow King's blow had been severe, it hadn't been fatal.

She smiled, then dropped her eyes to watch the foot soldiers limping into the bailey of the keep, now cleared of the dead. Kive had buried every deceased man. He hadn't eaten them — she'd insisted on that. Not one mage or soldier within that courtyard would be disgraced in death, for all had fought valiantly.

Kive hadn't argued, though perhaps that was because he preferred live prey.

The mounds of the fallen spread across the frozen earth surrounding Talbethé. Rocks covered them, for which Kive had searched long. But Lawen had been buried apart from the rest. His lone grave lay within the stand of trees where Gwyn's party had waited until true night on the evening of their infiltration. There, Nathaera had watched the brothers embrace a final time before they'd ridden to the keep.

Last night she'd told Gwyn her choice, and he'd softly thanked her before he fell into silence in an armchair before a blazing fire. Later, he'd asked if she would show him the spot once he'd mustered more strength. She'd agreed.

"Should we head down?" she asked now as Gwyn's arm trembled against her shoulder.

"No. I'll remain here until they're all inside the walls."

Together they waited, watched, while a freezing wind carried snow from the north. As the last contingent reached the gate, one of the bedraggled soldiers glanced up, and his step faltered.

Those around him paused and raised their eyes to find the Winter King upon the wall. Whispers seeped through the ranks, and then noise ascended. Cheers. Cheers for their king who had conquered Keep Talbethé.

Gwyn bowed his head and closed his eyes. Nathaera smiled and drew his arm tighter around her shoulders.

"They love you, Gwyn. They believe in you, just as I do."

He said nothing. His eyes opened as the rattle of the closing portcullis filled the air, but he didn't look down. Instead, his eyes searched the horizon.

"Aluem is returning."

Nathaera squinted against the midday sun for a long moment before she spotted what might be a galloping unicorn afar off. "I wonder where he's been. Shall we head down to meet him?"

Gwyn nodded. Together they descended the stone stairs to the bailey proper. Assembled at the bottom step, Gwyn's officers waited.

"Sire," said Mershen ahead of the others who all drew breath at once to speak. "We offer our heartfelt condolences on the parting of your brother. Lord ren Terare's loss is keenly felt by all, especially within the Order of Cygnus."

Gwyn smiled weakly. "Thank you, my friend. How are the men?"

"Heartened, now we've taken Talbethé. Food and proper shelter will do them great good. I've already sent Aleteer and Rohkye to take stock of our pilfered provisions, and I'll draw up a plan of rationing this very evening if that's agreeable to you."

Gwyn nodded. "Yes. Quite. Thank you."

Perhaps sensing Gwyn's distance, the officers took their leave, and Nathaera helped Gwyn to the gate.

In that moment, Aluem arrived at the portcullis.

*'Greetings, Gwynter and Nathaera,'* said the unicorn. *'I bring good tidings from far and from near. Shall I enter?'*

"Open the gate," called Nathaera.

The portcullis lifted. Aluem trotted in, hooves and horn glistening in the sunlight. He tossed his head, then rested his horn against Gwyn's arm. They conversed, though Nathaera heard nothing of their exchange. She turned her eyes away to offer some privacy until Aluem took a step back.

His voice rose like a gale in her head. *'You already know I traveled first to the Winter Army to deliver your word of the keep's taking, Lady. From there I traveled southwest to Londolin.'*

Nathaera furrowed her brow. "Why there? Hasn't it fallen to the Crow King?"

*'Nay, for long before the Crow dispatched doom upon the Silver City, a force of light took up arms to defend it. And now that same force, led by Celin'Laen of the Ilidreth, marches to Talbethé to aid the Winter King of Simaerin.'*

Gwyn's shoulders squared. "Celin?" He laughed, a clear, bright sound. "Celin has come after all. Afallon be praised."

*'He comes not alone, Gwynter. In company with his three hundred bowmen rides a contingent of fifty Crowsmen, now defectors. Their leader is Cadogan ren Silverard.'*

Gwyn tensed. Nathaera glanced at his face to find wonder and horror in tandem in his eyes. "Cadogan, defecting? Impossible."

Aluem said nothing, but watched Gwyn with steadfast, prismatic eyes.

Gwyn wrestled with himself. The storm in his eyes attested to it. For a long moment he stood silent, brooding, brow drawn.

At last he inhaled and nodded. "I gave to Bened Arnnor a chance he did not deserve. That chance cost my brother his life. It's possible Cadogan comes at the Crow King's behest to fool me once again, yet if I cannot take a man at his word, what manner of creature am I? I don't trust Cadogan — but if Celin does, I *can* trust his word and *must*. But Afallon help the next man who calls me friend as he spears me through. My fury will not be soon sated."

"Believe me," said Nathaera, catching his eye. "Nor will mine."

# Chapter Thirty-Six

Rindermarr Lorric had welcomed Nathael with open arms. More than that, he'd supplied him with priest robes to wear as he roamed the streets seeking information.

For days now all anyone could talk about was Talbethé. Was it true the keep had fallen? Was the Crow King dead? Had the Winter Army been swallowed up by the wrath of Talbethé's restless spirits? Had Afallon struck them down?

This morning, Crow Castle issued a proclamation reassuring the frightened citizens. The Crow King had dealt the traitor and his army a heavy blow, possibly a decisive one. There was nothing to fear.

Nathael wasn't convinced. Neither was the population of Crowwell. Foremost among the rumors were eyewitness accounts claiming Bened Arnnor had been spotted fleeing into Crowwell, having been discovered as a spy and driven from the conquered keep. The wrath of the Winter King had followed him as a hound upon the heels of a flagging fox, they said and seemed content with the idea.

At first, Nathael couldn't understand why. Shouldn't they consider Bened Arnnor a hero?

He listened more closely to discover the why of their mockery. It soon became apparent Bened Arnnor was no more loved than the Crow King himself, who inspired fear and even awe, but loyalty bred of such was a fickle thing. Many of Crowwell's citizens were ardent loyalists — Crowsmen through and through.

Indeed, most of the royal city hated Gwynter ren Terare ren Wintervale with a burning fervor. But others appeared to fancy the idea of shifting power.

"Perhaps a bitter winter's what Simaerin needs on the heels of a blistering heat," one merchant had remarked in the marketplace. Others echoed the sentiment.

The context was clear, for little else besides war was spoken of these days. Even at social functions, where Nathael attended as Rindermarr's acolyte, the subject of civil upheaval came up.

The city was split in two. Loyalists tended to be wealthy, but even among them were those whose families had suffered from the Crow King's massacre of mages. Where once those families had rejoiced at the unholy of their number being purged, now it was common knowledge that the Crow King used magic, had his own mage force of arms, and only eliminated those he deemed worthless to his service.

"He sacrificed the whole of them. Every mage of Corvus at Talbethé was murdered, but it still couldn't kill the Winter King."

Nathael paused at a refreshment table and glanced toward the source of that statement. As dusk fell over Crowwell, Nathael had joined Rindermarr at a noble house for a winter dance. Now, as Nathael wandered about, he picked up tidbits of conversation, most of them political.

A well-dressed nobleman stood in the darkest corner of the ballroom, and with him stood a younger man in apparel just as grand. Drinks idled in their hands, untouched. Nathael recognized the older of the two: Lord Penden ren Targeth, father of the much talked about Lady Arianwen.

"Are you certain, my lord?" asked the younger man, incredulous.

"Not entirely. I tried to confirm it with Arnnor, but the tight-lipped brute finds himself my superior these days, though he ran from the field as a coward."

"Has the Crow King promised her to him yet?"

"Nothing official," said Lord ren Targeth with a sigh. "The better question, Sir Huwin, is shall the king give her in marriage, or does he desire her for himself?"

The stringed instruments faded away as a dance ended. The lords glanced toward the floor, conversation dying with the music. Applause ensued, and Nathael caught up a pastry and moved on before they noticed him eavesdropping.

House Hithren hosted tonight's ball, in honor of its heir's coming of age. The boy led each dance with such solemnity, a stranger might mistake the event as a wake rather than a celebration, despite the colors and music. Young Lord ren Hithren was a plump, miserable soul, quite Nox's opposite in disposition, though his rotund form put Nathael in mind of his absent friend.

Homesickness gripped Nathael. He turned from the dance floor just as the ballroom doors opened to admit a latecomer.

Nathael had never seen Sir Bened Arnnor before, but word of him had been so frequent, the sight of the man was strangely familiar. He was a grim, imposing figure, with dark hair that framed his face and an ill-favored light in his eyes. An almost supernatural aura enveloped him, eerie as a boneyard.

*The Crow's touch*, Nathael thought with a shudder, as though tendrils of blackest hues writhed and strangled the knight's limbs.

If Bened Arnnor had once been an honorable knight of Simaerin, sworn to its throne and people, he'd now transformed into a creature, a slave to the will of the Crow King, shackled and broken. A marionette on hellish strings.

The music had struck up again, but it died upon the knight's entrance, and the crowds parted to give him a clear path to the head of the grand chamber. Bened Arnnor strode to the heir of Hithren, whose eyes widened as the man approached.

The heir lifted his pudgy hands to shield himself. "My lord. S-Sir Knight. You needn't—"

The knight drew his sword. With a swift, steady lunge, he pierced the heir's breast. Withdrew. The heir fell amid screams and the crowds pushed back.

Bened Arnnor wiped his blade on the heir's clothes, then swept a glance around the room. Fierce. Challenging. "Are there any other ambitious fools who would dare to make an offer for my lady's hand? Speak now, so I may quicken your death."

No one dared move. Nathael studied the knight, fists clenched. Bened Arnnor's eyes met his. Nathael knew he should look away. He should cower as the others. But a fire seethed within him, and he held firm against the knight's dark scowl.

"You," Bened Arnnor said, pointing his finger at Nathael. "You're not a priest."

Nathael nodded. "True, sir. I'm an acolyte merely."

"Liar." The knight strode toward him, the crowd shifting to give him space.

Across the room, Rindermarr pushed his way through the lords and ladies to come to Nathael's aid.

Bened reached him first. "I know your face. I read its message clearly. You're a traitor. You've sworn service to the Winter King and have come to spy on Crowwell."

Nathael started. He'd not seen Bened Arnnor before this moment. How could the knight know him? How could he guess Nathael's purpose?

Shaking his head, Nathael tried to think. "Nay, sir. You accuse me unjustly."

"My lord," called out Rindermarr, and his voice divided the crowd to give him passage. The priest hurried forward. "Forgive me, my lord, but this is my acolyte. If you have a grievance against him, address me and I shall see it righted."

Bened's scowl deepened. "You're the priest who once advocated for the Winter King at trial. Do you think to aid another traitor now?"

Rindermarr bristled. "Your words are hard, sir. I advocated for a boy not yet come of age. He was no traitor then."

"He used magic outside the law."

"An offense for which the king acquitted him, as I recall," said Rindermarr.

"Do you still defend him?" Bened's sword hand twitched upward.

Rindermarr glanced at the blade, then met Bened's eyes. "I'm defending my acolyte. Nothing else."

"Your acolyte is a traitor to the rightful king of Simaerin."

"Is this a trial now, sir?" asked the priest. "I see no judge and no committee to weigh his actions."

"You wish for a trial?" asked Bened. A smile crept upon his lips. "Very well. I shall present him before the Crow King and see what comes."

Rindermarr sucked in a breath. "There's no need of anything so drastic. The church shall—"

"The church is compromised. Priests at Londolin aided the Ilidreth. Be grateful we don't put you all on trial. Stand aside now, Rindermarr Lorric, and allow me to escort the young man away to await the king's justice."

Rindermarr's eyes flicked to Nathael, who understood well what it would mean to go with this man. He wouldn't survive long enough to stand trial. Nathael dropped his pastry and fled toward the door, pressing through the befuddled nobility. No one tried to stop him, though he heard Bened bark the command.

He rushed out into the corridor, sprinted along the flagstones, and darted into a side passage to leap from a window and land in the thorny rosebushes beneath.

Arms and legs stinging, he heard voices ring out from within. Nathael crept through the bushes and started for the gates of the estate. He pulled the cowl of his robes over his head to hide his face. No one at the entrance stopped him.

He slipped into the milling crowds of the street beyond House Hithren and disappeared in the growing night.

## Chapter Thirty-Seven

Arianwen glanced toward the bedroom door as it pushed open, her heart staggering. She expected to find the Crow King standing in the entrance, but instead she met the dark gaze of another dread specter.

Struggling to keep her expression smooth, she curtsied. "Sir Bened."

He entered, clutching a burlap sack in one gloved hand. He slung the sack to drop it at her feet. She peered down. It was stained with blood.

"Whose head do you bring me today, Sir Knight?" Already he'd brought the severed head of Windsur ren Cloven. What poor fool joined the black knight's collection now?

"The heir of Hithren," answered Bened. "He sent the Crow King an offer to take you in marriage."

"Is such an offer now a crime?" she asked, tone sharp as an icicle.

"When that offer is for you, yes. None but I shall possess you, Arianwen. You're the loveliest maiden in Simaerin, and thus best suited to be the wife of the Crow King's Talon."

She lifted her gaze from the soiled sack. "I believe Lord ren Lotelon is already married, sir."

"Traycen is dead," Bened said, a cruel smile on his lips. "He died at Talbethé by the Winter King's hand. I now fill the vacancy, as the Crow King has long promised."

"So," said Arianwen, "at long last the ever-underestimated knight claims glory for himself, but at what expense? You think the people will love you, as unfeeling as you are? You think the Crow King will do more than use you as a pawn in his conquest of the world? Does glory taste as well as you dreamed, Sir Knight?"

Bened marched forward and caught her wrist to pull her close. "You shall taste well enough, my lady. *You* are my reward."

"I will die first, sir."

Bened laughed, a dark, bitter sound. "You think he'll let you? The Crow King holds you captive, Arianwen, and none escape him."

"The Winter King did," she whispered, and winced as his grip on her wrist tightened.

"The *Winter King* is all but crushed. His heart is broken, and fever racks his body. He won't survive both assaults at once."

"You mustn't measure a man against your own strength," said Arianwen, pulling against him. "You might find yourself lacking much."

His smile deepened, and he caught her chin, pressed his hand to her back, and forced his lips over hers. She wrenched against him, but his grip held. Dropping her arms, she merely stood there, unmoving, unyielding, cold as a statue made of ice. She wouldn't respond to his insistence; she would give him nothing at all.

He drew back. Sneered. "You think yourself superior to me, but I'll show you which is the master before long." He struck her face.

She stumbled sideways. Lights flashed against her eyes. Warm blood trickled from her lips. She straightened and glared at him, frigid.

He laughed, stooped to claim the bloody sack from the floor, and tramped from the room.

# Chapter Thirty-Eight

The clouds over Talbethé swelled, but they carried no snow or rain. Sunlight glanced through them now and then, coloring the world in shades of gold and gray.

Gwyn stood upon the outer wall facing west to watch the approaching wagons and Ilidreth cavalry. The Swan banner billowed in the chill wind, heartening, even as Gwyn contemplated his torn emotions.

Coming along with the wagons, bedecked in the armor and heraldry of the Crow King, rode Cadogan ren Silverard.

Lawen had respected his commanding officer in bygone days, before the man had threatened him into performing acts of murder and cruelty. Gwyn hadn't known until recently about the threat against his own life; how as a lad he might have died had Lawen not agreed to execute child mages and feed the remains of Ilidreth prisoners to others in bondage.

A vise clutched Gwyn's heart, searing it. His breath caught and strained. He slumped against the nearest merlon, vision foggy with tears. As he blinked away the wet haze, the white world beyond the keep gained focus.

"Afallon, lend me strength," he whispered through a sob. "Lawen, sustain me. I must go on without you."

A horn sounded from the watchtower. The gate rumbled open.

He pushed away from the merlon, drew a breath, and inched his way to the stairs along the wall. He'd regained a little of his strength, but it would be some time yet before he trusted his legs to keep him upright over distances. Even now, approaching the bottom of the stairs, his limbs trembled with fatigue and he stumbled twice.

Once upon solid ground, he leaned against the stone wall to catch his breath, and looked to the gate as the first wagons rolled in. General Cadogan rode beside them.

The man's eyes swept across the bailey, appraising every detail, from the snow-crusted flagstones and grand towers and battlements, to the ragged Unicorn banner limping against the wind, to the barefoot, ill-garbed soldiers stationed at various doorways, to Gwyn, who must look beleaguered and sickly, for he was certainly both. Cadogan's eyes lingered on him, then the man inclined his head.

Gwyn stared back, unmoving, suspicions screaming in his mind. Don't trust this man. Don't do it, fool.

"They've arrived!" exclaimed Nathaera, bringing Gwyn around as she sprang through the doorway from the kitchens and raced across the slippery bailey. Kive loped at her side. The girl spotted Gwyn halfway and changed direction without the faintest trip. "There you are. I've been worried."

Gwyn smiled and said nothing.

"Isn't it odd," said Nathaera, turning back to the wagons as they continued to roll in, "how General Cadogan has given up all his great wealth and rank and everything to join us? Yet Bened Arnnor and Haratin both ached so much for the same rank, and lost all reason and honor to pursue the very thing Cadogan forsook?"

Gwyn frowned. "Perhaps Cadogan's forsaken nothing."

"You think he's tricking us?" She glanced at him. "But Celin—"

"I know. But I still have doubts."

"Doubts are natural," she said gently. "Just don't plant them so deeply they remain rooted even once they're proved false." She peered toward Kive. "What say you, my dear Kive? Is the general there a fly or a rat?"

Kive considered Cadogan as the man barked orders at his men, positioning the wagons for inspection. "No, Fairy Wren. Not a fly or a rat. Not a snake either. He might be...a stallion. Yes. He is a stallion, Fairy Wren."

Nathaera nodded and turned a shrug on Gwyn. "You see? Stallions aren't suspicious. We really ought to heed Kive's instinct more. If I'd done so before, we'd have taken no stock in Bened's word and, well..." She didn't finish.

Gwyn caught her icy hand and squeezed it. "You're not to blame, my lady. We did the best we could. What more can be done than that?" He angled back to the general and heaved a sigh. "I suppose I must play a courteous host and bid the dissenters welcome. Afallon knows we need every able man we can find."

He strode across the bailey.

Cadogan turned his horse and gazed down at Gwyn, searching his face. "Hail the Winter King." He swung from his saddle and tapped a fist over his breastplate. "I don't seek you in service, for I suspect you would struggle to accept me. Instead, I've pledged my sword to another king at least until this war is decided." His gaze flicked past Gwyn. "Is *this* the incumbent king of Ilid?"

Gwyn glanced at Kive and nodded. "The Swan King, by rights. Kive, come here."

The fallen fae loped forward and halted beside Gwyn. "Yes, Shiny?"

"This is Cadogan ren Silverard, now your liegeman. What say you?"

Kive blinked at Cadogan. "Hello, Stallion."

The general's mouth twitched upward. "So, it's true he's mad."

"Aye," said Gwyn. "Courtesy of his brother, the Crow King."

"Which is the elder?"

"Kovien."

Cadogan nodded. "I've served one form of madness or another all my life. 'Tis fitting I continue along that course, though in this, at least, my honor shall remain intact." In a fluid motion, Cadogan stooped to one knee. "Kive, prince of Swan Castle, from afar I swore fealty to you and was cut loose from the bonds of the Crow King. Now a second time I vow the same. What life remains to me is yours."

Kive patted Cadogan's head. "Nice Stallion."

Cadogan shrugged and rose. Snow clung to his boots. "I will take that as acceptance."

"That's wise." Gwyn shivered as wind billowed across the bailey. "Shall we take refuge from the chill, my lord? A fire blazes within."

He gestured to the main keep looming at the center of Talbethé. Cadogan nodded, and they walked together as Aleteer and Rohkye emerged from the kitchen passageway to count the new stores.

❧

"After all we've been through already, can any man blame me for my mistrust of the Crow King's left hand?"

Gwyn considered Mershen. "Does anyone else feel the same?"

The war council sat along an oaken table within the keep's central tower. Gwyn occupied the chair at the table's head, and he gazed down its length at his officers, studying their expressions. Most wore pinched scowls as they bore holes in the polished oak before them. No one spoke.

Gwyn waited, lifting his eyes to the emblems of the Crow adorned throughout the torch-lit chamber upon shields, hanging banners, and above the door lintel. His throat closed. After this meeting, he would order Rohkye to burn the heraldry.

Swallowing, he reached with his mind for the Weave. Its current danced around him like wind torrents. He tapped his reservoir of power. Nearly empty. Likely it would be weeks before his magic replenished itself.

"I must agree with Mershen."

Gwyn started and looked toward Colonel Cluv. "You protest Cadogan joining us?"

Cluv nodded, gnarled face fierce in the guttering flames of the windowless room.

"Any other opinions?"

A knock rapped against the door. Gwyn frowned. A guard stationed there opened it to peer out into the hall. Whispers followed, then the door swung wide to admit a familiar figure.

Gwyn smiled. "Towwen, welcome. Please come in! You look well, my friend."

Towwen Stone entered, followed by another man. They both bowed. The door shut behind them and they seated themselves at the far side of the table.

Towwen Stone gestured to his companion. "Your Majesty, this is my friend, Remien, a faithful and hardy fellow of considerable candor."

"I welcome candor," said Gwyn, nodding at the stranger, "and so I welcome you, Remien."

"Thank you, sire," murmured the man. "'Tis an honor to serve the line of Wintervale."

"We were discussing General Cadogan ren Silverard," said Gwyn. "I've asked all to share their thoughts on his arrival and shifting loyalties. Do you have anything to add to the matter, Towwen? Remien?"

Both men fell still.

With a sigh, Towwen nodded. "I do, sire. Afallon taught that all men are fallen, and it's by his mercy that we're redeemed. I spoke with Cadogan once upon our journey here, and what he said rang true and sounded remorseful." He lifted his hand as several chairs creaked. "I won't fault any man who mistrusts him. We've all heard the stories of the Silver War, where he triumphed again and again against whatever foe. Such power lends strength to fear."

He tapped the table with a finger. "I'm a mage. My talent is words, and though my preference is Scrawling, still I hear the hum of truth when it's spoken. I heard it in his voice. I *saw* it in his face. His eyes were steadfast and resolved—not against our cause, but for redemption. How he feels about the Winter King, I know not, but his honor is genuine and his respect for Lawen ren Terare is real. If for no other reason, I don't believe he'll betray us. He can be trusted. That's what my heart tells me."

Gwyn studied his friend, then nodded. "Anything to add, Master Remien?"

The man frowned and considered the table. "Only this, sire: I agree with Towwen's observations."

"But he's served the Crow King for twenty years!" cried Mershen. "Lest we forget, the Silver War was a bloodbath. Cadogan ren Silverard *slaughtered* women and children without just cause—"

"That's mere speculation," cut in Towwen. "Before you shout out accusations, be certain of your source, General Mershen. We *know* only that a village was wiped out and ren Silverard reported it so. Wives' tales have always been embellished and often fabricated. Reference only what you know."

Gwyn spoke up. "I'm not concerned with the events of yesteryear so much as I am with today. That Cadogan has committed atrocities in the past we know already. Who here hasn't? I've killed more than one man upon the battlefield, and while I called it necessary, yet it was still the taking of a life. By Afallon's decree, that's a sin—at times pardonable, even justifiable — yet still a sin. I only wish to protect my men and Simaerin from further harm. So, I will ask again: Do we accept Cadogan's aid in our cause, or do we banish him?"

General Grene spoke for the first time. "The Crow King wouldn't give him a chance were your positions reversed, sire. Something to bear in mind."

Gwyn eyed him. "Perhaps that's true, though it's just as likely false. The Crow King finds all men inferior to himself, and if they can be used in any way he'll keep them close. If they've betrayed him, all the more reason to accept their apology and punish them in close proximity."

"Yet Haratin was banished from Simaerin," piped up Remien. "News is all over the countryside of his disgrace."

Gwyn felt a twinge of satisfaction. "Justice shall have her way."

"Sire?"

Gwyn looked down the table to Colonel Cluv, who held his hand up, waiting. "Yes, Cluv?"

"While we're addressing concerns, I must speak of my own. The Ilidreth, sire. Can we trust them? Only recently we discovered that the Crow King himself is of their race. Most are fallen, savage creatures now. Even your Kive is a terrifying specter to most, though I don't wish to offend you by saying so." He shook his head. "I fear having too many of them at our very backs. If the Crow King commanded them, would they not heed their rightful liege?"

Gwyn's hand clenched as fire surged through his chest.

*Keep your temper.*

He let out a long breath. Cluv had every right to express his concerns without reproach.

Gwyn nodded. "I understand your fear well. Within the True Wood of Ilid, I met several of the fae kind, and found they were not all alike. One was truly savage, and stalked me for my life. As for Kive, he's harmless to anyone I call my friend. The Crow King betrayed his own, just as he betrayed us. I count Celin among my friends, just as I do each of you. He's been as wounded by his king as have we. Should he *not* fight against the very man who felled his kingdom? Slew his liege lord and lady? Tortured the younger prince to madness?

"I won't ask Celin to stand aside so that others may wage his war. Let him ride with us, sir. Any Ilidreth who desires it, let him also come. Frankly, my lords, we can't afford to turn them aside if we want to win."

"But..." Cluv hesitated. "They're heathens, sire. Surely Afallon will curse us if we fight beside them."

"If you think that," said Gwyn, "then you know nothing of Afallon's teachings. Does He not love all men? Even our enemies? Even the Crow King in his darkness? We fight, not because we're holy, but because we love holiness, liberty, and justice, rather than cruelty, tyranny, and death. I'll hear no more prejudice spew from the lips of my officers."

He rose and rested his hands upon the table. "My decision is this: We shall allow Cadogan ren Silverard to remain in our company to prove himself a friend. As for the Ilidreth, they're welcome and must be treated with respect and dignity as becomes any honorable man."

He allowed himself a soft smile. "You've each served well and faithfully, and I thank you heartily. Rest now. We'll meet again on the morrow."

# Chapter Thirty-Nine

Nathael sat upon the roof of Quee'avv Cathedral under a waning moon in a sullen sky. He studied the black-stone castle stretching its towers like claws to rake against the heavens. The stones of Crow Castle gleamed with water from a recent rainfall, painting the abode in a weak, sinister light.

One of those claw-like turrets held the much-sought Lady Arianwen. What was her significance? Was her use spent now that Bened Arnnor had betrayed the Winter King, or did she remain motivation for his continued service to the Crow?

Nathael frowned and sighed, breath misting before him. The night chill sank into his bones. He tasted the crisp threat of snow on his tongue.

Rindermarr had been placed under arrest for defying a servant of the king. He would probably be executed for treason like so many others. Like Nathael if he were caught. He shuddered, hands curling into fists. The thought terrified him, but he mustn't let it keep him from his task. He'd come to Crowwell to aid King Gwynter.

Evidently, his warning of Bened Arnnor's betrayal had arrived too late if it ever reached the Winter King. He mustn't let such failure happen again.

Perhaps Nathael could discover what part the fair Arianwen played in the Crow King's schemes.

Lightning broke over Crow Castle, crawling across the sky in hues of red, violet, and blue. Thunder rumbled, deafening, booming.

Lightning replied, searing the heavens. Thunder rolled like drums of war over the city.

Nathael froze, mesmerized, as though he watched a battle playing out above.

Lightning emanated from two directions, meeting just above the castle's highest tower. Striking. Raging.

A scream sounded from that height. High-pitched, full of pain and fury. Lightning blossomed again, but now it streaked away from the castle, toward the city, downward to strike the ground a few streets away.

Nathael stared wide-eyed, hair lifting, heart galloping. Something — some*one* — had been attached to that thread of light: A figure, not unlike Nox's dragon, with burning wings and a long, lithe body.

Had he imagined it?

He leapt to his feet and clambered along the clay tiles to the ivy climbing up the side of the grand edifice. He scrambled down the vines, jumped to the lawn, and stole across the courtyard. Rindermarr had provided him with a key to a side door high priests used when they wished to avoid the fawning masses.

Slipping through the ornate carven door, he entered a narrow, cobbled street and trotted to its end to peer into a wide thoroughfare. The lightning had struck three blocks southeast. He must hurry before others arrived at the scene. It was late enough, perhaps few had noticed.

He passed a crowded tavern and caught the last few bawdy lyrics of a sea ditty, before he hurried on, raucous laughter ringing in his wake. The wisping odor of ale taunted his nose.

Battered houses and naked trees sagged into the wending street where the figure had fallen. Windows gaped, dark and silent.

Nathael saw no sign of a dragon. Perhaps he'd guessed the wrong street, or perhaps the dragon's enemy had come already to finish its work.

No. There.

Something gleamed in the dismal moonlight. Nathael inched forward, heart in his throat. Brow perspiring. Hands clammy at his sides.

A figure lay in the street, but she was no dragon. A lady sprawled across the paving stones, black hair threading the ground, surrounding her red robes.

He gasped. Blood pooled around her, thick and glistening.

He raced to her side. Knelt. Hesitated. Had she fallen from the sky? Should he touch her?

"M-my lady?" His nerves hummed.

She moaned.

A gasp exploded from his lungs. "My lady, don't move. I'm called Nathael, and I mean only to aid you." He laid a hand on her shoulder and felt her trembling frame.

She turned her head until she could see him from the corner of one dark eye. "You...would help...me?"

He nodded. "Where's your wound? I must bind it."

"Go," she whispered through clenched teeth. "Hurry. The Fiend is coming fast."

Fear danced across Nathael's flesh. He peeked toward the sky. He'd heard whispers of the Fiend. A dark, winged beast that prowled the air and feasted on human flesh.

Some whispered it was the Crow King's pet.

He swallowed and slipped a hand around the woman's waist. "All the more reason I must assist you. The cathedral will offer us sanctuary."

She cried out as he lifted her.

"I'm sorry," he whispered, "but we must be swift."

Wind rushed along the street. Silence rang in Nathael's ears, as though every noise in the city had been snuffed out on that breeze. He shuddered and turned, keeping his arms firmly around the woman.

Ahead in the street, a specter of smoke and starlight pawed the ground.

Nathael's eyes widened. The Fiend possessed a lithe, deer-like body, with a black mane and an obsidian horn glinting in the dark.

"A unicorn?" whispered Nathael. "But it's impossible."

"Nay," hissed the woman through her pain. "'Tis unlikely, but possible. Purity itself has been corrupted. The Crow King taints all that he touches."

Nathael's heart twisted. He wheezed in a breath. "But why? Why destroy something so fair?"

"Because the Crow King fell long ago, and that which has fallen cannot abide beauty, purity, *goodness.* Yet it must subsist on it, swallow it up, or the fell thing shall fade into naught." The woman closed her eyes and drew a rattling breath. "Leave me, human. Depart from this place, else you too shall be devoured."

She wasn't human? Could a dragon take on the shape of a woman? It didn't matter.

Nathael tightened his grip. "I won't leave you."

"The Fiend has challenged me," she said. "I must fight until the end, which ending is welcome now." She turned her black eyes on Nathael and snared his gaze. "Would you do me a service in my last hour, Nathael?" She caught his hand and pried it from her waist to press something cold into his palm. "Take this. Bring it to Lady Arianwen. Tell her Demréal has paid her debt and flown home."

"No," said Nathael. "Bring it to her yourself. Come with me now."

"*Go.*"

Nathael released her and backed away, clutching whatever gift she'd given him. His eyes wandered back to the Fiend who waited, patient, unconcerned with him. Its eyes carried the same pearlescent shades as Aluem's, but there was nothing of warmth or light in their depths.

This Being, this *Unbeing*, had become tainted. A tragic wretch, deformed even as it remained beautiful in its imagery.

"GO!" screamed Demréal again.

Nathael turned away to race toward Crow Castle. Toward the service he must provide this magnificent creature in her final hour.

Long minutes passed before the crack of thunder sounded again in the sky. Nathael didn't look up to witness the battle. He paused to catch his breath and opened his palm. And stared.

A diamond — glittering and bright in the flashing stormlight — lay in his hand.

A scream cut across the air, long, harrowing, beautiful.

Nathael caught the edge of a building and heaved a sob, then he pushed off and darted toward Crow Castle. She wouldn't die in vain.

Whatever her purpose in bringing the diamond to Lady Arianwen, he would see it done.

❦

HE COULDN'T CLIMB the outer wall. He couldn't walk through the front gates and up the stairs to the lady's room. He would never make it.

But still he must try.

Nathael had grown up on the streets, barely surviving until a portly boy offered him half a loaf of bread. That same boy had brought Nathael to his home and urged his parents to take the waif in. They had, and Nathael had become part of their family. He'd learned to read and write. Learned to bake. Learned to smile and laugh.

Others were less fortunate. Under the Crow banner, how many had been slaughtered, burned, maimed, imprisoned, enslaved? If Nathael could do something now to change the fates of others, he must try.

Still, plunging blindly ahead did nothing to thwart the tyrant king. He must think of some clever means to enter Crow Castle.

His mind ran through every possibility as he trudged toward the front gates, heart racing.

What could he do? He wore the garb of a priest, but was it enough? The church now quarreled with the Crow King. Even should a guard let him enter, he wouldn't get farther than the vestibule.

He squeezed the diamond in his hand, wishing it would provide some answer.

Warm wind breathed through him, like sunshine and bright meadows. The world around him, the road under his feet, the guardhouse ahead, the looming wall beside him, faded into dim shades. His limbs lightened. His mind and heart eased. His stride grew longer and doubts rolled away. He could enter Crow Castle. He must simply walk on.

As he crossed the drawbridge and entered the castle courtyard, the armored guards remained stationary. The way ahead lay clear. The doors opened before him and he stepped into Crow Castle.

On instinct he turned left and entered a passageway of stairs leading upward. These he took, calm and certain. His steps fell light and swift. He never tired as he ascended the long flight and came to stand before a corridor of dark stone and cold torches.

At its end stood a wooden door.

Nathael strode forward, took the handle, and pulled against it. Locked. He tried again, and it groaned then gave way.

Moonbeams and lightning pooled into the room through a window across the way. Near the door stood a four-poster bed swathed in curtains. Lying under the coverlets, Nathael could perfectly see Arianwen's features, stark and lovely against the faded hues of the distant chamber.

She stared back, bewildered, her fear drumming the air in waves.

Nathael shut the door and lifted a hand. "Don't shout. I come as Demréal's friend and messenger."

Arianwen sat up, eagerness stealing across her pale blue eyes. "Pray, what message does the dragon send?"

"This." Nathael held aloft his fist. He uncurled it, and the room fell into the space around him, dark and gloomy. Arianwen's features grew hazy in the nightscape. Panic rolled over him, sharp and throbbing. But the diamond in his hand shone bright and clear.

The lady rose, silken nightgown whispering against the coverlets. Her feet padded across the cold floor. She neared, eyes illuminated in the diamond's light.

"Demréal sent this to me?"

"Aye," answered Nathael, his voice thick.

Arianwen looked up into his face, catching his breath with her fierce beauty. "What's happened to her?"

"She fell." Nathael's voice caught. "The Fiend has defeated her."

A faint cry escaped Arianwen's lips. "My dear friend! Alas that I could not save you."

"Take it," said Nathael, heart hammering in his ears. "Take the diamond. I don't know its purpose, but it was intended for you. Somehow it got me into the castle. Perhaps with it you can escape."

She plucked it up and stared into the glowing cuts of the precious gem. "Come with me. We should go now." Arianwen closed her hand around the diamond — and gasped. "*He's coming.*"

The door creaked open. Nathael backed away, wondering if he might escape through the window.

"It would be your death to run, child," whispered a wistful, haunting tone. In stepped a figure dressed in robes lined with crows' feathers. A black crown glittered on his head. The Crow King stood fair and tall yet dark, so like a fae. How had none seen it before now? "I am deeply impressed you made it so far into my castle, but alas, you've cornered yourself. For what? The Lady of Ice? You think to rescue and woo fair maid?" He smiled. So gentle, so nearly kind.

Nathael stared. *This* was the dread king who had murdered so many children? Left his people to starve? Waged war against the world? How was it so? The same sorrow touched this man as the Fiend. Two fair and fallen creatures, tainted and cruel.

*Why*? Where was the sense in it?

"Let him go," said Arianwen in wintry tones. "He only came at Demréal's behest to let me know she's been killed."

The Crow King considered the lady. "Did he? How very brave."

Nathael stared between them. As the king's gaze returned to him, he steeled himself. He mustn't show fear. This was no king, whatever his presence, whatever his blood. Nathael owed this tyrant no deference.

"Come to me," said the king, spreading his fingers in a beckoning fashion.

Invisible cords wrapped around Nathael, and his legs moved on their own until he stood before the tall and stately figure.

"Tell me your name."

"Nathael."

"I see courage in your eyes, Nathael. It lights your very soul. The same soul I will snuff out as a candle under my breath, for I also see in you an oath sworn to the Winter King."

"If you kill me," said Nathael, "my only regret shall be that I can die but once in service to my country."

Fire burned in the king's eyes. In a fierce whisper, he issued one command: "*Die, peasant.*"

Nathael tumbled back, growing light and unburdened. Death wasn't dark and cold as he had imagined as a starving child on the streets of Charquae.

It was bright as fire and lovely as a spring morning.

## Chapter Forty

"What thoughts dwell in your mind tonight, Kive?"

The fallen fae glanced down from where he crouched on the nearby merlon upon Talbethé's wall.

Gwyn hefted himself onto the next flat-top merlon and folded his legs before him, then drew his cloak tighter around his chest. The stone beneath him felt colder than the chill night air, but he welcomed the opportunity to sit. He'd had a long day overseeing the keep's conditions.

"Shiny, a new star is in the sky. See?" Kive pointed eastward to a twinkling array of stars. "That one was not there before."

Gwyn smiled. "Was it not? Perhaps it's a good omen that spring will come early."

"No, Shiny." Kive drew his knees to his chest and fingered his bare toes. "Spring will come only when it comes. Never soon. Never late."

Gwyn chuckled. "That's reasonable." He studied the Ilidreth for a long, quiet moment, trying to imagine how this poor, absurd creature had existed in a former life. The prince of his people, second born of noble parents, fair and light and whimsical. Had he loved to dance or sing? Hunt or explore? Had he been prone to fits of laughter or bouts of melancholy?

Shadowed now by nighttime, it was easier to ignore the horrors that marred Kive's mind. To imagine instead pale hair and silver eyes in a fae face.

Those eyes might light up under an incorrigible idea, while a gentle yet mischievous smile brushed at his lips. What mirth he might feel as he walked under a younger sun and contemplated the freedoms of youth, wise enough to appreciate them before they were lost; foolish enough to waste many on simple pleasures: the ones that matter. For such foolery is no sin.

Gwyn turned from Kive and eyed the sky, wondering which star the fae meant. "Kive?"

"Yes, Shiny?"

"Do you ever remember? Not the dark times, not the pain. Do you ever let yourself walk among the sheaves of memory, golden and warm as an early autumn day?"

Kive turned to Gwyn, eyes wide, uncomprehending, innocent despite their sinister shade. "Kive doesn't eat wheat, Shiny."

"No. But I think you misunderstand on purpose. Do you remember your parents, Kive? Do you let yourself love them even when it hurts? Or have you shuttered and locked away those feelings forever?"

Kive turned away. Didn't answer. The wind rose and howled, then died away and left the world silent. Dark. Dreary.

"Beautiful," said Kive in a muffled voice. "All the Shinies sparkled like dew in the grass at dawn. Bright. Light. Beautiful."

Gwyn held his breath.

Kive went on, tones low and laced with agony. "Aaalll the Shinies died, Shiny. All of them. First, Shiny went away, sad, and afraid. He never came back. The Crow came in his place, and he ate them all. All the Shinies, Shiny. All of them. Only the Swan survived, and she wept beside Shiny Father as he stared. Stared, Shiny. Just stared and stared, *and he will never stop staring*."

Hunching, Kive buried his hands in his hair. Silent sobs racked his frame.

Gwyn rested a hand on the Ilidreth's shoulder. "I'm so sorry, Kive. I know it hurts. But didn't you love the Shinies? Don't you want to remember Swan and Shiny Father even still? It hurts because you love them — but, Kive, that pain won't ever go away. Isn't it better to remember them and make the pain worthwhile?"

The Ilidreth shook his head, though he remained buried in his knees, hidden.

"Tell me about the Swan, Kive," said Gwyn softly. He'd seen her, over a year ago, at Swan Castle. She'd appeared and spared his life when he lay dying. Never had he seen anyone as beautiful before or since.

A low moan answered Gwyn's request. "Oh, Shiny." Kive lifted his head to stare into the abyss of his broken mind. "Swan is lovely. Such a lovely, lovely Swan. Her voice is fair as moonlight, clearer than faery song. Swan is wise and sad and full of fire that never burns. Oh, Shiny. Swan is *swan*. She glides and dances, merry and somber. Rich and humble. Such grace shall never again be."

Gwyn stared, transfixed by the change wrought across Kive's face as memory transformed him. His eyes shone silver again, deep, ageless; his hair gleamed pale, long, and untangled, shimmering like spiders' threads.

The madness had fled, though sorrow lingered to crown him in wisdom. Almost, Gwyn perceived the ghost of such a device upon Kive's head, delicate and sparkling with starstones like those of the Crystal Way. Against his slight frame flickered the phantom reflections of kingly raiment, light and silken.

Dumbstruck, Gwyn bowed his head to this lordly creature. He dared to look up, hardly breathing, fearful the vision had already faded. But memory still snared Kive, and Gwyn beheld the ruler of the Ilidreth: The Swan King.

A shout rose from the watch at the gates below. Someone replied with laughter.

Kive started and blinked. The kingly figure shrank back into the hapless wretch crafted by Kovien's hand. "Hello, Shiny."

Gwyn offered a faint, sad smile. "I'm sorry, Kive. I'm so deeply sorry."

Kive tilted his head. "Shiny, do you say sorry because you ate one of Kive's rats? But Shinies don't eat rats, Shiny."

"I wasn't speaking of rats, Kive. You've endured more than any living soul ought or can. If only I could offer a balm to soothe your hurts. To heal your mind and spirit. You must have been remarkable once."

"Kive is Kive," said the fallen fae in a chiding tone.

"Yes, but do you remember all that means, my friend? Might there be a way to gather all the shattered pieces of your life and put them together again? To forge them as a broken sword renewed?"

"While the Crow King stands, nay," answered a familiar voice from the darkness beyond Kive.

Gwyn peered past the fae until he could make out the silhouette of his Ilidreth friend. "Hail, Celin. I've looked for you long upon the battlements since your battalion arrived. Where have you been?"

"Elsewhere," said Celin wryly.

Gwyn smiled. "That much I did surmise on my own."

The Ilidreth stepped into the illumination of the torchlight. Garbed in fine cloth of motley hues, wearing no armor at all, with a single sword at his hip, light and delicate to wield, Celin looked like a prince. Nothing of fatigue showed on his brow. His blue eyes lingered on Kive, perhaps searching for a hint of his king's former grace.

After a moment, Celin looked away. "A dragon has been murdered this night."

Gwyn started. "Parsha?"

"Nay. Demréal, a she-dragon. She fell over Crowwell, defeated by the most unholy creature born of the Weave. It is called the Fiend, though once it walked the same vales as your unicorn brother. The Crow King goes too far. He has corrupted the purest of any fae Being. Why, I cannot fathom."

"He tainted a unicorn?" asked Gwyn, shuddering. Aluem was so *good* and *just*. To twist such beauty, to mold it into something of darkness... "How did you learn of this?"

Celin sighed. "The stars hold the fate of this life. Just as Prince Kive witnessed a new star appear, so did I. In truth, there were twin stars born this night: each for the ending of a hero slain by darkness. The Weave pays homage to the fallen."

Gwyn nearly asked if Lawen, too, had a star, but pain choked his words and he held his tongue.

Celin eyed him but said nothing of his unspoken question. The Ilidreth lifted a finger to point toward the heavens. "Just there, a star once hung bright and true. But one hundred years ago it fell, not as a starstone compelled by the fae, but as a warped and blackened husk. Beforehand, it had represented the wisest of the unicorns: Arastet. No sign of the Being has been found since, though Aluem looked long — as did I, for Arastet was my friend. Now at last I have found him, or what has become of him. The Fiend is more wretched by far than his lord and master, for the brighter the Being the farther it may fall."

A groan brought Gwyn's gaze back to Kive, who huddled again, face buried in his knees. Black tangles of hair cloaked him against the night.

Gwyn laid a hand on the fallen fae's shoulder. "Don't despair, Kive. Even what is fallen may rise again."

"Can it, Wintervale?" asked Celin. "Don't offer false hope where there is only broken sorrow."

"Hope, by its nature, isn't false," Gwyn replied. "Hope exists to dispel the gloom."

"Hope dies in the dark." Celin sighed. "Forgive me, Gwynter. We Ilidreth are nearly fallen, and what threads of hope you cling to have all but severed for my people. I shall have to trust to your faith."

Gwyn smiled. "That sounds awfully like hope, my friend."

The Ilidreth searched his face, then turned to consider the waning moonlight. His eyes glittered under the stars. "You live such fleeting years. Is that the reason you still harbor hope even in a sea of sorrow? Does your brother's death matter so little? Is your grief as fleeting as your life?"

Gwyn flinched and clasped his hands together. Sorrow and anger swelled up to drown him. "Nay, Celin. My pain is eternal, though my mortality will end. No bond of man, or Ilidreth, or unicorn could be deeper than mine with Lawen. Don't think me unfeeling to find hope when I need it most desperately. A torrent of rage fills my breast when I think of Lawen's end. I *hate* the Crow King for taking my brother from me. Perhaps *that* is where my hope was born. I know I shall overthrow the mad tyrant, for my grief and anger will allow nothing less. Each fuels my hope, lending strength where without it I would be nothing.

"Don't mistake me, Celin: My hope isn't some child's prayer for a pleasant holiday. It's for the force of arms to *destroy* my foe. I cannot rest until I see that madman fall. I shall bring winter to the Crow's threshold and call his days numbered."

Celin remained still, eyes locked on Gwyn's. He nodded. "Gone is the child I met near the Vale of Life. On that spring day, I warned a listless boy that his vision was fading as he grew into manhood. So it is at last: Before me stands a man of strength, his vision funneled as all the rest, but what he sees he views well and justly. Perhaps it is merely the fate of Man to lose full sight, else his heart would not remain steadfast upon his purpose. Gwynter, last of the Wintervale line, First King of Springtime: I am honored to know thee and witness thy work. The Weave has chosen well."

# Chapter Forty-One

Toward middle night, Gwyn left the two Ilidreth upon the wall and traipsed up a flight of stairs leading into a tower far above Talbethé. Here he sought solitude on sleepless nights.

Tonight, memories of Lawen's death plagued his thoughts, brutal, vivid, unrelenting. Sorrow had given way to anger on the heels of his conversation with Celin, and now he nursed it — let it fester and brood within him.

The Crow King had tainted a unicorn. Destroyed the Ilidreth kingdom. Enslaved and burned Simaeri citizens. Waged war against Fraelin. Murdered his brother.

Gwyn clenched his jaw and stalked into the tower, vision dark with wrath.

"Oh. Hello."

Gwyn froze to stare into the startled eyes of Nathaera. She stood at the window, bathed in moonlight, bundled in matted furs. For a long moment, neither moved.

Wasn't it late? Shouldn't she be asleep in her private quarters below?

"I couldn't catch a wink of sleep. I've been waiting for you." She took a breath. "Do you mind?"

He blinked as he realized he'd been glaring at her. He tried to smooth his lips into a smile. "No, I don't mind. I'm sorry. I was lost in thought."

She nodded. "Yes, so I saw." Her mouth played with a smile, bright and warm and full of mischief. "You really don't mind my invasion of your tower?"

"'Tisn't mine."

She only smiled wider. "I saw you speaking with Celin as I made my way up here. How is he?"

"Well, but worried. Just as everyone else." He padded closer, and she stepped to one side of the window to invite him nearer still. He leaned against the stone sill, heartbeat quickening. "You didn't come here to discuss Celin."

She shook her head. "I didn't come here to discuss anything. I only wanted to see you. Alone." She flushed and turned to study the keep's outer wall below. "You're very busy lately."

"Nathaera."

Her eyes darted between the wall and the wintry fields beyond the keep. Back and forth.

"Nathaera."

She glanced his way, but her eyes retreated again. "Yes, Gwyn?"

"You said you don't love Adesta."

She nodded.

"Did you mean that?"

Her gaze flickered back to him for a sharp second, then retreated again. "Yes."

"You said you love me."

"Mm-hm." She bit her lip and trembled.

"Nathaera." He reached out and caught her hand where it rested against the windowsill. Ice cold. He brought it to his lips, slowly, snaring her eyes as he tenderly kissed her fingertips. Her knuckles. Her wrist.

She watched him, unmoving, breathless. Her eyes were bright

and wide, glorious in the glow of the distant moon in its faraway sky.

"I love you, Nathaera," he whispered. "My steadfast, brave, foolish lady. I love you dearly."

She stood as still as the tower walls. Gasped. Flung her arms around his waist and buried her head in his chest. "I'm dreaming! Only dreaming. But what a lovely, wondrous dream. Sweet Afallon Above, let me never wake."

Gwyn caught her chin in his hand and lifted her head until she met his gaze. He bent down, caught her lips with his, and kissed her. She answered, tentative. It was a sweet, lingering kiss.

After a moment, the two pulled back and stared into one another's eyes, content to find what burned there. Adoration. Devotion. Love.

"Goodnight, Gwynter," whispered Nathaera, tears slipping unchecked down her cheeks.

"Goodnight, my dearest lady."

She withdrew and left him alone in his tower. Though his cracked still heart ached, warmth cocooned his soul, and his hope burned a little brighter.

# PART IV
# CROWN OF THE BLIGHTED

# Chapter Forty-Two

The first thaw of spring brought an army to the gates of Talbethé.

Dripping icicles made their last stand against the ramparts of the keep while Gwyn stood before the open gate to receive the approaching force of arms.

The musky scent of the horses floated into the Bailey as the Crane banner bobbed above a forerunner upon his steed, beside which merrily danced the Swan banner.

Celin stood next to Gwyn to welcome his kin.

At the head of the five hundred Ilidreth bowmen, Gwyn spotted a familiar face. He smiled at the memory. The Ilidreth commander bore the same amusement in a vivid smile and twinkling eye. He raised a hand in greeting as he reined in his horse. "Hail, Winter King, once my captive simply called Gwyn. Do you still claim not to be a mage?"

"Be welcome in the company of many mages, High Lord Bowrin of the Ilidreth allied forces under the Crane King's banner," replied Gwyn with a broad grin.

Celin looked between them, eyebrow arched. "I see you are

already acquainted. Your Majesty, you have not been idle a day in your life, I suspect."

"Some years were more eventful than others," said Gwyn. "I had the high honor of accompanying Lord Bowrin through the woods of Ilid for a few short days before Kive and I escaped. It was shortly after I made your acquaintance, in truth."

Bowrin laughed. "High honor indeed, though that honor belonged to me. Forgive my ignorance of your heritage." He bowed his head.

Gwyn's smile slipped a little. "We were both ignorant — and I long often for those days when I was but a fledgling mage. Please, dismount and refresh yourselves. Be welcome. You've had a lengthy ride."

Bowrin made a hand signal, and his men dismounted in unison.

As Gwyn's aides rushed forward to provide whatever the new troop required, Gwyn and his Ilidreth allies headed for the inner keep.

"The Crow King's ranks are daily swelling," said Bowrin as they walked along the flagstones. "Two Simaeri cities who openly swore fealty to Your Majesty were torched a fortnight ago. The flames burned black. I would venture to guess it was the Fiend's work."

Celin sighed. "Yet more tragedy is heaped upon the soil of this ancient land. How much more darkness can the Crow King invoke?"

"Darkness begets darkness," said Bowrin. "His magic grows stronger with every act, Lord Celin'Laen. He has also ordered an attack on the borders of Ilid, but none of his soldiers will march to the True Wood. They still fear the Ilidreth."

"That will be advantageous," Gwyn murmured.

Celin nodded.

Bowrin went on. "Fear also drives the Simaeri to adhere to the Crow's wishes. He demands more men, and more men bend the knee to his tainted throne, heeding the call. There are rumors and stories he has circulated about you. The Winter King is now a dark tale ringing like a dooming knell across the whole of Simaerin.

You're a dread specter used to frighten the most wicked child into submission. The Crow King has decreed that the very world will burn under your tyrant hand should you ascend the throne of any land. Ignorance, fear, and prejudice work in his favor, leading many to take up his *holy* cause with zealous fervor."

Gwyn swallowed hard against this bit of news, though it shouldn't surprise him. The ancient line of Wintervale had long been anathema to the country and its people. No doubt the Crow King had wished to banish any notions that previous rulers were better than him. If the people of Simaerin thought the Wintervale kings were tyrants, then the Crow King was free to oppress them meticulously, like a slow poison over time, and none would be the wiser, for days of old were deemed far crueler.

The question remained: Why? What purpose did the Crow King's machinations serve? Was madness the only reason for his careful schemes? Did he have an ultimate goal, a point he meant to achieve? Or was this but a game, and Gwyn was only the latest contender to be crushed under the king's talons?

*Well.* Gwyn's hands curled into tight fists. *This contender will not succumb.*

This wasn't a game to him. Nor would he let the Crow King continue in his evil course.

Spring had come. It was time to march on Crowwell.

# Chapter Forty-Three

'Gwynter, will you ride with me?'*

Teeth gritted, Gwyn blocked his opponent's sword as the voice rushed through his mind. *Anywhere, Aluem.*

The unicorn tossed his mane. '*Now?*'

Gwyn lowered his sword.

Prince Fayett stumbled to a halt midcharge, hair stuck to his sweaty brow. "Are you all right, Your Majesty?"

Nodding, Gwyn sheathed his broadsword. "Enough training for now. I thank you for your time, Your Highness."

Fayett waved that away with a casual hand and nodded toward Aluem. "Does the unicorn call you?"

"He does."

"Then go. We can spar another day."

Gwyn bowed his head and trotted to Aluem's side. "Where do we ride?"

'*Across the Weave.*'

Gwyn raised an eyebrow. "I'm afraid I don't understand."

'*Come and I shall show you.*'

Gwyn mounted. Aluem cantered toward the keep gate, which opened as they neared. Beneath the portcullis and out into the open fields they rode, and here Aluem broke into a full gallop. Gwyn hunched forward and let the wind toss his long hair as it might.

The unicorn rode south for nearly an hour, then his pace slowed to a canter, a trot, and he halted before a grove of willow trees whose thirsty vines dipped their heads into a little spring at their center.

Reverently Aluem started forward again, hooves silent against the earth. A sacred hush drifted through the grove, and Gwyn held his tongue, afraid to break the stillness.

'*Dismount and peer into the pool.*'

Gwyn slid from Aluem's back, and picked his way around the tree roots until he gazed upon the reflective surface to meet his eyes in the water. Those eyes widened, for though his image stood within the pool, his surroundings there were vastly altered.

"Swan Castle?" whispered Gwyn, recognizing the spires of that once-grand edifice. His voice thundered within the grove, far too loud and coarse for such a realm.

*I'm standing inside a Vale*, he realized.

It felt much like Celin's secret home within the northern woods of Ilid. This pool belonged to the Ilidreth.

'*Few Vales remain in the mundane world, and fewer still serve the purpose of this place. This is a pool of memory.*'

Gwyn glanced at Aluem. "Am I to view the past?"

'*If you deem it wise. I cannot say. Perhaps it shall reveal what answers we need in this age of war. Or perhaps it will show only sorrow. I thought to give you the choice, for the dearest gift granted to Man above all else is Choice.*'

"Do I step into the water?"

'*Yes.*'

Gwyn searched the pool, studying the memory of spires belonging to a faraway age and place. He drew a breath, gathering his nerve. To learn the truth, to witness the horrors he suspected would follow, enveloped him with chilling fear.

*But if this might offer a chance to win against the Crow King, I must try.*

He slipped into the water. It swelled up to swallow him, warm as an embrace, caressing as a mother's touch, welcome and sweet.

His vision blurred. He could still breathe, though air filled his lungs languidly. Black leeched away color, air grew scarce, and then the water receded back down to his ankles.

Here the world shone brighter. Memory had crystallized light and color, encasing it in vivid detail too profound to be real. Flowers shimmered. Birdsong floated on streams of sweet, aromatic wind tasting like flowers and honey. Life hummed all about him, bursting with joy.

Laughter sounded on the succulent breeze. Gwyn's heart tightened. He strode from the pool, out of the grove of willow trees, and entered the courtyard of *Shaeswéath*, throne of Ilid, home of Prince Kive.

Beneath the fountain of his grandfather sat the prince himself robed in rich motley patterns, crowned in silvery light. Beside him, exquisite and graceful and human, sat the lady queen: Shalesta of Crane Castle. In her hands she held a lily pad from which she sipped golden water.

A presence stood beside Gwyn. He started, and glanced right to find Aluem there, pearlescent eyes sorrowful. *'Long has it been since the world was so full of light and wonder. Do you sense the innocence of this age, Gwynter? Do you taste the succor of beneficence? Of fair trade, tolerance, and kindness? 'Tis a cup sweeter than the purest water to sip once more from such a time. My soul longs for these tender moments—for they are never more than that.*

*'Alas, Gwynter! How bleak the world is. How foolhardy its inhabitants. How steeped in greed and warmongering. But that is the way of it, for it is in such turmoil that we can come to love and honor tender memory and feelings. I must endure.'*

Gwyn rested his hand on Aluem's neck, hoping to convey some meager measure of consolation. "If only the innocent weren't the ones most wounded in conflict. But I suppose that which is good and wholesome is targeted most ardently by evil." He frowned. "If only I understood what *makes* evil. How does the choice to do harm penetrate a man's heart? Is he born to it?"

'*Nay,*' said Aluem. '*Choice is given to Man, as I said before. Never is he born to play a certain role upon the stage. He must choose to rise to such or to play some other part. You, Gwynter, were not required to oppose the Crow King. You* chose *to do so.*'

"I didn't choose to be a king," Gwyn whispered.

'*Aye, but your parents and their forebears made the choices which led to your birth. And even so, you could walk away from your birthright.*'

Gwyn smiled wanly. "With a glad heart, I would."

'*Then why do you not?*'

He hesitated. "Because I must do all I can for Simaerin."

'*Indeed. For* this *you have chosen.*'

As they spoke, Gwyn and his unicorn watched the queen and prince bask under a warm sun, enjoying the faint breezes.

Another figure strode into view, as familiar as the first two: The Crow King — or rather, Kovien, as he was once named.

This long-ago shade of the Crow King had already chosen evil as he walked toward his family, his gait rigid, his mien dark, his hair flowing long and black as a crow's wings. In one hand he gripped a sword. In the other he held a crown of obsidian black bedecked in blood rubies glittering with malevolence in the sunlight.

Gwyn started forward, sensing the bloodlust and rage within Kovien, but he stopped himself.

*This is only memory, long past.*

"Aluem, can I bear to watch?"

The unicorn didn't answer.

Kovien reached his kin. Shalesta rose from the fountain's edge with concern written in the lines of her brow.

Kive rose in the next heartbeat, gasping. "My brother, you are ill!"

Kovien said nothing. He reached up and placed the jagged crown upon his own head.

Shalesta and Kive shrank back.

Gwyn felt the malignant force radiating from the crown. "What is that?"

Aluem pawed the earth. '*An ancient relic molded from the blood of thousands. 'Twas the same artifact which ended the divine life of your beloved Afallon, for he who wears the Crown of the Blighted wields the unholy magic of Hell itself.*'

Gwyn recoiled. His heart flinched as he understood. "*That's* his weapon, Aluem. That's how the Crow King will end magic. But if he wields such a force, why hasn't he already succeeded? Why has he waited so long, and why doesn't he use it now to defeat my army? Are there limitations to its power? Rites or magics required to work its ruin?"

'*It killed a god. It ended the line of Wintervale. It purged the Ilidreth. I do not think the Crown itself lacks strength, but rather its wielder does. The Crow King, for all his cunning and all his magic, is only Ilidreth. No doubt it has taken its toll with every use. Perhaps he is loath to use it unless he absolutely must.*'

Gwyn lifted his eyes again to the scene. Shalesta begged her son not to use such blatant evil — to cast it aside.

Kovien remained still, unmoved. "Father is dead," he said. "I slew him within the throne room. Behold." With a flick of his wrist, King Roth appeared against the grass, limp and pale as fallen snow.

The queen let out a cry and fell to her knees, pressed a hand to her face, and wept.

Kive remained standing, eyes wide as he shuddered. "Why, Kovien? I do not understand."

"I am called to this purpose," answered the Crow. "I must heed the voice."

Kive shook his head. His eyes, so pale and innocent, shone with tears. He trembled harder. Gwyn understood. The specter before Kive was his brother no longer, but a creature molded in madness.

"I must stop you if I can," Kive said.

Kovien smiled softly. "Behold, Kive. Your betrothed." He pointed his sword to the ground, and there at its tip formed a coffin of rich wood cloaked in a banner newly familiar to Gwyn. A silver tree against a black field bore two swords crossing before it. The royal crest of Wintervale.

Kive stared at the coffin.

"I would caution against opening it," said Kovien, "but I suspect you shall all the same. What remains of her lies within. The Simaeri princess was compelled to jump from the heights of Londolin three days ago."

Kive sprang to the coffin to throw aside the banner and wrench open the box. Gwyn couldn't see within, but Kive's expression confirmed the truth.

The fae prince sank before the wooden casket and sobbed. "Why, Kovien? Why did she jump?"

"She was inconsolable when I informed her that her family had died. That you were mad. That the Vales of Ilid had been destroyed. All this was too much for the fair Liliaé. She fell."

Kive sprang to his feet, bounded the few yards to his brother, and snatched his tunic. "*Why?*"

"Because it is all true. I have foreseen it, brother. All shall come to pass, for it is required to purge the world of all its injustices. To end the human race, with its unquenchable cycle of corruption."

"But *we* are human! Our mother is human!"

Kovien's eyes hardened. "We are half human, true. Long has this truth plagued me, but at last I understand its necessity. Only someone born of both races — a human mage and Ilidreth combined — could wield the Crown and survive. Its wrath would otherwise consume a mage at the first use. An Ilidreth would shrink from the task, for we have become frightened of our birthright. We were meant to rule this world, Kive. Meant to guard it against corruption and suffering, yet what have we done but look on and see each running unchecked through every epoch of humanity? I say enough! This task I shall gladly undertake. And you, brother, shall witness this world's end."

Kive released Kovien and took a step back. "You are mad. Something has driven you mad. What happened upon the south seas?"

"I told you," said Kovien. "I heeded the voice."

❧

NIGHT HAD SPREAD its long fingers across Simaerin when Gwyn stepped from the pool, shivering, weary to his core. He knelt in the wet grass along the bank and stared into the shadows before him. Aluem stood at his side.

He had watched it all. Watched as Kovien cursed Shalesta with eternal slumber. Watched as he locked Kive away in the dungeons of Swan Castle and began his mad tirade against his own people.

He slaughtered many. Fed them to Kive. Fed Kive's betrothed to him. Humiliated him in unspeakable ways, all to break his mind.

Kive remained resilient. He staved off madness for years. Years that flew by in awful moments before Gwyn's eyes. And then, under the scourge of time and imprisonment, at last Kive crumbled. His mind and spirit joined his shattered heart in the darkest recesses of his soul. He bent the knee to his lord and master. The fearsome Crow became his world, his one constant, the thing he loved and hated most.

The memory racked Gwyn's soul. How could anyone commit such atrocities? To murder and maim his own kin? His lifeblood? To slaughter countless thousands.

"Why?" Gwyn growled. "What was the point, Kovien?"

'*Gwynter, behold.*'

Gwyn turned back to the pool. He expected to find the night sky reflected on its surface. Instead, he found the image of a ship upon a storming sea. He understood at once what he must do, and he slipped back into the water to learn the reason for Kovien's crusade against the world.

# Chapter Forty-Four

"Has there been any word from your father, Prince Fayett?" Gwyn set his eyes on the Fraeli heir and waited.

Fayett shook his head. "Nothing, Your Majesty, though it's possible the channel remains impassible. The spring thaw is late this year."

Gathered within the council chamber of Keep Talbethé, Gwyn's officers and allied commanders sat around the table — including High Lords Celin'Laen and Bowrin, Crown Prince Fayett of Fraelin, and General Cadogan ren Silverard. Aluem had also come and stood near Gwyn at the table's head.

Gone was the Crow heraldry that had once adorned the chamber. In its place hung the Swan, Unicorn, and Crane banners, swaying in a faint breeze wafting from a window whose drapes had been tied aside to let in the fresh spring air.

"We can't wait any longer," said General Mershen. "Supplies are low, and the men are restless. Some have threatened to return to their homes, for all they've done since enlistment is 'cower in this den of filth' — their words, not my own."

"None would dispute them on the part of filth," quipped Remien down the table.

A few men grunted in agreement.

Gwyn pinned Mershen with a sharp look. "The weather's warmed, and the thaw can supply water in plenty. Let the men cleanse this den to liven their spirits and chase away disease if they feel so restless. But I do agree we can afford to wait no longer. Food in particular is my concern. The Crow King is content to let us rot in Talbethé if that is our wish. He'll make no open move against us. We must march to *him*."

"Sire, without the aid of Fraelin, we stand no chance," said Cluv.

"My country will answer," Fayett said, "but they cannot yet move. If we could but wait a week or two more—"

Cadogan stirred. "I'm afraid that's out of the question, Prince Fayett. As the Winter King said, food is scarce. Either the Winter Army marches now with what food remains to it, or we stay here to eat one another as the cannibals of the isles. Anyone who deserts now will be cut down the instant he returns to his village. The Crow King won't forgive a single soldier who has served King Gwynter. Not one."

"You would know," said Cluv with some heat.

"Aye," Cadogan said above a murmur of assenting voices. "I would know."

Gwyn slapped a hand against the table. "Gentlemen, if you would turn a sword against your allies, I would turn my sword against you. The traitor in our midst is only he who acts against our cause."

He swept his gaze over those at the table. No one stirred.

"Preparations for our march must begin at once," he continued. "We have three days. After that we'll move out. Not only do we need food, but if the Crow King continues to swell his ranks, we'll be cut as wheat beneath a sickle."

"Wasn't that already likely?" murmured Grene.

Gwyn fastened his gaze on the man. "Aye, that's true. But under Afallon's protection we stand a chance. Should we wait, I doubt we'll receive his blessing — for I suspect he isn't eager to bless cynical fools."

"Sire, what is our strategy once we reach Crowwell?" asked Remien. "Do we mean to besiege the city and pray for a miracle?"

Gwyn smiled faintly. "I wouldn't begrudge the prayer — but no, we aren't waiting on a miracle. I believe we must make our own miracle and let the rest follow. I've sent Towwen Stone on ahead at Cadogan's suggestion. Towwen is setting the stage for our arrival. A frontal strike is only a fragment of our plan. The Crow King expects an army, and so we'll supply one. We also need to weaken the number of our enemy, thus the army is crucial. The Crow King will anticipate magery, and we shall supply that too. But we also know the Crow King sacrifices lives to strengthen his own magic. We can't allow him to use our own men against us.

"Most of you understand the Weave on a fundamental level. It keeps the world vital. Keeps *us* vital. Priests call it the substance of divinity or the touch of Afallon. I'm inclined to believe them. If this is so, the Crow King's magic was once divine and is now corrupted. One might call its new form the substance of damnation. Quite literally. If the Weave in its natural state *feeds* the world, then the Crow King's magic in its tainted state *stoppers* the world. Cuts off the flow of magic. Kills whatever it caresses."

"Most of this we understand, at least a little," said Mershen. "Are you implying that we need to shore up the Crow King's magic somehow? Yet its nature is to stop things. How can we stop that which halts, already?"

"You misunderstand me," said Gwyn. "There's a reason the fae have fallen. There's a reason they can't rise again. These reasons are connected to the source of the Crow King's magic."

Those assembled exchanged mystified glances — except for the Ilidreth High Lords, along with General Cadogan and Aluem. During the long winter months, Gwyn had been learning all he could of the Weave from the Ilidreth and his unicorn. It was under their tutelage and in viewing the pool of memory that he now understood what he must try to do.

"The source?" asked Remien.

Gwyn nodded. "The Weave *flows*. It cannot stop itself. It can only be directed or redirected. However, something *else* might stop it. Not a mage, for we're subject to the Weave's flow as much as the Weave itself is. Not the Ilidreth, for they're born of the Weave and are its children, as are the unicorns. But the Crow King found a tool. Something to manipulate the Weave. To make it *stop*. Yet the Weave cannot stay stoppered, for it must run, always. Should he dam it up, all of it, it will eventually burst asunder. His purpose, gentlemen, is to destroy magic."

All fell silent. Gwyn studied each pale face, each pair of troubled eyes, each furrowed brow. The breeze picked up, dallying with the banners overhead.

"What tool did he find? Where could he discover it?" asked Remien.

"Ages ago," said Celin, in his rich, melodious voice, "High Prince Kovien left the lands of Ilid on a journey to find answers to his private fears. Somewhere across the sea he found a new, dark purpose and the tool to implement his purging of the world. Now we stand upon the brink of undoing. We must discover what he is using, though we do not understand how it is possible. We must *try*."

"But how?" asked Mershen. "Could the tool be some tangible object hidden within Crow Castle? Would the Crow King keep it in such an obvious place?"

Celin gracefully shrugged. "Where else would he keep it but near himself? Where else might it be better guarded?"

"What sort of object would it be? And how could you even approach it?"

Remien chimed in. "I'm still having trouble believing there could be a tangible tool of such power. How might it be forged? Where would he have found it upon the sea?"

"On that matter, I'll keep my peace for now," said Gwyn. "Suffice it to say, there's one means of forging such a tool, and there are stories of fell places where such things might be kept. Places better left unexplored, but which might truly yield such horrors as would drive even a noble fae to the blackest purpose." He glanced at Aluem, who nodded. They'd discussed long what they'd seen within the Vale's pool and determined not to reveal the source of the Crow King's strength, for what sane man would defy such overwhelming power?

"Even should you locate this vile tool, sire," said Grene, "how can you destroy something so dreadful? If it can dam the Weave itself..." He shook his head.

Gwyn sighed. "As to that, I have no answer yet. I can only pray when the time comes, I'll find a means to do it."

Cadogan's voice rolled along the table, a commanding rumble. "Enough questioning of your liege. He's given a command to prepare for your march. *That* is your aim. Are there any other relevant questions?"

Silence replied. Gwyn nodded. "Please go about your duties, gentlemen. Be sure our Heshi prisoners are comfortable. The Winter Army leaves this dread keep in three days."

❧

WIND TOSSED Gwyn's loose hair about his face. He prowled along the top of the keep wall. Beyond the keep, patches of snow dotted the earth, painted orange under the withering glow of dusk. On the morrow, Talbethé would be emptied of its army, and the march on Crowwell would begin.

He had spent the past two days looking over supplies, addressing his soldiers, planning with his officers for the weeks' long march and subsequent siege. His heart hung heavy. So many men would fall in battle against a foe who could easily wipe them from existence if he chose.

That thought still plagued Gwyn. Why didn't the Crow King end this now? Was he truly bound by his own limitations as Aluem had suspected?

Kive's voice drifted above Gwyn. "All the world's blood spreads across the snow."

Gwyn located the fae standing on a merlon farther along the battlements. "Kive, come here."

The fallen fae leapt across the merlons until he stood before Gwyn upon the stone edifice. "Yes, Shiny?"

"Why do you say that, Kive? What thoughts run through your head?"

"Rats, Shiny."

"What else? Kive, did the Crow tell you things? Did he ever mention what he intended to do to the world?" He leaned a hand against the merlon and gazed up into Kive's red eyes. "Do you remember the Crown, Kive?"

The fae's eyes widened and he flinched back. "Hush, Shiny. Shhh!"

Gwyn felt the familiar seizing of his will. His mouth sealed shut. He sighed through his nose and caught Kive's ankle to keep the fae from bolting away. Gwyn shook his head, and Kive slowly relaxed and crouched before him.

"Shiny, some things mustn't be spoken. The Crow wouldn't like it."

Gwyn held his gaze and waited.

Kive exhaled and nodded. "Very well, Shiny. You may speak."

His jaw unlocked. "Kive, tell me what the Crow said. If you don't try, I — and all the other animals — will likely die. Can't you help me, Kive? Can't you try to be brave for Shiny?"

For a long time Kive held still. Then he stirred, eyes wide and unfocused. "The Crow needs blood, Shiny. Always he needs blood. Always."

Understanding dawned as chill as midwinter. Gwyn shivered. "The Crown needs fuel. Wars feed it. Massacres feed it. He can't destroy magic without sacrificing life, any life, his people, his enemy, doesn't matter... He wants us to march on Crowwell. Death is his answer."

Kive shook his head. "Not all death, Shiny. Not old death. Not natural death. Only bad death. Young death. Sacrificial death."

Gwyn clenched his hands. Rage rumbled through his frame. "Like Lawen." His voice drifted out low and trembling. "He would dare to use the deaths of the innocent to break the Weave. By Afallon, I won't abide it. I must stop him."

He reached up and Kive leaned closer until Gwyn could rest his hand against the fae's cheek. "Help me, Kive, please. Do you know where the Crown is?"

Pain and fear lit in Kive's eyes, bright and deep. His frame shuddered beneath Gwyn's hand.

"Shiiiny," moaned Kive.

Gwyn smiled gently. "Kive. Tell me. Be brave."

"Always he keeps it near him." Kive gasped out the words, body shaking with the struggle. He bowed his head and let out a sob. "Oh, Shiny. Master will be furious."

"I won't let him harm you, Kive. Not any longer."

"Always he hurts me, even from afar. Shiny cannot change that. The Crow is my master."

"I know, Kive. I saw." Gwyn released the fae and stepped back. "Come with me. We must ride ahead of the army. We must face the Crow King alone."

Kive looked up. "We're going to my master?"

"Yes, Kive. One last time."

# Chapter Forty-Five

The past winter had been a trial for Nox, bound to the streets of Charquae, living off rations, uncertain of how the war waged beyond the gates. Each morning he climbed to the top of the city wall and visited Parsha who had taken up residence on the battlement heights.

This morning, in a light rainfall, he climbed the same steps, less winded than he'd been last autumn. That wasn't surprising, as he'd spent most of his days through the long winter honing his sword skills and climbing up and down this same flight of stairs. While Nox wasn't skinny, he had become more fit, and that rather satisfied him. His arduous work had paid off.

"Good morrow, my round friend," Parsha said, with a toothy grin. He perched cross-legged on a merlon, arms folded, wearing the guise of a human as he often did these days. He'd assured Nox that he endured wearing the form because it decreased his appetite.

While the granaries still held food, the winter had been brutal and spring planting would start late. Rations must continue. Parsha usually ate venison, but there was none to be had within Charquae, and he couldn't venture far outside and maintain his protective magic. Instead, he dined on barley and oats like most of the city. If he despised the fare, he said nothing.

"Do you see anything?" Nox leaned through a crenel to peek over the wall.

"There is movement in the east."

Nox perked up. "What sort?"

"The clouds of battle are gathering. The Winter King makes his move."

Nox blew out a breath, his heart dancing a jig. "It's finally coming to a head."

"It is time for us to leave Charquae," said Parsha. He unfolded his arms and rose to his bare feet. "Come, Nox. Climb onto my back and we shall start for Crowwell and the tyrant king."

"Now?" asked Nox, glancing toward the city below. "What of Charquae's protections?"

"The Crow King shall be too preoccupied with the Winter Army to heed this city at present. It will remain safe until this war is decided. Make haste. We must catch the Winter Army."

Nox clambered onto the crenel and then up onto the merlon beside his dragon friend. He caught Parsha's robe sleeve and waited.

Wings spread fluidly from Parsha's back first, and then he transformed. His face grew long and fanged, changing color as green and blue scales spread along his muzzle. His arms lengthened. His legs stretched. It took only seconds, while Nox clutched what became Parsha's foreleg.

Despite the transformation, Parsha wasn't his usual tremendous size — not yet. He was instead the size of a horse. Nox climbed onto his back and leaned forward, wrapping his hands in the dragon's silken mane.

"Ready?" asked the dragon in a rumbling voice.

"Ready."

The dragon beat his shimmering wings and lifted into the sky. As he pulled away from the city wall, his body lengthened and grew, until he became his normal, massive size, and Nox was but a tiny passenger upon his back.

Parsha headed southeast against the rain, but though the downpour grew worse, Nox remained warm against the dragon's heated scales.

## Chapter Forty-Six

Arianwen meant to escape. Each night she drew the diamond from the toe of her slipper, gazed into its prisms, and resolved to run away. But fear stayed her hand.

Even as she held the diamond close and felt its pulse, drinking in its savor, her dread of the Crow King clung stronger still.

What chance would she have to evade the king's far-reaching eye? Even with the diamond, Demréal was dead, fallen to the Fiend. And the young man who'd brought the gem to her — what good had it done for him? On command he too fell at the very feet of the king, courageous but dead.

Lying on her bed, fingering the diamond, Arianwen wondered if it might not be better to jump from the window and end her life. But that too was foolish, for the Fiend stayed ever watchful. He wouldn't let her die.

"Why?" she whispered, wishing the diamond could provide the answer. What did the Crow King desire of her if not her body? What fell purpose did he intend?

Always she asked. Always there was no answer.

She shut her eyes. Emotions swelled, closing her throat. She curled into herself, clutching the diamond close. Wishing to understand. Fearing to know. Her eyes burned with tears.

He'd said he meant to break her. It was working, little by little.

"My lady, do not grieve so."

She gasped and sat up, hair clinging to her face. Through her tears and tresses, she glimpsed a figure, strangely bright, standing before the bed.

She clawed aside her hair, then lifted her chin to banish all emotion from her face. "Who are you?"

The man took a step closer. Arianwen gasped. She could see *through* him to view the window.

"You're a spirit?" she whispered, heart lurching in her chest.

"I am." The man smiled and bowed his head. "Lawen ren Terare was my mortal name. I'm here to offer solace."

She shook her head. "But how...? I don't..." The diamond in her palm warmed. She glanced down and found it glowing.

The spirit spoke on. "My brother is the Winter King. Even now he rides toward Crowwell to challenge the Crow King. All will soon be decided."

"Why are you here? Why come to me?"

"You wished to understand why the Crow King keeps you close."

"And you know?"

He nodded. "You bear a strong resemblance to his mother, Queen Shalesta of Swan Castle. Once, long ago, he couldn't bring himself to destroy her. Now, in his madness, he believes you are she."

Chills crawled down Arianwen's limbs. "Impossible. He knows my name. He knows my family."

"But his madness knows you differently. The Crow King desires to destroy magic. He will sacrifice however many people to do it. But you he will protect."

"He said he wants to break me."

"Yes. He does. So that you will understand him."

She bit her lip and looked away. "What can I do?"

"Escape, Arianwen. Run from here and use the diamond to defend yourself against the Fiend."

"How can I? Not even Demréal could win while she had the diamond."

The spirit sighed. "She didn't use it. She intended it for *you*." He stepped sideways and motioned to the window behind him. "Go, Lady Arianwen. Have courage and take the leap."

She stared at the open portal. Dare she try? "He'll find me."

"He may. But if you don't try, the only certain thing is that he won't *need* to find you."

She pinned her eyes on the spirit. "Why do you aid me?"

He smiled. "You asked for help and the diamond in your hand provided such. Go, my lady, while daylight prevails."

She rose from the bed and moved toward the window. He stayed still as she passed him to gaze down on the castle grounds far, far below.

"Where will I go?"

"The Winter Army approaches from the north. It will shield you."

"They'll all die. The Crow King can't be stopped."

"Perhaps. In the end, the army may fail and fall. The Crow King might destroy magic and then enslave what remains of humanity. When magic dies, so too will dragons and unicorns. The fae will fade into madness and become as the Crow King himself: tyrants, or servants to such. Or perhaps the Winter King won't fail. Perhaps he'll cut down the mad king and raise a banner of hope, preserving life, honor, and faith. Can we know what will occur? Nay, my lady. We can but hope until the Winter King triumphs or crumbles in defeat. Mayhap your perspective is more realistic, but I much prefer my own."

"You're dead," said Arianwen. "What has this to do with you?"

His smile returned. "Everything. You think the dead are unaffected by the living? You think we don't watch and care and hope? I love my brother. I would do all within my strength to buoy him up in this trial. I would see him take on the Crow King and prevail or die trying. For what is life without liberty?"

She stared at him. His words resonated within her, moving her heart. Tears brimmed in her eyes, but she blinked them away. "Life without liberty is death." She turned to the window, caught the ledge, and sprang up to crouch upon it. "I will take the leap, Lawen ren Terare. Afallon willing, I'll survive to taste this hope of liberty."

"You will find the flavor divine."

She jumped, eyes squeezed shut, heart in her throat. As she clasped the diamond to her chest and sent a prayer to Afallon, wind screamed in her ears. Her fall slowed. She dared to open her eyes and found herself soaring upon the back of a dragon glowing as Lawen had glowed.

"Demréal!"

*'My lady, I have been waiting to guide you.'* The voice rushed through Arianwen's mind, sharp and piercing as a bell.

Arianwen leaned forward and buried her face in the dragon's ghostly mane. "My dear friend, how I've missed you."

# Chapter Forty-Seven

Aluem's hooves kicked up earth as he raced toward Crow Castle.

Gwyn's knuckles tingled, white and numb from gripping his mane, and tears streaked his cheeks from the chilly wind.

Toward midday Aluem slowed to a canter, and Gwyn pried his fingers free to work the blood back into them. He wiped his eyes with the back of an icy hand, then looked south. Behind him, Kive pulled back from clutching Gwyn's waist, unaffected by the speed or length of his ride.

"Are we near Gond?" asked Gwyn.

'*We have passed it. We are closer to the city of Kellion.*'

Gwyn nodded and brushed back his tangled hair. Something in the western sky gleamed, and he turned his head. "It's Parsha!"

Kive sniffed the air. "Ooh, Lizard."

Aluem pranced a few paces and let out a chiming bay. The dragon opened his great maw and issued a rumbling roar in reply.

Gwyn laughed. "Is that Nox upon his back? Good ol' Nox!" He lifted his hand high and waved. The distant human figure waved back.

The wind picked up and Gwyn had to snatch Aluem's mane to

keep astride. Kive flung himself to the ground. The dragon landed with a gust of wind and tucked his wings.

"Greetings, Your Majesty!" cried Nox before he slid down the sparkling scales of his companion and touched ground. He'd lost some weight this winter, though his girth remained considerable. His round face beamed as he approached Gwyn on foot.

Gwyn dismounted, crossed to his friend in a few lengthy strides, and seized his shoulders. "How are you?"

Kive crept forward, gaze darting between the dragon and his rider. He stared at Nox. "Are you...a pigeon?"

Nox blinked, then smiled. "Well, a pigeon is better than a whale, which he thought I was before. I'll gladly take a pigeon."

Gwyn laughed despite himself. "I apologize for my fae friend, Nox."

Nox grinned. "No need, sire. I'm fat and there's no disputing it. He's only honest." He glanced at Aluem. "What brings you so far ahead of your army, sire? They're leagues behind you."

"Aye, so they are. I've a matter to attend to in Crowwell before they arrive. It may bring things to a close without the need for further bloodshed, Afallon willing."

"Wouldn't that be a blessing? Heaven knows we've suffered enough losses."

Gwyn nodded soberly and glanced toward Parsha. "What brings you both from Charquae?"

Nox answered. "The city is well enough defended for now, says Parsha, with the Crow King's gaze pinned on you. We thought to come and offer what aid a giant dragon might supply."

"I expect that will prove to be a tremendous help. You're most heartily welcome."

Parsha rumbled, drawing the gaze of both men. His thunderous voice cracked through Gwyn's mind.

'*We've another visitor on the winds. The spirit of Demréal wings toward us, bearing a human passenger.*'

Gwyn frowned. "Demréal?" He glanced at Nox, whose face had fallen.

"She was a magnificent dragon, sire. She fell midwinter to the Crow King, so Parsha said as he felt her passing."

Gwyn glanced in the direction the dragon's eyes were trained upon, south toward Crowwell. "Her spirit flies toward us now?"

A south wind welled up, forcing Gwyn a step backward. Something rippled in the sky, silver on blue, perhaps in the faint shape of a great winged beast. It flew past, but something plunged from its back as it swept low.

A woman landed lightly upon the ground, gowned in white, framed with raven hair that fell in soft curls nearly to her knees.

She stood quietly for a heartbeat or two. "Are you the Winter King?"

Gwyn hesitated. "I am."

She fell to her knees, gown settling around her. "I beg of you, Great Lord, grant me sanctuary."

"You run from the Crow King." It wasn't really a question. The earnest desperation of her tone left little doubt. "Are you the lady Arianwen, for whom many men have ardently sought?"

She lifted her head, eyes bright like ice in the sunlight. "I am, Majesty."

He smiled. "Be comforted, my lady, knowing that my heart is caught by another maiden as fair as yourself, though she's beautiful as a summer day, rather than a winter sky. I'll not hold you against your will for that or any other reason. I swear it upon my brother's grave. I gladly grant you sanctuary from the fell king. Nox here shall take you to my army, and the lady Nathaera will keep you safe."

She searched his face, then smiled faintly. "So, you are he who inspires such bravery as I've seen. I met one of your men, sire. A brave lad named Nathael."

Gwyn's smile grew. "Indeed? How does my friend fare?"

"I would know as well," said Nox, stepping forward. "He — he's my brother."

Her smile died. "Then I'm the bearer of ill news. He fell before the Crow King, but not without defying him. He never cowered in the face of death and died a hero for his king."

Nox gave a cry and Gwyn's chest squeezed.

The Winter King bowed his head. "Another brave soul, and one I sent alone to spy. I've killed your brother, Nox. Forgive me."

Nox's pain pulsed across the Weave in aching waves. He shook his head, eyes staring at the ground. "Nay, sire. The Crow King killed him, as he would kill us all. We *must* stop him."

Gwyn's heart clenched tighter as a familiar rage flooded his core. "He shall be, Nox. And he shall pay for every soul he's claimed. Every last one." He whirled to Parsha. "Take the lady and Nox to the Winter Army, please. Stay near them, and protect them however you can, should the Crow King make a move before they've reached Crowwell. I must ride on."

Parsha nodded his magnificent head.

Gwyn sprang onto Aluem's back. "Come, Kive."

Kive mounted behind him. "Is Shiny angry?"

Gwyn's eyes narrowed on the southern horizon. "Yes, Kive. Shiny is *angry*."

Aluem bounded forward, covering ground at such speed Gwyn could see nothing more than blurs of color all around him. He let himself seethe. Let his emotions roil and froth within. The Crow King must pay. He must be defeated, but not before he understood his crimes, understood their weight, knew why Simaerin stood against him.

To do that, the people must rise up and oppose their king.

# Chapter Forty-Eight

Towwen Stone had covered every inch of Crowwell over the past four days. He could only hope he'd missed nothing as he prepared to send a message to every soul within the capital city. If he had, the entire spell would fail.

Scrawling wasn't difficult magic. Scrawling on a large scale, however, was tantamount to a mage healer knitting someone's shattered bones back together. It required precision and power, both of which Towwen had — but Crowwell was a large city, and his message was crucial. His efforts had built a headache behind his eyes.

He sat now within the walls of Quee'avv Cathedral, tucked away inside a study apart from the acolytes in the lower hallways. Rindermarr Lorric, recently freed following a long stint in Crow Castle's dungeons, sat in the winged chair opposite Towwen's own plush seat.

"The tides are turning," Rindermarr said, staring into the flames glutting on giant logs within the ornate fireplace. "It won't be long before the church loses its weight at court. The people are scared, and the Crow King appears to be the one with actual power. Even releasing me was meant as a show of his beneficence."

"Incredible," murmured Towwen.

"You should hear the stories about the Winter King. He's practically a goblin these days."

Towwen frowned at the flames. "I've heard. If only Simaerin could meet a real goblin to learn the difference."

Rindermarr paused. "Have you?"

"Have I what?"

"Met a real goblin?"

Towwen met the priest's gaze and chuckled. "No, but I've little doubt they exist. Why not? Unicorns do. The Ilidreth do. Perhaps the Crow King himself has become a goblin. He devours enough life."

Rindermarr grunted. "So, when does your message..." he swiveled his wrist "*...hatch?*"

"Dawn. I must walk the streets one last time tonight to be certain. If I've missed a single etching, the message will die upon my fingertips and all my work will be for naught."

"Will *I* read it?"

Towwen nodded. "You won't have a choice. Everyone within Crowwell, even at Crow Castle, will receive the message and comprehend its meaning and understand its intent, like it or otherwise. I only pray it works. There's no time."

"The army's not here yet."

"It will be, and soon. King Gwynter was growing more impatient with each passing hour. Whether or not the Fraeli come to our aid, he'll march. He doesn't have a choice. He's running out of supplies."

Rindermarr started to reply, but a cry — high and piercing — broke across the chamber. Deafening. All-encompassing. Otherworldly.

Towwen's blood froze. His eyes met the priest's. "What in the name of Afallon and all his holy legions was that?"

Rindermarr shuddered. "The Fiend."

# Chapter Forty-Nine

"Enough of your tantrum. *You* let her escape."

Kovien's voice hummed low. He stood at the window within Arianwen's vacant chamber, gazing at the black unicorn standing in the sky.

The Fiend tossed his head, pawed the air, and snorted.

"Don't lose your temper with me. You were meant to guard her, not I." Kovien's hand rested on the windowsill, and his fingers curled into fists. Black flames raced through his frame. "Find her, Fiend. Find and bring her back. Out there she'll be wounded. She may die. If she does, you are to blame. She will try to reach the Winter King. You mustn't let her. He must not have her."

Kovien gasped as cold grief doused his flames, killing them. "He is trying to take everything from me, Fiend. We cannot let him."

The Crow King uncurled his hand and reached out the window. The Fiend dipped his head and let Kovien stroke his mane. His fingers climbed the unicorn's horn to rest one fingertip against the sharp tip until he drew blood.

"If she won't come, if you cannot save her, destroy her."

The Fiend's eyes caught fire. He let out a cry of indignation.

"Then see that she comes, and there will be no need to end her life. Go. Search well. Return swiftly."

The Fiend tossed his head again and danced away across the air on hooves wreathed in black flames. Against the clouds, the black unicorn shifted and broke apart, becoming of murder of crows. The birds flew in different directions to scour the world.

Kovien dropped his head. "Hurry back to me."

He choked down a whimper. He couldn't turn around. *They* were there; he could feel them. All his ghosts gazed at his back, boring holes into his soul. Accusing. Hateful.

"Stop it, stop it," he hissed. "I've been chosen. I must heed the voice."

The eyes looked on, burning into his flesh.

"STOP!" he screamed as he whirled to face the chamber.

Nothing was there.

# Chapter Fifty

Dawn sounded with the ringing of cathedral bells.

Towwen stood at the center of Crowwell, in a market square where merchants set up their wares for the coming crowds. His fingers itched to unleash his Scrawl. Perspiration pricked his brow. He waited. Waited.

At last, the bells fell still, though his ears rang with their echo.

"Sweet Afallon above," he murmured, "let the Winter King's message resound with truth in every heart."

He lifted his right hand, summoned the Weave, and let his pointer finger blaze with sparks of fire from his soul, gold as daylight.

The merchants stared. No one moved to stop him.

Towwen penned a single word:

*Liberty.*

The keyword ignited the spell, and all within Crowwell heard and felt and saw the Winter King's decree. It burned within each man, woman, and child. Even sleeping infants were infused with the meaning, for so Towwen Stone had Scrawled.

*'Hear ye the words of Gwynter ren Wintervale:*

*'Let he who values Freedom rise now to defend it. We the People of Simaerin cannot and shall no longer abide the tyranny of a Sovereign King whose hand does nothing but defile life and justice for his own Gain and Glory. The Crow King has murdered mere children to keep them from the use of magery, yet he himself commands an army of Mages in order to oppress this people and to scourge other lands.*

*'He lies and calls himself Simaeri, but his blood is of Fraelin and of the Ilidreth — yes, the very people he slaughters and decries. What proof is there of this accusation? None, save the Crow King's own actions and the source of his magic — the very same magic he has long outlawed in order to control any and all who may oppose his reign. His defamations against his own kingdom must speak for themselves.*

*Look! Look well, Simaerin, and See Truth, for evil cannot long be hid. Ages ago, the Crow King stole the Throne of Simaerin from the Kings of Wintervale. He declared them tyrants — yet what deeds more vile can a tyrant do than what the Crow King has done? Endless war, needless death, poverty, and inequality of classes haunt his reign.*

*'How much longer can Simaerin abide such abominations? How much longer will we endure his abuses?*

*'I say no more! It is our duty and our right to oppose such tyranny. Rise up now, take what weapons there may be at hand, and make a stand.*

*For our families, our homes, and our lands, fight!'*

As the words faded from Towwen's mind, he raised his hand again and stabbed the air with his Woven finger, again writing *Liberty*.

Again, the message blazed across the Weave to infuse every inhabitant of Crowwell. Sweat poured down his face and neck. He shook with the effort, but as the message died, he Scrawled the keyword to send the message once more.

As the words rang a third time within Towwen's frame, a

smooth, soft voice like velvet broke across the air to speak over King Gwynter's message.

The voice enveloped Towwen, safe and warm as a hearth fire in midwinter, yet tinged with coiling madness:

"Ah, Gwynter. Is this your design? Would you turn our people into rebels and traitors? Would you encourage the shedding of blood upon the soil of your beloved country? Is this the justice of Wintervale?

"My dear people, heed not the impulsive nudging of a stray youth hungry for power. For his sake as well, stay your hand. This is not war, but a mere skirmish which shall soon end. Let those of greatest courage lift their swords to defend you against the heir of Wintervale and the poor simple fools who follow his banner. Unless controlled, mages shall oppress this land. They cannot be left free.

"Which do you choose, my people? Freedom to die, or security to live? *What I do, I do for the world.*"

The voice died away and Towwen slumped to his knees, gasping. He'd used a great deal of magic to send his message thrice, but that was nothing to the nauseating feeling in his stomach on the heels of the Crow King's words.

Where once the king had seemed calm and even gentle, now, despite his silken tones, his words fell upon Towwen like a poison.

He smiled to himself. In the Crow King's fear, he'd done what Gwynter's words alone couldn't. Under such contrasting influences — a message filled with earnestness and hope, and a message gripped with fear, illness, and mockery — who would the people more eagerly follow?

"Arrest him!"

Towwen looked up. A handful of soldiers charged him, swords drawn.

Rindermarr Lorric slid to a halt beside him, yanked him to his feet, and pulled him away from the square.

Towwen staggered after him, vision swimming. "Leave me, priest. I'm too tired to run."

"Hush, Scrawler. Brioc Ffyr would never forgive me if I let you burn at the stake." He shoved Towwen into an alleyway and pushed him hard against the side of a leaning building. The wall gave way, and both men tumbled inside. The secret compartment was little more than a cramped and dank nook, but it hid the two as they listened to the slapping feet of soldiers rushing on down the street.

Rindermarr smiled at Towwen's questioning face.

"Smuggling nooks, Towwen Stone. They're all over the city. This is how we've been rescuing mage children."

# Chapter Fifty-One

The door to Kovien's private chamber burst open.

"Majesty, *where* is Arianwen?"

Kovien stopped pacing and glanced behind him at Bened Arnnor. "You are very free with my door, Sir Knight. Where is your reverence?"

Bened stood firm, arms planted at his sides, eyes dark and furious. "Where is she, sire?"

"Gone, Bened. Gone. Fled. The Fiend seeks her."

The knight's eyes widened. "Fled? How?"

"You recall the boy who broke into her room? The one sent by the dragon Demréal? Likely he brought a means of escape with him. I had suspected it at first, but she made no move for so long..." Kovien sighed and rested his fingers against his forehead. "It matters not. The Fiend shall find her or he won't. Gwynter is on his way here. He rides ever nearer on the back of Aluem."

"So, the boy king lived? Does he think to claim Arianwen for himself?" Bened gritted his teeth. "He shan't have her."

"No," snapped Kovien. "He shan't. Nor shall you, Sir Knight, nor any other human creature. You think to claim such a being for yourself? To cage such beauty? You think yourself equal? Ha!" He threw his head back and laughed. "Fool! Fool! Human fool!"

He whirled toward Bened and flung his hand before him. "Begone from my sight, filth. Any who defy me — any at all — shall meet such an end as you cannot fathom!"

Bened crashed to his knees. "Forgive me, sire. My king!" He dove forward to prostrate himself against the floor. "I would never defy you."

"Silence." Kovien stepped forward and kicked Bened's head with his boot. The knight grunted but remained still. "That is better, much better. Another moment of defiance, a single flash of rebellion, Sir Knight, and your life shall be forfeit. Not your soul, mind you. That remains mine forever. Do not forget it. You are *mine*."

"Yes, my king."

"I said silence."

Bened hardly breathed.

Kovien stooped and caught Bened's hair to tilt his head up until their gazes met. "Gwynter does not *want* your maiden fair. He has one already. A pretty creature you've met before, I believe. Lady Nathaera? Yes. She. Go, Bened Arnnor, and slay that pretty creature. Bring her head to me, so I may present Gwynter with a last gift before his execution. Hurry!"

He released Bened's head so fast, the knight's face slammed against the floor, but he made no sound. He climbed to his feet, nose bleeding. Bowed low, and retreated.

The door snicked shut.

Kovien moaned. "Oh, Gwynter. You know not the struggles of a king, or you would not be so eager to play this thankless role."

# Chapter Fifty-Two

Kellion lay in ruins.

The outer wall had been reduced to shattered stone and charred wood. The buildings within hunched, smoke-scarred and broken. Half the city had been obliterated, save for a dark mark against the earth — and bones, countless bones, littering the ground.

Aluem wouldn't approach the city's remains. Gwyn dismounted and picked his way over the crumbled wall to survey the dread work. Kive followed, somber and silent.

Gwyn clutched his sword, a sound like drums pounding through his ears. "Is this the Crow King's idea of justice? The massacre of any who would view the world differently than he?"

Aluem's voice drifted from afar off. '*This is the work of a black unicorn, Gwynter. The Fiend did this.*'

"Nay," said Gwynter in a low whisper. "This is the work of a coward." He sought the southern horizon. "A coward!"

A breeze caught his hair and pulled, and cold laughter laced the wind. Kive moaned.

Dropping his eyes, Gwyn found the skeleton of a child near his feet. Kneeling, he inhaled to hold back his emotions. "Why must he destroy children?" He stretched out a hand but couldn't bring himself to touch the grinning skull.

Rising, he again surveyed the site of Kellion. A city, one of few, who had openly opposed the Crow King. One of those loyal to Gwynter.

"I'm sorry," he whispered. "I hear your cries from the earth. You will be avenged."

He climbed back over the rubble and crossed the sweeping grass to Aluem's side, near a tall oak tree. Kive haunted his steps like a shadow, head bowed.

Aluem met Gwyn's gaze.

"I had to see."

'*I know.*'

Gwyn and Kive mounted and rode around the husk of Kellion to race on toward Crowwell. Gwyn's mind flickered with memories of what he'd just seen. He'd ridden through that thriving city several times while he'd served in the Crow King's army. It had teemed with life, with color and music, laughter, scents, and tastes.

He leaned forward to rest his head against Aluem's neck and squeezed his eyes shut. Kive's fingers clutched his shirt behind him.

"How can we recover from such horrors, Aluem?" he whispered.

'*We persevere.*'

Gwyn nodded, but his heart twisted. "What voice calls Kovien to commit such sins? Does Hell demand such numbers all at once?"

'*It does not matter what voice your enemy heeds, Gwynter. What matters is which voice* you *heed. That is all that you must know.*'

Gwyn opened his eyes to watch the world flying by. "How much farther?"

'*We shall reach Crowwell on the morrow. Rest, Gwyn, if you can. Do not tap your magic. Find harmony in the Weave and pray to your Afallon. Whatever strength may be had, you must seek.*'

He shut his eyes again and delved into himself. His center. His magic. The Weave was there, always: a humming song of life and nature. But now, it was frayed at the edges. Not within him, but without. The Weave of the world perished bit by bit under the

Crow King's ceaseless onslaught. Every death counted as a blow against its armor, chinking and cracking here or there.

*I won't let it end like this. Please, Afallon, aid me.*

THE GATES of Crowwell loomed against the predawn gloom.

Aluem halted several hundred yards before them, panting, trembling from his strain. '*The Weave has lost much of its succor. I am spent.*'

Gwyn stroked Aluem's neck. "Rest, my friend." He slid from the unicorn's back and leaned against the tree trunk which hid them from the city watch. "We must both get some sleep before we enter that place."

Kive slithered from Aluem's back and collapsed to his knees. "Shiny, we mustn't. Mustn't go on. The Crow is waiting. He is angry."

Gwyn knelt beside Kive and rested a hand on his shoulder. "Hush, my friend. You know I'll do what must be done, no matter the danger. I am resolved."

Kive moaned and bowed his head. "Shiny is stubborn."

"Yes, Kive. Shiny is very stubborn. Please stay with me. Don't run now. We will face the Crow together."

Kive folded into himself, burying his face in his knees. "If Shiny says so."

Aluem lowered himself to the ground and tucked his hind legs beneath him. Gwyn caressed the unicorn's back, then leaned against him, feeling the rise and fall of the unicorn's chest.

'*Gwynter, how do you intend to destroy the Crown of the Blighted? It is beyond your power to accomplish. It killed even your god.*'

Gwyn studied the swaying branches above him. "Afallon died to transcend mortality. He let Himself die, Aluem. Even so, I know the Crown is powerful, far more than I. Perhaps I can't destroy it. That isn't my goal. I intend to kill Kovien."

'*How? He wields the Crown.*'

Gwyn shrugged. "I don't know yet. I only know I must try."

'*Then why ride ahead of your army? To spare them? What if you should fail?*'

"Then another will try in my stead. Perhaps Celin or Cadogan. Perhaps Towwen Stone, or Adesta Gilhan, or valiant Nox. Maybe the Fraeli armada will arrive and Fayett will cut the Crow down. I don't know."

'*You are a brave man, Gwynter.*'

Gwyn lowered his eyes and stared at the ground. Terror surged through his blood, yet anger ran with it, and he could only hope that would make some difference. Survival seemed unlikely, for though the Crow King couldn't kill him directly, there were other ways to inflict death. He'd come so close to dying before. He reflected on the blue gem he'd found so long ago in Swan Castle, twice used to spare a life.

It had one use left.

"Aluem, where has Queen Shalesta's gem gone, do you suppose? I confess it would be a comfort to have when I face the Crow King."

'*It is very near, Gwynter. Ask Kive.*'

Gwyn blinked and glanced toward the fae who rocked back and forth, murmuring fragments of poetry he'd learned from Nathaera.

"Kive?"

The fae glanced up through his matted black tresses. "Yes, Shiny?"

"Do you have the blue gem that belonged to your mother?"

Kive stared at Gwyn, held his gaze, red depths unreadable. He looked away, unanswering.

Gwyn rested his head back and returned to his scrutiny of the branches. "I can't fathom how it's all come to this, though I've lived through it. Once, I journeyed to Swan Castle to save my brother's life. Somehow that single action set me on this path. I've lost the very soul I wished to save, yet I can't call this course a waste. It's so vastly important. But I can hardly believe myself to be a part of it or why. Surely there's someone better equipped."

'*Men are not chosen to accomplish great tasks based upon their skills,*

*Gwynter. They are chosen for their hearts. Perhaps there are some who would better plan against the Crow King — but would they endure all that you have, and continue to try? Perhaps not. It does not matter.* You *are here. You are fighting.*'

"I wish I'd used the blue gem to save Lawen again."

'*It might not have worked twice upon the same soul, Gwynter.*'

"I would still liked to have tried."

Silence wrapped around Gwyn and his companions as the sun appeared on the eastern horizon. Soon he heard Aluem's deep breathing. Kive continued to murmur poems, altered to include rats and Shinies. Gwyn smiled as he pictured Nathaera's exasperation if she were here.

He missed her. They'd shared a tender kiss before he'd departed, and though she'd wanted to go with him, he'd made her promise to stay behind with the army. To let Adesta protect her. For once she'd agreed, perhaps sensing he needed to face Kovien alone.

"Take Kive," she'd insisted. "Let him protect you."

"He's the one who needs protecting."

"Then he needs to see you take the Crow King down. To be freed from his trauma. Take him. He's meant to be with you."

Gwyn had already resolved to do so, though he harbored doubts. He wanted Kive to be healed. To shake off the shackles of his mind and stand tall and kingly as he was born to do.

But what if the Crow King's hold on him remained too great? What if in the end Kive was the one who cut Gwyn down? He wasn't certain that was possible. He didn't understand quite how the protective spell on the line of Wintervale worked.

"Kive?"

The fae didn't look at him. "Yes, Shiny?"

"If the Crow King told you to kill me, would you?"

Kive dragged his eyes from the ground. They were wide and clouded. "Shiny?"

"If he commanded you, would you kill Shiny?"

Kive shuddered. "No, Shiny. I cannot kill Shiny. Not Shiny."

"Are you certain?"

The fae faltered. "No, Shiny. Kive isn't certain."

Gwyn nodded. "Thank you for being honest, Kive. I don't intend to let you hurt me, so don't fret."

Kive moaned and turned his head away.

Golden streams of sunlight painted the budding leaves above like delicate filigree. Gwyn smiled again. "A new day dawns. Kive, please stay close by. I must sleep for a few hours at least."

"I will stay, Shiny. There is nowhere else to go."

Gwyn closed his eyes and fell straight away into dreams of golden fields and blue skies. Lawen stood before him, beckoning.

# Chapter Fifty-Three

Kovien summoned the Fiend to him.

Reluctantly, the unicorn obeyed, appearing within the empty throne room where the Crow King stood before his throne, his ebony crown clutched in his hands.

"Bened Arnnor has gone to meet the Winter Army, and claim the head of Gwynter's fair maiden. Likely, that is where Arianwen hides. He will find and return her to Crowwell. You and I must ride out to meet Gwynter in combat. He waits outside the city walls."

The Fiend pawed the floor.

Kovien turned to face the unicorn, expression cold. "Do not challenge me, O fallen one. You are *mine*." He heaved a sigh. "Of late, everyone wishes to challenge me. I grow weary of rebuking those who should be faithful." He raised his arms and rested the crown upon his head. "Young Gwynter thinks he stands a chance against me. Even with Aluem as his ally, we are stronger. It is time to crush this hindrance to my plans."

The Fiend nickered.

Kovien's eyes narrowed. "There are things far worse than death, or have you forgotten that? My crown will show him the truth of the world, and we shall see what becomes of his mind then. Come. We ride."

He strode across the stone floor and sprang onto the Fiend's back. "It has been an age since last we took to the field. My hands tremble with anticipation. Have I longed for such an engagement all this time?" He laughed to himself. "Gwynter's rebellion is almost welcome. It has quickened my goals, hasn't it? It seems we are indebted to him. We must pay what is due."

He nudged the Fiend on, and they trotted from the throne room, out into the corridor. Servants and courtiers shrank from the dread pair. Kovien spared them no glance.

The Fiend carried Kovien from the castle proper, down the drawbridge, and across the bailey. The castle gates opened and together they stepped into Crowwell. High noon had sent most citizens inside, for the southern clime had turned hot already.

Unattended by the Order of Corvus, he paraded through Crowwell, smiling as he imagined Traycen's disapproving expression. Too bad the man had died again.

*Why defend against the rabble? I've nothing to fear from these cowed humans.*

A swarm of peasants appeared in the street ahead.

"Go no further," boomed a voice from among them.

Kovien arched an eyebrow. "Hail, peasant swine. Do you dare defy your king?"

"Aye," answered the same booming voice. A burly man of middle years and balding pate shoved his way to the fore.

Kovien smiled at him. "Let me by, and I shall forgive your treason. Do otherwise, and my friend shall skewer you each in turn."

"We know we may likely die," answered the balding man, "but too long already we've cowered before a tyrant, and we would rather die standing tall than bent under the whip of slavery."

Kovien cocked his head. "Are you not free men? I see no mark of slavery."

"There's no mark, yet you treat us like cattle to be herded at your whim."

The king sighed. "I have no time for this. Time presses me. Stand aside, or I shall separate you from your legs."

The man widened his stance. "You killed my daughter. Called her a mage and executed her for heresy."

"Ah, so that is your grievance." Kovien nodded. "Magic cannot be allowed to run rampant. I have already explained this to you."

"Yet you and those you deem worthy are allowed to wield it."

"Yes. Those *trained* to handle its burden. Those chosen to protect Simaerin from invaders and traitors alike."

"The Winter King would've let her live."

Kovien smiled. "Indeed, he would. And then, when the streets were overrun with untrained, undisciplined mages, all fighting for power? When your daughter was murdered by one of those, or if she killed others because she could?"

"I'll never know if that was possible," replied the man. "You killed her when she was only an infant."

Kovien sighed. "This grows wearisome. Stand aside."

"Nay. We won't."

Peasants slipped from shadows and doorways to join those already assembled. The number reached two hundred, perhaps more. It was almost impressive.

"Fools," Kovien murmured and lifted his hand.

A flash of light leeched color from the world around him. The crown answered his call. When the light retreated and color returned, the street bled. All in his way lay in heaps upon the ground.

"I warned you."

He rode on, tracking blood far past the site of death. No one else came forth to challenge his rule.

Soon he reached the city gates, which creaked open to let him leave. He rode out of Crowwell. The road before him wended on, open and empty.

"Hail, Winter King!" he called. "I have come to meet you in combat mortal. Will you not ride forth to greet your adversary?"

He searched the rolling hills. Wind brushed its fingers through the treetops lining either side of the highway. The scent of blossoms wafted up from a nearby orchard.

The Crow King waited.

Minutes crawled by before movement appeared ahead of Kovien.

He smiled.

A single rider approached upon the back of a white unicorn. Kovien nudged the Fiend forward to meet his enemy.

Gwynter had changed since last they met. He sat taller, broader of shoulder, a man now rather than a boy. His gray eyes shone sharp and hard. He held himself like a king, straight and proud.

"Ah, Gwynter. No wonder there are some who follow you. What a sight you are to behold! Even in tatters, you look a king."

Gwynter considered him, lightning storming in his eyes.

"Have you nothing to say?" asked Kovien, tilting his head.

"Kovien Crow-King, you've murdered and desecrated Simaerin for too long. Bend the knee to your rightful ruler or I will cut you down."

Kovien laughed. "You claim to be my king, Gwynter ren Wintervale?"

"Nay," said Gwynter. "Your younger brother, Kive of the Ilid, is chosen by his people to rule."

"*Chosen*? Do the people now choose their king? Ha! Is this your plan for your own fate, Gwynter? Let the people decide? The weak, foolish, blind masses? So fickle in their feeling, so flimsy in their judgment? I am the king of Ilid, just as I am the king of Simaerin. As I shall be the king of Fraelin, and Hesh-Kasal, and all the isles of the sea, and what may lie beyond them! But first I shall slay you."

Gwynter lifted his hands to hold them out at his sides. "Slay me, Kovien. Pierce me through."

Kovien froze. "You mean not to fight?"

"You can't kill me. This we both know. So, take me into Crowwell. Present me to the people and try to burn me at the stake. Make an example of me if you can. I won't die, Kovien." The storm in his eyes blazed.

The Fiend took a step back. Kovien glowered. "You think to influence the people of Crowwell with your invincibility. Nay, Gwynter. Bring your army. Besiege Crowwell. Try to defeat me that way. I shall not fall into your trap."

Gwynter didn't blink. "You already have, Kovien." He lifted his hand and pointed it at Kovien's head. "I know your power. I know your secret. I know how to break it."

"Impossible. You're lying."

"I've seen you upon the isles of the sea. I've seen the altar upon which the Crown of the Blighted lay until you seized it in your hands and were consumed by its will. Alone, you stood upon the mount and declared the world yours. You seek to purge all magic from it. But I saw even more than that, Kovien. I saw your end. I saw you fail. I've seen my victory, and you can't stop me. You can't stop the Weave. You've lost."

Trembling before this creature of light, Kovien shook his head. "Lies. Lies! You cannot win. The voice has chosen me!"

"The voice laughs at you, Kovien. It's abandoned you."

Kovien threw his hands over his face. "Liar. Liar!"

"The world *will* burn, Kovien — but not with death and tyranny. It will burn with liberty and faith, bright and unquenchable. You've lost, Crow King. Your reign ends this day."

"No!" Kovien drew his sword. "I have not steeped Ilid and Simaerin in blood only to fail now." He urged the Fiend to charge forward, blade gleaming in the noon sun. Wrath filled his soul, writhing and torrential.

Gwynter raised his sword and blocked Kovien's blow. Aluem danced sideways. The unicorns backed up, then charged at the same moment.

Swords clashed. Kovien gritted his teeth. Gwynter was stronger. His mount pressed his advantage, forcing Kovien back.

With a cry, Kovien withdrew his sword and snatched a dagger from a second sheath with his free hand. He hurled it at Gwynter even as the young king brought his blade down to deflect it. The dagger struck metal and bounced away.

"In physical strength, I'm superior," said Gwynter. "Surrender, Kovien. Stand down and let Simaerin alone."

"And what becomes of me?"

"You will be executed for your crimes."

Kovien barked a laugh. "I will not bend to a human child to face my own destruction."

Gwynter's eyes narrowed. He nudged Aluem forward. The white unicorn lowered his head, horn pointed toward the Fiend.

Kovien lifted a hand and conjured wind, forcing Aluem off course. "You cannot die, and I cannot best you in combat, but I am the Crow King! I am chosen to win."

"How, Kovien?" asked Gwynter.

He clenched his jaw. *Let the frustration die. He is goading you to blind you. Think, Kovien. He does not have the power here.*

He smiled softly. "Simaerin is my hostage, Gwynter. Defy me if you must, but know that our people will suffer for it."

Gwynter's expression remained impassive. "If I do nothing, you'll still kill them all. I'd rather offer them a chance for escape. I must defy you. You must be stopped at any cost."

"Any?" whispered Kovien. "What of your lovely maiden? What of her fate? If that is the cost?"

"Kill her," said Gwynter calmly. "But know that I can resurrect her again, as I was once revived by your mother."

Kovien's smile slipped. "Liar. You couldn't resurrect your brother. You've lost the stone or used it up already."

"Nay, Kovien. Lawen had already been healed by the stone. I couldn't use it twice upon the same soul. But Nathaera I *can* save."

"Then I shall kill her twice."

"You won't." Gwynter sounded so certain.

Kovien scowled. "You have forgotten in all of this the most crucial point: The Crown of the Blighted is mine. How can you stop me? How can you win?"

"I told you already, I know your secret, your weakness." He leaned forward. "*You*, Kovien. All the magic of that crown will avail you nothing, because you're too weak to use its full power."

Kovien stared. His blood ran thick and hot. "You think so? You think my stores are depleted, do you? My time wasted? You think I have been idle?"

"No, Kovien. I think if you use all the magic you've stored within that crown through all your blood sacrifices, the crown will consume you. Does its source care who lives or dies? Does its source want magic destroyed when it's so useful to inflict pain and suffering on others?

"Nay, Kovien. That crown wants only one thing — a thing it's been grooming for ages now. *You*."

# Chapter Fifty-Four

On his own, Bened had little power. But the Crow King had granted him more, and with the paltry cost of several souls Bened traveled in a mere blink to the armory of Andonn, the garrison nearest to the Winter Army's camp.

Once at Andonn, he mustered a force of thirty five hundred cavalry. It should be enough against the rabble. The garrison captains were glad to act.

"We've been nervous since we spotted the Swan banner along the highway," said one captain. "Ilidreth aren't creatures you let pass you by. Bad luck, they say. Best to kill them before they can curse you."

Bened said nothing to correct him. If superstitions encouraged the men to march upon the enemy, all the better to feed such nonsense.

It had taken most of the night to ready the horses and gather accoutrements. Thankfully, the Crow King had poured most of Simaerin's wealth into outfitting his men and outposts, and not one man at Andonn rode without full armor, sword, and shield.

Bened beheld the orderly rows of horsemen below from the garrison walls. *This* was an army. This was power. Gwynter's hodgepodge force, made up of farmers, runaway slaves, and the savage Ilidreth, couldn't compare with this awesome sight.

The Winter Army would flee from true warriors before the new day died.

Bened drew a breath, then spoke, straining his voice to let it ring across the bailey. "At dawn we march upon the treasonous swine who dare to defy our noble king! Let none be afraid. We're superior in might and experience. Embolden yourselves and know that you serve the cause of right. We cannot let Simaerin be overrun with malcontents and heretics. We must purge our land of wild mages and Ilidreth savages. Ride with me and cut down the enemy. The blessing of Afallon rides with us. The rightful king of Simaerin shall never fall. Long live the Crow King!"

Cheers rose from the mounted men, and echoing cries for the king's health followed in discordant chants. Bened let the thrill of their enthusiasm course through him as adrenaline galloped through his veins. He smiled to himself.

While the Crow King hadn't told him to bring an army, this was the surest way to victory. Nathaera would be well shielded, especially by her man-eating fae. Bened wouldn't risk his life alone in the enemy camp a second time. He'd ride over the Winter Army and cut them down to the last man. Afterward, the Crow King would see his wisdom, his cunning, his strength — and Bened Arnnor would make Arianwen his bride, or no man would have her. Not even the Crow King.

Bened hustled down the steps with as much grace as impatience afforded. He pulled himself into the saddle of his borrowed steed, drew his broadsword, and cantered to the gates.

With a curt swing of his sword, he cried: "To battle!"

His army followed in unison — the perfect war machine to slaughter peasants.

THE ENEMY MARCHED along the plains, smaller than last Bened had seen. Unsurprising after a long merciless winter within the forsaken Keep Talbethé. Gwynter had been a fool to remain there after Bened's betrayal. But then, Gwynter was a foolish boy in every sense — far too reckless to long survive.

What had possessed the boy to ride alone ahead of his forces to meet the Crow King? Gwynter ren Terare might well be mad.

Bened Arnnor shook his head. What did it matter? Soon, the Winter Army would fall. This way the Crow King could cut the usurper down and obtain satisfaction even as Bened plowed through the rebel force. By tomorrow, Simaerin could lay this entire affair to rest.

Crouching upon the greening knoll, Bened watched the marching line along the highway.

"I count five hundred cavalry, three hundred foot soldiers," murmured Captain Brandivven. "That's half what we expected. This engagement won't take more than an hour or two, Sir Arnnor. We've greatly overestimated them."

Bened frowned. Where were the Ilidreth riders?

"Sir, your orders?"

"They're trying to trick us," said Bened half to himself. "But where are they?"

A new voice spoke behind Bened. "Sir?" The aide crawled up the hill, trying to press himself to the ground. "We intercepted a messenger pigeon, sir." He held out a rolled piece of parchment. "It appears the Ilidreth army is farther up the road, about two hours ahead. The human forces have lagged behind."

Bened snatched the parchment from the aide and unrolled it to read the elegant lines scrawled in golden ink. He frowned, devouring the words, trying to catch any hint of a trap.

The missive detailed the whereabouts of the Ilidreth army several leagues ahead, with a push for the stragglers to hasten. The Ilidreth would wait for three hours and then march on.

One tidbit brought Bened's heart to a halt:

*We are relieved that you have caught Lady A. Do all you can to keep her safe. Will be of benefit if W. K. is captured by the Crow and negotiations are necessary.*

*-Bowrin*

Crumpling the parchment up, Bened smiled. "Afallon favors us this day. We will wipe out this force first, then proceed south to destroy their Ilidreth allies. Mount up. We ride against the rebels at once."

# Chapter Fifty-Five

"It is not possible! The Crown of the Blight has not stained the world merely to claim my soul!" Kovien thrust his hand out, shaken, and furious that he was so. In his distress, the ebony crown hummed a single, prolonged note.

He dropped his hand and smiled. He was *not* wrong. The voice had chosen *him*, not the Winter King nor any of the Wintervale line of old. "Ah, Gwynter, how little you perceive. I shall not call your ruse a waste, for it might have worked upon another, lesser man. But I am not as other men."

He raised his hand toward Gwynter, palm forward. "Behold the truth of the world."

The crown hummed again. The sun lost its glow and bathed all in darkness. All save Gwynter ren Wintervale and his unicorn, swathed in the soft light of the Weave pulsing within their souls.

Kovien smiled. "Alas, Gwynter, were all the world as you are, I would not be called to purge it."

Gwynter's eyes searched the darkness for the Crow King's face. "I don't doubt that you were called, Kovien. I only doubt from what source the voice springs. You call my words a ruse, but I meant them: You're nothing but a tool for some unholy specter."

A laugh escaped Kovien's lips. "A tool? Yes, Gwynter. This I knew already. And gladly I accept my place. Long did I search for a purpose, a reason for what I was."

"And you found a purpose, yes. But does that make it right?"

Kovien shook his head. "Oh, Gwynter. You sound so *certain* of your course. So *righteous*. But I feel the same. Do you not see? Belief in something is not enough. There are too many paths one might take. This world is broken. Broken, fragmented. I mean to repair that once and forever."

"By murdering all life?" Gwynter's voice flickered with heat.

"It is the only course that ends the turmoil, Gwynter. No other way has healed the broken places. Nothing else will last. We've run out of time, Gwynter. The world has executed your god! Can you justify that? No, do not try. I know the arguments of your faith — your tenets of forgiveness and second chances. But this world has been so many chances, and remains yet corrupt. Cruel."

Gwynter's eyes burned. "You speak of these things as though you've committed no vile deeds, but who has enacted them most?"

"I confess!" cried Kovien. A thrill ran through him. "I have become the worst of all offenders. But that was the point, Gwynter. I must press the world a last time, and should it fall, then there was no hope at all."

"But I won't let it fall." The Winter King nudged his unicorn forward, casting light before him, growing nearer and nearer to Kovien's comfortable darkness.

The Crow King sighed. "This vision is not ended, Gwynter, but only begun. Behold!"

The ground gave way to swelling tides of deep red stretching on forever. A faint light illuminated the ocean of blood, allowing Gwynter to survey the awful sight. Both unicorns remained standing, their hooves hovering above the sea. Aluem sounded a mournful bay and staggered.

"All the world is bathed in countless gallons of blood, Gwynter," said Kovien. "This is the world's truest history. Smell it. Taste the iron upon your tongue. See how it weakens your unicorn. The innocent suffer most from such evil — yet evil thrives, *thrives!* The very instrument I wield to purge this world is made from such dreadful acts as warfare and wanton violence. Only such an instrument could end the cycle, potent enough to succeed. And so, I use it."

"Lies," said Gwynter, stroking Aluem's neck. "You're deceived. This is mere illusion, supporting one aspect of life. I'll grant you, Kovien, that this world is full of war and violence. Greed, hate, judgment. But there are other things, beautiful things. Light and wonder and laughter and liberty. *Those* are the source of healing you sought and never found, for the truth is this: You wanted a reason to destroy people. You were afraid, proud, and resentful. To destroy is easier than mending, and you chose the easiest course, as all tyrants before you have done.

"But let's not pretend you're as noble as even that makes you sound. You intend to wipe away all life from Simaerin — yet before you said you'd rule it along with all other lands. Which is it, Kovien? Purging or control? And if in your heart of hearts the answer is the latter, who shall live under your eternal banner? Who decides? *You?*

"By your own admission, you're the worst of all offenders. Does that not mean you must purge yourself from the world? Are you a hero, as you claim to be, or are you the mad tyrant your actions declare? Who is the Crow King, Kovien? What is your purpose?"

Kovien stared, breath laboring, heart racing. Who was this *child* to question his calling? Who was Gwynter ren Terare ren Wintervale but a youthful usurper who would claim the world for himself? A mere human *boy*. A greedy, clutching monster.

"Hypocrite!" He stabbed a finger toward Gwynter. "You want the throne for yourself! You ride against me to steal my kingdom and my crown!"

Gwynter lifted his chin, his eyes storming on. "I can't argue with a madman. Call me what you will. Say what you want. Truth doesn't bend or mold itself to the will of Man or Ilidreth, and the truth remains this: Anyone who tramples and destroys the freedom of another for his own gain is a tyrant. And tyrants, no matter their creed, are *wrong*. You're wrong, Kovien Crow-King. The voice you heed is wrong, your calling is wrong, your actions are wrong. Nothing, not tantrum, or sword, or enchanted crown, can alter that."

Kovien's vision flamed red. He caught up his sword and charged Gwynter, screaming. The Winter King lifted his arm and deflected his blow, forced him back, and parried with a swing of his own.

Kovien barely blocked. He must calm down. Must be calm.

*Be calm.*

He *was* right. This was the only path he could take. The only one to make a difference. He must cut Gwynter down, but how? The boy remained untouchable. King Roth's ancient oath saw to that. The line of Wintervale would not fail by the hand of any living creature. Not man or beast. Gwynter alone could take his own life, or natural sickness steal his breath, or old age devour him.

The Fiend rounded Aluem, but the white unicorn danced away. Gwyn blocked another strike. Swords clashed, forward. Up. Side. Block. Metal rang in the iron-scented air.

Unicorns pranced and glided around one another, letting their riders engage, throwing their heavy swords to hack and skewer.

It was a futile effort. They both knew it. Yet anger drove them on.

Kovien could feel the hum of Gwynter's wrath, as wild and venomous as his own.

It made sense. Kovien had executed Lawen. His goal had been to push Gwynter into utter despair — not to drive him to self-destruction, as Bened Arnnor had suspected. If it had, so be it. But Kovien had hoped for more, much more.

His heart lurched.

"Join me, Gwynter!" he cried, recalling his desire. His loneliness atop the world.

The young man started and drew back, lowering his sword a little. His brows drew together and through his panting breath, he growled, "What?"

"Join me, Gwynter," he repeated, all his anger bleeding away. He recalled the fondness he had for this human child. He remembered well the day Gwynter ren Wintervale was born. Snow fell that day, though the fields still glistened with golden wheat and the trees burst with autumn's apples.

Far away in Crowwell, Kovien had fallen where he walked, strength leeched in a single moment as he heard the cry of an infant. He understood at once. For two centuries he had kept the line of Wintervale under his watch, but it seemed at last to fade away on its own. To die off naturally. He had let it go gladly.

But the Weave was stronger than he knew, and it seeped into a mother's womb to cocoon her unborn child, to douse him in magic but keep him concealed until he came into the world.

Trembling, Kovien had taken the form of a crow and flown for Mount Vinwen and the waling cries of the mage child he couldn't slay. He had entered that tiny manor and gazed upon the face of beautiful innocence glowing with the Weave's protections.

Untouchable. Unattainable. So nearly perfect.

Something within Kovien had stirred when the infant boy opened his teary eyes and gazed into the Crow King's face.

Guilt.

Guilt for all he had done. Anguish for all he had lost. Loneliness for what could never be returned.

In that moment, Kovien loved and hated the boy named Gwynter. He fled. Flew far away and found himself standing in the crumbling halls of *Shaeswéath*, his childhood home.

He climbed the stairs of yesteryear and entered the chamber where his mother lay sleeping.

Dear, beautiful Mother. Ageless and safe. Not dead, not alive. He knelt before the high bed and wept.

*Wept*.

He had never done so before, not after he had resolved to end the world's madness. And never again since the day the Winter King was born. But the fondness and loathing for Gwynter had endured, growing as Kovien took the boy under his banner and made him his general. He knew then what would happen. Knew this rebellion would spring up to thwart him. Knew Gwynter might even succeed.

Perhaps a piece of him welcomed it. An end. An answer, though it wasn't one he relished.

But the strongest part of Kovien would never bow or bend to this human. Gwynter was no longer the pure and innocent babe wailing with the wonder of life. He had become a man, grown, hardened. Pure enough to ride a white unicorn, but blemished enough to hate. A flawed creature, inherently wicked. Defiled by life's ceaseless barrage. Mortal.

Gwynter would die. If not in war, still someday. And Kovien would live on, for the Crown of the Blighted sustained him. Even when his Ilidreth kin were long deceased, he would remain.

"Kovien," said Gwynter, recalling him to the present. The vision of blood. His enemy upon the white unicorn.

The Winter King regarded him with such coldness, such anger. His eyes thundered. "I won't join you in the destruction of all I hold sacred. Once, you made me serve you out of fear, but never again for any reason. Nothing could compel me."

The certainty. The disgust. Kovien drank them in, letting them spark his resolve. "Ah, Gwynter. Few things have moved me as you do. Moved to fury and even to compassion. You're a rare man. A rare human. My father would have cared for you very much, I think." Kovien sighed softly. "It is his oath which has spared you time and again. I could plunge my sword into your chest, and draw your lifeblood, yet something — some magic or device — would spare you in your final moment."

With a wave of his hand, the bloody ocean fell away, and sunshine returned, bright and glorious. A cool breeze played with Kovien's hair. The world had returned to its natural, deceitful beauty.

A new figure stood upon the highway, clothed in tatters, his hair a tangle creeping down his back like vines.

Kovien smiled. "Ah, Kive. Come to your master."

The pitiful creature cowered, hovering between Gwynter and Kovien, gnawing on his finger.

Kovien frowned. "Kive. Come."

Kive whimpered and took a step toward him.

"Kive," said Gwynter in a gentle, affectionate murmur.

Kovien's heart throbbed to hear it. Why? Why would Gwynter speak so kindly to such a wretch as Kive? Broken, maddened, filthy. Whatever grace once belonged to the princely figure had long been destroyed. Kovien had thrived on shattering Kive, turning him into the miserable beast he was now, ruining whatever goodness, whatever nobility had existed.

What could Gwynter possibly find to treasure in such a creature?

"*Kive*," Kovien said again. Kive bowed beneath his tone as one would beneath a cracking whip. The fallen fae gingerly approached, hands wringing, eyes lowered as they should be.

He halted just beyond Kovien's reach, waiting, breathless.

"You've angered me, Kive," said the Crow King calmly.

The creature flinched. "Forgive me, Master. Forgive Kive."

"Perhaps this time I will not. You lingered with Gwynter. Why should I forgive your betrayal?"

Kive's lower lip trembled. "But Shiny must stay safe."

"Kive," called Gwynter. Aluem took several steps closer. "Come away from him. He's not your master any longer. Come to Shiny, and I will keep *you* safe."

"Shiny said to stay in the trees," Kive mumbled, as though he couldn't hear Gwynter's voice, "but I saw Master and I came. I came, Master."

Revulsion shivered through Kovien's frame as he stretched out his hand. "Well done, Kive. Come closer."

The fae slinked nearer, furtive, frightened.

Kovien rested a hand on Kive's head, another thrill of disgust running through him as it always did. He had loved crushing Kive's spirit, but his handiwork sickened him just the same. To reduce an ethereal creature into something so ugly, so primal, required the worst tactics Kovien had ever employed. Even now it unsettled him to think of them.

Kive drew nearer still, hungry to be caressed by his master, to feel some sense of affection — though Kovien offered none.

"Oh, Kive," moaned Gwynter.

Kovien looked up to drink in the sorrow and pity on the Winter King's face. "He is mine, Gwynter. I made him into what he is, and he shall always serve me."

Gwynter looked up and caught Kovien's eyes to hold them fast. "No, Kovien. He isn't."

Kovien realized his mistake. Understood Gwynter's plan. But Kive was already springing at him, snatching his crown, wrenching it from his head. They tumbled together from the Fiend's back. Kovien cried out as Kive leapt again to his feet and danced away.

"Give it to me, Kive! Return the crown to your master!"

Kive sprinted to Gwynter's side, heedless, almost *jubilant*. "Shiny, do you see? See? Kive got the crown! I took it from the Crow! I took it!"

Gwynter reached out. "Give it to me, Kive. Hurry."

"Don't touch it," Kovien warned. "It will claim your life, Gwynter. You will not die, but it will be your undoing. You are only a human."

Gwynter considered him for a heartbeat. He caught the corner of his tattered cloak and wrapped it around his hand before he accepted the crown from Kive. Innocent, broken Kive, who gave it willingly to Gwynter, betraying Kovien. Betraying his *kin*.

As Gwynter hoisted the crown before him, expression troubled, Kovien unsheathed his second dagger and flung it hard at Kive's back. Unsuspecting, joyous Kive. Traitorous wretch.

Fallen brother.

The Weave blocked him. The dagger shattered against the very air before Kive's exposed back, and the fallen fae remained unscathed. Kovien sobbed as Gwynter's eyes pinned on him.

"You will take no more from me," said the Winter King with such fervor, Kovien flinched back.

Crownless, he sat upon the ground and waited. Wondered. What would the crown do? What would become of Gwynter, who thought he was safe from its clutches by a mere tangible bit of cloth? Kovien knew better. The Crown of the Blighted was more powerful than any mage, even one of the Wintervale line. Only an oath sealed with blood protected Gwynter — and then, only from death itself. Nothing else. The crown knew other ways to claim a life.

It hummed, even as Kovien smiled and leaned forward to watch. Darkness streamed from its spires like threads of the Weave painted black. Gwynter's eyes dropped to behold the sight, and he gasped and tried to fling the Crown away — much too late to escape.

The crown would claim him. It always did.

# Chapter Fifty-Six

S*pringtime isn't the best season for going to war*, Nathaera thought with a grimace.

Cold one moment, blistering the next, more prone to rain and sleet than sunlight, and even then, the sun sometimes burned a person when the air felt chilly. An all-around miserable affair, though she must grant it was a sight better than marching in winter.

Or, indeed, crushing a man's hopes.

Poor Adesta Gilhan had been as graceful and stoic as a gliding swan when he'd accepted Nathaera's news that she and Gwyn had reached a mutual understanding. But since that midwinter discussion, she'd seen little beyond the back of the Fraeli knight's head as he trained far away from her.

*I'll take a war any day over love,* she thought.

A smile tugged at her lips.

*That's a lie and you know it, silly girl. Doesn't Gwyn love you? Is there anything so grand?*

A cry brought Nathaera's head up. She gripped her stallion's reins.

There. Against the southeast hills, a host of horsemen charged toward the Winter Army. The Crow banner streamed in the wind.

Shouts rang down the column along the highway.

"To arms!"

"Make ready!"

"Steady, steady!"

Nathaera whipped her horse around. "Arianwen, stay with me." She kicked the stallion into a gallop even as the other woman nodded. Arianwen followed upon her own horse as Nathaera led her away from the highway and into the western hills.

"It's him, it must be!" Arianwen shouted above the wind noise.

Nathaera smiled grimly to herself. Bened Arnnor had come at last. "Stay close!"

The hills riddled the land for miles, dotted here or there with leafless trees, gray and soggy in the spring melt. Nathaera veered through the flat stretches and wended around the slopes to maintain as much speed as she could. Arianwen kept up splendidly.

Nathaera glanced back once and found a half dozen soldiers bearing down hard on their heels. The heraldry of the Crow blazed upon their chests and shields. Nathaera scowled and whipped her eyes forward again, fixing them upon the single tree atop a high rise a few hundred yards on.

Nearly there. Just a bit farther.

Her stallion perked up. Nathaera leaned forward as much as she could, letting the wind tear through her hair, ears aching, lips numb.

The horsemen were gaining. Thundering hooves rattled the air.

A voice shouted: "Arianwen, you shall never escape me!"

Nathaera's grin returned, sly, perhaps even wicked, but she suspected Afallon would forgive her a moment's relish. Her horse rounded the bend, and the hills gave way to a hidden valley filled with color — but the colors weren't natural.

Motley shades of red, blue, purple, green, and gold adorned the mounted army waiting with bows drawn. Behind them sat a dragon, steam rising from his snout. Nathaera charged into their midst as a pathway opened to her. Arianwen followed, and the path lined by Ilidreth closed to the enemy.

Nathaera heard Bened's cry of distress, followed by a scream of fury.

Her smile grew and she steered her horse around. "Celin, don't kill the knight."

"As agreed," the Ilidreth said, glancing toward her even as he unleashed an arrow. "But he will not be unmaimed."

Six soldiers in red lay unmoving upon the damp ground. Bened clutched his leg where a shaft jutted from the flesh between the joints of his armor.

"That's just fine." She nudged her horse forward.

Bened Arnnor looked up with pain bright in his eyes. His wince fell into a glare. "*You*."

She shrugged. "I told you I would make you pay, Bened."

He barked a laugh. "You sacrificed your main forces just to lure me into a trap?"

Nathaera arched an eyebrow. "Sacrificed them? How?"

"My men outnumber yours by several thousand strong. You think they still stand?"

Nathaera caught her hair and tossed it over her shoulder to emphasize her disdain. "What do you take me for? *You?* More importantly, do you truly underestimate the Ilidreth so much? Two hundred to one, Sir Knight. That's how much stronger the Ilidreth are than your king's brood. One Ilidreth can slay two hundred human knights, let alone enlisted men. By the way, how many Ilidreth do you see before you? Fifty? I confess, I chose that many only to frighten you, but that's not important right now. How many Ilidreth are missing, Bened Arnnor? Consider that, and then consider the odds I just gave you. Whose men are cutting down whose, I wonder?"

His expression hardened, though the color in his face faded enough to satisfy Nathaera. She motioned to Celin, who approached on horseback wearing a perfect mask of indifference.

"So, this is the dread right-hand of the Crow King?" His tone hummed flat. "How the mighty do fall as softly as an autumn leaf."

"Now, now," said Nathaera. "Be kind, my lord. He's much more impressive when he's standing upright."

"Is he. Well." Celin's eyes swept up and down the lame man's frame. He turned away and waved a hand to one of his scouts, who rode forward and bowed his head.

"My lord?"

"Bind him and bring him along. Bury the rest."

"Yes, my lord." The Ilidreth slipped gracefully from his horse and tied Bened's hands fast behind his back.

"Why let me live?" growled Bened.

Nathaera held his gaze. "Who said you will?"

Approaching hooves brought her head around. Arianwen's mare trotted near and halted before the prisoner.

Bened's eyes brightened with greater fury as the raven-haired maiden considered him with a countenance of deep winter.

"Sir Knight," Arianwen said in frosty hues, "gaze upon me and know that you shall never see me again. I'm not yours. I shall never be. Die knowing that." She turned away.

His eyes narrowed, and he trembled. "Don't forget, I kissed you. I tasted the untouchable lady of ice!"

She glanced at him with indifference equal to Celin's, then with perfect ease she moved away on horseback, as regal and self-possessed as any queen Nathaera might dream up.

"We must go," Celin said, drawing Nathaera's focus back to the situation at hand.

She shook herself and nodded. "Of course. At once."

"You won't win," cried Bened after them. "The Crow King is far more powerful than your woeful army!"

Nathaera patted her ear as she rode away. "I'm sorry, Celin. Were you saying something? A bug was snared in my hair, you see, and all I could hear for a moment was its tiny buzzing. Such a nuisance. I do hope that's the last of his noise I shall ever endure."

They moved east toward the Winter Army. As she rode,

Nathaera plotted the most poetic end for Bened she could think up, a gleaming smile lighting her countenance. Though she knew the surest way to humiliate the man was to turn him over to the Winter King as soon as she had the chance.

That thought made her smile brighter still.

# Chapter Fifty-Seven

A force seized Gwyn, unseen, clutching. His lungs constricted and his body convulsed.

*The crown!*

He tried to throw it away, tried to escape its pull, but his limbs refused to obey. Magic surged through him, cold as ice, burning like fire. He buckled against Aluem. His vision blackened. Scent and sound vanished.

The last noise he heard was of Aluem calling out to him, but a torrent of hollow despair cut the unicorn off.

It swallowed him up, poured into him like a raging flood, filled every thought and feeling until he screamed beneath its crushing weight.

The strength of the crown's power, far superior to his magery, would break him. He couldn't resist. Couldn't fight. He would fail and go mad.

*Afallon!*

The single word rang through his mind, faraway, as he tumbled. Down. Down. Into the growing abyss of his soul.

But no. In the depths where all should be dark, a light burned before him. His light. Not magery or the Weave, for neither could resist the Blight.

Something else. Something distinctly human.

*Choice.*

A thrill rushed through him. The freedom to choose either to remain in this unyielding vast desolation or not to remain. To return to life, with its horrors, its sorrows, its pain.

He knew already what he would choose: *Liberty*.

Gwyn reached out, not with hands, but with his heart. He took the light into himself, let it burn brighter and brighter, until it could chase away all the hopelessness.

Sound tore through his ears. His eyes opened. The fragrance of loam, greenery, blossoms, attacked his senses and made his eyes water.

He sat up.

"Impossible!" cried Kovien.

The Crow King stood now where he'd fallen, though Kive blocked his path to Gwyn lying in the tall grass beside the highway.

In the field nearby, the unicorns danced and dove around each other, horns blazing with magic, dueling. Gwyn turned from the fight.

Kovien gripped his sword, eyes narrowed on Gwyn. "It claimed you."

Gwyn hefted himself up on his elbows. His arms quavered under his weight. He gritted his teeth, and shoved himself up until he sat, gasping. His bones ached with fever. He swallowed and ran a hand over his face before he answered.

"I chose not to let it."

"No. *No.*"

Kovien charged forward, but Kive threw out his hand. "*Stop, Master*!"

Kovien froze in his tracks, seized by an invisible hand. His eyes widened. "Kive, *release me*."

Kive shook his head. "No, Master." He paused. "No, *Crow*. You will not hurt Shiny."

Kovien seemed to wrestle with himself, torn between fury written in his eyes and terror trembling on his lips. "Kive," he gasped, forlorn.

Kive's shoulders hunched. "Master?"

"Kive, let me go. Please don't hold me captive." The plaintive cry hung so soft, so sweet, upon the air. Gwyn shuddered at the contrast between that sound and the blazing eyes of the mad king.

Kive whimpered and took a step forward.

"Kive, don't listen. He's fooling you." Gwyn staggered to his feet. "Kive. Look at me. Look at Shiny."

The fallen fae turned slowly to find Gwyn's face. A faint smile touched Kive's lips, but his eyes filled with tears. "Shiny! Shiny, it's Kovien. Kovien is trapped. Do you hear him?"

Compassion swelled in Gwyn's heart for this wretched soul. "Kive, Kovien is no more. Here stands the Crow King only: your brother's murderer."

Kive stood still, lines etched into his face. He blinked and understanding lit in his eyes. "The Crow murdered my brother?"

Gwyn nodded. "Yes, Kive. He murdered him on an island far away, and then he took up the Crown of the Blighted and came to this land. He killed your betrothed next, and then came to Swan Castle and killed your family. He's not your master, Kive. He's your enemy."

Kive's shoulders shook. "The Crow did this. He did this. He took them all away." He spoke as though memory dawned, and his tone heightened as he whirled on Kovien. "Traitor!"

Kovien flinched. "Kive, release me. I am your master. *Release me*!"

The cry of a unicorn ripped Gwyn's eyes from the brothers, and he found the Fiend staggering away from Aluem. The latter's horn glistened with silver blood. The Fiend charged again, head lowered to deliver a blow of his own.

Kive's defiant voice seized Gwyn's attention. "I will *not* release you."

Gwyn realized only now he didn't hold the crown anymore. He

glanced down to find it lying in the grass, teeming with threads of black. What should he do? He couldn't let Kovien have it back, for while it was a thing of evil, alone it could do little. In Kovien's grasp, it could do nearly all.

*Afallon, lend me strength. Help me know what to do.*

Magery couldn't break or seal the crown. Nor could the power of the Ilidreth. A unicorn was too pure to touch such wickedness unscathed. The Fiend was proof of that.

What did that leave? Nothing temporal would suffice. Only the divinity of Heaven could combat this vile thing.

"Gwynter."

He looked up from the artifact and found Lady Shalesta, Swan Queen of Ilid, standing before him, wreathed in light.

She held out her arm and uncurled her fingers to reveal the blue gem. "Behold, a starstone crafted for a mortal queen's crown, twice used to save a life. It has one last use."

Gwyn plucked it up. He stared down at the crown upon the ground. The surrounding grass had withered.

"A crown against a crown," he whispered, "and one last life spared: The world."

Gwyn knelt and pressed the starstone against the Crown of the Blighted. What would become of him, wielder of the stone, a mere mortal standing against immortal magic? Would this be his end?

Kovien screamed. Broke free of his invisible chains. Raced toward Gwyn with magic flowing on his fingertips. But his stream of magic rebounded, broken by protections put in place in ages past.

Kive tackled Kovien in the next second, drawing him to the ground.

Surging power resonated from the crown and the blue gem, pulsating and trembling. Pressure caught Gwyn in a kind of ethereal grip. Light and dark collided in a conflict unseen by mortal senses. He squeezed his eyes shut against a blinding stream of prismatic light. Yet he witnessed the struggle even still.

The ground quaked and rumbled. Lightning crawled across the

sky, and the sun dimmed. The Weave leeched celestial strength from above to charge the stone.

The crown hummed a last furious note of wrath and ruin — and cracked in half.

Kovien screamed the same ugly, piercing note, then fell limp beneath Kive's grip.

The sun returned.

Birds trilled a question.

Gwyn sank back against his ankles, frame racked with shivers. His blood ran cold and sluggish through his limbs. He gasped for breath.

Gazing down, he found the starstone too had cracked in half. His heart throbbed for the loss of a star. It had sacrificed itself for Gwyn's sake, because he'd asked.

"Thank you," he whispered, stroking a finger across the polished surface.

Kive dragged himself to his feet. "Shiny. Shiny, are you well?"

Gwyn looked up and offered a tremulous smile. "Y-yes, Kive. I'm well." His eyes slid down to gaze upon Kovien's motionless body. "Is he dead?"

Kive glanced at the Crow King. He bent toward him, cautious. "He does not—"

The Weave pulsed. Kovien's eyes flashed red, then he disappeared in the next instant. A crow stood where he had been. In a flurry of black feathers, the crow took flight with a cry.

Gwyn reached up, summoning the Weave to spear the Crow, but the magic sputtered and died upon his fingertips. His arm fell with a quiver to his side.

"Shiny, Crow is getting away!"

Gwyn tried to command Kive to stop Kovien from retreating, but his vision distorted. He careened forward. Arms caught him.

He resisted sleep, urging himself to rise — to give chase, but his body wouldn't respond. He turned his head enough to watch the Fiend bolt away while Aluem looked on. The black unicorn didn't race toward Crowwell as Kovien had, but along the highway northward, away from his master.

Gwyn's lips stretched in a smile. Perhaps the Fiend had been freed of Kovien's grip. Perhaps he could find some measure of healing.

Perhaps...

He slumped forward and let oblivion claim him.

# Chapter Fifty-Eight

"Tell me there are no new stars in the sky tonight."

Celin'Laen turned from the heavens to watch Nathaera approach, wrapped in her matted furs, hair braided over one shoulder. Her eyes carried a familiar glow of concern.

He smiled to reassure her. "None, my lady. While a change has taken place, I do not yet understand it. Something has shifted."

She sat in the grass beside him. "A good or a bad shift?"

Celin'Laen frowned and turned to regard the swaying wild grass of the hill where he had taken up the night's watch. Moonlight transformed the grass into silvery feathers. "A good shift if I must guess. But I cannot say for certain."

"It's Gwyn," Nathaera said. "I woke from a dream about him. He defeated the Crow King."

Celin'Laen shook his head. "The tyrant yet lives."

"I didn't say he killed him. He *defeated* him."

The Ilidreth smiled patiently. "If you insist, though you are not a soothsayer, my lady. Your dream may only have been that: A dream."

She shook her head. "I don't profess to be clairvoyant. But I *know* Gwyn, and I know he defeated the Crow King."

"Yet dark clouds gather on the horizon, and the Weave speaks of war." Celin'Laen turned his eyes southward. "Defeated or otherwise, the Crow King is not done fighting."

"I know that too. But Gwyn is alive."

He glanced at the human girl. "Yet you asked me about the stars."

"I had to be sure." She drew her furs closer. "He's the sort of man you expect will give his all to the cause he upholds. I fear he'll fall before it's over. I pray otherwise, but if Afallon claims him, what can I do?"

"You place great faith in your god. Do not doubt that he will reward that."

She smiled and drew her legs to her chest. "I don't. Not really. But Afallon's rewards aren't always what we covet." She sighed. "Gwyn is a great man. A good man, but also great."

"Yes, he is."

"Such men are rare and often martyrs. But such men are needed after wartime, too. Surely, Afallon raised Gwyn up not just to fight and win, but to rule a nation justly. To teach other men to be good and great men, too. I believe that, Celin."

"As you should. Such faith is noble."

The faint thunder of light hooves down the highway drew his eyes toward the sound. "Hush a moment, lady. Something rides this way. If my ears do not deceive me, it is the graceful gait of a racing unicorn." He listened a moment more. "It carries two."

Nathaera let out a cry of joy, and she leapt to her feet. "Does he return so soon?"

"We are much nearer to Crowwell than before. It is possible the unicorn could cover the distance if his strides are long and true." Celin'Laen rose to join her. The hooves were familiar. "Yes, it is Aluem. He is but a few leagues away and riding swiftly. Come."

Nathaera pranced after him toward the silent encampment.

They passed the dark tents and stood at the borders of camp to wait for Aluem's arrival.

Nathaera tugged on her braid, while Celin'Laen remained still, though the same needles of concern pricked his insides.

There. A white shape appeared against the pitch-black night.

Celin'Laen started forward. Nathaera sprang past him, racing across the wet grass until the unicorn slowed before her.

"Gwyn!" she cried, soft enough that the camp didn't stir, though her voice rang through Celin'Laen's sharp ears like a tolling bell.

Aluem reached her side in the next second. Kive shifted on the unicorn's back to let them both see Gwynter's face. The king lay unmoving, draped in Kive's arms, limp and deathly white.

"Kive, oh Kive, what happened?" asked Nathaera.

"Shiny broke the crown, Fairy Wren. Shiny broke the crown, and the Crow flew away."

Celin'Laen's soul shuddered at the implications. "The crown, Kive? Do you mean the Crown of the Blighted?"

*'Indeed, he does,'* answered Aluem. *'He broke its power using the star-stone of the Swan Queen. Alas, he is wounded from his action, and his arm needs tending to at once. It may already be too late. Behold.'*

Celin'Laen turned his gaze to Gwyn's right arm. His fingers and hand were black, and already his arm darkened.

"Prince Kive, give him to me." Celin'Laen reached out his arms.

Kive handed Gwynter down without complaint or inquiry. Celin'Laen hoisted Gwynter, turned, and sprinted lightly toward camp. The others followed, anxiety taut on the wind.

Celin'Laen brought Gwynter to the largest tent, where Prince Fayett sat up with a start and blinked at him sleepily from his bed. It took a moment for the young prince to comprehend what he saw. Celin'Laen was already laying Gwynter out across a plush pillow on the floor when the prince cried out and bounded from his bed.

"He's returned!"

"He is tainted," said Celin'Laen shortly. He whipped around as Aluem entered the tent.

*'I am here. We may begin.'*

The unicorn trotted near and bent his head to touch his horn against Gwynter's arm. Celin'Laen knelt, rubbed his hands together to banish the cold, then rested his palms against Gwynter's icy fingers.

"The star could not banish this?"

*'The star gave its life to destroy the crown. It could do no more.'*

Celin'Laen nodded, closed his eyes, and drew upon his essence. The Weave flowed through him like a warm stream, light and laughing. It traveled down his arms at his urging — and recoiled as it touched Gwynter's hand.

Celin'Laen pressed it onward. The Weave coiled around Gwynter's fingers, humming as Aluem's horn ignited with purest light.

"Will he live?" asked Nathaera far away. Celin'Laen ignored her, and gently pressed the Weave into Gwynter's blackened limb. The Winter King remained still and cold, chest rising and falling faintly.

"Can I help?" Fayett asked. "Can I do anything?"

Celin'Laen ignored him too, and drew from deeper within himself as the Weave weakened. The world's magic was weary already from combating the crown's taint. He pressed harder, even as his body trembled.

Aluem's horn flashed with colors, all colors, some named and others not.

As Celin'Laen thrust the last of his strength into Gwynter's arm, the unicorn sank to his hindquarters and bowed his head.

With a shuddering sigh, Celin'Laen bowed his head and gasped for breath. "We have...done...all we can..."

Nathaera stepped between the two of them to rest a hand against Gwynter's forehead. "Will he live?"

"It was never a matter of death," the Ilidreth answered. "At least in the sense you understand. Whether he shall remain Gwynter as we know him, it is too early to tell. We will know with the dawn."

"What do you mean, as we know him?" asked Fayett "What else would he be?"

Celin'Laen curled forward to rest his head against the pillow. "The crown began to taint him. Should it have reached his heart, he would become fallen. Not as Kive is fallen, for fae fall differently than humans. It was the risk he took to break the crown's power, and the cost might have been his identity. If he wakes and knows us, we have acted in time."

"He might have forgotten us?" whispered Nathaera.

"He might have forgotten *all*," Celin'Laen murmured. "A fae cannot truly forget what he is, no matter how hard he might try. But a man is changeable, fluid, able to grow or to digress as no other creature. Unfortunately, this allows magic to write itself *over* him, given the chance. The Weave of itself would not — but a tainted magic like the Crown of the Blighted, whose purpose is to override the will of its wielder, would wipe away a man's identity should it enter his heart."

"Did it?" asked Nathaera. "Did it enter his heart?"

Celin'Laen lifted his weary head to meet her wide, frightened eyes. "Not so far as I can tell, but as I said only the dawn will bear the answer. Now, my lady, prithee, let me rest."

Her feet retreated a step or two. "Of course, Celin. I'm sorry. Sleep. I'll watch over Gwyn until the morning."

Fayett spoke, his voice distant and fading. "Help me move him to the bed, my lady. We should make him comfortable."

# Chapter Fifty-Nine

The dawn had never been so slow to arrive.

Nathaera sat beside Gwyn, where he lay unmoving upon the bed. She'd prayed through the hours of night, making every promise she could think of that might improve her character — if only sweet Afallon would let Gwyn remember her.

She'd gone from promises, to silent weeping, to more promises, to pacing, to more weeping. Now she stared at Gwyn's face as the first rays of morning painted shadows across the canvas walls of the Fraeli prince's tent.

Fayett stayed close by, maintaining his own silent vigil, but he moved forward now as she leaned in. "Any sign?"

She started to shake her head, but a faint moan escaped Gwyn's lips. His eyes fluttered open.

"He's stirring."

Fayett closed the distance from his bit of floor and the bed, and leaned over her to watch the king's eyes flutter open again. "Your Majesty?"

Nathaera scowled. "Don't confuse him." She leaned closer still and smiled. "Hello, Gwyn. How do you feel?"

He blinked a few more times, then turned toward her. A smile spread across his lips. "Hello, Natty. I feel terrible."

Nathaera squealed and flung her arms around Gwyn's neck, showering his face with kisses. "You're all right! You're all right!"

He laughed weakly. "Of course I am." He stiffened. "Nathaera."

She pulled back. "Yes, Gwyn?"

"The Crow King got away. I broke the crown's power, but he escaped back into Crowwell. We must continue our march. We must take him down."

She opened her mouth to protest. Let the Crow King wait a day at least. Gwyn must recover his strength. But the firmness of the Winter King's eyes told her that any attempt to dissuade him would waste time.

She closed her mouth and nodded.

# Chapter Sixty

It began with rumors. People whispered that the Crow King had murdered over three hundred men and women in the main thoroughfare before he rode out to duel the Winter King. There he'd been defeated, and many claimed they had seen him flying in the form of a crow back to Crow Castle to die.

Too many reports agreed about the massacre in the streets and the subsequent duel for Towwen Stone to write them off as hearsay. But whether the Crow King was dead, he was far less certain.

His gut insisted the Crow King wouldn't die so easily, so quietly. And if it were so, where was the Winter King? Shouldn't he ride into the royal city to declare his victory?

Some whispers insisted Gwynter had died. That he'd defeated the Crow King by sacrificing his own life.

The only fact Towwen knew was that the city gates had been shut and no one could leave. After that, the looting began. Fear rode the winds. The people grew uneasy, then restless, then bold. Soldiers existed, but they appeared almost aimless, uncertain. Headless.

Blood ran in the streets for days. Most people hid in the cathedrals and churches to escape the chaos.

So it remained until a horn sounded from the gates. Towwen looked up from the letter he'd been composing and set aside his quill.

Rindermarr's eyes met his across the prayer room of Quee'avv Cathedral.

"The Winter Army is here," said the priest.

Towwen let out a breath. "Blessed Afallon be praised. Could it be true?" He rose and bolted for the door, Rindermarr on his heels. They clambered down the passage steps and across the vaulted hall, out into the courtyard.

Priests and refugees dared to venture forth, joining Towwen and Rindermarr in listening to the second volley of notes from the gate.

"He's truly come," cried a voice, half-hysterical. "He's come to free us!"

A smattering of cheers echoed across the courtyard.

Towwen looked at Rindermarr. "We need to reach the gates. We have to open them."

"Impossible. We'll be cut down before we can get close."

The horn blasted a third time.

"That's the call to arms," said Rindermarr. "Every soldier in the city will head for the gates. It's a death sentence to go there now. We've done our part. We can only watch and pray."

Towwen shook his head, heart pounding. "I can't be idle in such a moment. Shall the city stand by while others fight our battle? Nay, sir, I'll not abide it. We must fight. We must call others to rally and take the gates." His eyes widened. "The Scrawl!" He whirled and sprinted for the cathedral gate.

"You're mad, Towwen!"

Towwen didn't look back, but he laughed as he raced for the center of the city.

It didn't take long before a soldier noticed him sprinting through the streets. "You, stop!"

Towwen barreled on, barely feeling the slap of his own feet against the hard ground. The pounding of pursuant boots stayed close behind him, and he prayed he could keep up his stamina. He wasn't much of a runner, inclined to study and thought rather than physical prowess, but if he survived this madness he intended to take up a sword and learn to use it to defend others.

Not because he relished the thought, but because if his countrymen were plowed under by a tyrant's merciless war machine, he wouldn't stand by to see it done again.

Puffing for air, Towwen staggered through a jostling throng of frightened citizens intent upon the distant gates. The soldier barked orders for the people to stand aside, but no one heard.

Towwen broke free of the crowd and threw the last of his strength into one last dash to the city center. He careened to a halt when he reached his goal and glanced back to find the soldier fast approaching.

Towwen summoned the Weave and etched the keyword into the air. No message was attached to the spell now, and so his own visage projected into the minds of all within Crowwell.

Wheezing, he spoke as quickly as he could. "Citizens and countrymen, we the people have been silent too long at the ax and plow. What becomes of Simaerin forthwith is upon our heads. Sit and watch or rise to fight — those are your only choices. You know the nature of the Crow King. You've seen and felt his tyranny for far too long. Yes, those who opposed him have died, but even now an army stands outside the gates of Crowwell to resist such oppression.

"Rise, Simaeri, and grasp liberty with your very souls! Go to the gates and open them for our new king!"

He let the message fade, too weary to send another. Drawing a steadying breath, he turned to face the soldier, to face the sword and feel its sting. But the soldier merely stood there, regarding Towwen with wonder, just a lad, perhaps even younger than himself.

The soldier lowered his sword slowly. "Do you think we could win?"

Towwen smiled faintly. "Aye. But only if we try."

# Chapter Sixty-One

Kovien stood within his tower room and stared out upon the army at the gates of his city. So few, yet so vast. Three united banners rose above the allied forces of men and Ilidreth.

How had it come to this?

He hunched into himself, frightened, weakened, alone. Below, in the streets of Crowwell, the ranks of his army formed to resist the enemy. Even besieged, Crowwell would stand. But what was the point of it? His power was gone; the voice had retreated.

Kovien had already lost.

"No," he whispered. "No, *no*. It came so very near. I can't have lost so close to the end. What was the point of it?"

She was gone. Gone with the starstone. Kovien had protected his mother from death by tying her soul to her crown, to the same blue gem Gwyn had stolen and used to defeat the Crown of the Blighted. Yet she had sacrificed her life to thwart her own son.

Kovien's hands pounded the windowsill, then curled into fists.

"Why? It cannot end this way. If I lose now, all I have done, all I was asked to destroy, will have been for naught."

A single tear rolled down his cheek. Despair enveloped him,

cradling him, keeping him safe from guilt. But it could not spare him rage. It churned within his soul, deep and abiding — the strongest force of his life. Rage. Anger. *Hatred.*

These filthy humans would *not* take his victory. Not even their beloved Winter King could rob him of his purpose. He would kill them, *kill them all.* Rip from Gwynter all that he loved. Kovien should have done so from the start. Had he broken Gwynter as he had Kive, this would not have come to pass.

"You will not win, Winter King!" screamed Kovien out the window.

With a tolling note, a message rolled across the Weave: A call to arms. A plea for the human scum of Crowwell to stand and fight. To take the gates. To resist their king. The figure in the message was a youthful man, and in his eyes burned the same hateful resolve, the same pure intent, as in Gwynter's.

The streets below swarmed with people, so many of them, rushing to the gates. Rushing to die. Rushing to freedom.

An emerald dragon appeared to circle across the sky overhead, threatening. Powerful.

Kovien clutched his face and screamed, screamed, screamed against such defiance. Such human hope. Foolish. Useless. Why did it inspire its fellows?

*What was the point?*

Roth's quiet, soothing voice cut through his cries. "Behold, my son: The seeds of hope have traveled far indeed."

Kovien lowered his hands to find his father standing beside him at the window. The ghost's finger pointed out, but not toward the northern gates. It pointed to the southeast.

Kovien's eyes followed that finger until he found the channel that poured into the Vaymeer Sea. The faint scent of brine nipped his nose. Out there, spread across the vast water, banners billowed in a warm wind.

Kovien beheld his downfall.

The Fraeli armada had come. They surrounded him. Crowwell would fall.

Kovien sank to his knees with a sob, buried his face in his hands, and wept.

All his efforts, all his sacrifices, all for naught.

Hatred seized him again, murdering despair. He would not abide it. He could not remain in such a cruel and unforgiving world. He would not let them lock him up to keep company forever with his ghosts.

He had one escape. One chance of it.

Kovien leapt up and caught the edges of the window. He smiled a last hopeless smile, and threw himself from the tower.

He could not remain here for one more hateful moment. If he couldn't have the world, the world would not keep him.

His last thought as he closed his eyes was of Gwynter. Pure, headstrong, reckless, noble, foolhardy boy. Let the Winter King have the throne. Let him rule Simaerin. Let him feel the weight and grief and suffering of kings as Kovien did.

Let him ask the same question Kovien always had: What was the point?

## Chapter Sixty-Two

Gwyn swallowed bile as he rode Aluem along the bloodstained thoroughfares of Crowwell.

Behind him, streaming through the shattered gates, marched the Winter Army. Their losses had been few. Indeed, Gwyn had lost more men to sickness and winter's hand than to the battlefield. His heart throbbed to think of it.

The arrival of the Fraeli fleet had turned the tide, but that alone would not have been enough. Even now his eyes searched the crowds of bedraggled people, eager to find Towwen Stone among them. Afraid he wouldn't.

Gwyn had heard the man's message — everyone had. Many of the Crow King's soldiers had thrown down their weapons as Towwen's words faded, and the citizens of Crowwell had overrun those who resisted.

The brave rebels stood now on either side of the street, broken bottles, mallets, the odd rusted sword, and other worn tools still gripped in their hands. Many grinned broadly, while others wore gaunt or bewildered expressions, eyes interrogating Gwyn.

He wished he knew the answer to their silent question.

Amid the siege, energized by the Fraeli armada's arrival, Gwyn's men had heaved battering rams against the gates, and shot arrows at the city guards with fervor. Just then, a scream had cut across the wind — mad and forlorn.

The siege had faltered as eyes turned toward the looming towers of Crow Castle. The scream came again. And again.

As Gwyn watched, a faraway figure had pitched itself from the highest tower window. He could guess who it was, but Kive confirmed it. Kive, who had loped beside Aluem as Gwyn charged across the field, barking orders.

With a cry of his own, Kive had fallen to the earth, trembling. "Oh, Master. Master. Master, you're gone at last. What shall become of Kive?"

Despite the surrounding chaos, Gwyn had flung himself from Aluem, and pulled Kive to his feet. "Stand, my friend, and know that you're free."

Kive had regarded him with shock and confusion, eyebrows drawn, eyes dark with emotion. Tears tracked his face. "Kive must fall with his master."

"No. No, you mustn't. You must stand, Kive. Stand now. Fight. You're *free*. The Crow is dead."

Kive's eyes had widened, and a tremor had racked his body. With a cry of terror, he'd wrenched free of Gwyn's grip and thrown himself into the fray, disappearing amidst the clatter and whistling of arrows. Gwyn had called after him, but the fallen fae never returned.

Now, with victory in hand, Gwyn tried not to think of Kive and his fate. Had he too leapt from some high place to end his life? Had the Crow King claimed his brother in death?

"Sire!"

Gwyn perked up and managed a smile as he spotted Towwen Stone racing down the street. "Towwen!"

They met when Aluem pranced to a halt.

"Sire, the city is yours. Simaerin is yours. We've won." Towwen's light eyes shone bright as sunbeams.

Gwyn answered back with a grim nod. "So we did. What news of the Crow King?"

"His death is confirmed. He fell from the tower into his courtyard. Why he fell, none can say. Was he pushed, or did he jump?"

"He jumped," said Gwyn. "See that he's buried, but not with the other fallen. Hide his grave, so that none may claim his remains. Evil like his mustn't come to light again."

Towwen nodded and took off to obey his liege lord's command. Gwyn continued along the thoroughfare, flanked by Cadogan, Celin, and Prince Fayett. Soon he reached the open gates of the castle proper.

In an even line, Ilidreth arrows pointed at their hearts, stood the Crow King's unarmed officers.

Gwyn considered them. "Your king is dead, and your city is conquered. Which of you shall offer formal surrender?"

The officers exchanged dark looks. One strode forward. "I, Sir Drinald, Knight of the Crow, shall do it."

Gwyn nodded. "Return his sword to him."

An Ilidreth marksmen came forward and offered a sheathed broadsword to the knight, who took it with a flash of pain in his eyes. He unsheathed the blade and started toward Gwyn, who held out his hand.

"Not to me. Your king would surrender directly. In his absence, an officer shall accept your surrender in my stead." He gestured to Cadogan. "If you please."

Cadogan inclined his head and rode forward, dismounted, and stood before the knight.

Several of the Crow King's officers muttered, and one spat at the ground. "Traitor."

Gwyn's gaze fell on the man who spoke. He was a general Gwyn knew from his time in Kovien's service. "General Broven, hold your tongue. You're now considered traitors, not General Cadogan. Your king abandoned you for death. I now rule in Simaerin."

Broven tried to hold Gwyn's gaze, but after a moment he lowered his head, saying nothing.

Sir Drinald held the broadsword toward Cadogan, hilt first. "The Crow Army surrenders to the might of our enemy. Let this act sever the threads of war. We have lost."

Each word hit the Crow officers like physical blows. Their shoulders hunched lower and lower, eyes turned downward.

Cadogan took the sword. "In the gracious names of the Winter King and the Swan King alike, I accept your surrender. Let the promise of peace be forged in the fires of life."

He turned and strode to Gwyn's side, lifted the sword, and smiled. "Your Majesty. The day is won."

# Chapter Sixty-Three

That night, Bened Arnnor was tried and executed for treason by members of Gwynter ren Wintervale's council and several church officials. Alongside Bened, every other Crow officer who refused to swear fealty to the new king of Simaerin was sentenced as well. Those who would swear an oath of loyalty were pardoned of any war crimes and knighted under the Unicorn banner.

Arianwen didn't watch any more of the proceedings after that. It was enough to know her dread specters were both gone now. She wandered from camp where the Winter King held court. He seemed unwilling to take the throne of Crow Castle for himself. She couldn't blame him. The castle reeked of dark magic. Even now, so far removed from it, she felt as though its towers surveyed her every movement.

Picking her way around the rocks and trees under the velvet night sky, she traveled toward the dense westward woods. Walking, walking. Free, but still troubled.

Could she trust anyone ever again? Dare she believe the Winter King was different from his predecessor? Such thoughts plagued her steps while the woods grew before her vision, thick, ancient, and safe.

A sound broke the stillness ahead. She froze in her tracks.

Was it a deer?

Something moved toward her, black against the night. "Who's there?"

A faint snort sounded. Plaintive. Pain-filled.

She gasped, recognizing the Fiend coming nearer. "Stay back!"

The black unicorn halted in his tracks.

"His name was Arastet once."

She whirled around with a cry and found the Ilidreth named Celin'Laen standing in the gloom, motley clothes blending with the night.

A faint smile touched his lips. "He was a magnificent unicorn, wise and kind, until the Crow King stole his purity and thrust him into darkness beyond mortal reckoning. Yet he is not so fearsome now as he was, do you not think, Lady Arianwen?"

Heart pounding, she looked between the Fiend and the Ilidreth, wishing she could run away. Surrounded. Caught.

"Be at peace, fair one," said Celin'Laen. "I am not fallen. I would not harm you."

He moved toward her, and she flinched back, but he passed her by and lifted his hand toward the unicorn. He whispered, his words foreign. Smooth as water. Sweet as a spring wind through an apple orchard.

Those words moved something deep within Arianwen, and she inched toward the fae despite her fear. "What are you saying?"

Celin'Laen looked toward her, his blue eyes vibrant in the faint moonlight. "I am reminding him of what he was. Calling him back to himself. But he does not desire my attention. He is here for you."

She recoiled, heart leaping into her throat. "He wishes to imprison me."

"Nay, Arianwen. He seeks forgiveness. He seeks light. He seeks what once he was beneath a full sun."

She trembled, yet staring at the black unicorn, she could see his change. No longer was he a raging creature filled with black fire, but a wretched thing, hanging his head low, eyes filled with remorse deeper than tears.

With a pang, tears filled her eyes. Before she knew what she did, she wrapped her arms around the unicorn's neck, kissing it, weeping. "I forgive you, poor thing. I forgive you."

Her heart warmed as the unicorn nuzzled her face, baying a sound like a sob.

Celin'Laen's soft voice stirred the wind. "You have both suffered beyond what others understand. As kindred you stand 'neath the hallowed moon and heal each other's hearts. Come with me, Arianwen and Arastet. Come away to *Shaeswéath,* and find peace at long last."

Arianwen lifted her head and turned to the Ilidreth. "Swan Castle fell long ago."

"Then help me to restore it." Celin'Laen extended his hand. "Come to the northern forests, and peer upon the Vales. They will heal now. The paths of old shall reveal their secrets, and the swans shall return to the waters. Come away with me, and find solace in ancient memory renewed."

"What of the Winter King?" she asked. "Doesn't he need you?"

"I have bidden him farewell for a season, but the season is fleeting as mortal days. The Winter King is an ally to my people. The Unicorn banner, the Crane banner, and the Swan banner fly free in the same sky. No king alive shall tear this alliance asunder." He smiled, and music swelled in his silence.

Compelled, she accepted his hovering hand. "I will come. I desire to see this memory of ancient days."

"Ancient days are come again," said Celin'Laen. "Ride upon Arastet, and you shall keep my pace."

She climbed onto the black unicorn's back and rode after the Ilidreth as he bounded into the woods. She never looked back on the scar that was Crow Castle. It lay behind her forever.

# Chapter Sixty-Four

ONE YEAR LATER

Londolin shone against the Vaymeer Sea. It was there, within the Winter Castle, that Gwynter ren Wintervale was crowned the Winter King of Simaerin. It was also there that he wed Queen Nathaera on Midsummer's day before the banners of three united countries, and the dignitaries from each. Prince Fayett, Lord Adesta Gilhan, and High Lord Celin'Laen stood among them.

As Gwyn strode through the grand courtyard of the castle, his gaze swept over his many guests, his heart full. Full, but for two holes from which he would never heal. Lawen was absent, as he would always be. Where Mother stood in the throng, Gwyn's half-brother ought to stand too, but only memory remained.

Kive was also missing.

Poor, mad, frightened Kive had never been found, though Gwyn had ordered a search. Celin'Laen had agreed to seek him among the trees and Vales, but discovered nothing of the fallen fae. Gwyn had used magery, and asked his mage allies to do the same, but the Ilidreth was well hidden or long dead.

Finally, Gwyn gave up the search, but he'd prayed to Afallon that Kive still lived. That he was mending somehow, and might someday return to Simaerin and seek Gwyn out. For now, that was all Gwyn could do.

Brioc Ffyr bowed his head near the refreshment table, catching Gwyn's attention, before returning to a conversation with General Cadogan, Towwen Brym, and Towwen Stone. They were among the leaders of the Order of Cygnus, Gwyn's mage council, obliged by oath to maintain peace and represent the voice of the people.

By Gwyn's decree, his power as king was not absolute, but subject to the will of those chosen by Simaerin's citizens. He hoped this would prevent such tyrants as the Crow King from taking power ever again.

A hand gently caught Gwyn's arm, and he turned to smile down at his beautiful wife. Nathaera beamed back at him, glorious in a gown of white, her flaxen hair woven with flowers.

"Hello, Gwynny," she murmured.

"Natty, my love," he replied.

Together they laughed, and he ran a hand along her cheek.

"You seemed awfully glum just now for your wedding day, sir," she said, holding his eyes.

His smile faded a little. "I was thinking of Kive."

Tears sprang into her eyes. "Poor dear Kive. I wish he were here. Funny, isn't it? He was so horrible at first. Eating rats and people, so terrifying and pathetic, yet life is hollow without him now. Do you think he could've healed from what was done to him? Do you think he's found some kind of peace?"

"I hope so." Gwyn's gaze turned skyward just as Parsha the dragon streaked across the sky to land on the city wall far across Londolin proper.

Gwyn let a fond smile brush his lips. No doubt Sir Nox rode upon the mighty beast's back now that the wedding ceremony had finished. Nox and his dragon were inseparable as they went from city to city and village to village, helping to rebuild what was broken, teaching the people how to defend themselves. Simaeri were becoming rather accustomed to dragons and unicorns these days. Gwyn often rode across Simaerin, letting the people know him, coming to know the people.

The war had ended, but battles continued. Not upon a field with swords and shields, but within the halls of the Winter Castle where men brandished ideas.

Some wished, as he did, to end slavery and make all men free. Others resisted the idea with vehemence. But Gwyn wouldn't give up — not until liberty had been obtained for all, or he died in the effort, and others took up the same cause. For he knew there would always be honest men who fought for right.

"It's time for our dance," Nathaera whispered.

Smiling, Gwyn took her hand, and led her to the center of the throng. As the music played, he swept her off her feet. Nathaera laughed, a sweet singsong sound that filled the Winter King's soul with light.

Far overhead streamed the banner of Simaerin: a unicorn racing across a blue field, while behind the fair creature stood a silver tree framed by two swords.

Magic and fae and humans, united.

# Epilogue

Snow fell from the heavens.

Gwyn stepped out onto his balcony, wrapped in a warm fur to fight the bitter chill. His breath curled against the midnight sky in wisps of white.

Something had woken him from a deep sleep.

Pulling his fur closer about his shoulders, he stared into the darkness and waited. Waited.

*Gwynny, look.* The voice, so much like Lawen's, whispered on the wind.

He looked below. There.

Against the night, he noticed a figure in the snow-covered courtyard.

'*Gwynter, come.*'

Gwyn obeyed the rush of Aluem's voice at once, leaping from the balcony. The wind caught and lowered him to the ground, and he moved toward the grand fountain in the center of the courtyard.

Aluem stood waiting for him, horn glowing faintly. As Gwyn neared, he turned his head toward the figure he'd spotted before.

His heart swelled.

Alone in a swirl of snow, tangled tresses of hair whipping about in the wind, stood a long-lost friend.

Gwyn gasped. Five years. Five years had come and gone since Kive had vanished at the battle for Crowwell.

"Kive!" He raced forward, afraid the figure would bolt and melt into the night. But Kive remained still and Gwyn caught him in an embrace. "Kive, my friend."

"Hello, Shiny."

Gwyn pulled back to peer into the Ilidreth's face. He was the same, just the same.

But no. Gwyn looked closer and tears pricked his eyes . Kive's eyes had changed. The bloodred color was gone, replaced by a beautiful silvery hue.

He wasn't wholly healed. Not yet. His clothes hung in tatters. His smile hung broken. But there was hope, for Kive was no longer bound to the Crow.

At long last, the Swan King stood free.

The End

# Dearest Reader

Thank you for picking up this book, and for supporting a starving author in the process. Your efforts mean more than you may ever know.

If you've enjoyed Gwyn's journey, along with all his dear friends, please consider leaving an honest review on Goodreads and/or your favorite online retailer. It's one of best ways to support an author.

Please feel free to visit my website at www.mhwoodscourt.com and sign up for my newsletter to receive updates, exclusive short stories, and more! You can also follow me on social media and say hello.

Thank you kindly,

*M. H. Woodscourt*

# Appendix

## People

Adesta Gilhan [*uh-DES-tuh gill-han*] – A knight from Fraelin.

Afallon [*ă-fall-on*] – The god of Simaerin and Fraelin. Also referred to as Sweet Afallon or Blessed Afallon. According to church doctrine, he sacrificed himself to redeem all men.

Aleteer Hemonn [*ăl-uh-teer HEM-awn*] – Gwyn's aide.

Aluem [*ă-loo-em*] – A unicorn who dwells in Ilid.

Arastet [*air-uh-stet*] – A unicorn who once dwelt in Ilid.

Arianwen ren Targeth [*ah-ree-AWN-wenn ren tar-geth*] – A lady of the Crow King's court.

Bened Arnnor [*ben-ed ar-norr*] – A knight of Simaerin.

Bowrin [*bow-rin*] – An Ilidreth commander allied with the armed forces of the Crane King.

Brandivven [*brăn-divv-VEN*] – A captain stationed at Andonn Garrison in Simaerin.

Breye [*bray*] – A magistrate of Bayton.

Brioc Ffyr [*bree-ock fīr*] – A philosopher and printer in Charquae. He is part of the Winter King's council.

Brisht [*brish-t*] – A soldier in the Winter Army.

Broven [*bro-ven*] – A general in service to the Crow King.

Cadogan ren Silverard [*căd-oh-gen ren sil-ver-ard*] – A general under the Crow King.

Celin'Laen clo Vae'nan [*sel-LIN-lay-in klo vay-năn*] – An Ilidreth High Lord. Also called Celin. [*sel-LIN*]

Chiaven [*chee-ah-ven*] – A dread lord 1,000 years before the present day. He slew Afallon within Keep Talbethé. *Also see Afallon.*

Cluv [*cloo-v*] – A colonel in the Winter Army.

Crane King, The – Ruler of Fraelin.

Crow King, The – Ruler of Simaerin.

Cygmund – A king of Crane Castle of Fraelin and brother of Queen Shalesta of Ilid. He lived over 300 years ago.

Delyth ren Cryven [*dell-ith ren krī-ven*] – The recently widowed wife of Charquae's former governor.

Demréal [*dem-ray-all*] – A red dragon.

Dontri [*don-tree*] – A Fraeli duke quartered at Keep Montré.

Douva [*doe-vuh*] – A high priest of Afallon stationed in Londolin.

Drinald [*drin-ald*] – A knight in service to the Crow King.

Dura [*durr-uh*] – Rafer's son and a runaway slave turned soldier in the Winter Army. *Also see Rafer.*

Fayett sae Marqwen [*fay-ett say marr-kwen*] – Crown Prince of Fraelin.

Fiend, The – A servant of the Crow King.

Freyder [*fray-der*] – Sovereign Prince of Hesh-Kasal.

Grene [*grenn*] – A general in the Winter Army.

Gwynter ren Wintervale [*gwin-tur ren win-tur-vayl*] – The Winter King, he is the rightful ruler of Simaerin through his mother's line. Formerly of Mount Vinwen. Also called Gwyn [*gwin*] or Gwynny [*gwin-ee*].

Haratin [*hawr-uh-tin*] – A general in the Winter Army.

Hemm – Father of Nox. A baker in Charquae.

Henris [*hen-riss*] – A member of the Winter Council at Charquae.

Huwin [*hew-inn*] – A knight of the Crow King.

Kive ave'ar Edelin [*kīv ah-vay-air eh-dell-in*] – An Ilidreth now fallen.

He views people as animals, and eats those he sees as rats. *Also see Fallen under Terms & Phrases.*

Kovien ave'al Edelin [*ko-vee-in ah-vay-all eh-dell-in*] – A prince of Ilid in former days, now revealed to be the Crow King.

Lawen ren Terare [*law-wen ren tur-RAIR*] – Lord of Mount Vinwen in Simaerin, elder half-brother to Gwynter.

Leelin [*lee-lin*] – A general in the Winter Army.

Liliaé [*lil-ee-ay*] – A Wintervale princess of Londolin 300 years ago.

Mershen [*mer-shen*] – A general and doctor in the Winter Army.

Nathaera ren Lotelon [*nuh-thay-ruh ren lot-TAY-lawn*] – A young noblewoman of Simaerin, and Gwyn's dear friend.

Nox – A citizen of Charquae and formerly a baker's son. He is part of the Winter Army.

Parsha [*pär-shuh*] – A green and blue dragon.

Penden ren Targeth [*pen-den ren tar-geth*] – Father of Lady Arianwen ren Targeth.

Rafer [*ray-fer*] – A runaway slave, now a soldier in the Winter Army. Father of Dura.

Remien [*rem-ee-ehn*] – A member of the Winter Council.

Rindermarr Lorric [*rin-der-marr lor-rik*] – A priest of Afallon in Simaerin.

Rohkye [*row-kī*] – Gwynter's aide.

Roth ave'al Edelin {*raw-th ah-vay-all eh-dell-in*} – High King of Ilid in former times. He is now deceased.

Shalesta {*shuh-LESS-tuh*} – A princess of Fraelin in former days, and queen of Ilid before its collapse. She was the wife of Roth.

Succunder {*suk-KUHN-der*} – A magistrate of Bayton.

Thiavos {*thee-uh-voss*} – The Devil according to the doctrine of Afallon's church.

Towwen Brym {*tau-wen brim*} – A printer in Charquae and associate of Brioc Ffyr. He is a member of the Winter King's council.

Towwen Stone {*tau-wen stone*} – A childhood friend of Gwynter from Vinwen Province. He is a member of the Winter King's council.

Traycen ren Lotelon {*TRAY-sen ren lot-TAY-lawn*} – A member of the Order of Corvus under the Crow King. Father of Nathaera.

Tull {*tool*} – A magistrate of Bayton.

Windsur ren Cloven {*wind-sir ren klo-vin*} – A knight of Simaerin and formerly betrothed to Nathaera ren Lotelon.

## Places

Andonn {*ăn-don*} – A southern garrison in Simaerin.

Bayton {*bay-tunn*} – A port city in Simaerin.

Charquae {*char-kway*} – A trade city near Mount Vinwen in Simaerin. It now houses the Winter Council.

Crane Castle – The castle of the Crane King in Fraelin.

Crow Castle – The castle of the Crow King in Simaerin.

Crowwell [*cro-well*] – The capital city of Simaerin situated on the southern coast of the kingdom.

Delesar [*DELL-uh-sarr*] – A river running near Trayton & Phinion.

Dilian [*dill-ee-awn*] – A town on the east road to Crowwell.

Dorshen Heights [*dor-shun*] – Northern cliffs above Bayton.

Fraelin [*fray-lin*] – A kingdom to the northeast of Simaerin constantly at war with its southwestern neighbor. The Crane King reigns over these lands. Its people are called the Fraeli [*fray-lee*].

Glashon [*glă-shun*] – Home province of Sir Bened Arnnor.

Gond – A city in southern Simaerin.

Hesh-Kasal [*hesh kuh-SALL*] – Eastern country whose paid mercenaries (Heshi) have allied with the Crow King against Gwyn's forces.

Ilid [*ill-id*] – The wooded northwestern kingdom of the fae-like Ilidreth [*ill-id-reth*], it has fallen into ruin and its fae are becoming wild and violent. *Also see Shaeswéath under Terms and Phrases.*

Keep Arch – A fortress near the northern Simaerin-Ilid border.

Keep Canad [*kuh-NOD*] – Northern fort of Simaerin.

Keep Hathoss [*hă-thoss*] – A fortress on the east road to Crowwell.

Keep Montré [*mon-TRAY*] – Northern fort of Simaerin.

Keep Talbethé [*tăl-buh-thay*] – Where the Order of Corvus makes its home, it is considered unholy but significant as the place where the god Afallon was executed.

Kellion [*kell-ee-awn*] – A city in southern Simaerin.

Kender [*ken-der*] – The location of a lost campaign of General Haratin.

Lemlin [*lem-linn*] – A southern province near Crowwell. Most of the Crow Army's supplies come from its granaries.

Londolin [*LAWN-doh-linn*] - The abandoned former capital of Simaerin from the age of the Wintervale Kings.

Misoril [*miss-or-ill*] – A far western province of Simaerin.

Mount Vinwen [*vin-wen*] – The agricultural estate where House ren Terare resides within Vinwen Province.

Phinion [*finn-ee-awn*] – A village near the bridge spanning the Delesar river near Trayton

Quee'avv Cathedral [*kwee-aw-v*] – A prominent cathedral within Crowwell.

Simaerin [*sih-MAY-*rin] – The southern kingdom ruled by the Crow King. Its people are called the Simaeri [*sih-MAY-ree*].

Suffon [*suff-AWN*] – The location of a lost campaign of General Haratin.

Swan Castle – The human term for *Shaeswéath*, the legendary castle belonging to the Ilidreth.

Trayton [*tray-tunn*] – A hamlet east of the Delesar, where Heshi forces make camp.

True Wood – The human term for the fae kingdom of Ilid.

Vaymeer Ocean [*vay-meer*] – Also called the Vaymeer Sea, it is the southern ocean in Simaerin. Crowwell and Londolin sit upon its shores.

Yastport [*yăst-port*] – A prosperous port city in direct trade with Crowwell. Windsur ren Cloven's home.

## Terms & Phrases

*Chesevwé* [chess-eh-vway] – The Crystal Way; a path leading to Swan Castle.

Corvus, Order of [*kor-vuhs*] – An order of mages under the Crow King.

Cygnus, Order of [*sig-nus*] – An order of mages under the Winter King.

Fallen – A term used to describe the state of the Ilidreth when their souls darken due to the blight that has overcome their people and kingdom. A fallen Ilidreth loses his or her sense of reality and usually becomes violent until they fade into nothing.

Feast of Afallon (*also called Afallon's Feast*) – A celebration for the birth of Afallon. The eve of Afallon's feast is also celebrated. *Also see Afallon under People.*

*Shaeswéath* [shay-SWAY-auth] – Swan Castle and its enormous grounds within the fae kingdom of Ilid. *Also see Ilid under Places.*

*Sui* [swee] – Fraeli tongue for "yes."

Weave – The source of magic, both of fae and of human mages.

Winter Army – The army that is risen to oppose the Crow King. It is led by Gwynter, rightful king of Simaerin.

Winter Camp – The transient headquarters of the Winter Army as it slowly heads south toward Crowwell.

Winter Council – Stationed in Charquae, this force is lead by Brioc Ffyr, Towwen Brym, and Towwen Stone. *Also see Charquae under Places.*

# Acknowledgments

First of all, I express humble thanks to my Father in Heaven for giving me a heart too full not to write its contents.

Fellow American Revolutionary War history enthusiasts will undoubtedly have noted the battles and events borrowed from actual historic incidents of that era, but they will also recognize the many deviations from said events — and I hope they will forgive me for taking creative license often.

*Yes*, the crossing of the Delesar is certainly inspired by, and largely replicated from, the famous crossing of the Delaware during Christmas of 1776. Other events are less obvious because they aren't as well known. Others still are pure fiction. Even so, I hope those with a love of the cause of the American Revolution have enjoyed my fantastical tipping of the hat to those wondrous, even miraculous, moments that altered history forever.

I ardently acknowledge — and express my deep gratitude for — the people and sacrifices that inspired the shaping of this book.

I also want to thank my family — in particular my parents, Duane and Deborah — for letting me spend so much of my time growing up cultivating my writing. And for letting me dream about one day becoming an author. They never discouraged me, and that means *everything* to this appreciative daughter.

I'd be remiss if I didn't pour out my gratitude for my beta readers and ARC readers for both *The Crow King* and *The Winter King*, without whom I wouldn't have braved publishing this dear little series.

In particular, I wish to thank Laura A. Barton, CJ Farley, Mandi

Oyster, Heidi Wadsworth, and Tawnee Wadsworth, for your tireless efforts and enduring support of this duology. My characters and I are deeply touched by your affection for the *Wintervale* duology. This has been an immense labor of love.

Huge thanks to Sara B., a marvelous editor and even more lovely human being. You're amazing.

Lastly, I must again acknowledge my love and admiration for George Washington. He inspired this story at its earliest conception, as he also inspired my personal efforts to be a better, braver, more resolute person in all aspects of my life.

To him, I dedicate this duology with all my heart.

## About the Author

Writer of fantasy, magic weaver, dragon rider! Having spent the past two decades devotedly writing fantasy, it's safe to say M. H. Woodscourt is now more fae than human.

All of her fantasy worlds connect with each other in the Mithrinn Universe, forged with great love and no small measure of blood, sweat, and tears. When she's not writing, she's napping or reading a book with a mug of hot cocoa close at hand, while her quirky cat Wynter nibbles her nose.

Learn more at www.mhwoodscourt.com

 facebook.com/mhwoodscourt

 x.com/woodscourtbooks

 instagram.com/woodscourtbooks

# Also by M. H. Woodscourt

Mark of Valliath

*High Fantasy/Young Adult*

The Storyteller True

The Shattered Arch

The Marked Prince

The Blood Fountain

Record of the Sentinel Seer

*Science-Fantasy/New Adult*

Prince of the Fallen

Rule of the Night

Song of the Lost

Paths of the Broken

Heart of the Sentinel

Paradise Trilogy

*Portal Fantasy/Humor/Young Adult*

A Liar in Paradise

Key of Paradise

Beyond Paradise

www.ingramcontent.com/pod-product-compliance
Lightning Source LLC
Chambersburg PA
CBHW020529310726
48979CB00014B/2265/J
* 9 7 8 1 9 5 9 6 1 9 0 8 6 *